IN THE MEANTIME...
COMPLICATED
BOOK ONE

LOVE BELVIN

MKT PUBLISHING, LLC

in the
MEANTIME...

THE *complicated* SERIES 1

ISBN: 978-1-950014-73-6 (Paperback)
ISBN: 978-1-950014-72-9 (eBook)

MKT Publishing, LLC
First print edition 2024 in U.S.A.

Cover design by **Visual Luxe**

ONE

February

ISHAAN

Something feels peculiar about this night...
    "Don't forget we're entering the Laguna Street side," I called out to Earl, my driver.

"Yup." He nodded. "Got it, boss."

Munchie, in my ear, sighed, "Why not the main entrance—or at least Parklights Drive—where you can possibly see some of your guests arrive?"

"Because, tonight, I'm a fly on the wall." I observed the droves of people out enjoying the nightlife of Las Vegas. They were all clueless to the under workings—the backend—of what made this town so magical. As *HAYDAR Resort & Casino* came into view, I was reminded of a gazillion fucking things on my list of shit to do. "Speaking of which, was Donald able to secure the EUR40 cords?"

"For the..." Munchie stalled, and I knew it was because she was checking her handy notes. "...new *Boise* speakers? Yes. They were installed."

"Installed when?"

"Minutes before soundcheck."

"And the lights?"

"Which ones? The IP65s were installed last week. The..." She must have searched again. "...sconce brushed LEH1s for the bathrooms in *Flare* are still on backorder."

"Damn," I murmured, ducking my head.

"But I'm on it. I've called the company every day for over a week. The production manager knows my name. We'll have them installed as soon as we receive them. We're ready, Ish. I swear we are. Just... attend. Your mere presence will assure they won't fuck up. Our team is one of the best around."

That was the problem. I didn't want to attend. This event wasn't for me. It was for a client. I had no desire to party with the client. My satisfaction came from exceeding expectations.

"Alright, Munch. We're pulling up."

"Oh, shit!" she squealed. "Okay. Wait!" Then she took a loud ass breath into the phone. "The Laguna Street side should be cleared of the prostitutes. Lieutenant Graves assured me. And didn't you speak with Madam Needa, who knows the women populating the area?"

"I did." Prostitution in Vegas—and even Atlantic City—went with the culture. In my line of business, I needed relationships with legitimate people from the community, which I had. However, having random hookers hanging around one of the most successful, Black-owned casinos in the world could set a bad precedent. My partner operated in a state of excellence. It has been my pleasure to bring him just that. "We're good. I gotta go."

Before Munchie could return the bid, I'd disconnected the call. By the time I'd fired off a text to food and beverage, Earl was opening my rear door.

I'll be damned...

When I rounded the black, diamond, tri-coat *Escalade*, I saw three women, all in heels, loose overcoats, a shaggy shawl, and scantily clad clothing. One wore a fur scarf and another, visible thigh-high hosiery. I halted in step and could feel Earl freeze, too.

"One had her thumb out when we pulled up," Earl whispered to me.

They were still here. But these broads didn't give "street-versed" energy. Collectively, they stared. Clearly, they appreciated what they saw among the walker-bys passing the smaller guest entrance of the casino. They must have been newbies, because while each woman gaped, none solicited.

Continuing toward the door to the vestibule, my mind began to flow with how to address yet another glitch at *HAYDAR Resort & Casino.*

love
belvin

Hayden

Sundryia:

Sundryia:

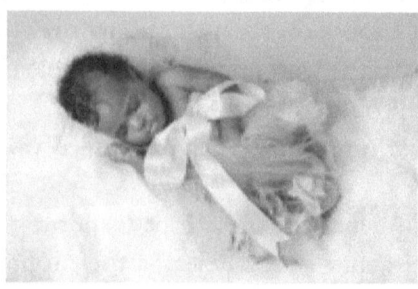

Scrunched over on a cognac-hued suede bench, I smiled toward my phone.

Me: They're so stinkin cute! 😍😍

My heart opened temporarily, thrilled by the sight of my brand-new cousins. I still couldn't believe my cousin, Sundryia, was a mom, much less one with twin babies. A boy, Isam, and a girl, Imani. At just three weeks, they were so tiny and new. Even with unsettled faces, they resembled their grandmother, Cheryl.

Sundryia: *They are. I was so happy the photographer caught Isam with his eyes open.* 😍

Me: Why? He's been alert since they pulled him from your open belly.

Sundryia: *That's exactly why. So when he's older we can prove to him how alert he's been since day one.*

Another text populated on my screen from a friend since high school, Letisha, saying they were outside on the Laguna Street-side of the resort. I knew this. The girls were just outside the door of the plush vestibule I sat inside of, texting my cousin. It was our last night in Vegas, a girls' trip it took what felt like forever to coordinate and execute. We'd been out here for three days. Tonight would be our fourth and final, and I was grateful. This venture overwhelmed my typical tempered social battery.

"Haydeeeeeeen!" Mika playfully shouted from outside when one of the twelve feet tall, tented glass vestibule doors opened from a middle-aged couple entering. When the door closed, the chorus of laughter from my crew muzzled.

They thought I was still upstairs in my suite. Letisha sent a text to our girls' trip thread, saying tonight would be our role-play night. We were to put on our hooker ensembles, high heels, and meet in the Laguna Street lobby. She asserted we'd end our trip with an unregrettable bang.

Hmmm.

Well, after I forced myself to put away my laptop, I took my time getting dressed while enjoying two glasses of some fancy ass tequila furnished by the resort. I made it down here, yes, but *after* the appointed meeting time. I was here, though not wanting to be. From the darkened glass, I could see their glam. High heels, fishnet hosiery on one, faux and shaggy furs, long and dark lashes, striking colors, and bare flesh were all visible from my purview. My girls looked the fuck good.

"She ain't coming," Lucy, a colleague, told the group of three. "Knowing Hayden, she's upstairs working. She's ready to get back home!" she shouted.

Me: I miss them already.

After a good laugh, Mika performed a seductive spin. "I'm ready to hit the town." She stuck her thumb out toward the street to the moving vehicles. That made me snicker. Mika looked every bit of a zaftig prostitute. "If she wants to join us, she'll call. Come on, ladies."

Sundryia: *When do you come back?*

Me: My flight leaves out just after ten in the morning.

Sundryia: *Come up next weekend? Rayna's supposed to be flying out Friday.*

I rolled my eyes and chuckled quietly at that. No matter where Rayna Jacobs was in the world, no matter what she was doing, if she said she was flying in to visit Sundryia and her brand-new babies, I was sure she'd follow through on the promise. I guessed Sundryia was still adjusting to having our cousin in our lives. I could dig it. It was still new. But hell. She followed through with her word on aiding my girls and me on this trip.

Me: …

My thumb, in strange haste, hit the send button as my attention drew up and over to the tall, tinted, glass door. Coming through was a force felt viscerally. He was tall, athletically lengthy in a black suit and black dress shirt. His skin was the hue of sandpaper, odd, but fucking palatable if I'd ever seen it before. He had long, dark hair. A thick, wiry mane box-braided and pulled back into a ponytail. The sides and back of his scalp were faded and lined with precision. I didn't like men with hair, but it worked for this guy. Jarringly, he stopped in the middle of the vestibule and gaped at me with full audacity. Etched into his warm-toned face was a deep scowl, transforming the muscles on mine into a darkened expression. Silently, I begged his pardon.

That didn't break his absurd gape. He flipped his chin, the bristled ends of his slender beard groomed and even. "How much?"

I blinked. Slowly, I swallowed then glanced into the lobby through the gradient glass. A surge of energy radiated from my spine, and I turned my attention back to him. "I beg your pardon?"

His inspection dropped to my heeled shoes; one bare leg crossed over the other. His eyes lifted as he perceptively sized me up. When our eyes reunited, he inquired again throatily. "How much for your... services?"

The thought caused me to glance down at my risqué, fitted, black midi dress with circular cutouts on one side of my waist and hips and high-heeled PVC *Red Bottoms* ensemble. Hooker ensemble. Then my neck whipped toward the glass doors. My crew was gone. I dropped my head toward my chest.

He thinks I'm a prostitute...

Why was I not offended? The faulty assumption didn't humor me, but I didn't find it insulting either. However, I was damn sure irritated by his blatant judgement. I took a few seconds more to inspect his countenance. He was quite handsome...and obscure. There was a darkness to his aura.

"You can't afford me."

Now his brows shot up in surprise, begging my pardon. His head tilted, big hands pushed up his lower arms to expose his cold wrists. One was cuffed by a sizeable, radiant mosaic diamond tennis bracelet. The other was—I could easily assume—a *Richard Mille*. I only knew this from a conversation I observed between Sundryia and Rayna about watches when Sundryia was shopping for Maaz's Christmas gift a few months ago. Rayna was extremely knowledgeable as her million-aire-husband was a timepiece aficionado. In the span of a couple of hours, the pair went over several *Richard Mille* pieces and their distinct commonalities. So, from a few feet away, I could only assume.

"Try me." The baritone-thick croakiness could have been a prognosticator of the clashing of our worlds.

My eyes blossomed wide at his wild, confident tenor. "What do you have in mind?"

His eyes rolled toward the lobby. "Just your company at a private event I'm about to attend."

"So, just a sit-down dinner?"

"And mingling."

"As in with others?"

His eyes sparkled wickedly. "Of course. I'm proposing a low-risk opportunity here."

Opportunity.

Oh.

My eyes closed in recollection. *I'm a prostitute.*

"But nothing more." I wanted to be clear as I considered it.

Hell, yeah. I'm crazy...

The "john's" nod was soft but definitive.

Sundryia: So...?

My eyes roved up to my "client" as I considered my cousin's request. He was handsome. Damn handsome. His confidence was louder than his captivating scent.

Slowly, my attention returned to my phone.

Me: I'll call you tomorrow after I get settled in at home and will let you know then.

I pushed my phone into my purse. "Lucky for you, my schedule has just opened up. How many hours?"

My john shrugged. "Two hours at best. We can call it then."

I pushed my puckered lips into the air and rolled my eyes against the ceiling, pretending to think. "Two hours. I can give you that for one thousand-five hundred dollars." I enunciated each syllable to rush this exchange along. This man was out of his goddamn mind and, clearly, so was I.

He gave an assured nod. "For the night?"

"Per hour." I straightened my spine.

His eyes lit up. A sleek grin warmed my face at the same pace. He reached into his pocket and pulled out a lit phone. I watched him read then type. He put it away, stowing it back into his suit jacket. "You better be the best companion to ever walk the floors of *HAYDAR Resort & Casino*." He tossed his head toward the lobby. "We have a party awaiting us."

I didn't move. "Jane." My john questioned me with his eyes. "Jane. You need to know my name before parading me in front of your associates."

"Jane is a bit..."

"Generic. Yes. But Janie isn't. You can introduce me as Jane and reference me as Janie. Please tell me you know how to force chemistry."

A gorgeous smile opened on his appealing face. God, I wanted to see all of his teeth. "For three bands, I'm sure you can coach me as we move along."

"Judging by your ability to 'identify' me with ease," I stood to my feet, "I can safely assume you've forced chemistry lots in the past."

He moved to open one of the lobby doors for me. Immediately, we were hit with agreeable Muzak floating above us. The waterfall near the entrance was a captivating show and beautiful display. I followed at his side, matching his pace as he pulled out his phone again and tended to it. It made me think I should responsibly let someone know where I was. Then I thought, he wasn't inviting me to a private room. *The event is here at Azmir's casino.* The minute I felt unsafe, I'd make a beeline.

We took an escalator to an upper level, ascending to the excitable jingle of casino slot machines and a playroom's signature tobacco fragrance. None of those distractors of my senses overpowered that of the energy belonging to the man just feet ahead of me.

"Ish."

I braved a glance his way as we promenaded down the plush hallway on cushioned carpeting with intricate design. "Come again?"

"My name. You need to know my real name." His eyes brushed over me before looking ahead again. "It's Ish."

"Oh. Right. You know these people." It dawned on me how I needed to know his real name. "Just 'Ish'?"

We made it to an elevator when his eyes swept up toward the ceiling. My john exhaled, "Patterson. Ish Patterson."

Incongruent to the vibe of the moment, I smiled widely. "Okay, Ish. How long have you and Jane known each other?"

When he pivoted to face me, I noticed how thick and expressive his dark brows were. "What's your last name."

This time, it was me brushing my eyes against the ceiling to think. "Doherty."

"Doherty?"

I used my hand to cover my mouth as I snickered. "It's close to Doe. Get it? Jane Doherty."

"Or, for me, Janie Doherty."

I winked. "You know me."

I could see the cogs of his brain working. "We're...new." My john was sizing me up. His inspection seared each inch as it traveled from my blue toes in four-inch *Christian Louboutin* "Just Nothing" sandals to my legs. When his sights made their way to my exposed hip, butterflies erupted and my groin churned, scaring the fuck out of me. Immediately, my abdomen contracted, and lungs slowed. Unapologetically, my john's eyes remained on my breasts for seconds long before ascending to my lips then eyes. "I'd say a few months."

My throat was tight when I inquired, "Where did we meet?"

His dark, ebony irises smiled. "At a fundraising event."

How apropos...

My heart blossomed and so did my face. "I think I can do that."

Shit...

As I glanced around the room, a waiter approached me with a tray of champagne. There was nothing I needed more as I read the big ass banner over the stage at the head of the room. "*Blakewood State University Panthers.*"

Fucking *BSU*? The most prestigious, historically Black university on the planet. This was the event my john hired me to attend with him. I'd never been in a room so beautifully Black. Trumping the food, the space smelled like royalty—money. Not that I imagined everyone attending was rich. However, it was known that graduates of this esteemed university, statistically, either were successful entrepreneurs or held executive-level positions at *Fortune 500* companies.

"You look so familiar." Two women appeared. One with a sparkle in her eyes I hadn't earned. She was my complexion with the old Halle Berry cut from *Catwoman*. "Did you stay in the *Winnie Dorm* on campus?"

The woman with her gave masculine energy as she peered at me over her wine glass while her other hand was stowed into the pocket of her pants.

I forced a smile and sighed, "I didn't attend."

The Halle Berry haircut woman, who was considerably short compared to my five foot-eight-inch frame, mimicked my expression, but giggled nervously. That's when the masculine-appearing woman paid me the longest onceover, making my skin crawl. "Oh! Are you current staff for the *Panthers*?"

My eyes blossomed again. "No. I'm a plus one." I wanted this exchange over with ASAP.

"With who?" The masculine woman finally spoke, face screwed tight with curiosity.

"Ish," rolled off my tongue with pride.

The two women regarded each other. I guessed deciphering that information.

Masculine bae snapped her fingers then elbowed Halle Berry haircut. "Ish." She circled her index finger in the air.

It took a few seconds, but Halle Berry's haircut shrilled, "Oh! Patterson."

I nodded. "Patterson."

My john didn't lie.

Yay, me!

This meant I wasn't as crazy as I thought downstairs.

"You two...?"

With an even bigger smile, I nodded. Of course, I'd claim my john. It was clear to me these two women were interested in me for reasons beyond a school reunion. "In fact, let me go find him. Nice chatting with you two."

I took off without awaiting a single response.

A waiter stopped at our table and handed me what was my third flute of champagne this evening. It was delicious. Beyond that, the conversation I'd been privy to between my john and his peers had been interesting as hell.

"I don't know," Fatima, a middle-aged *Panther*—now that I knew what a *Panther* was—shook her head while twirling a wine glass in a lifted hand. She was a track phenomenon during her tenure at *BSU*. She's since gone on to become a footwear engineer. "It's becoming increasingly difficult to support this endeavor. These kids don't want help. They want to go viral."

Her partner, Rodney, an alumnus, but not an athlete, added, "It's a different experience in EPS."

"EPS?" I asked.

"I'm sorry, Jane," Rodney offered with a snort. "That's so ungracious of me. Earth and Planetary Sciences."

I felt heat shooting to the side of my face. My john was staring at me again.

Oh. Right.

He'd mentioned that was his area of study at *BSU*.

"Got it."

"Yes. So," Rodney continued. "...those students are highly motivated to have the full experience in that program. They come in knowing about the benevolence program and apply for it right away. I believe the superficiality is exclusive to the athletes."

"Yup." Fatima's eyes swept the room. "And yet, we're here, donating over one million dollars to the lost generation." She hiked her brow line.

"The Lost Generation," I echoed in almost a whisper. "What brought about their ruin?"

"Pardon?" Fatima straightened her spine.

"The Lost Generation. The Stein lady." I snapped my fingers, trying to recall. "Gerry Stein. She coined the phrase in the early nineteen hundreds but with an understanding that the cohort, the Lost Generation, came from uneducated families highly inundated with the media. They were hit with historically known phenomena like the Spanish flu. She was able to define the group by their experiences."

"I thought Hemmingway coined it." Fatima appeared unsure.

Swallowing champagne, I nodded then explained, "He popularized it."

"Oh!" She balled her lips.

"What's ruined this generation?" I landed my question.

Rodney shrugged. "Shared parenting with electronics?"

"I'd say no cultural or political leaders," Fatima answered. "Where's this generation's Malcolm, Marcus, or Nat?"

"This isn't the only generation without those leaders," Ish surprisingly added. He hadn't spoken much during this conversation. I'd come to believe he was an introvert. This couple had been carrying the conversation since we'd finished dinner. "There hasn't been a leader in the Black community since the baby-boom era."

"Not you forgetting about the Reverend Al Sharpton," I quipped.

The couple fell into laughter. I did, too, cracking my drunk self the hell up.

"In your jest, could you have used a worse figure?" Rodney snickered.

"Yup." I nodded. "Pastor Jamal Bryant."

And that's when my john burst into a chuckle, hanging his head. He'd laughed. My client demonstrated satisfaction, to some degree, with my services. I played it cool and didn't express how affected I was by his reaction to my fucked up sense of humor.

"These kids are über-obsessed with social media," Rodney, a mid-level executive at *NASA*, argued while trying to stop laughing. "Their values are in numbers on an application created for a mobile device. There's no social responsibility or an obligation to those who fought so they can have the liberties afforded to them. The seventies were the best decade."

"No," Fatima pushed out a breath. "The eighties get my vote."

Then my john turned toward me. His long lashes met, and eyes sparkled again when he asked, "Which generation gets your vote?"

"Well, you know me. I can be bought." His eyelids lowered, smile broadened. *Damn.* He was beautiful. If I was going to get through this experience, I knew I couldn't stare at him all night, getting lost in whoever he was. Then I continued, "My preferences change day by day. Experience by experience."

He sounds even better in person...

R&B balladeer, Ragee, was belting Keyshia Cole's *Love*. As a true artist, he made it his own while remaining true to the original rendition. He walked off stage shirtless, singing his ass off. The sweat from his thick, carved frame had accumulated during his performance tonight. Imagine my surprise when the host for the evening transitioned us from dinner to a performance from the one and only "whore-maker." He sang several of his hits, rendering the conservative crowd to their feet in no time.

Ragee handed the microphone over to a stiff, gray-haired man with wiry glasses. He had money. I could tell by his demeanor and conservative ensemble. The man stalled a bit, giggling his cautious nature. Then he accepted the mic and howled, "*Loooooove!*" He sounded awful, but the room found it funny and in good fun.

I wanted to take pictures. The girls would die if they knew who

I'd been sharing a room with tonight. But then they'd want to come. And if I shared this with Sundryia or Rayna, they'd call me crazy and would clock my every move for the night. Rayna may have even put a security guard on me.

Hell no.

Absolutely not.

Tonight, I was Jane Doherty, lady of the night. A courtesan.

But no harlot...

Smiling wide, I glanced over to my john, who didn't move much, but had been taking in the talent of the crooner as well. Not wanting to lose a moment of this, my attention returned to Ragee. Hearing this song brought back memories of an eleven-year-old, who watched too much television, believing the world was a safe place. I would reenact all the videos and the performance of the day on *106 & Park*. Damn. Those were the days.

Then Ragee was nearing me. He stopped to serenade Fatima. She was taken and I understood why. The man smelled damn good, even drenched in the result of his hard work. Then, the man was approaching me, eyes locked and microphone first. I had only half a second to think, and what did I do? I grabbed the mic and was transported to my mother's living room where no one was around besides my imaginary audience. Admittedly, I sounded coarse at first, but soon I warmed into the notes.

And Raj liked it. I could tell by how his spine reclined and he rolled his neck. His brows narrowed as he watched me intently. When he decided I was done, Raj grabbed the mic, continuing the song, then dapped it up with my john and moved on. I couldn't feel my feet, in total disbelief at what had just happened. I watched him finish his show in complete awe. His last selection was an old hit, *No Bed Needed*. And yes, he was sure to include the closing line, *"Be my whoooooooore!"* fluidly while falling to his knees. The entire room was on their feet, hooting and hollering.

It was official: move over Dale. Ragee was now my favorite male R&B artist.

I adjusted my dress, shifting it in place as I ambled out of the luxury stall toward the vanity. When I glanced up and ahead, I stumbled.

"Oh, come on! When are you going to let up off the necks of us mediocre girls?"

Tori McNabb's head swung up from the vanity as she washed her hands. Right away, a soft chuckle pushed from her lungs as she resumed her duties. "Says the girl in what's probably the sexiest dress and voice in the place tonight." That caused me to look down at my exposed hip. The faint stretchmarks decorating my skin were visible. "You look amazing." She straightened to reach for a paper towel to dry her hands. "Tori Spencer, by the way." She offered me an elbow for a bump now that I'd begun washing my hands.

"Yeah." I reciprocated with my arm as best I could. "Spencer with kids, but still shaming those of us without children with your mere existence." I knocked my elbow into hers. Yup. The champagne had given me a new identity. "But you're doing it right. Retire the work but keep the body. Doherty." I had to remember. "Jane Doherty."

Still drying her hands, the retired boxing champ's head swung backward. "You're a mess! So, you're a singer and bathroom motivation influencer."

"I'm in admiration. I blast your female bestie's music just about every day on my commute into work. Tonight, I performed alongside your male bestie. How many can say they've accomplished that? And to learn you're a *Panther*." I'd even become conversant with the community at this point of the evening.

"I was. How about you? What did you play?"

I shook my head. "I'm a loser plus-one who gets to see up front and in person that Tori McNabb can still walk a runway *and* beat my ass."

Intoxicated or not, I needed to remember this night. I'd never been so socially forward. Then again, I was not Hayden Washington. My name was Jane Doherty.

Tori and I freshened up our faces and ended up leaving the bathroom together. She held the door for me as I scooted past her.

"So, you and Ragee's *Protecting Love* foundation," I broached the topic.

"What about it?"

As we sauntered back to the ballroom, I inquired, "Who is responsible for receiving grant proposals?"

Tori's face wrinkled, eyes rolling up to the ceiling. "I believe the new girl's name is Kawanda. The last guy, DeVaughn, left a couple of months ago. Do you want to be a donor?"

And reminding me just how much the universe was aligned for me this night, my john came into view, robbing me of my attention. He'd been watching me. As he stood next to a man nearly his same extreme height, yet with a slightly broader frame, two things dawned on me. As the gentleman next to him spoke, my john's tongue swiped his lips before they rubbed together. Was that a sign of his attraction to me? I glided toward him as though on a conveyor belt wearing a beam warming my girlie parts. The second thing I realized was I'd broken character with the former undisputed heavyweight champ. Hayden Washington reared her over-worked head.

As I arrived at my john, I glanced over to the man he'd been speaking with. I recognized him right away. Ashton Spencer. We'd received generous funding from his multi-billion-dollar corporation over the years. But there was no time to slip out of character again. I was here for my john. And by the way he reached for my hand, not removing his attention from me, the man was devoting some of the evening to me as well.

"You played basketball."

His brows met as humor and, perhaps, admiration crackled in his eyes. "What?"

"Basketball." I reached for his upper arm and squeezed gently. "You played basketball at *BSU*."

"Hoopin', hoopin!" Ashton Spencer jeered.

"Nice friend, Ish." Tori shifted her weight into her husband's chest. "I like her."

My john gazed down at me. "She's lots of things. So much for me to explore." He pulled me closer into his torso and murmured, "Let's go dance."

"Oh, damn. I don't get an introduction?" Ashton Spencer feigned offended.

Ish turned on his heel. "Later, Spencers."

Behind me, I could hear Tori's thick titter.

The dance floor was filled with couples, cozying up on each other's bodies. There was a natural comfort to his chest and abs when I leaned into him. His virile, floral fragrance caused my lashes to meet. No more champagne for me. Character-immersion had become too heady for me from this proximity.

"Basketball," I spoke toward his ear.

I felt him pull in a breath, letting it go as he confirmed, "Basketball. Three years of D1. That was the extent of my *Panther*-ship." He pulled me closer, and my spine shivered, causing my breasts to heave twice into his abdomen. "No more questions. I'm pleasantly in heavy deliberation."

I waited a spell before asking, "Deliberating on what?"

The sound of his heavy exhale aroused me. "If I'm going to shell out more money to see if your pussy is as talented as your mind and practiced personality."

My lungs collapsed and liquid spilled onto my inner thighs. I closed my eyes to slow the pulse in my ears and clitoris. "You can't afford me intimately."

"Try me," he droned over my head.

With closed eyes, I blurted, "Seven thousand."

His powerful chest reverberated against me. "You're expensive."

"We're at *HAYDAR*. Everything's luxury here."

Still swaying with me attached to him, his arm shifted, and hand was at my pelvis. His fingers were gentle in their navigation through the thin material of my dress. My hips stiffened. They outlined the triangle of my private area and found the slit of my vaginal lips.

"I see." His aura was calm. That, I could read. "You value your services, I see."

Lifting my head, I peered into his eyes. "I hope you do, too."

Two

February

Hayden

Chlamydia.

Gonorrhea.

Trichomoniasis.

Mycoplasma Genitalium.

Fucking yeast infection.

Gardnerella.

The big fucking HIV, and two more I couldn't recall.

I cleared my throat and straightened my dress as I sat in an examination room inside a clinic here at *HAYDAR*. What casino had a damn medical clinic inside? Why was it even necessary? I'd been sitting here for over twenty minutes awaiting the rapid results of my sexually transmitted infections tests and my john's. On the one hand, 'safety first' being his motto and practice made my john appear responsible. On the other, after being pricked, having to piss in a cup, and orally swabbed, the arousal had waned greatly.

The door opened and the nurse stepped inside first with my john towering in behind her.

"Ms. Doherty, your results are available and yielded no infections found." She handed me several documents. "You'll see that where there are yellow highlights." Then she reached for the papers between her arm and side. She glanced over her shoulder at my john, who responded with a faint nod of approval. "And with Mr. Patterson's consent, I'm sharing his results as well. As you'll see here..." she pointed to his name. "...is his name, and not dissimilar to your documentation, the negative and or normal results are highlighted. Do you have any questions for me?"

Stuck, my gaze went between the two people before me. His scent. I knew it, though the name wasn't coming to me. That allowed me to snap back into character.

"Actually, I do."

The young nurse of Asian descent nodded. "Sure!"

"Do I get a lollipop for my good report?" Her eyes grew wide, and she exhaled. Then I winked.

Giggling, she bowed. "Thanks for your patience. Have a good night." The nurse offered my john a neck bow as well before leaving the room.

He was sure to close the door behind her and lean into it as he peered my way through slit eyes. Damn. He was so fucking handsome. Tall, bronzed, well-dressed, long lashes, and great teeth. I caught glimpses of them during the event.

"Still with me?" He beamed. Full lips and an aligned smile.

Trying to ignore my reaction to his features, I pushed out air and swung my hand in the air. "Please. I'm a pro. Minor deviation."

He didn't give me the humor I was attempting. Instead, his smirk waned, and eyelids remained low. Slowly, he pushed away from the door and promenaded over to me on the examination table. My lungs seized when he settled between my legs. His delicious scent deluded my mind as he leaned into me. Moist, pillowy flesh pressed into my lips. And without my permission, my spine inclined to feel more of him. His tongue was smooth, velvety, and measuring. He didn't move fast and not exactly slow either. I caught on quickly and tasted him. He was confident, cultured, and deliberating. And man, did that ignite my furnace.

When his fingers danced up my leg out of nowhere, I moaned between tongue strokes. He pulled at the elasticity of my dress to make it to my thighs. I managed to spread my legs, totally anticipating this stranger's hand in my secret space. The erotic sounds of our kiss reverberated from the walls of the sterile room. His fingers were gentle when they reached my wet flesh. He rimmed me as his solid body caused mine to recline. I should have been embarrassed to have this stranger in my private folds, discovering my bareness beneath the dress. At least inveigh against him in some way. But I couldn't. His strong energy compelled me.

Were we going to do it here? Would I?

I had no clue what I was capable of. If you would've asked me this morning if I'd pretend to be a prostitute and spend the evening with a stranger, I'd beg your fucking pardon. Yet, here I was. It took my body no time to respond to the demanding rubs on my clit. I warmed all over, kissing him with wild abandon. I didn't know I was melting until my stomach muscle flexed and shoulders jerked. My hand shot up and I clutched his shoulder blade. A helpless moan of betrayal escaped my lungs, but my body turned greedy, and I pushed my sex into his ministration. My orgasm made me fluid—*possessed*. My body behaved wildly, and feet curled in my heels. The muscles in my lips weakened, breaking our kiss. My john remained in my face, his tongue tracing the inside of my opened mouth.

I didn't recognize my breathing pattern and my eyes wouldn't open. The beat of my pulse was so loud and light spasms were active in too many places on my body. I'd slipped. I'd fallen out of character. When I struggled to open my eyes, my john's glistened. The muscles in his face were tight but his eyes confused me. They were radiant with an unnamed emotion.

"I think we're ready to execute your services for the night," he whispered with virile sensuality.

He quickly washed his hands then assisted me off the table. In no time, we were out of the clinic and back inside the golf cart we'd picked up some time after leaving the *Panther* event. Just as it was on the way here, my john took service routes, apparently knowing the bones of the resort. He must've been an employee of sorts. For much of our commute, I stared at my phone. I should have texted someone to let them know of my whereabouts just in case. I wasn't reckless. I never believed in throwing caution to the wind.

The night feels bizarre...

And I was okay with it.

We traveled down a hall of suites. These were for the high-rolling guests. I could tell by the concierge stationed at the elevator. We stopped at a set of double doors and my john gained us entry inside by a swiping of his wrist against a pad on the wall. The suite was dark and spacious from the foyer. I could make out the window walls and wondered about the view. There was no time for discovery. My john led me down the hall where my heels click-clacked behind his lengthy frame.

We turned into a room, which opened up to another floor-to-ceiling view. This was a bedroom, indicated by the over-sized bed resting on a low platform, topped by countless pillows. He didn't stop until we were at the windows. The view. *Wow.* Just amazing. Lights, streams of colorful water shooting up towards us rhythmically against the melodies performed by an orchestra sitting mid-level in a balcony of the four buildings. Separating my heightened senses, I closed my eyes and listened to the familiar tune.

"What are they playing?"

"Marvin Gaye." He circled me like a jaguar, remaining in my personal space. "*I Want You.*"

Oh.

My body was on sensory overload. The shooting water, lights, music, his scent and heat, and my proximity to it all had me going.

"Can I undress you?" His throaty request ensconced in the darkness of this strange place. His alluring scent I couldn't escape.

I wanted it all. But I had to remember to stay in character.

"How should I expect your payment?"

Those soft lips were on my right shoulder. "Which forms of payment do you accept?"

My spine shuddered. "Cash only." What was I saying?

"Then cash is what you can expect."

"When?"

A pocket of soft, cool air hit my hot skin. "Upon completion of your services. And in case you didn't know," he pulled me by the waist into his flagrant erection. "I've been wanting to see you naked since laying eyes on you in the lobby." My pulse shot up hard and my knees and hips trembled. I hoped like hell he wasn't aware. "Can I remove your dress now?"

Eyes closed, I licked my lips. "You rip it, you pay for it."

My john snorted through his nose. Then I could feel his slight squat to capture the hem of my midi dress. Slowly, with savor, he pulled the material up my thighs and over my hips. His hand brushed over my bikini-waxed pubic bed. Instinctively, my hips pushed back into his crotch. I lifted my arms as he pulled the dress up and over my torso. Now, only in heels and a strapless bra, my knees buckled when his mouth met my neck. His tongue swiped my flesh, causing a helpless mewl to expel.

My bra was unfastened, breasts spilled and, immediately, his exploratory hands clasped me. His tongue roved and roved over the sensitive flesh beneath my ear. His intrusive fingers thrummed my nipples and my hips swung, and ass rocked into his erection.

"Open this," he whispered in my ear, forcing my eyes to open.

It was a condom. Where he pulled it from, I had no idea. I'd been too busy enduring his sensual fluency. Obeying him, I took the square package and ripped the foil with a shaky hand and my teeth. I held it in the air, and once my john retrieved it, that palm slammed onto the glass window. Within seconds, his magical fingers abandoned my heavy breasts and were between my legs, guiding the wide crest of his dick inside of me. He was fucking thick and long—at least it was what I felt as he returned to my breasts. His mouth moved to the other side of my neck, busily stroking his tongue against my flesh as he rocked gently inside of me, not fully encapsulated. He worked and worked, gently massaging my pounding, swollen walls all while the orchestra performed a classic love song on the other side of the window.

My palms were plastered in a forceful grip on the glass as I held myself up against the mounting pleasure. He lifted my left leg, and with the push of his chest against my back, he leaned me toward the glass windows enough for my nipples to swipe against the cool exterior. And when one of his tireless fingers crawled down and found my throbbing clit, I was close to the precipice of losing my shit. It was not lost upon me that I was bare to him in only my heels while he hadn't removed a single article of clothing, just shifted his pants down.

His girth deep inside me stiffened my hips until the whirring pleasure loosened them. My head collapsed backward, landing on his shoulder where he took my mouth. His tongue moved around mine with evidential hunger. His tongue, too, was long and thick. He fed it to me with force. There was an energy behind it. He wanted me to catch his aggression. Oddly, I wanted to prove I could keep up with it. The kiss was intentionally sensual, intrusive, and indecent, eradicating the anxiety of my joints, loosening them as I curled into him. I felt small in his hold. Could feel the pounding of his chest resound against my nude back. His grip wasn't painfully tight. It was virilely secure on my frame.

My mind was turbid from wild sensations. Just as the horns from the orchestra striated from the ensemble, the thread which was me unraveled.

"Fuck!" pushed from my lungs in a helpless whisper as I exploded around his swollenness driving deep inside my quivering walls.

"Fuck," he grunted as I bounced into his hard body.

His chest bulged over me. Silky hairs, rounded pecs peaked at the apex, the hairs leading down to his delicious pipe thrusting into my core all enthralled me. My john was gloriously naked this round, and never in my life had I wanted to see a man's full, bare body more than I did his. As I lay on my back on the bed, spread wide for him, he was almost in a frog pose, only resting on his knees and lower legs. His thickness stretched me so good, massaging pleasure points I never knew were placed so deeply. The rolling of his abdominal wall was rhythmic with the orchestra playing in the courtyard. For a while, it sounded like Summer Walker's "*Karma*."

Who was this man I'd allowed to fuck me so randomly? His touch was gentle and passionate as he fingered me, spurring me along to an ascension just like before. I wondered what he saw when he watched me being fucked by him. Was he curious about me? The real me? Or was he just using the services of my womanhood like a commercial-grade machine?

I wanted to know all about my john at this point. *Ish. What was his last name?* His practiced, sensual talent was one I needed to hold onto. As I squeezed my boobs and rubbed my nipples, unable to see much of his face in the shadows of the room, I felt invincible.

"Fuck me harder," I wheezed, grabbing his left thigh. "Harder!"

Did I need him to go harder? Hell no! I was at a trembling squeeze around his girth now. But I'd thrown caution to the wind earlier tonight. There was no turning back now. I thrust into his powerful drives, feeling the defined muscles of his thigh. Our heavy breaths rivaled the orchestra's symphony. The darkness of the room, but for the festive lights from the shooting water outside the window, had awakened my inner prowess and emboldened her. I arched my back, while holding on to his flexing thigh. His circular stroke on my clit, my caress of my breast, and the feel of his hot flesh rubbing against my lubricated nerve endings all drove me over the edge.

My orgasm hit hard. It was so forceful, my body shuddered

uncontrollably and mewls pushed from the pit of my belly like a wounded animal. His subterranean grunts could have been a telltale sign of his submission to our sexual chemistry, but my mind was too far gone to know.

I didn't want this euphoric experience to end. I wanted to do it again and again.

"This is good, Daddy." I tried licking the escaping dollop of ice cream racing from the cone onto my little hand.

He's so big, brown, and handsome as he smiles at me. Holding his own cone of his favorite flavor, chocolate, Daddy's face tightens. "You need a napkin, Den-Den."

After a few more slurps and licks, Daddy stood then began to step off.

"Hey, wait a minute!" I lick my lips, feeling the stretching of my forehead. "Where are you going?"

The sun is out and shining so bright I have to tent my hand over my eyes. But Daddy's smile is still as radiant as it's always been. "To get you a napkin, baby."

"But I have something to tell you, Daddy!" Urgency and anxiousness, my common companions when Daddy's around, flared. "I did something last night."

Again, Daddy's head shifts my way, and he smiles. His brown, plaid button-up shirt gave cowboy vibes, which excited me. "You're ten years old, Den-Den. You're always doing something at night." With a dismissive snort, he finally takes off, rounding a brick wall.

Panic strikes again. "Daddy!" My heart juts. "Daddy, wait. But I didn't get a chance to tell you."

Immediately, I feel empty. The sentiment is familiar.

Daddy always leaves before I'm ready.

My eyes swung open. The room was dark, but a different kind of darkness than it was last night into the early morning. The sun crept through the hem of the long curtains. And his intrusive heat was gone. Immediately, I felt bereft of his erotic countenance. I rubbed my tight eyes, swearing to having just fallen asleep. We'd fallen into an exhaustive rest together after he shuddered from behind me before promenading to the bathroom on unsteady, powerfully-banded legs. My john returned to the bed where, with a swift roll, he yanked me into his fold by the arm. Within seconds, his breaths turned heavy, rhythmic, and soothing, and I rolled into siesta with ease.

It's morning...

That realization had me sitting up on my elbow to inspect why. The moment I shifted on the mattress, I felt modest weights around, pinning the comforter to me. Money. Banded stacks of cash. There were several of them placed around my body. I reached for one and thumbed through a count. Not believing my tired eyes, I counted again. *One thousand dollars.* All one-hundred-dollar bills.

Shit...

My heart thundered and I sat up fully. Did I take my impulsive, undeveloped, and patently promiscuous game I played with *myself* last night too far? My eyes were wild, swiping around the room to confirm my suspicion of being alone. I began collecting the bundles around the bed. Fifteen. There was possibly fifteen thousand dollars planted around me recently for my services last night.

"I can give you that for one thousand, five hundred dollars."

"For the night?"

"Per hour."

That was our exchange for the *Panther* event.

"Seven thousand."

"You're expensive."

Clutching the comforter to my naked body, my face fell into my available palm as the other held harlot cash.

Shit.

My john tipped me well, too.

Shit, shit, shit!

Here was the time in this charade I was supposed to exit. *My dress.* Where were my things? I slid across the mattress, holding my nude breasts with my arm. The moment I stood flat on my feet, my bladder began to protest. New issue. *Where's the bathroom?* Seconds into my search for an ensuite, I found my dress, purse, shoes, and STI report card carefully placed on a single sofa chair.

I dipped into the bathroom for a quick relief and then to wash my hands and spot clean my face. I was out and hopping into my bra, dress, and heels soon after. The cash. How was I going to take all the cash? Should I have taken it? Thinking fast, I click-clacked back into the bathroom where I found a robe. After arm and shouldering it on, I emptied the contents of my *Asè Garb* clutch into the oversized pockets. I then managed most of the bundles inside. The four I couldn't, I planted inside the pockets of the robe beneath my other junk.

With a pounding chest, I found my way into the hallway, trying to navigate the massive suite. Feeling confident I'd made it to the entryway, I heard noises. Nearby was the kitchen. An older woman appearing Hispanic peered my way. My eyes grew wild.

"Senorita Jane, would ju like breakfast?"

My head popped back. Breakfast? Was my john still here? Because if so, I'd broken character the moment I fell asleep a few hours ago. Frantically, I shook my head, telling her 'no.' With the door in sight, I hightailed it out of my expired fantasy.

His tongue was firm and wide, riding my spine from the opening of my ass to the nape of my neck. "You're moving again," *he chided throatily over my shivering body.*

I couldn't help it. His touch was a sensual mixture of pleasure and uncertainty. His heat was enriched with intimidating, masculine strength. His mind was a quiet collection of erotic treasures. The man watched me a lot, studying my reactions to his consummate touch. He was relentless with his pursuits and when I didn't hold steady to allow him his discovery:

WHAM!

"Uh!" I cried out from the sharp slap he lay on my ass cheek. As the pain withered away, pleasure knotted my nipples—

"Oh, shit!" The sharp swear had me blinking then glancing over my shoulder as I stood in line to board the plane. "Hayden!" Lucy paced quickly toward me, lugging her rolling suitcase behind. "Ma'am, I thought I'd have to stay behind and start a search for you!"

I pushed my sunglasses up my face. "Why?"

"We haven't seen you since lunch yesterday!" We moved up in line together as it was our group's turn to board. "I told them to leave you be last night." She waved off the notion. "I know how you can get. How many reports did you clear?" She jeered, laughing at her own joke.

Still able to feel the delicious weight of his hard and pulsing erection resting threateningly in the crack of my ass as I rested on all fours, I murmured, "Too many." Closing my eyes behind my frames, I softly shook my head. "Did you guys have a good time?"

"Meh!" She shrugged as we took a few steps up toward the door of the gate. "We went to eat at that restaurant Letisha just had to try out. Remember she said it was the rave with her yoga group? I've had better food at *B-Way Burger*." She turned to see if our crew was around to have heard that.

That warmed a smile on my face. "You have to stop. I'm sure it wasn't that bad. What time did you guys get in?"

"Oh, we haven't really slept. After dinner, we walked the strip a little until several Black people mentioned that club, *Flare*, inside the casino. We ended the night there, dancing and drinking. Mika scored. She met a guy." She giggled sheepishly then whispered, "I think they fucked in the bathroom. Then took the afterparty up to her room."

I choked on my saliva. Coughing and feeling my eyes mist, I tried warning her, "Lucy, I'm not supposed to know that."

She rolled her eyes, smirking. "I know, but you know…" When I thought she was stumped for words as I cleared my throat, she amended. "Whatever happened in Vegas stays in Vegas." Lucy conspicuously glanced around. "We're still in Vegas, woman." I held my face in my palm, smudging my sunglasses. "Anyway, it was a little concerning when you didn't answer the door when we stopped by to scoop you for the airport."

"I'm sorry." My eyes squeezed to a close at that blow, too. "I should have sent a text. I slept later than I meant to and rushed into the shower. Maybe that's when you guys were there knocking. By the time I was ready to head here, I knew you guys had left by then. Time got ahead of me."

That part was true. When I'd awakened in a strange bed, surrounded by fifteen thousand dollars, it was later than what was safe for my travel schedule today. I had no intention on spending the night there. I also didn't know my former john had such detailed plans for my body either. So, this morning, I had to get here early enough to deal with *TSA*. Traveling with so much cash could have caused me to miss my flight if they pressed me about how I got it. I had no paperwork from a casino win. I was lucky enough to be in Vegas and, at least, present like an unsuspecting civilian who simply got lucky in Sin City.

"Okay. I don't like to 'mother,' but we did travel here together and are accountable for each other." Lucy and Mika, colleagues as well, agreed to share a suite when Mika expressed being afraid to stay in such a big space alone.

Lucy was a counselor at *Christ Cares*, a non-profit organization where we both worked. The foundation was run under *Redeeming Souls for Abundant Living in Christ Family Worship Church* in Harlem, New York. At the helm was the pastor's wife, Lex Carmichael, who was more like the girl from up the block than a stiff ass old first lady. I enjoyed my work and was damn good at it. I was valued by my organization, too. My boss had consistently done everything legally possible to ensure my comfort. My pay wasn't competitive with my counterparts at the big non-profit hospitals or cancer organizations, but it was pretty much stone-knowledge that my wage was top three, and not number three, in the organization. I was needed. My primary role was to find and bring in money to serve the *Christ Cares* community.

"Excuse me!" I turned to find a petite white woman with shoulder-length chocolate hair and blunt cut bangs in an "I beg your pardon" stance while holding her luggage.

It was for my assistant, Mika, who had cut the line, stopping near us then sucking her teeth at the woman. "What? I'm with them. What's the big deal? I wouldn't be able to get on if I was in a later group, lady!"

I wanted to roll my eyes. This was Mika. Short, thick, and gutsy. She would not be backing down.

"I don't think that's her argument," I tried whispering. "Overhead spacing is an issue on flights. You could be rows behind her but get space and she doesn't."

"No, ma'am." Mika's neck rolled. "Respectfully, she's only two people behind. Ain't none of us in business class. We all got mediocre seats today. She'll be fine."

"Damn. Looking for a way to stay. *Huhn?*" Letisha was on her heels, snickering while cutting the line, too.

Mika rolled her eyes. "Don't start that shit," she murmured, hardly audible.

One brow arched high on my forehead. "What am I missing here?"

"I told you Mika got piped last night," Lucy chimed in. "We think she fell in love."

My head swung toward her, though she could see my shocked, bulging eyes. "In love? After one night?"

We were next in line to be scanned for the plane. I held my phone out, displaying my boarding pass.

"It's those fucking romance novels," my girlfriend, Letisha, snickered.

Lucy fucking hollered.

Mika was the first to be scanned. Holding out her phone, she hissed, "Y'all'll never understand." Then she stomped her way down the passenger boarding bridge.

From the final check-in to hauling our luggage overhead for storage, Lucy and Letisha giggled and laughed their asses off about a temperamental Mika. It became a little unsettling to see her downcast.

"Mika—"

"I know, boss lady, but not right now," she grumbled across the aisle as people were still boarding. "What I did was wrong but something I'll never regret."

Oh my, god!

Mika grabbed her face as though she was crying. When I heard her sniffle, I knew she was, in fact, sobbing.

Over a one-night stand?

I plopped down into my seat, immediately feeling the ache of my tender sex. Hell, my damn pelvis was even sore. I just hoped the pain wouldn't linger longer than the deed. I needed to get my head straight. Jane Doherty was dead. Buried.

Now, back to my real life.

"I can't believe the nerve of them," Kathrine, one of the board members, hissed from across the conference room table. She was a vigorous, elderly woman with warm gingerbread sagging skin, who'd been on the advisory board since Lex took over at *Christ Cares*. She was a devout member, making each meeting and being sure to add to the agenda. "I think there's something to them doing that." She tapped her natural, burgundy painted nail on the table.

"Really?" Lisa, a middle-aged member, asked. "I mean... It does sound awkward." Her skin was attacked by severe eczema over most of her body. Her casing resembled that of a crocodile.

She'd been with *Christ Cares* for three years and missed several meetings from hospitalizations. There was a patch of infected skin on her cheek and neck, and more on her hands. The sight of dry skin brought back a memory incongruent to my current setting.

When I draped the terry cloth robe over my body in Vegas, the deci-

sion was born of needing to sheath places on my body covered in dry secretions I was sure were my own. I'd never been so damn wet in my life during sex. My excitement for his prowess seeped down my leg as he plunged into me against the floor-to-ceiling window. Or when he draped my leg over his knee as I was on all fours, and masterfully used one hand to stroke my clit while wounding two digits inside my sopping canal. I greedily rode his hand in that awkward position until my pelvis stiffened, and the first splat of liquid left me. My leg wobbled over his, leaving me unbalanced until I collapsed in a fitful orgasm with uncontrollable jerks. In that posh suite, I was a gushing mess as Jane. Too messy to be so anonymous with intent. I would've been embarrassed if not so curious about his next erotic act.

"Earth to Hayden!" I heard yelped. "Earth to Hayden!"

I blinked hard and whipped my head around at the sound of hard taps at the table.

Mika snickered, "Ms. Ma'am, are you kay-kay?"

I cleared my throat. "Of course. I'm here." Then I tried for a sheepish grin.

My boss, Lex, shook her head, fighting back humor. "Kathrine said she's worried about *NYU* pulling our funding soon."

Shaking my head with my answer, I shared, "No. That's not what this is. It's common practice for some donors to want non-profit recipients to have relationships with other donors. It shows you're serious about your proposed mission statement. So focused, you're maintaining relationships with more than one donor. When companies give money, they want formidable recipients. It makes the donor look good to their constituents and doesn't waste their resources. They can be competitive that way. And for others, they don't like feeling your non-profit organization is going to go belly up if they pull out." With pouted lips, I jerked my palm in the air. "We'll be fine. I have my sights on another major donor."

"Who?" Lisa asked.

Studying me before deciding to answer, Mika shared, "*Protecting Love.*"

"Who's that?" pushed from Kathrine's belly with passion. It was her style of communication.

I explained, "A fundraising organization R&B singer, Ragee, has with the undisputed heavyweight boxing champion, Tori McNabb."

"*The* Tori McNabb," Lex emphasized with humor.

Mika followed with, "The one and never the two."

"You know her," Kathrine noted to Lex. "Bishop is good friends with that Ragee. Heck, he's been a member of *RSFALC* for a mountain of years. You ain't never ask her to donate?"

Lex sat back in her chair and sighed. It was a reminder of the late hour. She'd just closed the advisory board meeting minutes ago. Most had left the building. We were the few still lingering behind. And I was just as tired as shit as my boss appeared when she explained, "Never. I don't seek out funding from friends. I have a grant writer for that. A fund-hunter."

Her words may have seemed sharp, but I understood Lex carried a bone for the church culture. They could be brutal, and she refused to be a victim.

"But Hayden is going to ask them for money," Kathrine argued. "What's the difference?"

"*Christ Cares* will be applying for funding from *Protecting Love*," I qualified. "They raise money for underaged survivors of sexual abuse. We have a subset of our population falling into that category. I'm also writing a grant for *Bobby's Hope*, which is Tori's organization independent of what she has with Raj."

Kathrine wanted to know, "Well, how much more you got to go?"

"Not much." My head bobbed up and down.

"Alright now. We got one donor saying we need more if they gone keep funding us. Then we got two potential donors that's been under our noses all this time. I know you know what you're doing—" she flashed her manicured fingers over the table expressively. "—but let's not miss these opportunities. We've done some good stuff for this community. Can't stop now."

"I know the meeting was adjourned ten minutes ago," Lex interjected, head shaking, and eyes closed. "...but let me just put it out there. *Christ Cares* is by no means in danger of being underfunded. In addition, Hayden has worked tirelessly to increase our budget exponentially since she began here a few short years ago. She's here stark early and one of the last to leave the building. She's a door-knocker and seat-warmer while hunting for money—"

"Those lovely leather seats you rave about each time you're here," Lisa mentioned. "It came from that unusual grant the luxury furniture company provided from California. Remember how rare and specific the requirements were? How small the number of grantees they had in mind?"

"Yeah, but..." Kathrine appeared to have turned defensive, unable to get her words out.

"I don't mean to come off as argumentative here." Lex swiped an errant loc of her long, dark, wooly hair from her face. "I have a good thing going with Hayden. I'm constantly speaking with our non-profit peers out here and hearing nightmarish stories about inconsistent staffing for grant writers. So many organizations have to settle for inexperienced people just to have a dedicated person. More than I care to gossip about, there are constant issues with misappropriation of funds. We run a cohesive ship around here. So dedicated that I had to force a few of them to take their earned time off. Vacation. Do self-care. I can't afford to have anyone on my team burned out, especially the money-chaser."

Kathrine's little hand shot into the air. Her eyes were wide. "I wasn't trying to imply you aren't doing your job, Hayden. God help me, I wasn't."

"No worries. I understand the excitement behind success." I shook my head, blowing off her need to apologize. "With funding, we just want to stay aboveboard. We want to make sure we're answering to each requirement of the application."

Not to mention my stealthy research for the appropriate party at HAYDAR.

Of course, I wouldn't speak that out loud. It had been two weeks, and I was still struggling with forgetting my last night in Vegas. No amount of work cured my pathetic memory.

THREE

February

ISHAAN

My chest pounded, and lungs were on fire as I walked down the hall, leaving my home gym. I wiped my dripping face as a thought popped into my mind of calling Kia before the day was done.

"Mr. Patterson." The housekeeper greeted.

"Hey, Ms. Green." I stopped, wiping my face again. "Did you see I approved your time?"

"Yes. Thanks so much! I know it's a lot considering I was off last month on vacation, but I'd really like to be with my father for his first two weeks of chemo. I can't rely on my sisters or brothers to take care of him. I'm the knee-baby, always seeing about our parents' health while they run the business."

"No worries. I understand. A few friends of mine have experience with caring for family going through chemo and radiation. It can be fuckin' brutal. Just keep me posted. We should be alright around here."

She gave a neck bow. "Thanks so much, Mr. Patterson. I have quite a few things to do around here before I leave in a few days."

I nodded and continued to the kitchen, yanking off a scrunchie to release my hair. On my way to the fridge, I noticed my mother at the nook, an arched cove with tulip and bay windows, gazing out into the garden she'd planted back there.

I noticed a jar of banana peppers on the second shelf of the fridge. It was right in the front. "Who eats these nasty peppers?" I mumbled. When she didn't reply, I glanced her way "Sittin', reminiscin'?" I teased.

She turned just her head in my direction. "On when I had the choice of having you implanted in my womb or ingested. Maybe I should've been spittin' *you* in faces."

I lost grip of the crystal pitcher in the fridge. It slammed onto the glass shelf. "Aye!" I shouted. "Watch your mouth. *Please.*"

Unperturbed, she slowly rotated her neck back toward the window. "Who do you think you get your dry sense of humor from?"

Trying again, this time I successfully grabbed the pitcher and brought it over to the countertop. I plucked a glass, still jarred by her comment. "From you, woman, I've received lots of notable traits; however, my sense of humor isn't one of them."

"I can pontificate on my dominant genes at another time. Right now, I need to know if you've spoken to Mehki since you've been back from Vegas."

"Of course, I have. I've been home since Tuesday, Ma."

"No." She turned her entire body toward the open kitchen. "About the banquet. About the Winfreys being in attendance."

Damn...

"I will." I took a big gulp of the freshly squeezed juice, feeling the coolness of the liquid spill down into my belly. "I haven't yet," I panted. "But I will."

"When?"

"Ma, it's in a few weeks."

"Try two. If he finally invites them, their excuse will be it's a purposely last-minute invite."

I scoffed. "That's bullshit."

"Yeah, but we know the game now. We need to stay ahead of the drama. Talk to Mehki. Tell him how important it is to have all of his family at these milestone events in his life. He's growing up, Shan. He's seventeen already. We won't get these precious moments back."

"It's his decision, though, Ma."

"And he won't get them back either. That's why you need to speak to him. Having a seat at the table for the academy's recognition event is a big deal. I remember you getting invited. Your father cried the entire way there and home. He managed to hold it together during the ceremony and dinner, but it was truly an accomplishment to render your emotions to."

Damn.

I sighed, remembering my junior year at *Ellis High Academy – Hackensack* where I commuted to from Waldwick. I knew I'd get into *Blakewood*. It was my only motivation to keep my grades up. The academy held a banquet each year for students with proven academic success. In my case, I'd been accepted into the most prestigious *HBCU* in the country. *Blakewood State University* was offering me significant funding, too. You're allowed to bring family. My mother wanted Mehki's family to be there as well.

"I understand." I nodded politely as if I didn't have one hundred and two other fucking things to tend to. "I'll talk to him ASAP."

"Well, in the meantime, let me talk to you, sir." Those dark brows reached her forehead, letting me know how serious she was. I shifted my torso to silently give her my undivided attention. "You."

I gave her a nod. "Me."

"You need to evolve."

"Evolve?"

"Yes. I only have one child."

I swept my hand, motioning down my sweaty body. "Moi."

"Yes. And let me tell you how fast your childhood came and went. It happened so fast, I'm not even sure I made the most of it all. It made me realize a few missteps I made."

"As in?"

"For starters, I should have had more than one child." She shrugged. "When being realistic about your mortality, you have to know it's better to have more than one child to split the burdens that come along with issues of the parents. Look at when your father passed. You had to practically shoulder the responsibility of laying him to rest alone. You paid for everything. I was so beside myself in grief I could hardly pick out a suit for him. You were but a child your-self having to deal with your grief and bury your father at the same damn time. While your father and I worked, you were left behind without a peer to bond with in our absence."

"Because I didn't need anyone. Still don't. But I'm not alone. I've got you and you've got me." I winked before downing the rest of my juice.

"Ishaan Dawl Patterson." She shook her head determinately. "You're not absorbing. You're looking for a break in my words to fix whatever you perceive the 'problem' I'm presenting to you to be. Yes, I'm telling you there's a problem, but it's one *you* have to decidedly approach."

"Which is?"

"You have to partner up with a woman, Ishaan. You need more kids running around here. You need to spread your loins. You need a legacy. Family is the most underrated essential now for Black men and women. Whole families. You've amassed so much financially, but money isn't a value left behind when you're dead and gone. Family is."

"Why are you bringing this up?"

"Because I'm sixty-seven, Ishaan. I don't have many days ahead. And as I'm reflecting, and seeing my mistakes, it's my job to warn you of your own. Mehki needs more family, too."

I smiled. "I'm really good at lots of shit I do, but not even I can meet a good enough woman and have a baby with her by the banquet."

"Don't be an ass, Shan."

Successfully controlling my humor, I explained, "I'm trying not to be. But what does me finding a woman to have babies with have to do with the *Ellis High Academy* banquet, Dr. Patterson?"

She stood from the table. "Life can show you better than I can apparently tell you."

"Yirp!" his corny ass shouted, dropping down the last few steps of the rear staircase into the kitchen.

I could feel my mother's energetic gaze. The moment I peered her way, it was confirmed. Her lips were balled, and forehead stretched, as her head and shoulders bobbed.

Mehki rounded the banister wearing that killer light-skinned ass smile women, young and old, seemed to become beguiled by. The nigga had the fucking nerve to be only two inches shorter than me on approach while issuing me a proffered handshake I'd taught him over the years.

"It's been a minute," he joked, trying to erase his smirk.

"Nigga, I just let your ass drive me in my *R8* to school this morning," I reminded him, accepting his hand. When I met it in a firm shake, Mehki broke character and chuckled. "Fuck you mean, it's been a minute?"

"Language!"

I cringed. "Sorry, Mom." Then I looked Mehki dead in the eyes as he laughed at my expense. He knew my mother hated my work travel. It wasn't conducive to raising children. Thank god I had her, a decorated, licensed family therapist. "Where are you off to?"

"Meeting up with Johnathan at *B-Way Burger* to eat and play some video games."

"And he's picking you up?" I asked.

Mehki had only a learner's permit and couldn't operate a vehicle without a licensed driver. But already, he'd had a car in the garage, which we'd make sure he drove regularly to prepare him.

"You know this." He picked up a few clementines from the decorative bowl on the countertop and began to juggle them. "It's gonna be up and stuck tonight."

"I don't know why y'all prefer that fast food to homecooked food," mom grumbled. "Will he be bringing you home, too?"

Still juggling the fruit, he backed toward her close enough to plant a wet kiss on her cheek. "Sure is, Nanu, my favorite girl."

My mother rolled her eyes knowing damn well she loved that shit. "You know your Poppy here used to try to charm me the same way. Right?" Mehki laughed my way. "And I let him...until he came in past his curfew when I'd be waiting with my belt."

Mehki had to end his juggling act. He couldn't stop laughing. "I wonder if those beatings were worse than the spankings you used to give me, Nanu."

Mom put her hand on her hip. "You wanna find out. I don't give a good damn if you're an only child. Poppy here was, too."

"No, ma'am!" Mehki's smile didn't fade as he expressed, "I haven't gotten a pow-wow from you in almost ten years. No need to start tonight. I'll make my curfew." This time, he wrapped her in a bear hug.

Pinching the bridge of my nose, I shook my head. Mehki's had this woman wrapped around his finger since she first laid eyes on him.

Feeling her heavy gaze, I opened my eyes to confirm it was there and stapled to me. She was giving me a harsh cue.

Shit...

I took a deep breath, taking the towel to dap the back of my head. "Aye, Ki," I began. "About the *Ellis High Academy* banquet: did you invite the Winfreys?"

A pinch brought his dark brows together and his eyes rolled away. "Nanu said, but..." He shook his head, appearing annoyed. "For what? They're not going to come. They never do. First thing he's going to do is ask will y'all be there then say 'no.'" Mehki's throat bobbed as he shrugged. "I ain't beat for that."

"Your mom—God, rest her soul—" I cleared my throat and swallowed hard. "—would want all of your family there, not just my side."

"Yes!" Mom expressed spiritedly. "*Princeton, Yale, BSU,* and even

MIT wants you. Mandy would be in pain if they were not there in full support of you."

"Yeah. Then they need to sit with that."

"There's nothing like blood, baby. Good, bad, or indifferent, they're your blood. We have to keep giving them a chance to change their hearts."

He reached over and laid another wet one on my mother. "My stomach ain't changing easily right now either. I gotta go, Nanu. I'm as hungry as you were after your colonoscopy!"

This time, my head tossed back, and I laughed my ass off.

"Don't think this is over!" Mom hissed.

I pushed my palms into the air. "I don't imagine it is. I'll stay on his little ass. Don't worry."

She rolled her eyes and left for the back door to tend to her winter garden.

"You have a conference call scheduled with Zambada in Cape Verde in the morning at eight-thirty," Munchie murmured as we sauntered down the hall of *KAHRI Resort & Casino* in Atlantic City, New Jersey. "He seems really motivated to speak about us sponsoring dancers to do a residency here. And can I say how excited I am to see *ADJ Properties* open up opportunities to cultures who share our melanin. This will be groundbreaking," she applauded dryly. It was her way.

"I'm sure the montage we sent over to illustrate what the experience would be helped." I adjusted my tie. "Now, let's see what the head honcho has to say about it." I slowed to trail behind her as the door was opened by the security guard.

Munchie didn't utter another word. She pushed the frame of her glasses up her face and straightened her spine as we entered the mammoth conference room in the administration wing of the facility. Most of the room was empty. There were several assistants at work, performing their various tasks. At the head of the table was the CEO of the company, Azmir Jacobs.

"Patterson," he shouted me out, removing his reading glasses. "What it do, brother?"

"A little bit of this and a little bit of that, sir." Munchie and I took our seats, hers right next to Rob's.

"Rob here," Jacobs pointed down the table. "...was the first to arrive. He mentioned the Marino family. I asked him to hold off until you got here."

My attention fell hard on one of the hosts I'd hired for the clubs here in Atlantic City. Rob Whitter was a *Hampton University* dropout who had earned a reputation of being the party king, had been with me here at *ADJ Properties*. In his late twenties, Rob was young enough to have his finger on the modern-day pulse of entertainment. He was also old enough to know protocol and hierarchy.

"You're not on today's agenda with Mr. Patterson and Mr. Jacobs."

"Yeah." Rob hesitated. "Okay, but I knew they'd be meeting today and thought now would be a great time to discuss this."

Munchie's shoulders dropped. "That's not how this works. Mr. Jacobs and Mr. Patterson have hectic schedules. We stick to an agenda here."

Nervous, yet obviously determined, Rob cleared his throat and sat up in his seat. "But Ish said we'd talk and since the big man was on the property today, I figured—"

Munchie was shaking her head before he could finish his sentence. "That's not how things work around here. The Marino family will not be discussed today. In fact, you don't need to be here."

Rob peered my way. My response was a blank stare. Jacobs sat back in his chair with one elbow propped up on an armrest while stroking his chin. His associates around the table were now frozen.

"You can't tell me to leave," Rob finally spoke. "You don't have the authority."

Without looking my way, Munchie explained, "I think you know I do. Please wait for Mr. Patterson in his office, Rob." Rob didn't move. He stared petulantly across the table, mouth tight with agitation. "Rob—"

He shot from his seat. "You are not my fucking boss! You are a fucking assistant! I will—"

Leaping from my chair, I took him at his shoulders, twisting his body to face me and rocked his nose with my dome. Rob stumbled backwards, narrowly missing Munchie due to Jacobs' swift movement of pulling her away. I didn't allow Rob to fall, holding him by the lapels of his jacket. He was able to find his balance as I walked him backward toward the door. On alert, security had just pushed through the doors.

Rob was awakening from his temporary stupor. "Wait. Hold on." He blinked. "You just head-butted me?"

I pushed him toward one of the security guards. "Go to medical then go home. You'll hear from human resources regarding your status with *ADJ Properties* in a day or two."

As the guards rushed a disoriented Rob out, he shouted, "What the fuck?"

I closed the doors behind them then returned to my seat. On approach, I saw Jacobs standing with one hand in his pocket while doing something strange with his mouth where he pushed his tongue into his molars. There was a spark of humor in his gaze.

"I apologize for that," I murmured to Munchie. "I can assure the shit won't happen again."

Licking her lips while her head was toward the conference table, she nodded. She took her seat as I did. Jacobs followed.

"Domestic issues spilling into the boardroom, Ish?"

"Just a case of an overzealous talent." I rubbed beneath my bottom lip as I considered it. "Damn!" I whispered. "The kid was promising, too."

"Aren't they all," Jacobs remarked.

"Rob has been getting to know the town and players," I began my explanation. "He'd mentioned to me the desire to introduce me, and ultimately you, to the Marino family—"

Jacobs began to laugh and loudly. "Introduce?"

It was insulting, I understood. Azmir Divine Jacobs was no novice at setting up shop for business in new terrain. *KAHRI Resort &* *Casino* had been operating in Atlantic City for about five years now. We knew the "neighborhood" from the councilmen and women to each gang affiliated with the city. This included the Marinos, a family with mob ties whose tethers ran into shit I couldn't have associated with the *ADJ* brand. There was an information recovery program I ran here at *ADJ Properties*. It all tied into my role as chief operating officer. Disquisition was a key element to keeping the residents and patrons of each property safely engaged. Therefore, through extensive investigation, we learned years ago of the Marino family's involvement in human trafficking.

Rob, courting the city and its cultural metropolis, happened upon the family who'd convinced him of an alliance, which would unlock the city's government to *KAHRI*, eliminating long waits for permits and guarantee friendly inspection. In turn, the Marinos would have broad access to the property. Rob had no authority to even encourage that arrangement. He was a resort ambassador, not an executive. He was to be out on the circuit, meeting movers and shakers and influencing them to party at our clubs and to eat at our restaurants. Similar to how I'd found him in the *Hampton University* community, he was to be an influencer among a demographic in this region.

Rob had overstepped his job requirements by ignorantly rubbing elbows with a nefarious crime family. My answer to wait until I had time to meet with him about it was not good enough for Rob. He thought he'd jump over me and speak to the big guy about it today. I wouldn't tolerate capsizing of my authority, and certainly not in front of my partner, hence my reaction.

"Right." I took a deep breath. "Rob is aware of our knowledge of the family. Or his egregious ignorance of, not only the Marinos, but the culture of *ADJ Properties*. I apologize for that." In this moment, I wished I'd escorted Rob out myself. My anger was cresting. I wanted to beat his ass. "If it's all the same with you, I'd like to move on to the agenda. I know you have a tight schedule."

"To be honest, this was the highlight of my damn day." He winked. "Next time, let's allow them to walk out untouched—at least, in front of the ladies."

Reaching for my forehead where I used my area of choice to subdue the kid, I acknowledged him silently.

"Can we begin with the *Sun-Bronzed Maroon*?" Munchie asked, flipping through pages in her agenda.

A wide beam stretched Jacobs' face. "Our new baby. Nothing would please me more."

"The head of agriculture out there," Munchie referenced me. "After Mr. Patterson increased the offer, he's still not budging."

Jacobs sat back and let out a deep breath. "Talk to me, Ish."

And I did because I was never short of a solution.

love belvin

Hayden

"Oh, no! Isam, don't cry." I lay the newborn over my shoulder. Sitting with crossed legs on a plush beanie bag, I lamented, "We were doing so well."

From across the nursery, his mother snickered. "That lil guy is persnickety after feeding. He likes to be held how he likes to be held." Sundryia motioned over to her newborn daughter, Isam's twin, Imani. She was being held by our cousin, Rayna. "She's so smooth and easygoing."

"*Hmmmhmmm*," Rayna sniffed Imani as she held her in her hands. "Her aura is so chill, and she smells heavenly."

Sundryia scoffed while folding their clothes over the changing table. "Don't all babies smell good unless they shit?"

"Newborn poop doesn't smell too bad. Maybe later in their infancy stages—definitely by the time the little boogers become toddlers—you'll start to gag."

"Shoot." I rubbed Isam's back as he quieted. "I imagine that's when they're eating the same foods we eat."

"Ding. Ding. Ding." Rayna confirmed. "But you, my dear, are so precious. You're a doll." Then her eyes narrowed. "She favors my Divine."

"Who?" Sundryia asked. "Divine as in your husband?" Her lip curled.

Rayna snorted. "My son, Divine. Divi."

"Oh!" Sundryia snorted. "Girl, I was about to say: don't start no damn rumors of me being with your old man. Maaz would kill Divine and worry about having all of Brooklyn and Compton after his big ass after."

That made us all laugh. I tightened my grip on Isam as my abdomen drummed, I laughed so hard. Rayna reclined in the rocking chair.

Even Sundryia grabbed her temporary pouch, created by the twins, as she chortled. "I'm serious," she tried, hardly able to breathe. "Since Christmas, this nigga has turned into this...bodyguard."

"Girl, don't get me started." Rayna rolled her eyes and I immediately realized how dope this was. I'd been back from Vegas for five weeks now, and finally had been able to drive up to Connecticut for the weekend to see Sundryia and the twins again. Rayna's husband, Azmir, had flown to the East Coast for work at his casino in South Jersey. Rayna decided to tag along, since Sundryia and I were together. We'd been seeing a lot of each other lately as a group. Before then, it was pretty much just Sundryia and me. I'd grown fond of the inclusion of our cousin, Rayna. "Azmir was like a damn watchdog from the moment he pieced together my pregnancy with the twins. Even to the point of banning heels from my wardrobe."

"Heels?" Sundryia's eyes blossomed wide. "And you obeyed?"

"Was my father's name Eric?" Rayna rolled her neck sassily. "Well... We had to compromise. All these women after him and he expected me to look like an Oompah Loompa? I begged his pardon."

"Right!" Sundryia added spiritedly. "The same with Maaz. All these football-crazed heifers. Girl, they're even family members of the players! How 'bout they be friends of some of the girlfriends and wives."

I blinked hard. "You'd think there was a code. Like...the players would for sure be off limits to their people."

"It's the je ne sais quoi," Rayna casually murmured, eyes admiringly on Imani. "It's attached to his celebrity. And let's not leave his handsomeness out of the equation. But men don't even have to be good-looking to have women fawning over them like that. I see it with some of Azmir's associates. They're better seen at night, but because they either have wealth or are celebrities, women are constantly flocking to them. It's disgusting."

"So, how do you deal with it with Azmir?"

Sundryia scoffed. "Yeah. Hook me up."

She shrugged, now smiling at Imani. "I don't think I've arrived at a solution yet. I've raised some eyebrows on red carpets and at corporate gigs with having to check women on their fake familiarity with my husband. And white women are the worst. They carry a sense of entitlement to his personal space."

Sundryia sucked in a breath, "They do! They're all around the *League* and love to be touchy feely with those guys. It's so damn annoying!"

"You know what, Isam?" I pose to the baby who'd returned to a calm, restive state. "I think I'll start dating again when you do. Even then, I'd be ahead of your sister because she won't be allowed to start until she's thirty."

My cousins laughed.

"Damn. I was going to give her till twenty-one and look at cousin-auntie, Hayden, tacking on nine years," his mother, Sundryia, remarked.

"Did you wait till you were grown to date, Mommy?" Rayna asked, eyes playfully tight.

"That ain't the point." Sundryia's nose flared, causing us to snicker.

"How was Vegas? That was what?" Rayna asked, "Three weeks ago?"

I thought for a minute. "Almost five. A distant memory."

"Damn. That's it?" Sundryia asked. "I was beastin' for you to come up to share what I missed. All that time you were out there, I was here with a set of twins, living vicariously through you in my head."

I snickered, while I brought Isam from my shoulder to cradle him. He'd dozed off. "It was nice. Thanks for the hook up, Rayna."

Sundryia gasped. "And what about me? I set up the whole shit."

Smiling, I agreed. "You did."

Rayna, Sundryia, and I shared the same great-grandmother, Louise Tempest. Our mothers were first cousins. We hadn't always been this close and casual with one another—well, Sundryia and I had maintained a relationship growing up. As both of us were sexually assaulted by a relative, we'd often jokingly refer to it as a trauma bond. It was dry humor at best, but it worked for us. Funny enough, Rayna and Sundryia shared a trauma as well. Both their mothers struggled with drug addiction. Sundryia's mother, Angelica, had been struggling most of Sundryia's childhood with drug and alcohol abuse until her passing. We'd always known Cousin Angie's struggle and neglect of Sundryia.

On the other hand, Rayna's mother, Samantha's, addiction blossomed when Rayna was in high school. I remember hearing my mother speak of it and felt sorry for Rayna. It was devastating for her. The pain of it all was one of many reasons she fled New Jersey for *Duke University* and never returned. She ultimately landed in California where she began a career, got married to a millionaire, and had his babies.

She'd done well, meeting her person, and traveling the world. It was her husband, Azmir's, resort my friends and I stayed at in Vegas. He owned another in Atlantic City, New Jersey. Sundryia pushed me to ask Rayna for help in getting the best rooms for the fairest price. Rayna did us one better. She arranged for us to have luxury suites and access to all the lush restaurants and clubs free of charge. It was a dream. Rayna had vowed to spend more time with Sundryia and me, and since the fall, she'd kept her word. Though living in different states, Rayna made trips to the East Coast to be supportive of Sundryia's pregnancy.

"Did you guys visit the aquarium at *HAYDAR*?" Rayna asked. "I love that place. Did you make it to *Flare*? I haven't been into clubs for years, but I make sure to drop in there each chance I get. It reminds me I'm still young." She and Sundryia giggled.

"The aquarium is magical," I returned. "I heard the one at *KAHRI Resort* in A.C. is even bigger." Then my attention dropped to a sleeping Isam. "I didn't make it to *Flare*."

"I thought you said the girls loved *Flare*," Sundryia posed, confused.

"They did." My mouth twisted. "I didn't." A hush fell over the room. Upon that realization, my pulse began to race. I knew. I'd known since I spoke to Sundryia when I returned home, I'd have to tell her. "I met a guy."

"Where?" Rayna chirped.

I took a deep breath as I thought. "In the lobby."

Sundryia dropped the t-shirt she was working on and shifted closer. "And?"

"And..." I shrugged. "We caught eyes...and, clearly, we both liked what we saw. So, after a few drinks and a little food, we decided to... You know."

Sundryia's eyes blew the hell up. "*You* fucked him? That night?" She blinked. "The same night?"

"Whoa..." Rayna appeared to be in disbelief. I stood from the beanie bag and walked Isam to his bassinet. "Are you a one-night stand type of girl, Hayden?"

"Hell no, she ain't! Girl!" Sundryia supplied protectively as her head fell to the side. "Who is he? What's his name?"

"Was?" I corrected. "Who he was." I shrugged rubbing my upper arms. "He was just that 'something' for the moment."

"Like fun." Rayna's tone was now defensive. "I mean... You're young and, I believe, always responsible, Hayden. It's not a bad thing. Right?" Her chin dropped. "Did he make you feel uncomfortable at any moment?"

I shook my head. "No—I mean, yes. I was totally off my game. I was a completely different person. I didn't even give him my real name."

"You guys didn't exchange names?"

"Are you surprised, Sundryia?" Rayna asked. "There's no need. One-night stands are with the intent of never seeing each other again. There are only two rules to the game: protection and fun."

"And I know your ass used a condom!" Sundryia low-key demanded confirmation.

"Condoms." I stressed the "*S*." Then I scratched the side of my head. "We even got tested beforehand."

"Where?"

"There are clinics at both resorts," Rayna explained. "They're there for obvious reasons, but his team felt the importance of having adult testing and counseling as a major spoke in the clinics' services."

Sundryia's jaw dropped. "I didn't know that."

"It's not something advertised, exactly. Mostly high-rollers, employees, and locals know about it."

Sundryia's eyes cut over to me. "So, who the fuck was your name-less guy?"

I smirked. "Does it matter?"

"No!" Rayna was insistent. "If he didn't mistreat you. It doesn't matter. We can talk about his skill set and hang time over drinks tonight." She winked.

"Hang time?" I asked.

"The size of his wood," Sundryia explained.

"Oh!" My brows shot up.

"Yeah. That or how long his cum stays in the air before landing when he busts." Rayna beamed while biting her red-stained lip.

"Damn," Sundryia mumbled. "That one's new to me."

Rayna sighed, gazing into the distance. "Life-changing, too, if he knows what he's doing."

"Damn." It was my turn to whisper.

A phone sounded. Within seconds, Rayna was pulling hers from the pocket of her blazer. "Hang on, baby girl," she answered the phone. Then she appeared to put the call on mute. "This is Erin. I need to chat with her." She sighed, rolling her eyes. "She and Azmir have been beefing hard."

"For what?" Sundryia asked as Rayna left the rocking chair and handed Imani to her.

"She wants to color her hair and get her nose pierced."

Sundryia gasped, watching Rayna head toward the door. "How old is she again?"

"Fourteen."

"Oh, hell no!"

"Exactly. But my baby's a quarter white and is being raised mostly by white people. That's her extreme side." She snickered. Leaving the doorway, Rayna tapped then brought the phone up to her ear. "Hey, baby girl." Then she was out of listening range.

"Who is Erin?"

"Basically, Rayna's first child. I haven't met her, but she told me about the little girl a couple of months ago. Rayna had a best friend—she was mixed—who passed away from cancer. She left behind a daughter. Rayna's been like her godmother or auntie."

"And she's mixed?"

Sundryia nodded. "That's what she said. But let's go back to this shit in Vegas. What the fuck happened?" she whispered.

Pulling in a deep breath, I shook my head. "Every time I think about it, my stomach does somersaults. I was acting crazy as hell that night. I told him my name was Jane. Jane Doherty."

She wheezed, "What?"

My eyes circled the blue pewter walls with off-white mounted circles and the twins' names in gold metal calligraphy. "We—" I whispered, conscious of the twins' presence. "—fucked all night long. He wouldn't stop getting hard, Sundryia," I grunted hard, trying to control the visceral feelings conjured each time I allowed my mind to go there. I closed my eyes, haunted by the memory. "And I didn't get sore—at least, I didn't feel sore—until I left the bed the next morning. The more he touched me, the more I wanted him to touch me more. I don't know. It was like we had this...insatiable need to connect physically. I don't think he was prepared for that night any more than I was."

"Why?"

"Because we ran out of condoms so soon." I met her eyes.

"*Hay*—"

"We were careful."

"You fucked raw—"

"No!" I was now dishonest, defensive, and insecure as a mother-fucker. "I'm going to get tested again." I stared her dead in the eyes. That's when I decided to keep the other reckless, wanton details to myself. I'd already been kicking myself in the ass. I didn't need my cousin to jump in. "I got tested just before and I'm going to get tested again." That was the truth. "The recommended testing timeframe for HIV is two to four weeks after, then three months, then six. I wanted to wait out the first four weeks to be sure. I have an appointment on Monday afternoon. I'm getting the full menu of tests."

"Girl, you ain't got no damn HIV!" she whispered hard. "Knock it off. Just don't do it again!"

My eyes narrowed as I challenged her. "Why?"

She turned toward the bassinet to lay Imani next to Isam. "Because that's not like you. You ain't built for that."

"How do you know?"

"Because you *just* got around to doing that shit at twenty-nine." Her head twirled, daring me to challenge her again.

She was right. I'd never behaved so recklessly. But still, I shook my head. "You're sounding judgy. I've never judged you."

"Judged me when?"

"Last summer, when I found you and Maaz doing shit Norma-Jean taught you in his mother's beach house."

Sighing, Sundryia collapsed against the dresser. "Yeah. That's me. I'm the risk-taker. Not you. You go back into *Sam's Club* when you realize the scanner at the door missed an item you didn't pay for. You go back and pay. When you got laid off before working in Harlem, you wouldn't even wear the *Red Bottoms* and *Louis Vuitton* bags you owned because you didn't want to feel like a fraud. You keep your nose clean, Hayden. Always the ethical one."

"You can take a six-hour break from your high-held integrity to have a little fun and it not change your character, Sundryia," Rayna hissed, entering the nursery. She resumed her seat. "Live a little. So, if a man ever comes your way, wanting forever with you, you can have something to grade him against." She winked at me. "No foul. No regrets." She sat up, taking a deep breath while a smile spread across her face. "Now, where's the spot for good food and exceptional drinks here in Connecticut."

"*Arch&Point*, baby," Sundryia singsonged.

That's when Rayna grunted, body falling into the rocking chair. "Y'all really wanna see Mr. Jacobs pull up to Connecticut and show his ass tonight. Don't you?"

Sundryia and I caught eyes. In less than a second, we squealed, "Yup!" And cracked the hell up.

FOUR

March

ISHAAN

"If you weren't the COO of the fastest expanding outfit in the hotels, casinos, and resorts industry, what would you be?" Ebonee's lids were low, and her pink-stained lips shined beautifully. Her smile bedazzled the best of us.

I pulled the glass of brandy to my mouth for a sip. Then I swiped the dew sprouting from my face. "Right now, I don't know if it's the television host asking me this question or the attorney."

She snickered, twirling her champagne flute in the air above the jacuzzi's water line. I reached for her leg then pulled her foot toward me and began to knead.

"Shit," she moaned, not taken aback by my actions. "You're going to have me ask follow-up questions like, 'Why are you single and why didn't we work out?' Damn. This is nice." Her eyes swept against the glass ceiling displaying the stars of the night sky. "You have access to the best properties and rooms."

It was nice. Eb had almost always been a good time. "What would you be doing? You miss practicing law?"

"If I wasn't doing what I do. *Hmmmm...*" Her eyes swung to the right as she pondered that question. "Two years ago, I might have given you another answer. But tonight, I can say with zero reservation, I'd be a mother of two."

My hands steeled.

Ebonee's palm shot into the air as she busted out laughing. "No! No! I'm not trying to start any shit with you, Ish. I swear!" She laughed her ass off.

"A mother. Wow..." I nodded, fighting my humor.

"Yup. And, of course, a wife. That would have kicked the shit off."

"I can see you as a wife."

"Bullshit, Ish. If you could, then we would have worked out."

Ebonee Williams, a former attorney turned popular night show host in Canada, had been swimming in my friend zone for over six years. We tried the romance thing and quickly hopped out that bitch like it was hot fish grease. She was in town for an event, and I invited her to my suite at *KAHRI Resort & Casino*. Although we weren't intimate, we tried making time for each other when possible. I met her in one of the lobby bars and noticed her wincing. I asked her about it. When she explained it was a minor injury from a Krav Maga class, I suggested we soak in the jacuzzi with the skyline view.

"The old lady's been on me about not taking on your alternate life."

"Dr. Patterson?" I nodded. "She's a mother. Of course, she wants you to settle down. You didn't answer my question, by the way." She took a sip of her champagne.

I thought for a minute. "If I wasn't in this entertainment-cultivating culture, I'd..." Several scenarios ran through my mind. "...definitely still be an entrepreneur—well, you know I have a few businesses now. But...I'd likely own a barbershop."

"Cut hair?" Her eyes went wild. "You'd cut hair, Ish?" Her expression turned doubtful.

I shrugged with my lips. "I'm a cultivator. There's lots of potential for inspiring dreams and manifestation in a Black barbershop. It's a secret place for giving game and networking."

"Would you be married, too?"

I scoffed, rubbing the center of her foot. "What does my relationship status have to do with my occupation?"

"You wouldn't be traveling as much. Your schedule would be regular. That would leave more time for cultivating a bond with a woman."

"You think being single is mandatory to keep my job? Like...it's in the bylaws or some shit?"

Cowering beneath the bubbling water line, Ebonee tried hiding behind her flute with batting lashes. "I don't know," she whined.

I let her foot gently fall back into the water. My arms stretched over the lips of the hot tub. Inhaling, I realized, "You want to know why I'm decidedly single."

"Yes. Please."

Shit.

I had no problems having real intimate conversations with mature women—and Ebonee was just that. It was just that I wasn't used to having them often. The women I encountered didn't require such a personal explanation. This shit was never an easy thing to do, even with a beautiful spirit such as Ebonee's.

"My reasons have evolved over the years. But keeping it simple; you're kind of right. Settling down with a woman is wholly incongruent with my work."

"So, it is simply because you have no time to give to a relationship."

I reached for my glass and took a long pull before licking the honeyed brandy from my lips. "I didn't say it's just about a lack of time. I'm saying it's about the impossibility of a commitment. What many people get fucked up is thinking they can do several things and perform them all well. It's not true. We, humans, are limited with our greatness." I swung my palm.

"I'm on a journey of excellence. Everything I pursue must be done with all of me. Relationships are no different. Taking on a wife—because that's the destination for most women—would have to be pursued with the same level of passion and vigor as my work. I win at everything I pursue. The key is, I don't pursue a lot. I don't have the capacity to give a woman what I give to my work in the same proportion. One would have to come second in place of the other." My head swung left to right. "I can take on but so much to accomplish that greatness. I choose work. And because I do, I'm irreplaceable at work."

There was a pause before she asked, "Have you ever been in a monogamous relationship?"

I chuckled at that. "You know I have. Mehki's mother."

"Mandy! Right." She cringed. "I'm sorry. I..."

"No sweat. It's in the past."

"But does she have something to do with your decision to choose work over a committed relationship?"

"Maybe. Maybe not."

Ebonee went quiet again. I understood why. There was a lot of murky shit still lurking about Mehki's mother and my relationship. I didn't prefer the lingering suspicion or curiosity, but Ebonee was a neutral party. I'd allow it.

With her eyes toward the bubbling water. "It's hard to believe it isn't. Sometimes—well, in the past when I'd do a little obsessing over it—I wondered if she was the reason things didn't work between the two of us."

I pulled in another deep breath. "You could've just asked. You can always ask, Ebonee."

"But then asking requires hearing the painful truth."

"What? That if I wanted to settle down, you would've been the woman I'd have done it with when we had our run?"

Her eyes met mine again as she adjusted the strap of her bikini top. "*I*—but... *We*—you've never said."

"There was no need to."

"All this time, I thought it was because I was too needy or something."

My face tightened as I thought about that. "Needy? I'm not sure about that."

Ebonee scoffed. "I snapped. You can be honest about it. We finally fucked and I snapped like I'd never had dick before yours."

That made me laugh. Honesty can be refreshing to a man like me.

I nodded. "You introduced a side of yourself I didn't know existed, yes."

It was bad, but something I could have handled better if I were in a place where I wanted to settle down.

"So damn cringy," she whispered, gazing away from me.

"Ebonee, you're the elite in terms of women who are ideal to marry. You're esthetically pleasing, fit as hell, impressively educated, attractively cultured, well-spoken, and incredibly accomplished. You do queen shit every day. Any man, including me, would be lucky to have you to build with."

"Okay. So, you just answered for yourself. What about the other four billion men who are attracted to women?" I didn't have an answer. When Ebonee realized that, she scoffed and scratched beneath her ear. "You know, in my line of work, there is a lot of journalism. We research relevant topics to open conversation in hopes of bettering peoples' lives. I've often covered monogamous relationships and its attractiveness to humans.

"I know I'm hyper-independent and understand how, in my thirties, I have to accept that the man may come with lesser pay and possibly children. I listen to all the social media conjecture about high-valued men versus the depreciating value of women due to age, weight, parental status, and education. I pay attention to the fifty-fifty lifestyle split. I hear it all. I'm open to it all. And, invariably, each time I reflect on why I'm still single, I remember how I behaved when we finally fucked. I went bananas."

I chuckled, rubbing the tip of my nose. "Yeah. A little bit."

"But you held back a lot about who you are sexually!"

"And what am I supposed to do? Go around telling women what I like to do in bed?"

"No, but you can forewarn them of your ability to make them orgasm."

"I can't make every woman orgasm. Some can't." But I damn sure loved convincing the other sector they could.

"That's what I thought until crossing paths with you," she hissed, her head rounding her shoulders.

"Oh, stop it." I shook my head, chuckling.

Then sobriety washed over her face. "I'm sorry. If I've never said it and meant it, I'm saying and meaning it now. I acted a complete fool. The amount I've paid in therapy unpacking my shit, man." She shook her head. "Your mother is a real one. I'm pretty fucking lucky we were able to salvage the friendship."

It was a bad situation. Ebonee and I had kicked it for almost eight months before she decided she was ready for that next step. Upon hearing that shit, I was excited, so I mentally and physically prepared for the big night. It was fun. *We had fun.* Ebonee's energy pathway was really open to exploring. Then over the next few days and weeks, she became extremely clingy and jealous.

She flew down from Canada and showed up to my house unannounced. My mother was hosting an old buddy and her daughter that afternoon. She called me down to introduce me to them. At the same time, Ebonee was being escorted to the solarium where we were. Ebonee took one look at us and assumed we'd been dating. She was able to make it out without too much of an explosion. But when I walked to my car to leave the house that night, my *Urus Lambo* was keyed up.

I'd never expected a well put together woman like Ebonee Williams to behave so unhinged. It took months for me to get over that shit. She sent a check in an attempt to cover the damages. I never accepted her money, taking it as an 'L,' and moved on. But unbeknownst to me, my mother reached out to Ebonee. And in her professional realm of psychology, she embraced Eb and coached her on a search for a practitioner. When my mother finally came around to telling me, enough time had passed for me to be open to speaking to Ebonee, hearing her out, and remembering why I'd fallen for her as a friend in the first place.

My mother emphasized grace since I could understand it. She narrowed it down to the Black community as I mentally developed. I went to predominately white schools, so she would always highlight the unparalleled beauty of Black women and my expected allegiance to them. She would explain Black came in different flavors and cultures. Some are not as favorable as others. But don't let the hurt in them masked by anger make me feel women of other races were better. I was to work within the bounds of Black women and give grace to their scars and wounds—those who had them, at least.

That was Ebonee. Even if I had no desire to be with her romantically again, she was a beautiful and exceptional Black woman. It was my obligation to give her grace. She'd earned back my friendship, creating a safe space for me to share and for my confidence to exude. For that, she'd maintain my allegiance.

I pushed my glass into the air. "And you are, too. Here's to the right man finding your precious heart."

Ebonee met my glass with her flute then bit her lip. There was a pause before she whispered, "Promise me something."

"What's that?"

Her voice trembled when she proposed, "If you ever decide to settle down, I'd have the right of first refusal."

My head fell to the side, and I smiled, processing the sincerity in her beautiful eyes. "It's a bet."

Hayden

"Okay," Lex exhaled, exhaustion all in her presentation as she pushed her long, thick, dark hair from her face. She studied the meeting's agenda. "Funding. Oh!" She chirped then found me leaning against the doorframe of the small conference room. A few of the staff occupying each seat at the conference table peered up and over to me. "Well, Hayden isn't even supposed to be here." I winked her way. "So, Mika, in her 'wake,' what do you have for us?"

"Money!" Her eyes blossomed before her expression went blank ruefully. The table went up around her.

I was happy to see a semblance of her playful persona again. It had been absent over the past couple of weeks. My assistant had been "off." She was sluggish and an uncharacteristic introvert. I'd finally asked her about it last week when she'd returned late from lunch and clearly appeared to have been crying. She said she didn't want to talk about it but promised she'd explain when she was ready. What could I do? Nothing. So, I accepted it and moved on.

"From where?" One of the counselors asked, elation lacing her tone.

"Well, let's see." Mika's mouth curled. "Try *Protecting Love*, the charity super star, R&B sensation, Ragee, has with heavy weight champion, Tori McNabb—"

"Holy!"

"We got it?"

Excitedly, people were speaking over one another.

"Let me finish!" Mika laughed. "Let me finish! Our girl didn't stop there. She got the *Bobby's Hope Foundation* to not only hand over a chunk of change, but they've committed to funding for the next five years!" she shouted over the small group bursting into a merry ass cheer.

My job was done. I rolled off the metal frame to leave, catching my boss' gaze. She patted her chest in a silent gesture of gratitude and approval. As I headed to my office down the empty halls, I felt the victory from a big battle. However, the war was still in motion. After this late, evening meeting, my boss may have been heading home to her husband and children, but I'd be driving down to Atlantic City by way of the Parkway, two hours south of here. There was a *Grant Writers Association* conference happening this weekend. If I were lucky, by the time I arrived, I'd catch a restaurant that didn't serve takeout via a drive-thru.

Lying on the center of my desk was a white business envelope with *Boss Lady* written on the front. I knew right away, from the calligraphy style, who'd addressed it. Inside was a letter. It was from Mika. When I initially thought I was reading a letter of resignation, I soon learned just how wrong I was.

I walked around to the front of my desk and collapsed my ass onto it while holding the letter.

Fuck.

Mika shared she was pregnant.

Suddenly, Lucy appeared in my doorway, holding her trusted *Stanley* cup. Her shiny lips were twisted to the side of her face while her brows were hiked. "Let me guess. The coward finally told you why she's been throwing up all over the building, trying to keep it from you."

My eyes closed and rolled behind their lids. "Mika!"

It was her one-night stand guy from Vegas. He'd gotten her pregnant.

ISHAAN

"Take me to camera six," I ordered, standing over the mechanical board where my team of surveillance staff worked the cameras. This was one of three reconnaissance offices here at *KAHRI Resort & Casino* in Atlantic City. The general office was the largest and surveyed the entire property. Second to that in size was the one for gaming, maintaining the integrity of our gaming. "Now to two."

"There," Munchie called out. "Approaching the elevator." She pointed toward Lavonte Harris, a top-ranking runner for the Marino family.

He'd been a pain in my ass since the opening of the resort. Elusive, he didn't comply with the rules Azmir Jacobs established in the Atlantic City region as it concerned enforcement and safety for guests of *KAHRI Resort & Casino*. As a Black man working for an Italian family, he was able to convince Rob to allow him access to the resort, which got Rob fired and kicked out on his ass. The Marino family, via Lavonte, brought human trafficking into *KAHRI*, a relative nuisance to the business. Azmir Jacobs yielded on some illegal plays in this industry, but human slavery and exploitation was one he wouldn't support.

I murmured into the walkie talkie, "Get me two soldiers near the east escalator on the lower level." I knew it was him. My hand went to the shoulder of my head camera controller. "Charlie, take me to camera twelve. I want to see if he has friends trailing behind them."

We watched, studying the camera for a while. My eyes intermittently went back to follow my subject. Surveillance took lots of patience alongside a watchful eye.

My unit arrived to trail the subject, appearing non-distinct.

"Damn. I love when Srey and William tag-team like a couple. They look so cute," Munchie whispered.

"Yeah," Corey, an officer, snorted while controlling several cameras. "What's funny is Srey is Cambodian, and Will is Korean."

"And unless you knew, you wouldn't know," fell slowly from Munchie's lungs.

My eyes narrowed when a familiar—or not—subject amongst hundreds in one window came into view. I shifted nearer to Charlie as if that would bring a closer view. There was that tingle in my gut I'd come to trust. Tall, light-skinned figure with an aura of uncertainty covered by a metal cage and effortless beauty. She had high cheekbones, heavy-lidded eyes over chestnut irises. Her lips were slender yet attractively shapely. Her hair was jet-black, straight, and parted down the center, framing her face just as I'd met her. And her pussy was an underutilized talent.

Remembering my job, I requested, "Charlie, has he made it to the third level yet?"

He snorted, "This guy's got eyes in the back of his head." I didn't react. My eyes remained glued to the beauty in a crowd of people looking to be a part of a group event. "Yes, sir. Subject A is seconds away from landing on the third level nearby. Go to camera twenty-three near the *B-Lounge & Bar*."

"He doesn't have anyone following him." I'd decided. "Have our foot crew break up and head to the third level. Let the couple have a drink while Tom window-shops at the *Asè Garb* boutique. When Subject A and his affiliate take a seat at any of those gaming tables or machines, be ready to have them accosted and detained." The beauty headed toward the conference center, and I glanced toward my team. "I'll be in the C detainment room awaiting my impending guests." Then my attention went to Munchie. "I need you to look into something en route."

love ∞ believe

Hayden

"So, you want to utilize as many fields as possible. My theory is, if it's there, it can only help if populated." I pointed to the grant form on Larry's laptop. "Unlike the state, private donors aren't as fluent in the bylaws of our particular industry. They want to have all the information at their fingertips in the event something goes awry on your non-profit's end legally. They don't want the liability."

"Shit. That's going to take a lot of time," Larry sighed, swiping his silk tresses from his face. I'd known him for about three years. A young, white male graduate from *NYU*, we belonged to the same credentialing body. We met at a conference similar to this one where Larry told me about *Christ Cares* looking to hire a full-time grant writer. He wanted to pursue the role but had aging parents and knew he'd have to move in with them eventually, making a commute from Delaware to New York implausible. "Lots of work."

We were outside of a quaint coffee shop inside *KAHRI Resort & Casino* in Atlantic City. It was situated in the middle of the lobby, a tree house structure with a table and chair surrounding it. We'd just ended a day of back-to-back courses and I was completely exhausted. Larry appeared drained, too.

"Not really," I disagreed. "When I have a request for application and there are 'extra' fields, which is the donor requesting unsealed information, I complete it all. Then, for those unusual questions, I copy and paste them in case another donor asks for the same or similar information. Therefore, I'm not completely recreating the wheel."

"Damn, that's smart," Larry murmured, staring at the screen. "My program manager is on my ass about getting this grant." He scrubbed his face with his fist from frustration.

"You can do it. I promise." Absent-mindedly, I glanced around the mostly empty courtyard. There was a peaceful aura to this place. "You have about another twenty-four hours in the hottest casino there is in town to brace yourself for it."

"Speaking of which," he grunted, stretching his arms over his head. "Are you going to the banquet tonight?"

I checked the time. It was almost three in the afternoon, and I'd been in educational sessions since eight. The day had been damn long.

"I brought something to wear but haven't fully committed in my mind. Did you hear about the aquarium here?"

Larry nodded, brushing his pink hand down his hairy face as he exhaled from apparent frustration. "It's bigger than the one in Camden. I wonder if it rivals the one in Baltimore."

"Well," I pulled in a breath, trying to catch my second wind. "There's only one way I'll find out—"

"Excuse me." A zoftig woman with smooth almond skin and wire-rimmed glasses was at my left side with her small hands clasped. "You mind if I speak with you privately?"

"And you are?" I asked in the politest way I could.

"Munchie." Her smile was perfection and matched perfectly with her green A-line skirt, white blouse beneath a coral cardigan, and a wide, black belt emphasizing her voluptuous, feminine shape.

After giving her a long onceover, I turned to Larry. "You mind giving me a second and watching my things?"

"Oh, of course!" he assured as I stood.

We walked a few feet away, off the marble path around the coffee house, when she turned to me.

"Thanks for speaking with me." Her voice was controlled, volume professional. "If you recall, you met a gentleman last month in Vegas. He asked you to attend a *Blakewood State University* Athlete Alumni event with him and you agreed." My heart thundered in my chest. Her eyes bounced between mine. "You should recall supplying Jane Doherty?"

I cleared my throat. "What's the purpose of this conversation?"

"Because he's here and would like to...see you again."

"Again? Where?"

"Here, Ms. Doherty, at *KAHRI Resort*. He asked me to give you this, which will detail your meeting." She handed me an envelope the size of a greeting card.

My face hardened as I tried to reign in my temper. "And who are you to pass along this message?"

The Munchie woman reclined, and her defined brows raised as a soft smile coated her face. "You'd like to maintain your anonymity; I think it's only fair he maintains his." Her head cocked coolly to the side. "Right?" Stumped. I couldn't respond to her polite sarcasm. My eyes fell to the envelope. Responding in any way could have my reckless night in Vegas exposed. I had professional peers floating around in this area. "There's a telephone number in there in case you have any questions. Okay?" She nodded before taking off. "Enjoy the guided aquarium tour."

Fruitlessly, I quickly turned to see if anyone had caught on to our exchange. Larry was on his laptop, likely going over the application I was helping him complete. His face was screwed tight, mouth appearing beaver-like with his two front teeth breaking through his thin lips. He looked a sight and I felt like one. Taking a deep breath, I ambled back over to the table.

"This is one of the elite of the elites in the aquarium world. As you can see, there are two, and there are only three recorded in the country in aquariums. Small little things at no more than two and a half inches. They're called the Peppermint Angelfish. They live in tropical reefs and are found in the eastern-central Pacific."

The fish were tiny. They were red with white stripes. Cute little babies, swimming mindlessly around a reef inside the floor-to-ceiling tank. Their little existence in this big facility reminded me of how precious life is. It made me think of how significant each moment should be pursued no matter how small we are in the grand scheme of things.

Then, my attention failed, and eyes dropped. I glanced over my shoulder, once again in search of him. When I'd arrived at the aquarium over an hour ago, I was greeted by a tour guide who'd been awaiting me. I thought at some point the person who invited me—and clearly arranged for the visit at the famous aquarium—would be here, too. We were almost done with the private tour.

Oh, well. At least, I've seen the KAHRI aquarium for free...

Peering back over to my guide, I saw he was on his phone, brows furrowed. "*Okaaaay...*" he enunciated. "It appears I'm being summoned back to my office. I'm told to remind you about your full access to our facility." He pointed to my arm. "Your bracelet there gets you access to the exhibits as well as the petting zoos."

I glanced down at the yellow plastic strap band he'd snapped onto my wrist when I'd arrived. "Okay." But I was confused.

"Okay." The young man, who had to be no more than twenty-three, smiled. "It was my pleasure being your *Aquarium at KAHRI* guide today." He offered a neck bow before taking off.

I pivoted, glancing around. There weren't many people at this particular exhibit. A few adults and children scattered around the dark room lined with water tanks showcasing the ocean's treasures. My unease continued. This was a mistake, and I was impulsively carrying an insane amount of cash on my person right now from my trip to the bank earlier. Stupidly, I checked my phone again. Then I felt an uncanny sensation of heat penetrating the back of my body. The hairs on my neck stood straight. Suddenly, I was afraid to move. But...then I had to. Someone was—

"Hey, Boo-baby."

It's him...

The guy from Vegas. Delicious. Sucking on a damn lollipop, the man looked fucking delicious. Just as before, he wore a dark suit with the first few buttons undone. Today, I could see the ink he hid when I'd first laid eyes on him in the Vegas lobby. His long, boxed braids were pulled back into a ponytail again; his shape up was edged to perfection. I didn't get his "look." Long, dark, and apparently healthy hair with formal suits. But it damn sure worked for him.

He stood so close to my person. So damn close, I smelled him. My fucking god, he was good-looking. Those dark eyes glistened between curled lashes. The upper and lower lashes were stark, giving him an appearance of insouciance. I couldn't tell if his dark suit was black or blue in the room lit by the aqua tank. His white dress shirt was opened at the neck, and he looked so...damn manly towering over me. A portion of the generous ink on his neck was visible from my vantage point in the dim area.

As I backed out of his space, I realized he was better looking than I gave him credit for back in Vegas. I'd done unbelievable work of putting that night behind me before today. And here we were, sharing the same air again. Then it happened. The same spell overcasting me in Vegas began to blanket me again. His presence was that mesmerizing.

"How did you get here?"

He reached for my earring, stroking it gently. "You look cute." His hand retreated. Slowly, his cheeks lifted into a smile, eyes narrowing. "The entrance."

"No." I shook my head, trying to gather myself. "I mean to New Jersey. Why are you here?"

He sucked the lollipop from his thick lips then cupped his hands together at his pelvis. "The same thing I imagine brought you here. Work. But I must say, I didn't know your portfolio was that wide-spread." He reached for the ends of my hair, studying it before leaning in for a sniffle.

"So, you just so happen to see me a few hours ago and sent a random woman to address me?"

"I saw you with a prospective client." He offered me his candy on a stick. Without thought, I opened my mouth. All I tasted was sugar, trying to process his words and our chemistry. "I didn't think it would be appropriate to approach you myself. And no. I actually saw you last night from afar." He rolled the lollipop on my tongue, studying his actions.

Last night?

I pulled back from his candy. "And why didn't you address me then?"

"Because I was in a meeting and couldn't leave for some time."

A meeting...

"So, what is it that you do?"

His brows raised and beam widened. Then he put the lollipop back into his mouth. "For a living?"

"Yes. You know what I do." I swallowed. "I can ask you. Right?"

"Of course." He inhaled, locking his long arms behind his back and rocking on his heels. "In short, I make sure people have a good time and are safe doing it."

"You get paid for that?" my tone purposely doubtful.

With a concoction of humor and humility in his beautiful eyes, he nodded. "I do. And I'm good at it. In fact, you can vouch for me." He stepped into my personal space again. "Right?" His voice was so smooth. Low. Seductive. "Are you free tonight?"

What?

Was he seducing me? Is this how it worked in this industry? He made a request, and I was to simply accommodate him?

I swear. Doing shit like this was not in my nature, but the ease at which I interacted with this guy, and in such a high-risk manner, should have concerned me. I was not this girl. I was not promiscuous or free with my body or time. I did not sell my body. Then why did I want him to just...have it?

"I know I was able to accommodate you on a whim in Vegas, but I don't work that way. The day is running late now, and I'm sure we've both been at risk since our last..." I cleared my throat. "...encounter." What was I saying? I scratched my head while shaking it at the same time. "I don't think I can accommodate you. I need a recent record of your status..." I was rambling.

My john's smile deepened, and those pearly whites glistened as he began to bite the lollipop, chewing it until the sugar dissolved and disappeared down his throat. He walked off. I soon learned to discard the stick in a nearby trash can. When my john returned, his phone appeared, and he swiped until he found what he was looking for. He held the phone in the air for me to see.

"I can send it to you, but..." he droned, chords husky. *But he has no contact information for me*. And I wanted to keep it that way.

"When were you tested?"

Did he do this shit all the time?

"Yesterday. After seeing you here."

My eyes flashed wide before I was able to gather myself. "Oh."

"And you?"

"Me what?"

He leaned down close to my ear to ask again, "I'm sure you get tested regularly in your line of work. When was the last time?"

Peering up to him, I squinted, mistrustingly. "Monday."

With that same gorgeous grin, he asked, "Do you have documentation? I'm sure you have something."

My john was right: I did. But not for the reasons he'd assumed. It was because what I'd done *with him alone* put me at high risk for many things that could irrevocably change my life.

I pulled my phone from my purse, thinking of the timing of it all. I was tested less than a week ago, and today, I'd run into the irresistible creature who'd put me at risk. He was different. My john behaved more familiar to my being. He gazed at me with amazement glittering his eyes. In Vegas, I was something convenient to do, considering my "occupation." Today, he emitted energy making me feel like I was someone he had to have.

I pulled up the results in my phone, being sure to conceal my identifying information as he had moments ago.

The beam on his face brightened, revealing more of his beautiful, white teeth; and his eyes sparkled in quicker sequence. "My Boo-baby's clean for me. I told you I make sure people have a good time and are safe doing it. Good. Get me on your clock."

"My time will cost you." I'd hoped my expression and aura pulled that declaration off. I tried avoiding the tattoo of an eagle's wing covering his neck and those layering his carved chest.

His eyes rolled away from me first. Then he moved into me while pulling in an audible breath, torturously expelling his masculinity along with the scent of fruit-flavored candy. "I'm willing to meet your price." His conversant tongue ran the rim of my ear.

My eyes closed in helpless, sensual assault and my spine shivered disgustingly. "You don't know my price."

He reared his head and upper torso away from mine. A sensual smirk spread across his soft lips. "Sure, I do. This ain't our first rodeo."

"It isn't. But our last was local for me. I'm all the way out in Jersey now. My rate is higher."

He stepped back into me headfirst, gazing away again with that smirk, and murmured, "Bullshit. You have no West Coast accent I can identify. I'm between North Jersey and New York."

Shit...

I couldn't give up my identity. And was I really doing this again? I swear, I'd never been so risqué in my life. But I'd been coated by his sensualism. Tased by his decisive nature.

"Which has nothing to do with where I currently reside."

"Didn't I tip well?" There was eroticism pleading in his undertone.

I swallowed again, mouth as dry as the *Kalahari*. "You did. But my base price is my base price."

"Which is?" He pushed his big, hard frame into me, leading with his pelvis. Immediately, I felt the heat and fullness of his erection. Images of his perfect penis flashed through my mind. They kept coming in spades. Why the fuck couldn't I forget the hue of it, the weight and width? The impression it made inside of me.

His hand clasped my waist, and he backed me into the floor-to-ceiling tank. Panicking, I blinked and craned my neck to see how much of a disruption we were causing. No one. I looked to the left and right of his broad being. How did those patrons disappear as a collective? I was sure more would wander in.

But I was given no time to contemplate that. My john took me by the chin and planted his warm, heart-shaped lips on mine. His smooth tongue followed next, and my knees buckled. At first, my entire frame froze, in pure shock of his audacity. Helplessness coated me, but deep inside my groin ignited. It took long seconds for me to kiss him back, but I did. So soon, I lost reality around me and leaned into the passion he quickly thrust me into with his mouth and tongue.

Slowly, he turned my body, and I was pinned against the cool glass, breasts first. It was so reminiscent of our first encounter. There was an amazing view in front of me—the various sea animals swimming and some just being. My body steeled again at the sight of people on the other side of the tank. Small, red and blond-headed children were pointing into the tank with awe. My john's mouth retreated to my neck and my eyes struggled to remain open. With audacious familiarity, my spine curved, and ass pushed into his hard frame. It was final for me. I wanted my john again. He soon learned when his hand pushed down the waist of my dress pants and beneath my body suit. My legs clamped together reflexively before relaxing into his touch. He found my damp folds and fondled his way into my canal where he, too, discovered my willingness.

At the urgent sensations of his fingers, I fell into a dangerous mental and emotional cove with my john. *This shouldn't be.* I didn't trust men emotionally. They were entirely unreliable and fucking selfish babies. While I hadn't tried out all of the men in the world, the number I had were a good enough sample to glean an empirical conclusion. Men were bred to lie to and manipulate women—good women like me who were raised to love, nurture, and be loyal to one guy. My john's worldly appearance and behavior told me he was no different. In fact, he was more hazardous than I'd ever experienced.

So, I needed out of this. The erotic hold was too much and nothing I'd ever faced before. Plus, we weren't alone—

My eyes flashed wide at the splash of reality, and my pelvis steeled as I peered through the massive tank for the children on the other side. There were none. Not one child or adult. Around us had been quiet, too.

He took me at the chin, rounding my face to his. "They're all gone, Janie," he whispered into my lips. "Until you cum for me, it's just me and you. Now, cum so I can remind you I'm a V.I.P. client. And it don't matter if I encounter you in Vegas, Jersey, or the Sudan: I get time on your clock and inside this weeping pussy."

At my body...

That's what my john meant. He wanted access to my body whenever he said.

My eyes closed again, partially in shame. The other half of it was bracing for the tsunami stirring in my groin. Fuck. I was preparing to orgasm in a public room. There could be someone—or people—in the exhibit area. But it was too late. With a strained neck, my back bowed into him before I began thrusting into his big hand. I bit my lip to keep from crying out loud, but my mews couldn't be controlled. My nipples stung and titties felt so heavy—caged by clothing.

My hand covered his but through my pants, ensuring he'd stay right there. He pulled in a slow, sensual, audible breath in my hair as I began to lift off. The encasement of his arm tightened, and I felt his crotch push down and into my ass. There was that impression of his endowed member as I ascended blissfully. For seconds long, I couldn't feel my lungs. The pads of my feet heated, and all of my feminine parts felt heightened in unspeakable sensations with harmony. My spine wouldn't stop jerking, even when my pelvis thrusts slowed. With his determined fingers, my john milked me until the tormenting ride of ecstasy ended and I was left boneless. My lungs were the first to return with a vengeance. My head dizzied from the brief lack of oxygen as I held onto the glass.

Breathing almost as animatedly as I was, he droned in my ear, "Now, Boo-baby, what's your price?"

Breathlessly, I quoted him, "Ten thousand."

FIVE

March

Hayden

We made it to the penthouse level after my john punched in a code on the elevator's keypad, gaining us access. Then I followed him, click-clacking in my heels with a churning groin to the door of the suite. How he got these exclusive ass suites was any guess to me. Maybe my john was a high-roller gambler. Those folks received top-tier accommodations for free. He used another keypad at the door of the suite to let us in. Sauntering inside, the place was dimly lit and seductively scented with masculine wood-earthy tones and the breeze of the Atlantic Ocean just ahead of us.

He moved to an electrical panel mounted on an adjacent wall to turn up the lights. We were in a posh living room. The décor was minimal, indicative of a man. It was also modest, which was appropriate for a high-end resort. He moved fluidly, deeper inside the space, his steps confident and pacing.

"Can I get you something to drink? Water, wine, beer...*1211 EllleBee*? I have a couple of bottles of that, I believe," his volume teetered off as though he was unsure.

He entered the kitchen which was separated from the massive living room by a peninsula with overhanging cabinets.

"Sure." I spun on my heels for a full view of the place.

"Sure what?" his tone sharp. I swung around and saw the colorful crass in his expression.

I blinked at his audacity before replying, "Water would work."

I'd been fasting from alcohol for over three weeks now. My goal had been to go until my birthday, but I knew that wasn't realistic, so I kept the endpoint open in my mind.

"Flat or sparkling?"

"Flat please." I ambled over to the floor-to-ceiling window with the ocean view. It was dark out there, but the water was loud as hell. The clashing waves were visible, too.

"You aren't getting cold feet, are you?" He was in my ear again, lips so soft against my face.

I leaped, grabbing my chest. "You scared the shit out of me." Feeling foolish beneath his tall frame, I snickered at myself while receiving the glass of water.

He didn't pour anything for himself, I noticed.

Instead, he studied my features, head leaned to the side. "Would you feel more comfortable with a deposit? I can *CashApp* you." His beady eyes glimmered with mischief.

"Like you said: this isn't our first rodeo. I'm not concerned at all. Just a little anxious. It's a human experience. Right?" I took a sip of the water. Him drugging me was an afterthought.

"You didn't seem so reserved in Vegas."

Because I drank a lot that night in Vegas...

I supplied a smile and lied, "That's because I was home." And now, I'm horny, curious, and stupid. "Can we get started?" I glanced around, gesturing for the bedroom.

My john didn't answer right away. He simply smiled. He carried his measured beam to the sofa chair directly facing the view. He aired his jacket out then lowered himself into it and stretched his long arms over the rests. Those long legs spread wide, and he nestled himself into a comfortable space.

"I got in pretty late last night." He sighed. "It was a long day at the office. When I got off, I came in and sat right here to ponder my day. I realized the work was different. That wasn't what drained me yesterday." I pretended to want another sip of water as I listened to him. His delivery revealed vulnerability. "What drained me was learning you were here, and I couldn't get to you. It frustrated the fuck out of me to know we were in the same 'building,' and I couldn't see you. Talk to you. Feel you...or kiss you," he whispered.

"That's what hit me sitting right here, looking out at the water. I wanted a better view."

"What's a better view?" I placed the water down on the table and lay my purse aside it.

He brought his fist up to lay his chin on. "You."

"Are you going to just stare at me all night?" I snickered quietly.

He pulled in a long, audible breath before rolling his head upright. "No. But for the next few minutes, I want you to stand there and watch me. I fantasized about you doing it last night. Now that I have you here, in the flesh, that fantasy can be fulfilled."

I was confused as hell. The moment almost turned awkward until he stood from the chair to remove his suit jacket. He tossed it onto the sofa adjacent to him. My john watched me as he unbuttoned his dress shirt, including at the wrists. He shouldered out of it, gaping at me offensively. I had to transfer my weight on one hip, clenching my Kegels. Next, went his shoes. They were toed off with ease. He unraveled his belt then unhooked his pants. They went down and off, landing on top of the jacket. His undershirt peeled from his bubbled torso.

Goddamn...

There were cuts, grooves, and swelling everywhere in between.

Tattoos damn near covered his neck, shoulders, and breastplate, but everything below was smooth flesh until the trail beginning his pubic hair. *Man.* I missed all of this back in Vegas. Even leading down to the band of his boxer briefs, his swollen obliques were just as defined as every other muscle. And his dick was bucking at the cotton of his boxer briefs. The shit was intimidating.

His socks were next to be removed and discarded on the sofa. My john moved gracefully as he pushed down his boxers, leaning forward to pull them from his ankles and feet. It gave me a brief peek at the indentations on his broad back. When he stood straight, his member did, too. It arched into the air at an angle against his abdomen. It bobbed in the air so visibly, my john reached to stroke it. His energy was that of a trainer, controlling its vicious pit bull.

The sight of him stroking himself in front of me had me switching the weight on the other hip. He peered at me straight in the eyes, his passion unapologetic. Stepping back, he resumed his seat and maintained his stroke pace. Hot blood began warming in my body, my palms growing clammy.

"I want you to watch how I had to take the edge off while I waited to see you today," he delivered tautly, tortured by eroticism.

My clit began pulsating to a degree competing with the drumming of my heart. His head rolled back, exposing the graphics painted into his skin. His cords bulged and each muscle of his beautifully carved body cried out. Watching his big fist run the length of his veiny thickness introduced a new facet of masculinity to me. His bare feet were spaced apart and planted on the rug. His long thighs were hairy, inkless, and thickly striated. His abdomen was swollen and layered with silky pubic hairs. Those globular shoulders were broad and defined as he worked himself.

I was hot with boiling passion as he peered me in the eyes, stroking himself. I wanted to be in lechery with him. Once again, losing my damn mind, I began removing my clothing. My suit jacket and shoes went first. Next to go were my blouse and pants. My knee-high hosiery followed. His eyes bounced all around my body and I wondered if he was half as impressed with me as I was with him. I wasn't in shape like I'd aspired to be but was pretty toned. Only having half of my abs visible was the biggest thorn in my side. I needed to commit more to fitness was the biggest thorn in my side. I needed to commit to fitness, dredge out the time in my busy days.

But standing here, seeing his abdomen jerk each time his hand made it to the head of his dick when stroking, my john appeared arrogantly vulnerable. And if he could put himself out there, I could use the wonder in his eyes as he looked at me to meet him there in the middle. Desire welled in my groin, and I unclasped and removed my bra with trembling hands. My panties were a less complicated removal. Then I found myself toeing over to my john. When I arrived within inches, his virile thighs opened blatantly. I lowered myself between them and grabbed him. Together, we massaged the satin skin over a thick, pulsating rope with ridges. The lip of the mushroom head was wide.

He was hot and swollen as I included my second hand to stroke the posterior, or the spine, as I liked to call it. He was thick and responsive as I ran my thumbs the length of it a few times. His beady eyes sparkled and strained. Then I used one hand to ring just beneath the head, tightened to apply pressure, then stroked the lip of him.

His head tossed back. "*Ahhhh!*"

He liked it. So badly I wanted to use my mouth but couldn't. My john was a stranger. I didn't go around giving out blow jobs or my body. But a hand job was less personal to me—a "skill" taught by one of the most reprobate minds I'd ever encountered. Cousin Billy. It was either use my hands or he'd take my body. After some experience with the act, stroking a man's dick with my hands could be performed with my head and heart in a different room. With this act, I could be the prostitute he believes I am.

The singular difference was, I liked stroking his sensitive member. I enjoyed each grunt and groan produced by the pressure, direction, and cadence of my movements.

His torso leaped up in the chair as his hips shifted back, abandoning my grip. His face was inches away from mine. "You're about to make me explode." There was an indictment against me in his tone. "I'm not ready."

Then he stood and heaved me into his chest. My legs wrapped

around his waist. The man smelled so damn good, felt so warm. He pulled my head back by my hair and tortured me with his mouth, licking and sucking on my chin, neck, and bare shoulders. I could feel we were moving but didn't give a damn where; I was attached to all I wanted to be entertained by. I enjoyed his masculinity, the way he carried me without straining. My hands gripped the back of his neck and head, holding him to me.

Suddenly, I heard and felt, "Shit," reverberating in my chest when he stopped abruptly. Then a light was turned on, causing me to squint.

I shivered then glanced around the darkened room. Abruptly, it was cold as hell.

He muttered, "I left the patio door open." He motioned to let me down. "I'm gonna close the door and light a fire. "You can grab a few rubbers." He kissed me so conversantly on the forehead and groped my ass cheek. Then my john directed my attention toward the closets along the wall. "Third one, second shelf."

Covering myself, I hopped over to the closet and opened it. I glanced back to see him going toward the balcony. His ass was cute and blemish-free. Inside the closet was a camera, gum, *ChapStick*, a few keyrings, and a sealed box of condoms. I ripped open the box and reached for a strip of packets. Before closing the door, I grabbed the camera, too. My john was in the sitting area and dropped to his nude hunches in front of the fireplace. Within seconds, a flame was lit. It was small but growing.

"Come here." He stood and waved me over. "You take flicks?"

I raised the camera to see it was a polaroid. "With my phone now, but I had one of these in high school. They're fun."

"Are you fun?" Reactively, I gazed down at his resting member. He snorted, "Sorry. We can't do the cold." He reached for me. "Come warm me up."

He sat on the sofa and pulled me on top as I searched for the button on the camera. I straddled his hard frame, dropping the condoms next to us. "You mind?"

He lengthened his neck and squinted his eyes, answering in favor of the picture being taken of him. I snapped a picture and waited for it to eject before taking another. "Now, give me real. Relax. Tell me how you feel without words."

He rubbed my back in the freezing room. "A model?" I shook my head. "You a photog?"

I shook my head again, staring at him through the camera. "A lover of art. Art is you." When he didn't respond right away, I found what I was looking for and snapped a picture.

I wasn't able to see the print result because he took the camera and tossed it onto the couch before pulling me into his chest. "Kiss me."

He left me no time to think. His soft, heart-shaped lips were on mine. His kiss was slow yet demanding. His tongue stroked mine and he moaned into my mouth. It was sinuous and rhythmic...intentional. His big hands grabbed my cheeks, massaging them gently.

He pulled back. "Look at me when you kiss me." His voice was soft yet demanding.

How? I'd be cock-eyed.

When he took to my mouth again, I soon learned what he meant. When possible, I was to look at him. Appear in the moment with him. And shit, I had been in the moment with my john. I was the servicer, after all. Tonight was about his desires, his pleasure. Then why was it so damn fun for me? It had been. I could tell. I was warming up. Perhaps it was the fire catching behind me or the heat we created together on this sofa. But when there was an opportunity, I looked my john directly in his eyes.

"How often do you make exceptions for your clients?" He held me at the sides of my face, the flames of the growing blaze reflecting in his beady eyes.

I reached for the strip of condoms; my hand patted the sofa next to his bare hip. I found the foil material and brought it between us to rip one apart.

When I handed the single condom to him, I murmured, "You're my only complicated 'in the meantime,'..." My brows narrowed. "What's your name again?"

The most sensual grin grew on his face when he reached for the sides of mine and kissed me again. This time was hard, deep, and filled with palpable passion. My spine arched, bringing my taut nipples to his sinewy chest. My misted palms gripped his hard traps. His mouth was so welcoming, communicative without words. His passion boiled over, making this stupid ass game I'd been playing so easy.

So, when I heard him opening and applying the condom, my arousal heated up to dangerous degrees. The wide crest of him found my opening. He used his right hand to push me down onto his hardness. Remembering how well-endowed my john was, I reached between us and wrapped my fist to anchor myself and began rocking downward. I did this for a while, breaking him in and creating a cadence. Most importantly, I controlled the pressure.

"*Sluuuuuu...*" His eyes rolled up and head collapsed backward. "You feel fuckin' amazing," he whispered.

His thick bottom lip went slack, his head rolled up, and he gaped at me with lazy eyes. I watched as his abs rolled and lifted according to my action. This man was pure, virile perfection. He made me feel so powerful and in charge. Mindlessly, I released the base of his dick and pushed down farther to fit him all the way in. Determined, I plunged down onto him, pressure be damned. His big, hot palms clenched the fat of my hips, encouraging my strokes. His chestnut nipples were pebbled, neck strained, face distressed.

Then his neck gave out again and he grunted, "*Gaaaaaaah!*" Legs kicked out and shaking.

His abdomen trembled and jaw went slack. He had cum. I'd made my john orgasm. My job was done.

Why did that make me sad?

ISHAAN

When I walked out of the bathroom, I saw she was leaving the room.

"Heeeey," I whispered, taking long leaps to grab her arm. Gently, but with intent, I pulled her into my chest. "Where're you going?"

"Just felt...awkward without..."

"Me?" I smiled, laying my forehead against hers. Slowly, I backed up toward the fireplace. "Or your clothes?"

All she gave me was a grin. Her energy was less emboldened when she murmured, "It's still cold in here."

I ran my hands up her arms, across her back, and over the mound of her ass. Goosebumps were present, and I wished I'd been the cause of them.

"You are chilled. Let me warm you up."

That was dumb as hell. I had no method of warming her other than the direct heat from the fireplace. I felt off. A feeling of euphoria was blooming over me as I clutched her chin, angling her head before kissing her. In shock, she grunted, but didn't decline. Her tongue swept against mine, lips moved against my own, too. I couldn't stop kissing her. It felt like a fountain of life was in her belly and I needed to drink from her abundance.

Shit.

This was dangerous. I hadn't kissed a woman so much since Mandy. I was being reminded of how much I enjoyed kissing and soft touches. Beyond sex, it expressed so much fucking intimacy for me. The right temperature, scent, texture of lips and tongue, and emanating energy could have me losing my shit.

And this was happening. With my eyes closed and mouth busy, I lost account of fucking time. My hands were all over her: her scalp, narrow shoulders, and plump ass. At some point, a new sensation was introduced. My dick was hard again, pressing for room between us. Her small hands were gripping my arms—she was clinging to me. Fuck. She felt so damn good. I cupped her ass with my palms and dipped to feel her pussy against me—the strong of me.

In no time, she adjusted herself, bringing me between her legs. I didn't give a damn what she did with my body: as long as she didn't let go of my mouth...my tongue. I just let myself go and explored her mouth. The heat spread all over my body at this point and I had no idea if it was from ol' girl or the sparkling fire to the left of me. But kissing suddenly felt like fucking, and fucking with my tongue was my shit. It drove me wild.

Funny thing was, she was getting wild, thrusting into me. I felt the hairs of her garden and the slime of her pussy on my most intimate and sensitive place. She stood against me, straining on her toes. My knees were still bent, giving her access to the lower me while she invited me to her face...her mouth. She was building a tempo in a way my distracted ass wasn't aware of. Her pussy stroked faster, tits rubbed against my chest. I could feel her racing heart, which made me swell even more between her legs as we stood.

Her head swung back, detaching from my mouth. *"Oh, my gaaa... Oh, my gaaa!"* She squealed, pumping onto my dick.

Alarmed at first, I watched her wild expressions while still holding her face in my hands. All of her weight fell helplessly upon me without relent. She was fucking beautiful, unable to hide her ecstasy. Her eyes were closed, head resting in my palms, one hand squeezing my shoulder and the other the side of my abdomen as she rolled her hips around my throbbing cock.

Fuck.

I was cumming, too. My abdomen convulsed as I held her, and my own weight. Steadily, my seeds spurted into the dark air lit by just the fireplace as she clawed up my body. The feeling was amazing, but the sight of her was even better. I couldn't enjoy my nut because the moment wasn't about me. This wasn't planned. Still, she earned her ascension.

When her moans dissipated and hip thrusts stopped, her eyes eventually opened. She hiked in a breath while panting. "I'm so sorry!" she whispered hard. "I didn't mean to—"

I shut her ass up with another kiss.

About ten minutes later, she left the bathroom, fingering her jet-black, straight hair, parted in the center. Having freshened up, she gazed my way for cues. Pulling up my lounge pants, I tossed my chin her way. "Hungry? I am. I'm starving like a muthafucka," I mumbled then began toward the door. "I had food delivered."

"I guess I am," her voice un-spirited.

Her face folded and she stumbled then pivoted away. She seemed to struggle in thought with something.

"Everything good?"

"*Ah*—I... *Uhhh*..." She licked her lips. They looked kind of swollen, making me divert my eyes. "I don't have anything to wear besides my clothes." She crossed her arms over her tits and left leg over the right, balancing herself. Her chin lifted in the air as she cleared her throat. "They're out in the living room."

I scratched the back of my head. "May I make a suggestion?"

"Sure." She cleared her throat.

I reversed back over to the bed and pulled the comforter down to the bottom of the mattress. Then I yanked the flat sheet from the mattress, disturbing the pillows and comforter. Making my way over to her, I motioned for her to lift her arms. Once she did, I triple-wrapped the sheet around her tits, tucking the end inside beneath her armpit.

Then I met her eyes. "Good?"

She jerked her head at an angle, grinning. "I guess so."

Damn.

She was pretty as fuck. It made me idly wonder who she was as a little girl. Had anyone hurt her? Taken advantage of her beauty? But I quickly turned off my curiosities, knowing what this was. I then took her by the hand and led her out to the dining room where the table was set for two.

I pulled out a chair for her and pushed it into the table before taking my own seat.

"This looks great, and I'm famished." Her tone was polite as she smiled widely. Then her eyes met mine, catching the same dirty thought running through my mind. "I guess I have every reason to be. Huhn?"

I chuckled as she laughed.

"Please." I motioned the table. "Ladies first."

"Thank you." Her voice was soft as she leaned into the table to plate her food.

I busied myself with pouring wine. "Would you like some?"

"What is it?"

"A *Chateau Blevin* red blend."

"You're really trying to spoil a girl," her cords strained as she tried clamping her arm to the fold of the sheet and reach across the table. "Surf and turf, lit tapered candles, eating damn near naked and in private... I'd love some."

I poured her wine then served myself. In no time, I fell into a zone enjoying the food. My mind floated off to my schedule and the meeting I was missing while being here.

"Are we going to make this awkward?"

My head snapped up and I blinked. "Pardon?"

"Hearing the debris of Atlantic City against our smacking." She forked food into her mouth and giggled, covering her moving lips with her fist. "Something needs to flow between the two."

"I'm sorry." She was right. I was so used to eating alone, here at my place. Then I thought. "It's just kind of hard considering..."

"Our circumstance?" Chewing, I smiled while nodding softly. "Well, I hope it doesn't have to be."

"You like anonymity."

"And so do you."

"Then what's safe?" She didn't speak as she eyed me, obviously unsure, while sipping on wine.

Then she squinted my way. "Michael or Prince?"

Without thought, I shot back, "MJ."

"What's your favorite song?"

I thought while taking a sip of wine. "An impossible question."

"Try."

Something dawned on me. "What's yours from the King of Pop?" Then I thought to add, "And don't say 'Thriller.'"

"Never." She laughed. "*Hmmmmm...*" She pulled her glass closer and fingered the rim. "It was always 'PYT' when I was a kid. But for the past... just under a decade, I've uncovered a new appreciation for 'Off the Wall.' I don't know." Her shoulders lifted. "It's so...vibey. So invigorating. So universal." She shimmied in her seat. "Infectious. Who can't relate to ending a nine-to-five week?"

While chewing, I pointed. "You."

She shrunk in her seat. Then it seemed to be a quick recovery. "You think this is what I've done since graduating high school—assuming you think I'm capable of getting a diploma?"

"I don't know?" I continued forking from my plate. "Did you?"

With a dry smile and blinking, she nodded. "Yup. Many moons ago. I didn't play sports like you, though."

She remembered the *Panther* event.

"You like sports? That your thing?"

"I do, actually. Football, basketball, and boxing. Hell, I've even taken a liking to soccer in recent years. I love the live games, although I don't go as often as I'd like. I've been to a couple professional football games this season."

"Who's your favorite team?"

Her neck swiveled over her shoulders as she looked me dead in the yes. "The *Kings*, baby."

I waved my left hand dismissively as I forked a broccoli spear with my right. "Of course, they are."

"Why'd you say that? Because I'm a girl?"

"Well, first—," I lifted my head to face her, "—you're a woman. I need my perception of your physical and mental development to be expressed while we're here, alone, together under the occasion." Her breaking into a hard chortle had me tempted to follow. In spite of her infectious humor, I tried keeping a straight face. I was serious as hell about that. I didn't fuck young girls. They were thick and physically mature enough to fool you, if you didn't pay attention to the develop-ment of their minds, when trying to take their pussy. That was never my hype, and it wouldn't start with Jane here. "Anyway. What I meant by that is most Black women claim the *Kings* because they're Black-owned. It's cliché'ish."

"Who's your team?"

"*Dallas.*"

She spit out air through her lips and performed a hearty, fake laugh. "The *Cowboys*?" Then she abandoned the fork and brought her elbows to the table. "Let me guess. Either you grew up not really knowing your father who was a *Cowboys* fan, grew up living with your attending father who was a *Cowboys* fan, come from a huge family where lots of them are *Cowboys* fans, or had an influential male figure, like an uncle or somebody who smoked a pack of *Newport 100*s daily, drove a *Cadillac,* wore tight ass jeans cracking his nut sac, and a full mustache who was a *Cowboys* fan."

My eyes blew the hell up. "What makes you say that?"

"Because *Cowgirl* fans are inherited not earned. It's like a college legacy program concept: old and shriveled up, just like Jerry himself."

Damn...

I stifled a laugh. "We do have a legacy. It's unmatched. Count our rings. You don't have enough spokes in your crown to fit all of them."

Her head shot back as she smiled and appeared shocked at the same time. "As in the *Kings'* crown?"

"That's the only one in question when you're talking football." I pushed a piece of steak into my mouth.

"First of all, we're talking currently, not what happened in the nineties. Making the playoffs every year and not making it past the Conference Championship round is a 'red flag,' and I'm not referring to the coach's challenge flag." She cocked her head to the side and raised her brows.

I applied my poker face. "Really?"

"Really." We tended to our plates for a few quiet seconds. "Last, but not least. Until Jerry hires a real coach who's not afraid to make his or her own decisions, the team may win the Division, but will continue to fail to make it to the Big Game."

"Has anyone ever explained to you the penalty for hitting below the belt, Ms. Doherty?"

She blinked hard, chewing while fighting a blush. With food in her mouth she screeched, "Boy!"

We both laughed at that.

"Alright. Alright." I picked up the white cloth napkin and slightly waved it back and forth. "I've been learned. You know your football."

"And do," she hissed playfully, rolling her neck again. "Clearly, the women you keep around you do not."

That simple jab brought honest thoughts to mind immediately. It wasn't an appropriate headspace to be in, so I immediately changed the subject.

"If you weren't doing what you now do for a living, what would you do—if you had a choice?" I'd stolen Ebonee's question to me. Here it was more appropriate.

"A schoolteacher."

"Why?"

She shrugged, attention on her plate. "To help shape the minds of human beings before their brains are fully developed and injected with poison."

I couldn't help it. "Do you have kids?"

"Eww!" She cringed. "Never. And never will. Babies are cute. But they eventually turn into bloodsuckers and suck the life out of you."

I stared at her, trying to understand. "And you love your perpetual freedom."

She pulled in a deep breath. "I'm in constant search of me. Babies should only be experienced by people who are ready for them." She rolled her eyes and laughed. "This is going too deep. Change the subject."

"Nah. Let's stay deep, Jane."

"Oh, god." She rolled her eyes, continuing to giggle.

"What's your biggest fear?"

"Right now? Or in...life?"

"Either."

"Well..." A bolt of laughter erupted from her chest, and she leaned over in her seat, attempting to cover her mouth with a fist again. "My immediate fear is catching an STD or two or three from tonight." I chuckled as she laughed her ass off. When she slowed, she admitted, "I guess that will always be my fear. My life getting fucked up behind a man's inability to be honest." She flashed her eyes wide playfully. I guessed to softly acknowledge her stark philosophy.

"And what about women?"

"What about them?"

"Do you fear getting an infection from them, too?"

Her expression turned blank, lashes clapped. "I don't..." She licked her beautiful lips, something I found fascinating. "I've never been with a woman. I don't service them."

I angled my head. "Like...never?"

"Never," her tone resolute.

I nodded.

"Women are beautiful creatures, but I don't desire them."

"What do you desire?"

"Loyalty."

"Can you ask for that in your line of work?"

"This type of work won't last. I haven't always done...this. What I've done with you doesn't define me. Not even as a partner."

"So, do you want to settle down one day?" I wasn't propositioning her. I was just curious.

She shook her head. "I'm not in any rush."

"Why?"

Her eyes blossomed and neck swiveled over her shoulders again. "I said why. Men aren't honest. They aren't loyal."

"You've been cheated on."

She spit out laughter. "Duh! Of course. I *am* a woman who dates men."

"What's the worst part about being cheated on?"

She thought for a moment, eventually taking a sip of wine. "*Hmmmm...* Has to be when you can't compete with the other party he cheated with."

"I don't follow."

"If she's white, I can't compete. If she's a 'he,' I can't compete."

"Damn." I was stuck.

"Right."

"You've had one of those?"

"Almost. My cousin had and was able to help me to piece it together." She nodded then soon began squinting and placed her glass on the table. "That tattoo..."

"Which one?" I was shirtless. They were all exposed.

"The ones on your neck."

"What about them?"

"It's a lot."

Raising my chin, I reached for my neck, examining. "I like them."

"I see. But—"

"But what?"

Her eyes softened and lips puckered as she used her tongue to clean her mouth. "What type of job—*legal and well-endowed job*—accepts that presentation?"

A slow smile melted my face when she rushed the glass to her mouth. At thirty-seven, I had plenty experience with women. In my line of work, I was around them often. Their response to me varied very little. And Jane, sitting across from me, wasn't in a league of her own in terms of her reaction.

"What's it matter to you?"

"You pay me." Her eyes skirted around the room. "Remember? And left a nice tip, too. Just like you want it to be clear I'm of age for legal reasons, it would be nice to know I haven't been in business with Pablo Escobar."

I snickered. I couldn't help it. She vacillated between debutante, cerebral, and comedienne with short minutes in between.

"I'm actually a W-2 paid employee. No illegal business pays for your service. Speaking of which, do you have to be attracted to a man in order for him to be a client?" I watched her closely.

Immediately, her eyes fell toward her plate. "Of course, not. How else will I make a living? I'd go broke if I only serviced men I find attractive."

"Do you find me attractive?"

Her head swung up. "I do. Very much, I do." She stared dead into my eyes. "I've broken rules for you."

"Would you break more if I didn't have these?" I pointed to my neck.

Jane's head angled cleverly. "I don't know." Her eyes descended as she studied the ink. I lifted my chin to give her a better view. "Is that an eagle? What does that represent to you?"

"The ability to see sharper than most."

She tucked her chin, and her eyes went wild. "That has to be miserable."

"Why?"

"Do you mean you're observant?" I nodded. "I don't need to see more than putting one foot in front of the other. The ability to have eyes behind your head has to be lonely and depressing."

"Why?" I pulled my glass up for a sip.

"Because you see good and bad."

"In my line of work, I do."

"Some bad you can never unsee."

I swallowed the dry wine. "This is true."

"And you're powerless to let it happen."

"Not true at all." I noticed the diamond encrusted cross hanging from her neck as she adjusted the sheet beneath her arms. "Eagles have the wing capacity to soar so high, and the vision capacity to see far ahead. There are times where my sight allows me to see far enough ahead to prevent shit from happening."

Her head fell to the side. "Why do I feel like you're seeing something in me right now?"

My eyes rose to her face. "All I see is your next orgasm tonight."

Her jaw dropped and back collapsed in the chair.

Six

March

Hayden

"Here you go." My john handed me a packaged toothbrush plucked from a drawer here in the ensuite bathroom.

"Thank you."

He brought out a tube of toothpaste from another drawer. It made me wonder if he was a long-term guest at this resort. These drawers were packed, and it appeared to be beyond a standard guest's stay.

"Thanks," I murmured again. I, once again, caught the swinging of his braids. "I don't see many Black men with that hairstyle. Oddly, it looks...good on you."

It did. My john's bronzed, peanut buttery skin and voluminous hair box-braided made me question his ethnicity. I mean, his speech and mannerisms all gave Black man. But the beige-olive undertone and thick, long hair curling at the ends made me wonder.

He winked. "Thanks, Boo-baby. Be right back." I watched as he turned for the door to leave. His back was free of ink and impressively blemish-free just as his chest. But those tattoos were distinct, coloring his cut arms, shoulders, and neck. Odd for a pattern, I thought, as I went about brushing my teeth. He sauntered around, shirtless, with such confidence to say I was a stranger to him, and we were in a random hotel suite—a luxury resort suite to be more accurate. I needed to loosen up if I was going to pull this off.

I swear, if I make it out of this, I'll never try this shit again!

While leaned over the sink, brushing my teeth as I clutched my boobs wrapped in the sheet, my john returned with a strip of condoms. He flashed a smile before pulling out an electric toothbrush and applying paste. In silence, we cleaned our mouths, avoiding catching eyes in the mirror. It could have been weird if it weren't for his exuding confidence. He'd done this before, and lots. And I couldn't ask because in my alleged role as a prostitute, it would be inappropriate and unrealistic.

After rinsing my mouth and patting it dry with a hanging face-cloth, I turned to lean against the vanity. He was still bent over, brushing his teeth.

"Are they real?"

"What?" The word and his voice were distorted from having a mouthful of paste.

"Your teeth. Are they real?"

He didn't answer right away. I glanced away as he rinsed and dried his mouth. When he stood straight, I faced him again.

He gazed at his teeth in the mirror, checking himself out. Shaking his head, he answered, "Nah. This is the product of forty-thousand-dollar work."

Damn!

"For vanity?" They looked amazing.

He dropped the towel then crept up on me like a starved leopard.

His big hands cupped the side of my face and his hungry mouth followed. The coolness of his tongue wasn't lost upon me, but the passion in his kiss warmed me. Just like earlier under the fire, my john took special interest in oral play. His proximity was still new to me, but I liked experiencing a soft side to this stranger.

He managed to unravel the sheet from beneath my arms. Then his hands were at my feet, running my legs to loosen the cloth. He managed my thighs open and kissed his way to my neck, igniting my heavy ass panting. Those hands down low were still busy. They'd danced their way to my slit and swiped against my sensitive flesh. I felt myself swelling against his digits.

My spine curled backward, and I held him at his thick neck. I swallowed a thick collection of saliva, afraid to disturb the vibe—he felt so good. Then he brought his hand up to his face and licked his fingers.

His eyes rolled up toward the ceiling, and he whispered, "Not too bad." My john brought his fingers to my lips. Without thought, I opened my mouth. He fingered my tongue, introducing my personal, sensual musk to my palate. "Suck."

He studied me with hooded eyes and parted lips. The tip of his tongue pressed against the tips of his top teeth. Shit. He was so sensual. So bold. I sucked on his fingers, feeling my pussy lubricate, my nipples sting in need.

My john pulled his fingers from me and smirked softly in approval, it seemed. He pulled my legs up, my knees aligned with my breasts. The sheet was fully unraveled and splayed over the vanity and sink. I was now exposed to him. Why wasn't I embarrassed, ashamed of being bare before a stranger? Why was I so damn good and comfortable playing a sex worker?

I couldn't begin to unpack that. I watched as my john clasped onto my ankles, pushing my knees further into my chest as he descended before me. When his mouth hit my sex, my hand flew to my face. His tongue was wide and just as confident as the man himself. Unable to hide how good he felt, I slammed my eyes closed and continued to grab my mouth. I was failing. A professional would never behave like a damn virgin, especially when his tongue roved over every cell of her slit.

I knew I'd explode right away. This shit was illuminating. When was the last time a man had gone down on me? I couldn't think. Feeling my groin wound up, my head rolled to the side. I wanted to grab his head but pulling on his hair felt so cliché'ish, so I didn't. When he stopped, my heavy head rolled on a stiff neck, and I gazed down at him. Those long, dark lashes were closed over heavy eyes. His mouth and chin glistened with me. I watched as his lengthy and wide tongue darted out and caressed my clit, eliciting a helpless groan from my belly.

"You're about to cum," he droned, sounding just as close to the precipitous as I'd felt. Then a smirk appeared on his handsome face. "I didn't expect you to be so—" He licked me. "—responsive. You need for me..." His tongue swiped my clit and my belly lurched. "...to slow down?"

His full tongue shot out and expanded to swipe up, bringing with it a blob of my excitement. At the sight of that, my hands went to the back of his head, and I pushed my pussy in his face. And after three short thrusts, my groin imploded.

"Oh, damn!" I cried out helplessly, peering him in the face as my stomach visibly shuddered.

My spine jerked and back slammed into the mirror uncontrollably.

"*Mmmmmm...*" he goaded, still eating me.

His gaze into my soul was too much. I closed my eyes and rode through the fit my body threw during my paralyzing orgasm. He licked and licked until my tremors stopped and I could no longer endure his touch. I was too sensitive there, yet my body still convulsed, and heart pounded. Breathing riotously, I watched him kiss my inner thigh, smirking devilishly as he stood.

"Don't give up the ship," he chuckled with slanted eyes as he strolled over to the shower and turned the faucets on.

"Huhn?" I asked, still pinned up on the vanity with my legs in the air, exposing myself.

His sensual grin didn't waiver when he replied, "You keep abandoning the ship."

If that meant me consenting to sexual acts with him, I had no idea. But that would be dumb. It's what he'd paid me to do. Nonetheless, I had no capacity to ask. With rapt interest, I watched him remove his lounge pants, reminding me of his splendid fucking build. My john ripped a condom from the strip then managed me from the vanity and on to him in a straddling position. I clasped onto his strapping frame like a wounded solider.

Inside, he lowered me to the shower floor then positioned himself behind me. After applying the condom and tossing the wrapper to the floor, I winced as his fullness entered me. I spent the next few minutes savoring his long strokes with my face against the cool wall as my hard nipples brushed up and down the marble.

ISHAAN

My consciousness seemed to have snapped awake, truncating my sleep. I hated when that happened. *Shit.* I glanced around the dim room, finding the flame from the fireplace fizzling out. It was still dark out. I guessed it was before five in the morning, considering the time of the sunrise.

A muscle in my thigh pulsed, a sensation striking my groin. Then I felt soft, warm flesh on my stomach, causing my abs to flutter. The flesh was wet and soon accompanied by hands. Kisses trailed down my stomach. Then those hands—soft and warm—wrapped around my cock.

Jane...

Damn. She stroked me with her fingers first, running them down the structure of me. Her tongue came sneakily into play, tracing near the head of me. She didn't start with sloppy and harsh jerks. Nah. Jane knew how to grow my arousal. How to pace the buildup. She spit on me, and not in the gross way, but the sensual manner. It was her method of lubricating for her massage. The shit felt *so* fucking good. I stretched my legs out, relaxing into her work.

And the sounds. The oatmeal stir turned me the fuck on even more. Then, when I felt her tongue then lips on my balls... This shit was heating up faster than I was used to. My thighs strained on either side of her. Giving in to her talent, my head rolled on my pillow. Her flowery scent hit me suddenly. After a few minutes of this good sucking and stroking, my damn feet began to heat up. I burrowed my ass into the mattress, preparing to nut. *Shit*. I didn't want to.

Jane knew, so she lightened her grip and slowed her strokes. Her hard, warm breaths hit my wet dick. She was out of breath. But that wasn't why she stopped. Because after a few seconds, the woman went right back in. Tightening her palms, she moved slowly, only putting her mouth on my head. A few minutes more and I was ready to cum again. And just like before, Jane pulled back. She was edging me. When she sensed me about to orgasm, she stopped the shit again.

This shit was blowing my mind. She wasn't rushing it. Jane had this in her arsenal and wanted to pleasure me. It was probably because I ate her pussy earlier, something I didn't do with strangers. But Jane made fucking fun to me again. Explorative. She'd set a stage back in Vegas, and I wanted to play on it with her.

"*Fuuuuck*..." I cried out, feeling my explosion ready to top.

Then, swiftly, Jane stopped her cadence and pressure, forcing my orgasm to recede. With a vibrating pelvis from a weird ass sensation, I pushed my head farther into the mattress and swallowed deeply. I was fucking salivating at this point.

My Boo-baby...

I reached down for her head with a sting of pride. She was so damn good. Beyond good, she had a talent, shocking the hell out of me. The fire was almost fully out, lessening the glow and view of her.

Soft staccato notes asked, "You've had enough?"

I smiled, butterflies erupting in my damn belly from her aggression. "You tired?"

I felt her head shake. "Not with you." Her tongue lashed over the head of my cock. "You're inspiring."

My brows met. "Inspiring how?"

She didn't speak again, at least not verbally. Jane took me into her mouth again. Her fingers gripped the base of me, stroking with an intent grip. Before long, my head collapsed onto the pillow again. And so quickly, my hips pushed into her head on their own volition. She used a warm hand to caress my balls, massaging them. After a while, I could feel my sacs drip of her saliva. She kept stroking and sucking. Her soft lips, warm and sprightly tongue. Jane kept going, and it took no time for my orgasm to crest again.

This time, she didn't stop it abruptly and I was grateful. I was ready to blow. To release the anticipation she'd built, I had guessed from the critique I gave her earlier in the bathroom about her own immediate release.

Fuck...

I was cumming. My feet heated, and toes curled as I eased into it. I opened my legs even wider, bracing myself against the waves of bliss stemming from my balls and shooting up my belly and into my chest.

Then it stopped. Jane's mouth was gone, and her hands held still in a firm grip on the shaft of me.

"Boo-baby," I whined, out of breath like a fucking simp, and didn't give a single fuck. "I was cumming."

"And you'll finish. It's going to be stronger and soooo good," she whispered.

What the fuck?

Then she released me, jerked me faster and harder. Her head and mouth plunged on my pulsating cock. Out of nowhere, I got scared as hell. Is this chick crazy? What the hell does she think she's doing? Is she trying to hurt me? Is this her experimenting on my dick, confusing it as expertise?

Or is this broad a fucking master?

My entire body shuddered, forcing an animalistic cry from the bottom of my damn belly. And I couldn't stop shooting. I felt my shit jutting into her mouth as my hands gripped the sheets around me with misted palms. My ass lifted from the mattress, holding for a few seconds before collapsing and repeating.

Jane worked me over like a chef over a five-pot stove.

My mind was fucking blown.

The ringing of my phone was what had awakened me. At first, my eyes brushed around the dark room, remembering where I was and who I had been with. I then reached over to the nightstand.

"Yeah." I rubbed my eyes.

"Patterson."

I recognized her voice right away. "That's me."

"I have a proposition for you?"

My eyes squinted open. "Of what type?"

"One that will meet both our needs, directly and indirectly."

I had no fucking idea what Ebonee was talking about. I hadn't spoken to her since she was in town a few days ago. My brain was too foggy. I didn't even know what time it was.

"It's early, Williams—"

"I know. I'll be back stateside next Tuesday. Please say you'll be in the U.S., too."

"It's early, Williams."

"Okay." She squealed, happy as hell. "I'll try you back in a couple of hours. Wake the hell up. Our lives will be the better for it."

Then the line went dead. I peeped the time and saw it was a few minutes after six. Suddenly, I hoped I wasn't being rude to my company. After returning the phone to the nightstand, I reached for her. The opposite side of the bed was as cold and chilled as the winter air outside. I sat up to confirm. Jane wasn't in bed. My gaze rolled over to the bathroom. The door was open and lights off.

I left the bed for a leak. My bladder started to jump. After washing my face and brushing my teeth, I felt a little excited about my guest.

What the fuck was that shit she pulled last night? It was a first for me. I wanted to see if I could talk her into staying for a few hours this morning. The pay was of no concern.

Within minutes, I searched the living room, kitchen, and other bed and bathrooms of the suite. Jane had left. Fingering my drying lips, I felt confused as hell. How? I didn't hear or feel anything after dozing off last night. *My lip balm.* It was in the pocket of my pants. A thought occurred and I recalled where I'd left my clothes. As I drew closer to the sitting room off the kitchen, I saw cash. New, crisp bills. There were two stacks. One stack held fifteen one thousand-dollar bills. I didn't know one thousand bills still existed. Had actually never seen one. The other stack consisted of five twenty-dollar bills.

My hand gripped the back of my neck and head fell back. "This broad paid me fifteen thousand and tipped a hun'ed," I whispered to myself.

love belvin

Hayden

"Some say I'm fruity..." Lex beat the top of her desk, and I swung my hip.

"But he want the booty." She resumed, remaining on beat, and I did the same.

Then her fists continued in succession with the beatboxing on the desk and I went for it, swinging my arms and hips rhythmically. "And everybody knows how your man wants to do me."

I rounded my hips in the doorway, causing a stirring of laughter from my colleagues. We were cutting up. It broke the monotony of the afternoon. My boss, Lex, ordered a spread of pizza, sandwiches, chips, cookies, and cupcakes, which were laid on the table in the conference room. Along with my coworkers, she celebrated my third anniversary with *Christ Cares*. We were all intoxicated with the "itis" and secretly knew who wouldn't accomplish another work-related task today.

"Yes, mama," Eduardo, an outreach worker, cheered me on with saucy eyes.

He was my work cheerleader, often sharing lunch and chit-chatting with me.

"Oh, lord," Laura, another outreach worker, murmured, shaking her head as she scrolled past Lex's office door. "My virgin eyes."

Lex sputtered with a twisted mouth, "Virgin where?"

That made all of us laugh. Laura, an open lesbian, birthed five children. We knew she had some experience with her hips. Mika stood, holding a plate of chips and cookies. Her short, plump figure cupped the plate with her little arms as she gazed ahead, totally removed from the fun. The sight of her instantly dampened my mood, reminding me of what I'd been putting off since returning from Atlantic City over the weekend. I'd jumped heavily into work as soon as I'd hit the door on Monday morning. We'd reached the end of the week, and I couldn't continue to hold out.

I sighed. "Okay, folks. Let me go about finishing out the week." I rubbed my full belly. "Thanks for lunch and the touching card, boss lady."

"You just remember what I said," Lex hissed.

"I know." I rolled my eyes playfully. "If I get a more attractive offer for another gig, just remember, you can get me a stay at a beach house just a few houses down from my cousin."

"And I can get you burgers from *DiFillippo's* even if they're not on the menu!" she shouted to my back.

I walked down the short corridor and turned the corner. Mika's desk was in an open cubicle near my office. I tapped on the partition. "Mind if we chat a bit?" I tried to smile as she held a cookie sandwiched by two chips to her mouth.

"Sure."

I took off for my office. Mika wasn't far behind.

"Close the door. Please." She obeyed before taking a seat in my quaint space. I exhaled, "Mika, I don't know the protocol for this, but I feel I haven't handled your situation...supportively." Tears immediately began streaming down her round face. "I didn't know about it until I was leaving out—" My words stopped abruptly, and I stood to round my desk.

I wanted to hug Mika but didn't know the etiquette as she buried her face in her hands and cried silently.

"Can I hug you?"

When she nodded her head, I sat on the arm of her chair and wrapped her to my chest. Her body vibrated with anguish.

"It's hard," I whispered. "It's hard being a woman. The decisions we have to make. The respect we have to demand. And the sacrifices we make every day. I'm sure these aren't the circumstances you wanted it under, but you are going to be an excellent mommy, Mika." I felt her head shake against my chest. "Girl, please. You are. I can tell by how well you take care of me...always going above and beyond my requirements and being sure I'm comfortable around here with coffee, snacks, and cleaning my desk. You always ask if I've eaten and offer to pick up something for me if the answer's 'no.' You're going to be so attentive and loving—"

Mika shook her head again. Then she came up for air and wiped her face with her hands. I grabbed her a facial tissue from my desk. Sniffling, she murmured, "I got an abortion."

I froze.

Abortion?

"Is that why you took off on Tuesday..." And then I thought. "...and came in for a half day on Wednesday?" She nodded. "Did you go alone?"

Mika shook her head again. "My brother drove me."

"Damn, Mika. Why are you even here? You should be home, resting and healing emotionally."

"I don't have much paid time off left. I used a lot of them for vacation."

"But this is sick time. I would've let you work from home and had you send me random email reminders or some shit throughout the day." My heart twisted in my chest, my own damn belly churning.

Mika just cried in my arms, and I let her. She wasn't loud, but terribly shaken. I wish I could do something to mitigate the pain. I let her take her time. No one would disturb her.

Eventually, she whispered thickly through tears, "I know it sounds stupid. My mother keeps saying that. But it wasn't. It was real. I mean…" She cried. "…maybe if it didn't happen to me out in Vegas, I would think it's stupid, too, but we had something real, boss lady!" She borrowed the moniker from me. It was what I called Lex, my program manager. "That first night we got to Vegas, and I saw him in the restaurant, we both felt something. I felt someone staring at me and when I finally found him, he looked away." Mika sobbed more. "It was his eye. He's got a lazy eye, and I'm sure it doesn't make for the most confident dude when he sees something he likes.

"I didn't say anything that night. But when I saw him the next day at breakfast, I knew I wanted him. So, I went over to the fruit bar to give him the opportunity to say something." She snorted through her tears. "Then my fat ass went up for fruit a second time. You know I eat a lot, but not no damn fruit when there was pork at the bar a few feet away. But the third time I went, he made his move. We met up that afternoon when y'all went to the Strip."

Oh. That's where you were?

I continued rubbing her shoulder and back as best I could.

"I was in Vegas," she cried thickly. "You know. With the girls. It's when you're supposed to live on the wild side. Right? But it was more than that, boss lady. That last night, I split from the girls and invited him to my room. I knew Lucy wouldn't be back for a while. Henry said the sweetest things to me. He told me some personal stuff you don't just share with everybody. It was deep. So deep." She shook her head.

I wanted to ask if they, at least, attempted any birth control, but how dare I considering *my* time in Vegas. Atlantic City was more "responsible," if I could even make the claim. But Vegas?

So, I kept my big ass, irresponsible mouth shut and continued to comfort my assistant.

An abortion?
Damn.

ISHAAN

I constricted my arm wrapped around his neck even more as he tried to punch upward at my face. Applying patience, I pushed my head back, bobbing and weaving. His boys surrounded us on the dirt road, shouting to him in encouragement. It was useless as his face reddened, arm slowed, and the muscles in his neck turned pliant. This nigga was big as fuck, too. He had to be six feet, seven inches, and over three-fifty.

My whole body was tense with violent energy, but I had to remember the goal was not to kill him. And killing him was so fucking easy. In fact, it was just a matter of time. If this big motherfucker would tap out, it would make it easier on the both of us. I'd been in this situation more times than I could count, but tonight I felt each second of my physical exertion. The pre-gurgles began shooting from his closed throat. Very little air escaped or entered. The veins around his eyes thickened and colored.

Come on...

Come on...

Somewhere behind me, one of his boys shouted something sounding threatening. I couldn't concern myself with the prospect. My focus had to be on the thin line I was leading this buff nigga down. A few dollops of sweat from my face fell on his. One dropped directly into his eyes, forcing them both to close and squeeze.

No. No. No!

I needed to see his eyes. They helped me to measure his consciousness. Shit. I was going to kill this man and ruin an arrangement before it launched. His body began shuddering. It was fucked up, but I couldn't break my hold. This bitch was about to die, and I'd have to take a new approach to building an alignment with the top crime organization on *Red's Island*.

Oh, fucking well...

As his arms and legs began to thrash, I had no choice. I'd do what I had to do. The streets, be it back in the slums of Vegas or Atlantic City or here in the Caribbean, had its code. This was their decision. Either way, Divine would move forward with opening the resort—

"Enough!" Eli, the head of the *MC2* gang, made the call.

Relief hit my brain but took more time to penetrate my body. Eventually it did when I felt other rough hands and arms around me, prying dude from my snake grip.

"Ish! Ish!" I heard in an American accent.

"He called it bro!" That was Kell. I knew for sure.

I released him, stepping back, suddenly out of fucking breath. My attention left ol' boy as they were carting him off by his wrists and ankles, and swept over to Eli. His brows were tight, eyes low as he smoked on a big ass blunt. He was a shirtless, skinny ass, tall nigga with a ball of a belly. His locs were free-stranding and a brown-grayish color, looking dingy as hell. His eyes were large and yellow, but make no mistake, Eli had a sharp eye for his island. He ruled the underworld of *Red's Island* and nearly half the surface of it.

The problem was, where Azmir Divine Jacobs invested, he ruled. Either Eli would have to compromise his domination to make room for ADJ, or he'd get rolled over. Tonight was me playing by Eli's rules to assure we were about that fucking life. Tomorrow could be a matter of overthrowing the whole hood on this small island, using my men to descend on this bitch with semi-autos ablaze.

"Okay. Okay." Eli let out curls of smoke. "Much respect to ya now!"

With a heaving, bare chest and a stinging lower back, I backed away.

Inside the sprinter was a bumpy ride. I flinched, feeling my flesh being pierced.

"Calm the hell down, fuckin' baby," Lynn, my resident nurse practitioner, hissed as she worked on me. "It's ugly but you'll live. He didn't puncture it."

Shit...

I sat curled over on the floor while she tended to the "itch" I'd been feeling since leaving *Port Tesce* in a bullet-proof vehicle.

"Senior," Kell called out to me from the passenger seat. "...something didn't feel right back there."

"Yeah? Like what? I almost killed a fuckin' giant as a test?" That was some shit I was still trying to digest.

"Yeah and no." He scratched the side of his face. "You weren't sharp back there. I'm glad you secured your hair into braids. That would have been an instant grab had you not."

My head shot up toward the front. Kell's face was to the floor as he turned my way. Then I saw Carver, another combat-trained piece of muscle on my team, peer at me through the rearview mirror. Even through biker sunglasses, I felt his agreeance.

"Fuck you mean, Kell?"

He sighed, treading cautiously. "What I mean, sir, is your responses—though correct—were slowly executed. That shoulder roll when he was strong and aggressive at the beginning: it was slightly delayed—a technique you took me to *The Banger* to learn straight from the horse. The window was narrow and even your follow-up springing was slightly delayed, too."

"And you were winded a lot sooner than you should have been," Lynn critiqued.

I winced from another needle piercing. "Did you time it, too?"

Lynn snorted. "Just an observation, top dog. Your performance today was off."

"The kidney target was genius, but..." He shrugged. "...maybe it's because your diet ain't been clean lately? You scarfed down two ice cream sandwiches last night, back-to-back." He faced the road again, shaking his head.

We rolled over what felt like a pothole but was not. The shit made me howl in pain, feeling like my skin was being ripped from the muscle. "I slayed a fuckin' green giant on my own, managing a busted shoulder and a sneak slicing aiming for my damn kidney!"

That was what had me fold big boy into a chokehold. We didn't know it at the time, but the blunt force—although I had no idea what it was—made me fight to put his ass down. Now, I realized, if I'd killed the giant, I had every fucking right to. Ironically, when I kept attacking his kidney area with hard hooks to weaken him, he jabbed me with a blade he managed to make disappear as smoothly as it had appeared.

"Is your sleep still fucked up?" Kell asked from the driver's seat. Again, I could tell he peered back to me in the rearview mirror while trying to watch the road.

I didn't answer, so fucking annoyed.

"All I'm saying, Senior, is something isn't right."

"We'll give you a full workup back at the clinic," Lynn assured. "I'll run some blood tests for you, too."

My eyes closed, mostly from pain, but from fucking anger, too.

I beat the nigga's seven-foot ass, but y'all wanna tell me how mediocre my performance was?

Yeah. Tired as fuck, I was ready to get back to the resort.

SEVEN

April

Hayden

My real estate attorney, Frank, passed the gazillionth document across the table to me. "And finally, here's the mortgage decree. Listed here," He flipped through the papers. "...is the amount you're borrowing along with the interest rate. In this paragraph, the prepayment penalties are noted." He flipped again. "And around about here are the consequences for late payments. Yada, yada, yada."

I took my time poring over the areas he'd highlighted. The small conference room of his office was silent. I'd been floating on air since arriving and being shown to what the office referred to as "the closing room." That felt like a lifetime ago. I'd been signing my life away for what seemed like hours with document after document reminding me of the heady commitment. Affixing my signature after initialing while feeling as though I wasn't in the moment concerned me, too.

"Alright." Frank accepted the documents, tapping the bottom of them on the table into a stack. Then they were handed off to one of the women on his staff. "And here's where I have the pleasure of congratulating you on the purchase of your new home, Ms. Washington." His smile arrived. "This is a wonderful accomplishment. Our best to you."

The woman and man still sitting in on the process began to cheer with applause and congratulatory greetings. Frank joined them in clapping, awakening my giddiness. A goofy smile lightened my face and I turned to my one support system today. My mother's mouth was twisted to the side, arms folded, and brows hiked.

I put the car in park then turned to her. "What's the problem, Ma? Since when is buying a house a crime?"

"When you don't have plans to live in it comfortably. It's foolish!"

"I am living in it. I'll be moving in by next month."

"You're moving into the basement of your own home. A three-family home. Instead of taking the first, second, or third floor units, you want to live in the basement like a convict?"

My head tossed back, and I snorted at the visual of that. I hesitated, but that was when I shared, "There's nothing wrong with renting the larger apartments in the house. That's how I'll make money. Sundryia has done it practically from the time she purchased her first investment property until a few months ago when she moved in with Maaz."

My mother leaped around, the belt of the seat restraining her frame. "You can't do what other people do, Hayden! Why do you want to do what someone else has done? Someone who doesn't have even half the education as you? Half the brains! She's married to a rich football player. She has a family. And what do you have? A big house where you're content to take a small closet? It's utterly ridiculous!"

Sundryia was not married.

Yet.

My eyes narrowed curiously. "What's ridiculous about making money? Investing in me?"

"Investing in yourself while living in the basement of your own home like a peasant?" she charged back bitterly.

"Ma, I work hard. I've saved a lot of money over the years—saved even more when I realized I wanted to do this. I have no kids or a partner. I don't need multiple bedrooms. It's just me."

"You're in Paterson!" she spat. "I worked hard to keep you from places like that and here you are, trying to be like Sundryia?"

I squinted hard, lips poked. "What's wrong with Sundryia? She's your little cousin."

"I know she's my younger cousin. I'm not saying I have a problem with her. I'm saying I raised you better than to be making decisions based off what's she's done, Hayden. Angelica wasn't able to provide her with the love and guidance I have to you. I worked hard to make sure you didn't have a lifestyle or upbringing anywhere close to hers. So, excuse me for not liking to hear you're making a lifestyle choice she's had to make."

Staring ahead at nothing in particular outside of my car, I whispered, "Engaging in real estate is a bad lifestyle choice?" I nodded. "Okay."

"I'm not saying that—"

"What if I told you," I began gently. "I know, indisputably, Sundryia has made more in real estate over the years than you earned as a bank manager and me as a grant-writer?"

I knew I was pushing it, but seeing my mother's jaw drop was worth sharing Sundryia's flex. I didn't think my mother hated Sundryia, but since Sundryia and I were kids, I believed she looked down on her because of Sundryia's mother, my mother's first cousin. My mother thought she was better than her first cousins, Angelica and Samantha. Samantha was the mother of my other third cousin,

Rayna. I didn't spend as much time with Rayna growing up as I did Sundryia. And to me, Sundryia was treated like a friend of mine rather than my mother's cousin. It used to hurt until I saw Sundryia practically ignored it. She was so damn tough and unbothered by shit like that, whereas I felt everything. We both learned to accept my mother's strange ways.

"Young lady, do you think because someone has money, they have it all? Even Sundryia knows that! She's married with kids! And what are you? A migrant living in a damn basement. Meanwhile, you've got a bachelor's degree with double majors, two master's degrees, and countless certifications. And all you want to do is live in a damn basement in Paterson? You think about that before you come inside!" She hurriedly removed the seatbelt and grabbed her purse to leave.

Picking at my nails, I murmured, "I'm not coming in. I have an appointment."

"You never want to visit my home!" she shrilled. "You're too good?" Then she huffed her way out of my car. "Have a nice day, Hayden!"

The door slammed and I watched my mother take off up the stairs of her Passaic colonial, ignoring the greeting of a neighbor.

Monica Washington was pissed.

And I was left sitting with her anger, feeling a familiar foe. Inadequacy.

I'm never enough...

"Have a seat in here," the nurse pointed inside the examination room of my gynecologist's office. "I'm going to let her know you've arrived. As soon as she can break from her current patient, she'll be in here to chat with you."

I walked inside and turned to face her. "Did my urine come up dirty, parole officer?" I tried joking.

This was weird. I'd just been here yesterday, and her office called me first thing this morning to say Dr. Brown needed to see me today. The receptionist informed I'd be squeezed in whenever I arrived.

The nurse, who seemed to be about my age, chuckled. "I don't know. But in case Dr. B's a snitch, I'll keep the back door unlocked for you."

I shook my head, laughing as she closed the door. Expecting to do the waiting game, I pulled out my phone and began checking my emails. I started with my personal inbox and deleted a bunch of retailers' sale announcements. There was no way I'd be buying anything nice for myself for a while, having just purchased a home at a premium price. It was the route I wanted to take over a fixer upper. After being educated on the real estate game by my cousin, Sundryia, and a college-grad buddy of mine, Bruce, I decided on a contemporary property that had just been flipped. The units were turnkey, having been recently upgraded with new paint, appliances, and fixtures. Next week, I'd start my search for tenants.

I'd just opened the first email in my work account when there was a knock at the door before it opened. "Hayden!" her pitch was energetic, and makeup tastefully intact in the early afternoon hours as though it was applied just minutes ago. She stepped inside, closing the door behind her. I watched curiously as she strutted in her usual high-heeled shoes across the hard floor. "I'm with a patient but asked them to wait for a few minutes."

"Yeah. Everything okay?" My eyes were wide. "What happened since I left yesterday?"

I'd taken a battery of tests, still being vigilant since my reckless behavior, which started in Vegas but continued to South Jersey. I'd been tested and refrained from sex. Per usual, several of the results were instant and came back negative. There were others, sent to a lab, we'd been waiting on. Nothing about my visit yesterday was any different than the first after Vegas in February. I'd been regular. Responsible.

"Yes." She opened my chart. "And possibly 'no.' Our focus has been on your sexual health for the past—what? Two months, almost. I slipped up and didn't consider your reproductive health."

"What do you mean?" I blinked as she typed in her credentials on the computer in the corner.

"It means..." She leaned in and studied the screen, resting her chin between her thumb and index finger. "...you're expecting."

"Expecting what?"

"Was the first day of your last full period February fifth?"

I blinked again, so damn confused. "Yes—I don't know." I glanced down to my phone. "I told you a couple of weeks ago, it came and went—"

"You were spotting." She turned to me. "It's common during the first trimester."

"First what?"

A wry smile lifted on her face when she shifted to face me. "You're pregnant, honey. Your urine test revealed the results, but in my haste on yesterday, I didn't 'check off that box' because our focus has been on your sexual health. I'd like to test you again today for confirmation. But I have to tell you, I'd be greatly surprised if the results yield something different." She stood, went to a cabinet, and pulled out a plastic cup.

About thirty minutes later, Dr. Brown was back at the desk near the computer in the corner, typing again. "Okay. I'm recommending these now...in case."

I sat curled over my knees, body steeled, feeling so hollow inside.

Pregnant...

I hadn't been sick. Didn't feel anything different physically. How could I be pregnant? I'd been far more reckless with actual trusting lovers without a single scare.

But this one time...

A stranger had invaded my body. The thought of it made me shiver.

"Okay," she exhaled, turning to me on the rolling stool. Her aura warmed in an attempt to comfort me, though nothing could. "I know this wasn't planned, but keep in mind the risks we were facing, Hayden."

"A baby? I can't have a baby. This doesn't seem real." My feelings were similar to my closing earlier.

"Remember your first visit since coming back from Vegas? Then the one after Atlantic City?" I dropped my face into my hands, feeling my lash extensions crush. I told my doctor too much. *Clearly.* "We went over the risks. Maybe we focused too much on the pathology part rather than the whole pie in terms of what was at stake after..." Her hand extended.

Yeah. I knew what she meant. Me sleeping with a random guy. Twice.

She handed me a stack of pamphlets. All were about a woman's options in New Jersey regarding her fetus. "You're about eight weeks, which gives you plenty of time to make a logical and practical decision." She handed me a small paper. "A list of prenatal vitamins, if you're so inclined. And if you're not, abortion is still legal in New Jersey. Murphy declared it will always be a woman's choice."

I'd vote again for our governor if he was eligible to run, but it was his final term.

So glad I made the right decision the first two times.

There was a knock at my office door. When I glanced up, Mika's neck craned through the frame.

"Busy?"

I glanced down to my screen. I'd been working hard on the rough draft of a proposal for *Rutgers University*. It had been put off for a couple of days now, still...processing my shit. I was in a groove, not having the urge to cry since I'd begun. I was now on page six.

Damn.

I blinked several times and tossed my chin. "What's up?"

Mika stepped inside, leaping for the chair. "I need to go away!" she groaned through gritted teeth, lips tight as her chunky fists rose on both sides of her face.

I was confused. "Okay."

"I just don't know where to go."

"I thought you didn't have many more vacation days."

"I have two. And if we do something Memorial Day weekend, I can stretch those babies."

I didn't vacation with Mika. Listen, I adored her down to the bone, but Vegas had been the first of its kind. Last fall, Lucy and Mika were lamenting about needing a vacation. They wanted to get away from the office for a while; Harlem, too. So, as an impromptu game, they began writing out places they'd like to go.

About a month later, my girlfriend, Letisha, had been working in the area that particular day. She brought me lunch, figuring it would allow us to steal away girlfriend time together. Life had been so hectic for everyone, it seemed. We walked into the conference room and found Lucy and Mika already there but decided to stay anyway. One discussion led to another when, eventually, vacationing came up.

Playfully, Lucy shared her and Mika's list with my friend. Vegas was one of the destinations. Letisha shared with my colleagues how my cousin's husband owned *HAYDAR Resort & Casino*. That was all it took for the idea to come alive and pressure to begin about me asking Rayna for a hookup. It had taken a little more than a month, but my cousin, Sundryia, pushed me to ask Rayna. To my surprise, my cousin agreed, sounding so sincere doing it.

But that was that. So much had gone down in Vegas, leaving an astounding mark on both Mika and me. I had no interest in revisiting a scenario remotely close to what got me into the fucking quandary I was currently in. I was fucking eight weeks pregnant and stuck. Stuck. Vacationing right now was not on the radar, and especially not with the same cast.

"Oh." My brows shot up as I formulated my next thought. "Memorial Day is right around the corner, ain't it?" Reclining into the chair, I sighed. "My cousin invited me down to the beach. They're finally focusing on the new house. She wants me there to "interview contractors" to upgrade it. I told her I doubt I'd be able to make it. I have to move into the new house. I don't even have tenants yet."

"Congrats on the house again, boss lady!" Her eyes fell and mouth twisted in contemplation, it seemed. "Dang!" she murmured. "You've got a lot going on." Mika shook her head, sympathizing.

"You have no idea—"

"Hey!" Lex was at the door. "Lunch plans? I'm fuckin' starving!"

"Now, boss lady!" Mika warned.

Lex rolled her eyes. "My bad. But I am."

"Where are you going?" I reached for my vibrating phone.

It was Kenny. My belly flipped with anxiety.

"*DiFillippo's.* There's a revival at the church tonight, which means it'll be a long day for me. And I'm craving crème brûlée. I've been fasting and can break it. I need a big girl's meal. You feel me?"

Excitement burst in my chest as I coolly replied, "*Oooooh,*" unenergetically, thinking of the delicious possibilities. "I could go for their tiramisu. It's *sooo* good." I closed my eyes, tantalized by the memory of dining there with Rayna. "You're going fancy today. Huhn?"

"I deserve it," Lex declared. "Wanna come? That extends to you, too, Ms. Mika."

Mika's head whipped around. "My pinky toe can't afford to step inside of that spot. I'm good. I got my momma's seafood salad waiting for me in the fridge. Got some fried fish to go with it, too."

"You sure?" Lex asked then grumbled, "My treat."

Mika shook her head. "*Uhn-uhn.* And don't make me feel guilty about not offering y'all none."

I cleared my throat. "Mika, I think what boss lady here is doing is trying to prevent you from stinking up the whole building with your fishy fish."

Mika stood and whipped her body around. "Y'all go on 'head to the Italians and feast. Mine coming from my momma's kitchen and will be better." Then she rounded Lex, leaving my office.

While Lex and I both laughed—because that was Mika's intention —something about her declination didn't feel natural. Mika never turned down a good time or a free meal. She was likely still in bereavement.

"Are you okay?" Lex's concerned tone tore me from my thoughts. My gaze met hers and I was...stuck again.

Mika.

Will I grieve when I abort? I didn't think so. This pregnancy was a burden to me; it was nothing I wanted to be a part of. The thoughts kept rolling in as my eyes were locked onto my boss. I was...stuck, momentarily unable to speak. Confusion etched her bronzed face.

"*Ummmmm...*" I managed to slow my thoughts enough to close my eyes. I needed to get out of that damn headspace. *Don't think about it right now!* "I think I'm going to pass, too. I've been craving a bun-less burger. You know the ones without the bread? When you use sliced onions as the bun?" My mouth began to salivate at the mental image. I'd seen it on *TikTok* yesterday and hadn't been able to shake it. "I'm gonna see what I can work up from *B-Way Burger*." I shrugged. "Maybe ask for extra onions and take the bun off."

Lex pushed off the doorframe and winked. "*DiFillippo's* will whip you up one of those."

"That's an Italian restaurant like Mika said. I doubt if they even have burgers on the kids' menu."

"When I was pregnant, Ezra would have them make it for me four days a week." My stomach dropped. "Here and in Hackensack. Come on."

Pulling in a deep breath, I acquiesced.

He'd stopped speaking at least three minutes ago and the church was still going mad with harrowing screams and inspired shouts. I'd been here enough to know Ezra was likely closing out his sermon but wasn't quite sure. Either way, this was good. His sermons never failed, which was likely how I ended up here tonight.

Of course, my pitiful, confused, and angry ass was in church. After a delicious lunch with Lex earlier, where she fulfilled her promise of a juicy burger, and just the way I envisioned it, she invited me to their revival service. I'd come to *Redeeming Souls for Abundant Living in Christ Family Worship* a few times over the years. Shying away from church had never been my practice, having grown up on the same block as one. I simply wasn't a regular churchgoer, only attending every now and again. And since learning of Lex's husband's contemporary ministry not too far away from the office, here was where I'd attend when I did.

And my confused ass dumped myself in this pew a couple of hours ago, needing to *feel* something because I damn sure didn't feel a baby. As usual, Ezra came with a compelling word. I swear, this man couldn't preach an irrelevant message, in my opinion. He was a builder but to the point, smart in the Word, articulate as hell, and not hard to look at, at all up there. I'd never seen an attractive preacher before. Ever. While I didn't want to sleep with Lex's husband, I had to wait out at least ten minutes after the opening of his sermon to get the sexy Adonis out of my head and receive the message of God through him instead.

"*Shhhhh...*" He finally whispered powerfully into the microphone. A few howls rang out in the two-story nave. He extended a long arm into the air—the one with rosary beads. They were present for each of his sermons, something I found strange. "Stay right there. Don't be so quick to move. He doesn't need your help to help you."

The audience of, at least, a couple thousand people responded with emotional snickers. They were obedient to his pacing and responsive to his every word.

"Our God is a patient god. He was even on His own timing with His only begotten son. He didn't release Jesus into ministry until He was in His thirties, not as a toddler or tween with no life experience. Jesus was born as a prophecy fulfillment. But for those anticipating Him years before His birth, they had to think after His birth, 'now what?'" He glanced around the sanctuary, and some laughed at that. "Now what? Well, the Father's answer was, 'Just wait.'"

The church replied to that revelation collectively.

"Isaiah, the wise men...Micah. After the prophecy had come to pass, they all had to..." He acted as though he expected the church to complete his sentence before he did with, "...wait. Three decades would occur before the work began, but oh, when it did," he rasped. Ezra's smile was seductive, knowing. "Elijah struggled with depression. His suffering wasn't just for a night as some of you Christians like to limit the time of turmoil. The man suffered longer than he wanted, like the valley spells of many of our problems today. God didn't jump in the following morning, after the onset, and say it was over."

My face tightened. The people seemed to get excited, clearly familiar with the story.

"In fact, you know what the Holy One did? He sent an angel to comfort Elijah while he rested. Elijah ate and rested. Do you know what that rest and reprieve time is called?" The building fell silent. "It's called your 'in the meantime' tabernacle. Our trips to the valley are guaranteed. But it's what you do 'in the meantime' that makes or breaks you."

While people were, once again, shouting their affirmations, Ezra's face dropped toward the lectern. He took another moment to quiet the audience, pacing us.

Then he rasped, almost in a whisper, "Two years ago—I've never shared this publicly—but two short years ago, my baby, Lisa-Mare fell ill." He shook his head, thick brows pinched. "She suffered for some time with fatigue, unexplained bruises, easily bleeding, fever, swollen lymph nodes, loss of weight..."

What?

My eyes roved in search of Lex. She never shared this. I was very fond of her daughters, and especially wowed by the oldest, Lisa-Mare. She was incredibly gorgeous and bright-eyed. She was inquisitive and would often come search for me when visiting *Christ Cares*. We'd talk seamlessly, which was strange to say about an eight-year-old.

He pinched the bridge of his nose as the music began to play softly. "It went on and on, and the doctors tested and tested. Then, finally, we saw a specialist who tested and tested some more. After a few tests from the specialist came a diagnosis. Acute Myeloid Leukemia."

The church seemed to wheeze all at once. To that response, Ezra gazed in one direction of the church. You didn't have to know him to see he was trying to control his emotions. He applied patience again, pacing himself while thumbing those beads.

"So, when we got that, my wife was struck with grief and relief for an idea of treatment. And what did I do? I went to the Father. Then, I instructed my wife to join me in a fasting and prayer period. The symptoms didn't stop, but the Lord spoke to me. He reminded me of what I'd declared over her body since the day Lisa-Mare was born. One of those things was her health. He then said one word: 'Wait.' The specialist came with a treatment plan." He shrugged. "I said 'no.'"

Another gasp whirled around the sanctuary, mine included. Ezra lifted an upturned palm. "Rapha had spoken and told me what to do. I had to wait. This decision caused turmoil in my home. If any of you are familiar with the matriarch of my home, you know Remah is unapologetically impartial to my three girls. Her first grandchild was Lisa-Mare. So, each night I'd come home, I had two adversaries to face. One was from Harlem and the other, a cantankerous protector of said child, was from Portland, Jamaica. These two women glaring at me unnerved me each day I sat firm in my obedience." The congregation laughed while clapping. "I'm telling you! Even my alpha was challenged in an all-female household."

He shifted, chin dipping as he transitioned. "We waited for weeks. Ms. Remah cooked up natural remedies to treat Lisa-Mare's symptoms as best she could. Lex even filled in with over-the-counter meds when needed. But my baby girl was down, man," he whispered somberly. "Really bad. I'd lay hands on her in the morning then again at night. I'd pray throughout the day, recite His Word during my breakdown moments, and continue to trust God 'in the meantime.' I was like Paul and Silas. I prayed, sang, and praised through my pain. I drowned my fears in the Word of God."

The building erupted in an encouraging praise, causing my belly to flip over and over.

"Four weeks after the diagnosis, Lisa-Mare's condition didn't worsen, but it didn't improve either. While praying, fasting, praising, and believing, I had her tested by two other specialists: one here in New York and another in Philadelphia. I paid out of pocket for it.

Not even two weeks after consulting them, the results came in mirroring each other. No Acute Myeloid Leukemia. No cancer at all. The following day, after receiving the news from the second and third opinion, the original specialist called my wife and apologized profusely. Apparently, they ran my daughter's tests again and couldn't find the cancer. He said they ran it several times before contacting her—"

The shouts were so loud, I couldn't hear Ezra. There was no need, though. We'd all gotten the picture. Not many people were still resting in their chairs at this point. Although I had been, my face suddenly felt cool. When I swiped a cheek, it was wet. I'd been crying. I didn't know Lex's family intimately, but if something had happened to that little girl, I would have been deeply affected. As I wrestled with my thoughts, Ezra was patient once again, allowing the congregation their moment to respond to his personal story. It felt as though they'd never heard it. A lot of people were dancing in place, and a few were running around the sanctuary.

When he felt it was time to reel it in, he motioned to the musicians. The music slowed and quieted, and after a while, so did the church.

"God is faithful. Faithful!" he rasped, emphasizing. "He hears you —knew your predicament—before it fell on you, *or you* walked yourself into it. Focus on your 'in the meantime,' tabernacle. There's too much at stake. Too many elements making the wind blow. But there's only one Creator. One controller. Psalms forty-six and ten says, 'Be still and know I am God.' Focus on your 'in the meantime,' tabernacle. He will be exalted in the earth because He never fails to provide."

On that note, Ezra wrapped his sermon and offered prayer at the altar. I wanted to go, but didn't, not wanting to draw attention to myself. And what would I have told him? I was pregnant from a one-night stand? One that turned into a two-night stand? That would have been ridiculous. I didn't want anyone to know. And knowing how Ezra moved, he'd likely know anyway. I didn't want my boss' preacher husband to know I put myself at high risk the way I had. It wasn't a good look. *Christ Cares* was a spoke of *Redeeming Souls*. Having them know would kill my reputation. So, my dumb ass remained in my seat. Moved by his sermon, I reflected on it as people took to the altar in droves.

'In the meantime,' I'd stay right here with this dilemma until a clear solution populated in my brain.

May

They sat down at an empty, outdoor dining table. The water from the ocean can be seen behind them. I tried studying the surroundings from the television frame to see what I recognized. How could they be in Macen Beach during amenable weather and there not be a gang of tourists around? I knew they shot reality shows like this one, *Taking Tips from Tynisha*, months in advance, but where were the people?

"Girl, it's been forever," Tynisha expressed, placing her canary yellow *Chanel Boy* bag on the table next to Ebonee's mini, pink *Hermès Kelly* purse. It matched her jacket. Sundryia had a few designer bags and Rayna, I'd recently discovered, had a gang of them. I loved designer purses and shoes but didn't have the means to collect them yet. I had to save for a house first. "Where the hell you been? Swallowed the hell up in Canada?"

"No. I've been here in the States."

"Working?"

"Looking into new opportunities." Ebonee winked. She was beautiful.

I didn't know much about the mahogany beauty other than she was a former attorney and a big deal in television in Canada. She hosted a show, and a lot of popular names frequented it, including American talent. *YouTube* clips would often flood social media of her asking the stars the hard questions. She rubbed elbows with everyone, including the Obamas. She was a Black girl's goal, in my opinion. She helped us, young and old, see our potential was limitless. Yet, I had no idea she and Tynisha were personal friends. I'd been watching Tynisha's reality show since it began and had never seen or heard mention of Ebonee.

Tynisha's eyes went wild as I stuffed popcorn into my mouth while watching television from my bed. "You got a boo here, Eb?"

Exposing her blinding white teeth, which were perfectly proportioned to her full lips, Ebonee beamed so femininely, "Now that is more complicated than the career thing. I've been considering maximizing on relationships I've maintained over the years."

"Spinning the block?"

Ebonee laughed. "So to speak...maybe."

Tynisha shook her head and her eyes rolled to the back of her head. "You talking too much of that lawyer shit now."

After feeding herself a spoonful of ice cream, Ebonee licked her lips, glancing away while she allowed it to dissolve in her mouth. "I want to be a mum."

Tynisha blinked. "A mother? Since when?"

Ebonee suddenly appeared uncomfortable, but why? She was on a reality show. She knew what they'd discuss in advance. I guessed having the cameras rolling made it unnerving. "For about a year now. I'm only getting older, and with me losing my mother, who was my best friend, it only intensifies the desire. She couldn't wait for me to have kids. I remember telling her I wanted to go to law school and she didn't exactly like it. She said doing that would consume too much of my time, leaving none for marriage and children for a long while. So, after practicing for a while, I got the opportunity to do television, and I took it. My mother didn't think that was conducive for a family either, but she always supported. She didn't criticize or dwell on how I navigated life, she was always in my corner—"

"Rest in peace to Ms. Anna," Tynisha murmured almost incoherently, so the producers were wise enough to provide that comment in closed caption.

"Yeah. She was my rock. I dated two guys she loved—one, she

obsessed over. And when it didn't work out, she didn't judge, but was silently disappointed. I kept promising her I'd settle down. So, when she died from COVID, it awakened something in me."

"So, you bustin' it wide open for somebody?"

I laughed at that. Tynisha could be so ghetto at times. Ebonee was clearly sharing something personal, and here she was, with the shits.

"I wish. I've known for a while my uterine fibroids decrease my chances of getting pregnant and possibly carrying a baby full-term."

"Have you tried?"

"I did, actually. I got pregnant right after passing the bar. It was accidental, but I lost the baby almost as soon as I learned I was pregnant. My fibroids have been an issue since I can remember. So, for me, I'll have to try alternate routes in order to have a chance at all."

"Like what?"

Ebonee shrugged. "IVF."

"IVF? That's the one where you take all them needles in the belly or where somebody carries for you?"

Ebonee Williams snickered. "Kind of, yes. It can be either depending on the infertility issue. It's like artificial insemination. Four eggs have been taken from my uterus. One has been fertilized with sperm in a lab. I took injections to stimulate the production of healthy eggs and that was...a thing. And the expense of it is hellish." She dropped her face onto the back of her palm.

"Wait! Whose sperm?"

The smile lighting Ebonee's face made my damn belly flutter. "My partner."

"A partner?" Tynisha shouted. "So, you're really doing this shit?" Ebonee nodded, fingering her hanging *Dolce & Gabbana* earrings. "Damn, Eb! With who?"

Ebonee twisted her mouth, suddenly appearing extremely uncomfortable. "Now, Tynisha," she murmured with unease.

Dramatically, Tynisha's arms flayed in the air. "Are we talking? Or are we yapping?"

Then the screen transitioned to Tynisha's one-on-one where the camera was on her alone with her salon as the backdrop.

"I know it may sound like I'm being nosey with my friend,

Ebonee, but I'm genuinely interested. I got fifty-eleven chirren and ain't never heard of this stuff before. I was pregnant back-to-back for like four—five—years. Anytime I hiccupped, I was pregnant." She huffed expressively. Tynisha pointed over her shoulder. "Every time that **BLEEP** came off the road at the end of the season, I was pregnant. Every damn time I went to the damn doctor for a cough, I was pregnant!"

I laughed so hard at that, a tightening coursed the left side of my belly, and I grabbed it. Putting all of my weight on my left hand, I sat up even more against my pillows.

"So, if this bitch is telling me she's having trouble and get to use technology to do something my fertile-Myrtle ass did accidentally, I wanna know all the deets!" She folded her arms, and the frame went back to her and Ebonee on *Macen Beach* finishing their ice cream.

"Nope! Don't 'Tynisha' me. All my business is out there for everybody to see. Just tell me who. Anybody I know?"

"No."

"How do you know?"

"Because I know."

"Well? Who is he?"

Ebonee couldn't lose the grin when she weakly answered, "A Filipino cutie I met on set of a *Sprite* commercial I was shooting a couple of years ago."

"Oh, so you want exotic babies, Eb?"

Tynisha's shocked outburst had me laughing again.

Ebonee's head fell to the side. "Black babies are the most exotic on the planet. Just ask your rivals, the Ercegs."

At that, both women's' heads tossed back on a hearty laugh.

"Whoa," I muttered, scratching my lower belly. "Shots fired."

Once they were done, Tynisha reached over the table for Ebonee's hand. "I'm here for you—for whatever."

A dry smile lifted one side of Ebonee's lips. *Damn.* She was gorgeous. "Even if that means carrying the baby if my body can't?"

An unexpected cry burst from my throat.

Shit.

She's unable to carry her own baby.

Quickly, I paused the television using the remote and grabbed my phone to *Google* Ebonee's age.

Thirty-nine...

My jaw dropped and I glanced down at my belly. It was still flat in week twelve with no obvious symptoms. But for the past two weeks, I was aware of my body changing. My breasts were more sensitive to the touch, even in clothing. Usually, I'd work until well past four in the afternoon, which was my contractual end time. Since last week, I found myself taking naps as soon as I closed the door in the evenings from a standard, eight-hour shift. I also found myself wanting to be alone and not even talking on the phone as often as I normally did.

And Ebonee friggin' Williams was ten years older than me. She was established in two careers: law and television. Only god knew what she'd do next. She focused on her career in her youth. *Isn't that what I've been chasing, but on a smaller scale?* I mean, I was no lawyer or television personality, but grant-writing had been good to me. I was tremendously valued and respected at work by my colleagues and boss. I had a double-bachelor's degree and two masters' along with several certifications. I'd just closed on my first home four weeks ago and moved in last week. I'd been establishing myself before making the gravest mistake I had in all the twenty-nine years before it.

I rubbed my belly, considering my appointments for next week. One was with a women's health clinic in Fairlawn. Two days later would be a follow-up with Dr. Brown. I wanted her to take a look at what was left of me as my gynecologist. Work was about to load up on me soon, so I needed to make a call on this thing soon. Besides, between my mother finally asking to stop by the place for the first time and Sundryia pushing me for an answer about going down to *Macen Beach* for Memorial Day weekend in four weeks, I had to make a solid decision.

Rolling my eyes, I picked up the remote, resuming my "in the meantime."

EIGHT

May

ISHAAN

I got down with him, eye-to-eye as he handled the rock with pace. When he attempted a back dribble, I moved like lightning, stealing the rock.

"Yeah." I taunted, sweat dripping from my chin. Mehki was back on me, eyes glued to the ball. "Your eyes should be on me, son. You have to have one physical focus while studying the ball and other important factors."

His attention went between the ball and my face, trying to obey. Mehki was good at ball—damn good. But he still had a lot to learn. He attempted to steal the ball back. And on that move, I used a spin move with a crossover and drove it down the court before pulling up and nailing a jumper.

"You hear that?" I teased him. "Swish!" Gloating, I walked backwards. "You see that shit, man? You got swished on by an old head."

Humbly, but disturbed, Mehki went for the ball.

"Is this the type of discourse that takes place in here all the time?" my mother's voice pierced through my ego.

She was at the main doorway of my home gym. "Queenie!" I panted, out of breath, greeting her.

"How are you healing?" She looked and winced when examining my bare, upper body.

It reminded me of the big ass bandage I'd still been wearing. "Healing. I'm getting it checked every week."

My mother shook her head. "The things we do to make a living."

"Nanu, you see this?" Mehki was in a similar condition as me, just not as breathless and sweaty. He still had youth on his side as he approached her. "You see how he treats me?"

My mother giggled. "You today, but last week it was Jonathan, and you were the aggressor." She allowed a kiss on her cheek.

"Happy Mother's Day to my favorite girl." He greeted my mother, melting her heart, although she tried to play so damn hard. "You ready?"

"The question is are you two ready. Marsha is so excited you invited her to dinner at *DiFillippo's* again this year." She beamed. "She already knows what she wants to order!" My mother shook her head, speaking of her friend who'd moved to Chicago in her youth and had two children, both of whom died young. She eventually returned home to New Jersey alone. They attended the same church, and I invited her to be a part of my mother's celebration for the second year in a row. "Will we make it to service on time? You're playing basketball this morning."

After gulping down the last of my bottled water, I explained, "We have a whole hour before we need to leave for church." A wave of exhaustion hit me out of nowhere and I wondered if I could sneak in a twenty-minute nap. *Damn, aging ain't no fucking joke!* "Did you see the arrangement?"

"I did." She beamed again in her two-piece dark pink suit. "I saw them while having breakfast. They're gorgeous. Thank you."

"You're welcome, lady." Mehki grinned. "I picked them out."

When mom's curious gaze hit me, I nodded, confirming.

"Oh, my. I see your Poppy here is teaching you something about culture. They're beautiful, baby. Colorful and ample. I couldn't believe how they filled the kitchen." She pointed a pink oval nail on his chest as he towered her. "Now, let's see what your Poppy teaches you about having girls in the house after hours. And I don't believe it was Ms. Jessica either."

Mehki's face fell toward the floor. "*Nanuuuu...*" he cried.

"No, young man. You're not going to waste your youth on accidental pregnancies. Neither will you begin a path of infidelity."

Shit...

"Nanu," Mehki argued with intent this time. "Why you always gotta be extreme? Pregnancy? Fidel—*what*?"

"Because life's extreme, baby." She threaded her fingers together at her pelvis, standing her ground. "Consequences tend to be extreme, Mehki."

"I know, but—"

Dismissively, she turned on a heel with her chin in the air. "I'll leave it to your Poppy to explain."

Shit...

I wiped my face with a towel as Mehki glared down on me. Mom was on one first thing in the morning on Mother's Day. And she was dragging me into it. Having to scold Mehki today was not on my agenda when I went to bed last night or woke up this morning.

I sat on the bench, still catching my breath and wiping down my chest from the sweat. "Who you creepin' with, Ki?"

"When's her suite gonna be done?" The wise ass was referring to the mother-in-law suite she'd been considering having built on the property. For her, it was either that or her moving to a senior community once Mehki was off to college.

"You heard what the fuck I asked."

After a beat, he mumbled, "Sophie."

My head swung over to him. "The sophomore?"

"She's fifteen. I'm seventeen." He shrugged weakly, which wasn't Ki's style.

"Yeah, nigga. And when you turn eighteen, she'll still be a fuckin' kid. I told you: it gets tricky nowadays when you're fuckin' with girls. You're a junior: leave them freshmen and sophomores alone."

"We're just friends, Poppy," his voice was deep as he tried to defend himself.

I still found it hard to believe this dude was growing up so damn fast.

"But you're not just friends with Jessica."

Nose flared, chest puffed, Mehki turned away from me.

"Look," I continued, "You're young. I get it. You need time before settling down, which is what I told you when you said you wanted to lock Jessica down last year. But if you're going to step up and be committed to her, fidelity has to be at the core of it. No real relationship works when cheating is involved."

"Sophie and I are just..." He rubbed his head. "...cool."

"Oh. Word?" I stood. "Then there's no need for her to be at your crib, and definitely not in your bedroom."

Mehki shook his head then pretended to fix his shoestrings. "Poppy, I ain't out here wildin'!"

"You use a rubber?"

"We ain't fuck."

"Then what you do that required the privacy of your bedroom?"

He swiped his mouth, looking away again. "We just... You know, Poppy."

"She gave you head?"

"Yeah."

"That's it?" When he didn't respond, I knew. "You ate her pussy?" I was shocked as hell.

"I didn't mean to—"

"Nigga! You don't go around eating random pussy!"

"I know. But remember you told me sometimes the chemistry can take you there?"

I leaped around, looking for my mother before telling him through tight lips, "That ain't what I taught you, my guy. You don't eat random pussy. You don't eat pussy because she tops you off. And you damn sure don't engage with chicks when you got a girl, man."

"Poppy..."

I closed my eyes as I shook my head. "I never cheated on your moms, son. Ever. Was I ever tempted to? I'm a man—a damn good-looking one with money. Hell yeah, I struggled to make the right call a time or two. But I never cheated, my guy."

"Look, Poppy. Maybe I don't need a girl." He tried to stand firm, confidence resurfacing. "Maybe I tapped out too soon with Jessica."

"Okay. Then deal with that. I'm good with you not being in a relationship so young."

"What if I don't be in a relationship at all."

My head pushed back. "Like... Ever?"

"Yeah."

"Even once you're in college and out?"

"Yeah."

I shook my head and slowly answered. "Nah, Mehki. Settling down with a good woman is cool for a man. You see my pops and mom's journey. I wouldn't be half the man I am without them as a duo."

"You ain't wife'd up nobody. You're the most solid man I know. I'm turning out right. Being single can't be the worst thing for a man. You ain't got to be alone."

I sighed, seeing how far gone this dude was. Had I been traveling too much? "You know why I'm single, man."

"If the reason why you're single is still because of work, that means you ain't never linking up. You love your job too damn much." He stretched his long arm to gesture the space. "Your work got us living in Alpine. We live in a seven-bedroom mansion. I wake up and play ball with my pops in our indoor gym. I watch movies from a theater in here, too. Niggas like StentRo and T.B. live in my neighborhood. I go to one of the best and top-rated *Ellis Academy* high schools in the state. I've vacationed more places than my teachers and coaches, stayed at the best hotels, resorts, and villas. I personally know some of the top celebrities in pop culture—have been in the same rooms with many others. I'm the most blessed kid I know! And that's all because of one man. A man who ain't linked with a woman while raising me."

"Yeah. Yeah. All of that." I began to collect my shit. "Stop with the pussy-eating shit. You got so many years ahead of you to have fun with it."

"But you taught me—"

"I taught you as a rite of passage. Something to build your arsenal, not something to use on little ass sophomore girls as a one-off for sloppy top." Then I started to feel like a damn father and was turned off my damn self. I rubbed my face with the towel. "I know it's a big deal at your age to get your little meat licked every now and—"

"My shit ain't little, man!" Mehki snapped.

It's what I'd taught him to do. I'd worked on his confidence since I could remember.

Checking the notifications on my phones, I scoffed. "Boy, you don't want those problems with me. You better carry your ass up to your room and get ready to take your Nanu out for Mother's Day."

A burst of laughter ripped from his chest. "Poppy, you may be a killa, but I sleep good at night knowing that."

My head swung up and I caught Mehki turning away from me, walking toward the door as he cracked the fuck up. Suddenly, I needed a seat. My heart was pounding hard in my fucking chest.

Damn.

Dropping my face into my palm, I whispered, "I'm definitely gonna need a catnap."

We approached girl number four. Munchie lifted a picture next to the girl's face. She was indeed underaged. Just like the ones before her, she appeared happy and youthful in the picture. Before me was a child who'd played in her mother's closet and makeup bag. We moved on to the next, repeating the same confirmation process. Munchie would select the image of the girl and hold it up next to her face. This one in front of me had dark eyes, peaks into her troubled soul. She was angry with me, likely because she'd bought into her captivity. In her picture, which Munchie held, she didn't smile like the rest. This one looked more like a mugshot than a school picture or random selfie like the others.

By the time we'd made it to the seventh girl, I'd had enough.

"Have they eaten?"

"Not yet," Munchie answered. "The pictures came through and were printed out when we called you."

I observed the line of young girls, ranging in age between thirteen to nineteen-years-old. These girls rolled in packs and had been all over the country.

"Feed them ASAP. Put them in the gold suite. Have catering send up a hot and cold spread. No alcohol."

Munchie made eye contact with the onsite security of *Flare* at *HAYDAR Resort & Casino* here in Vegas. Paul got on his phone right away to implement the order. I glanced around the room of young girls and my men with guns. It angered me they had to be exposed to this, but I couldn't have my team here without weapons. These girls could be retroactive. I was sure several of them suffered from Stockholm syndrome or didn't want to be disbanded from a fellow captive they'd bonded with over trauma. I'd seen the shit enough to know. At least three of the twelve girls would revolt. God only knew the violence they'd seen and experienced firsthand.

"Take me to him."

"This way, sir." I followed Munchie around the corner and down the hall.

The room was covered by armed security who opened the door. Inside, was a man seated in a chair, restrained with cuffs. His back was to me as my men surrounded him with pistols drawn. I removed my jacket in the cold room as I rounded them, breaking into their cypher.

Even seated, it was clear to me he was tall, perhaps an inch or two shorter than my six feet, six-inch frame. He looked to weigh less than two hundred pounds. His dark, silky hair looked to be natural against his olive skin. He wore all black—dress pants, a collared shirt, leather jacket, and cap toe oxfords.

I handed my jacket to Munchie then approached him. "Don't forget about the puncture," she whispered, knowing where my temper was about to deliver me. "...and your meeting with Ms. Williams in the morning."

"Farhad Biswas," I addressed him, ignoring her. The nigga had the nerve to smirk as he bobbed his head arrogantly. I stood straight, arms folded over my chest. That made me smile. "Who told you about me?" He didn't respond. Farhad rolled his dark eyes away.

I glanced up at Lenny, one of my men behind him. "Uncuff his ass." Farhad switched position in his seat once his restraints were removed, but he still avoided eye contact with me.

"Who told you about me?" I shouted this time.

His gaze returned to me. "Why are you asking me such a question?"

"Because whoever did, told you fuckin' wrong if they didn't warn you." I hauled off and jabbed his ass. Farhad jumped to his feet, then quickly realized he was outnumbered. "Don't worry about them." I hooked his ass, causing him to stumble back onto the table. Lenny quickly moved to avoid breaking Farhad's stumble. "Yeah. Put 'em up," I encouraged when I saw anger flash in his eyes as he wiped the blood from his mouth. "They didn't tell you about fuckin' A.D. Jacobs either." I hit him with another jab followed by a hook kick, feeding him the heel of my *Tom Ford* loafer.

"This shit feels so good," LeRoy groaned, eyes closed, and head tossed back in the pedicure chair.

I scoffed silently, attention going to his nail tech, massaging his lower leg. The Russian man grinned deeply at him. Shaking it off, I decided to move on with the conversation.

"So, what do you think?"

LeRoy lifted a high-arched brow as he turned my way, opening one eye. "About the new resort on *Red's Island*?"

We'd talked about so much since meeting up for lunch and grooming, something I had to do to entertain LeRoy.

"That would be the topic, sir."

"Well, honey, Azmir Jacobs has been making a name for himself in the resort and entertainment arena. Hell, a buddy of mine from Botswana has been to you guys' Vegas property twice in one year. He claimed to have enjoyed it so much."

"Did he say what exactly he enjoyed?"

LeRoy rolled his eyes. "Honey, what do all you straights enjoy? The women and discretion. He said he had a blast, and the food wasn't too bad either." He shrugged. "Then there's my Turkish buddy." He snapped his fingers, appearing to recollect. "Oh, gosh..." The sight of his freshly manicured nails made me glance down at mine. I didn't get clear polish. Didn't get polish at all, though I enjoyed the grooming. Polish was where I drew the line. "Damn it, Ish!" He sucked his teeth. "Aksoy! That's his name! Aksoy—who I don't know if he's exclusively a fish type of guy—said he visited the Atlantic City resort and felt the gambling rules were too rigid."

"We're heavily state regulated. Aside from that, we have our own way of taking care of our high rollers with discretion."

"I told him I knew the man responsible for—" He cleared his throat. "—hospitality, and I could connect him with you."

"I'm sure his name has crossed my desk." I glanced across the room to Munchie who nodded while typing into her laptop. "Do you know what his betting range is?"

LeRoy shrugged with his head. "The millions, for sure. I really don't know the lingo. Gambling ain't my shit. American resorts ain't either."

"Which is why I need your endorsement for the *Sun-Bronzed Maroon Resort* on *Red's Island*." LeRoy had been a trusted friend for longer than I could recall.

He was best friends with R&B sensation, Ragee, which some say is how he got a name for himself. But the man worked hard at building a reputation for all things luxury. LeRoy was known in fashion and travel, and, recently, entertainment. He was a well-known socialite across and beyond the continental U.S. His friends—and lovers—extended beyond the pond and friendly skies. He knew wealthy people around the world. This was why I found time to nurture our relationship. Aside from that, LeRoy was a cool dude. Although gay as fuck, his mind was brilliant, always providing wonderful conversation and knowledge. When Mehki's mother, Mandy, died, LeRoy reached out and stood solid at my side. His advice and confidence fueled my survival during that bleak time.

"If I can get your help on this—just spreading the word and throwing contacts my way—I'd be appreciative."

"Oh, please!" He rolled his neck. "When do you not need me? How do you think my bills get paid, Ishaan?" He laughed loud as hell while inclining from his leather, padded chair.

"Aksoy," Munchie called out. "Baris Aksoy. He's in the gold range."

I turned to LeRoy. "He's not even a platinum-level spender."

LeRoy shrugged, rolling his eyes away. "Well, shit. I'm just telling you what the man said, Ishaan. Do with it what you may." He rolled his hand with a loose wrist.

"You're done, Mr. Patterson," the jet-black haired, ample-bosomed woman husked. Her lashes were long, and red lips greatly overlined. "Can I take you to the lounge or will this complete your services for today?"

I turned to LeRoy, "Tell Aksoy to contact me regarding his next stay at *KAHRI Resort & Casino*. All food and stay will be comp'd for up to seven people, and I'll also throw in a seven hundred-thousand-dollar voucher for our private gambling floors. I'll make it ten people and a milli if he wants to venture to the *Sun-Bronzed Maroon Resort* on *Red's Island*."

"Damn. And what about for me?"

"Oh, most def." I nodded. "Are you coming to *Red's Island* alone or will you be bringing your Saudi Arabian sheik boo?" I knew his latest breakup was a sore topic for LeRoy. He called me drunk with a throat full of tears, telling me about it last year. "How do you get these men with deep religious ties to..." I couldn't say it. Visualizing it turned my damn stomach.

"Your homophobic panties are showing, Mr. Man."

"What did Raj tell you about throwing that term out meaninglessly? Knock that shit off." My attention went to my phone vibrating with text messages.

"Anyway, are you staying for a little happy ending?"

When I looked over at LeRoy, he gestured with the nodding of his head to my nail tech. We were at a Russian spa in Connecticut. It was where I had to travel to, to spend face time with my friend. LeRoy was worth it in more ways than one. He was funny as hell, and not in your typical "gay boy entertaining" way either. The dude was quick witted, temperamental, yet smart as hell.

"Nah. We gotta be on our way back to Atlantic City tonight to meet with the boss. You enjoy yours, though."

LeRoy laughed hard as hell. "Well, I can't have none today either. I'm monogamous these days."

My face tightened. "Monogamous to yourself?" I moved to leave the pedicure chair.

"No. To my football, boo. You see I've been in Connecticut a lot lately. You're finally coming to see about me, with your overworked ass. This bussy belongs to a *King*, baby. I wanted you to meet him, but..." He shrugged, rolling his eyes again. LeRoy's mouth twisted, too.

"Let me guess: he's not ready for that next level of meeting your friends?"

"Well, Ishaan, I consider you a brother. Don't offend me."

I extended my hand for a shake. "Love you, bro. Keep your nose clean."

"I thought you'd like the women here. There are two Black beauties I was sure you'd find agreeable with your palate. You've been single for a fuckin' decade. Spread love a little, love." He reciprocated my shake.

"Until next time..." I glanced over my shoulder to confirm Munchie was ready to go. "If you need anything, you already know."

LeRoy patted his chest, giving me a silent gesture of understanding.

Munchie walked to the locker room where she waited for me outside while I put on my socks and shoes.

When I resumed her side, I commented, "This place is nice. Right?"

"It is. It's good to see you being pampered."

I scoffed. "You know how it goes with LeRoy. Either this or shopping."

We headed toward the lobby. "He has impeccable taste. He sent you those *Saint Laurant* shoes and cuffs a short while back from Milan."

I chuckled at the memory of that. He included a note saying I could hold off on wearing them for two months and still be the only man in my circle rocking them.

"They are dope. I need to break them in."

"I'm just glad you turned down the sexual service offer." That killed my smile and stride just at the door in the lobby.

Munchie ignored my response and continued to the door. Once out in the parking lot, I asked. "What's that about?"

She stopped at the waiting SUV. Munchie was a short and thick woman. She had fair skin and never wore hairstyles over her shoulder. Her shape was curvy, and her fashion resembled that of a Sunday school teacher. She was my reserved rock in that she knew her shit but maintained a humble delivery. I'd always felt she lacked self-confidence. Her devotion and skill as my right hand was invaluable. However, sometimes I had to force her to be direct. So, seeing her now licking her lips as she stared at something in the distance slightly annoyed me.

"What Mr. Goshay said in there is true. In all the years I've worked with you, you've never seriously dated a woman. I'm familiar with the rumors surrounding Mandy's death, but you've not really attempted another relationship—I know the short-lived run with Ebonee." She waved her palms. "So, when, in March, you asked me to retrieve the Jane Doherty woman and I learned you engaged with a prostitute, it concerned me—*concerns* me."

"Why?"

"Because..." She faced me. "...look at what you do for a living, sir."

I switched weight in my stance and narrowed my eyes with a grin. "Munch, we provide adult services every day in our jobs."

"Yes, but in a measured fashion. Ms. Doherty is unknown to us. She's not with a trusted madam or partner."

I opened the door for her. "Well, for starters, we know her name ain't no damn Jane Doherty. I had you look it up that weekend for shits and giggles—"

"I know, sir. I get it—"

We knew this because I had Munchie check that name against the list of attendees of the organization holding the training that weekend in Atlantic City, and there was no Jane Doherty or any variation of it. In fact, there was no registration for any event or room at the resort for it. I knew there wouldn't be. Jane—or Janie—told me why she proposed the name. I left it there in A.C., not needing to find her. I was good. Life had moved on. The most I thought of her was when I was tested during my regularly scheduled time.

And when taking meetings with Ebonee...

"It was an irregular occurrence." I explained as she shuffled into the SUV. "Forget about Jane Doherty. She's never existed anyway."

NINE

May

Hayden

"This is cute." I held up the welcome mat Sundryia gifted me. "Check your energy before entering," I read its message out loud.

"Child, I know that's right!" Rayna agreed.

"You better check your energy!" Erin, her goddaughter, slash niece, slash daughter recited playfully with attitude, causing us to laugh.

Even Rayna's daughter, Kennedy, cracked up standing next to her.

The weekend after Mother's Day, my cousins made their way to my new place. They both brought housewarming gifts, though I didn't have one. Neither was I planning to. But we'd been trying out this cousinhood thing for months and, so far, it had been working. Having Rayna in our lives lately made our relationship resemble a sisterhood. I'd been looking forward to today since we planned it. No, I didn't want to make a big deal about my basement dwelling, but I'd also been tired of being alone. I'd actually missed their face-to-face energy. Between Sundryia being a new mom to twins and Rayna living on a different coast, seeing each other couldn't happen on a whim. That's why having them in my little place meant so much.

"E, baby," Rayna called out. "You wanna put this in place for her outside the door?"

"Sure." Erin jumped up and took the mat from me.

She was so damn cute, and not because she was mixed either. The girl's features were soft and proportioned. Her blemish-free, peanut-hued skin, curly sandy blonde hair, and clear hazel eyes all meshed well. She was a smart and endearing fourteen-year-old. And she loved her "Auntie NaNa," as she referred to my cousin, Rayna. Rayna brought Kennedy and Erin to the East Coast, promising the girls a trip to *Melanated Girl Doll House* in New York City while here. Though there was about a four-year age difference between the two, you could tell they were very acquainted with each other as they deliberated on the placement.

I pulled another gift from the box Sundryia prepared for me. "Silk sheets? You're the shit, woman!" I winced right away, remembering the little ears being around.

Rayna giggled, catching on. "That's a beautiful color, too. Is that mustard?"

"Cognac," Sundryia answered.

"Yeah." I studied it. "I like it."

"You'll be slipping and sliding in them." Rayna cleared her throat, being mindful of the girls, too. "When you have a special guest."

My eyes blossomed and rolled at that.

Laughing, Sundryia added, "That sounds like so much fun." She grabbed her belly. "Wait until I get rid of this pouch, I'm going back to my whoring ways. I feel like I didn't give Maaz enough before catching two bodies and shit," she grumbled low so the girls, who were now placing the mat at the opened door, couldn't hear.

Rayna teased her with a pointed gaze, "You whored for Maaz before?" Her Red Bottom sole bounced in the air on a crossed leg.

Appearing unusually shy, Sundryia rolled her eyes toward the wall while giggling. "Girl, the shit I've done to that man over the years..." She sighed. "Let's just say, his mother is justified in not fuckin' with me like she used to...before..."

"Before you took advantage of my friend last summer." I added.

Sundryia and Maaz had been creeping around his family's back (and apparently hers) with a sexual affair. It all came out last summer when she was staying at his family's vacation home in *Macen Beach*, South Carolina. Maaz, a linebacker in the *League*, had always been close to his parents. He'd gotten even closer to them after the death of his older brother, who Sundryia used to date. I guessed it was true when they say secrets shred relationships because Sundryia and Maaz's mother were damn near best friends until the pregnancy happened, forcing her and Maaz to come clean. It had been five months since the birth of Maaz and Sundryia's twins, and the friendship between mom and grandmom was still stale, though they got along.

"Oh, no." Sundryia shook her head, sans a smile. "That man took advantage of me last summer. That's how we got the twins. I was cool on us living separate lives."

"Not if we let Mellie tell it," Rayna added.

Mellie had been Maaz's girlfriend since high school. Maaz broke up with her last year, before conveniently spending the summer with my cousin at his parents' vacation home. It was a fucking mess. Mellie was...young—in her mid-twenties—and so damn immature. She constantly aired her grievances on social media, which caused the demise of her relationship with a wealthy and handsome football player. As I observed Sundryia adjusting the straps of her tank, I fell into reverie.

I was dazed by Sundryia's comment about being caught off guard by her chemistry with Maaz and, as a result, getting pregnant. It rang familiar to me today in a way I wouldn't have been able to explain before February. Unbeknownst to me, my life had been irrevocably changed; I imagine Sundryia's had, too. Having not one, but two unplanned babies could send a woman to the nut house. It suddenly hit me how I'd never checked in on her mental health. I assumed, with Maaz's money and Sundryia's well-known resilience combined, it provided endless resources.

And Rayna. She'd had twins by a man new to her, too. Similar to Sundryia, her guy was wealthy. In both cases, the men wanted something real with them. One thing the three of us had in common was we were financially independent. Rayna was a physical therapist; though now, she worked when she wanted as Mrs. Jacobs. Sundryia had several, random certifications. However, she had a business acumen like no one else I knew. Real estate investing had done well for her. I wasn't much different. My journey brought me degrees and a job which pays on the higher end of the spectrum compared to my peers. No, I didn't earn six-figures, but bringing in just under eighty was something I prided myself on.

"Hey! You okay?" Sundryia asked, reaching for her wine glass. I could see she was trying to casually gauge me. "What's up with you? Has cousin Monica been by yet?"

Not interested in a conversation about my mother at the moment, I shook my head and whispered, "Hey... Would you two consider yourselves promiscuous before...Azmir and Maaz?"

Sundryia lowered her glass with a wrinkled forehead. "Shit."

Calmly, Rayna raised her phone. "Maybe I should have John bring Lisa back around to take the girls for ice cream," she murmured.

John was Rayna's assigned security detail. He had been for years, apparently. Lisa was one of her nannies. She traveled with a team, especially when her children were with her. What a life.

Sundryia's head fell back, and she hooted hard. Rayna tried controlling her humor as she typed into the phone.

My eyes skirted over to the little girls who'd just closed the door. "Just keep your language clean in your answer," I murmured to my cousins.

Sundryia was still laughing when she asked, "What made you ask that?"

Before I could answer, Rayna called out, "Lil E...Ken, Lisa's on her way to get you. Why don't you pack up your toys and pee before she gets here."

"I'll go first!" Kennedy, Rayna's biological daughter, shouted before skipping to the back of the apartment.

"Nice, Kenny. Just leave the mess for me. Huhn?" Erin sighed. "Just be lucky you're my only sister."

"Awwww!" Sundryia cooed. "She's so sweet."

Rayna grinned, shaking her head. "That's my first love right there. An old lady in a child's body."

"Now, answer my question."

"You want me to go first?" Rayna laughed. "Lord, why?" She reclined on the sofa. "I had a season, maybe. There was no button you could push to open my legs, but I'd fulfill my 'needs' when I wanted," she whispered.

"What's wrong with that?" Sundryia asked. "Why the *but*?"

Rayna twisted her mouth as she hummed, eyes focused somewhere on the wall across from her. "*Mmmmm...* Now, at thirty-seven years old...being married and super, super connected to my person, I realize it was high-risk behavior because my feelings were always removed. I've only..." She cleared her throat and glanced over at Erin, who was on her way toward the back of the apartment. "...loved two men I gave my body to: the first and last."

My head popped back in amazement. "Really?"

Rayna nodded her head. "I was really..." She reached for her phone again. "...messed up when I left Jersey. My emotions were cut off. The only human beings I managed to open to were Erin, her mother, and my guy." She shrugged. "So, was I a 'garden tool?' No. But was I reckless? Yeah. Probably so."

"And what about you?" I turned to Sundryia.

She poked her glistening lips out in a manner of shrugging. "I've lived, honey, and without apologies. I mean..." She seemed to not have her words together when she shrugged. "I've given more hand and blow job—"

"Girls!" Rayna shouted, jumping to her feet. "Let's hurry up and meet Lisa at the end of the driveway!" She strutted with urgency toward the bathroom for Erin and Kennedy.

Hayden

Twenty minutes later, I was sauntering from the kitchen to the living room where Sundryia was on her phone. "So, more hand and blow jobs. Huhn?"

Still engaging her phone, Sundryia laughed. "Yeah. But why I ain't never see Rayna move that fast, yo?"

That made me laugh, too. "She's a momma bear. You'll be that swift to remove Imani from dirty talk, too, as soon as she can understand what it is."

Sundryia sucked her teeth then exhaled, "Yeah. My princess. I'm looking at them now in my mommy camera. Imani's sleep, but Isam is going the fuck off. He always wake up hungry as hell. Cheryl ain't moving fast enough."

"Is that who's watching them?"

"*Mmmmhmmm.* Maaz, too."

Maaz at home with a set of infant twins—that belonged to him. I couldn't imagine it as I resumed my seat.

Then the door opened. Rayna came click-clacking inside, exhaling hard. "Y'all have no idea of the sponge both those girls are. They would drop a dime to Azmir in a heartbeat if they overheard something that felt inappropriate to their ears. He has them trained." She grabbed her glass of wine. "Anyway. Where were we?"

Sundryia hummed she didn't know as she typed into her phone. "I was just saying I gave out more hand jobs than my pussy."

"You said head, too." I recalled.

"Yeah, but that wasn't as much as my hands." She placed the phone down. "Rayna said when she fucked, it wasn't with her heart except with Divine and her first lil' boo. For me, the only man I gave head, hands, pussy, and my heart to was Maaz. He got it all. I gave his brother—*rest in power, Amir*—a hand job, though."

I gasped.

"Amir?" Rayna asked.

"Remember? Maaz's older brother," Sundryia explained. "That's how I met the Zyads. I used to run with Amir."

"Run?" Rayna's face wrinkled.

"Yeah. We were cool. We dabbled in street shit. I knew he was interested in me. He was fine as fuck, but...weird."

"Gay, you think?"

"Nah." Sundryia shook her head. "Just fuckin' trapped the fuck out. Amir was good peoples, but nothing got him off like street shit: getting money, robbing, and making his name known." She shook her head. "Never mind that. Did I answer your question?" I nodded. "What made you ask?"

"No." Rayna interrupted then pointed at me. "Now, you answer."

I took a beat to think, face tight. "I don't know. I've given out crazy hand jobs, too." I scoffed. "My head game has been critically acclaimed since I was in high school. I mean... Till this day!" Sundryia leaped over to hi-five me abruptly and with excitement. I had to scoff again, meaning what I'd said. "I will make a man lose his fucking mind, which is why I've fallen back from it. But like y'all—or more like you, Sundryia—hand jobs don't require much of me. I remember on my college campus, there were whispers about my hand game—nothing loud. But I was ready for it to be a thing. I prepared my emotions to tell them, 'Better my hands than my mouth and vagina being run through.'"

"Why are we discussing this?" Sundryia demanded, her head cocked to the side.

"And how funny is it that you do hand jobs," Rayna muttered thoughtfully with pinched brows. "Hayden, you grew up in a better environment than us. And we all know you ran them streets, Sundryia. But I thought hand jobs were a white girl thing."

Things got quiet. So much noise in my head. So much fucking doubt. Fear tripled in an instant.

Sundryia casually leaned over her crossed legs and grabbed a piece of diced cheese off the tray I'd prepared for their visit. Her tone was so emotionless when she shared, "Rayna, you ain't know Cousin Billy molested us?"

Rayna sucked in a hefty amount of air, eyes ballooned. "Molested who?" Sundryia swung her fingers between the two of us. "No!" She blinked then her eyes fell to the table; Rayna looked to be processing it all. "Wait! Wait!" She grabbed her head. "Wait!"

"Did he touch you, too?" Sundryia asked.

"No! I didn't spend much time over there as a kid. My mother had us in church."

I pulled in a deep breath and sighed of relief. No one deserved to share in that misery.

"Good. I'm glad his evil ass didn't." Sundryia's nose flared as she licked her lips. "But to answer your question about the hand job, it's what he'd make us do to him most of the time."

"Most of the time," I emphasized.

"Did he..." Rayna's eyes were wide on me.

I shook my head. "He would threaten to if I didn't do a good job with my hands...or mouth." I cleared my throat, hating to discuss this nasty shit. "But 'no.'" My throat closed up on me.

"Same." Sundryia seemed more comfortable sharing as she grabbed her wine glass. "He would say shit like, 'You ain't doing it right. Turn around.' Then I'd try something different, hoping he'd feel...good." She visibly shivered.

An unexpected, silent cry shot from my belly. I successfully caught it with my hand. The girls seemed to miss it, and I was grateful. I didn't mean to go there about my childhood abuse, but I was curious about their experiences.

"I can't believe this!" Rayna whispered hard, face crumbling. "Keeme always called him a weirdo. Even one trip when I brought Azmir out to meet some of the family, Keeme said he didn't want to go see Uncle Billy—" Her head swung up. "Is that why you two never called him Uncle Billy? I remembered that as kids. You two would say Cousin Billy."

"Uncles don't fuck their nieces." Sundryia shrugged emotionless.

"I know it happens, but 'kissing cousins' is a phrase. I haven't heard one for uncles, especially great-uncles. Sometimes, I wonder who else he did that shit to. It couldn't have been just Hayden and me."

That was followed by a crack in the air. Rayna began bawling her eyes out. "I'm so sorry you two had to go through that shit, man!"

"Rayna!" I called out. I wanted to reach for her, but my body locked in place.

Shit!

Sundryia was able to do it. "It's all good, shortie," she mumbled, holding Rayna.

Rayna shook her head. "It's just..." She cried, "We've...collectively, been through so much shit coming up, you know!" My folded legs began to bounce, my emotions were bubbling. "I still feel like shit for not doing this sooner. I always felt alone, especially when my father left and with my mother turning to drugs. When Keeme got locked up, something changed in me. I didn't want to connect with anyone! For years, I visited him in the pen but didn't tell him where I lived. Azmir and I got engaged and then I told him about Akeem. I ran from a whole ass billionaire because I was afraid to connect emotionally. I couldn't trust anybody. I hate that era of my life, yo!" She could hardly breathe when she shared, "I left Chyna here."

Shit. Shit. Shit.

I didn't know Rayna could be so raw. She was inconsolable. And I was sure the billionaire mention was in error. Her husband, Azmir, was indeed a millionaire with successful businesses galore.

But billionaire?

"I left my baby sister because I was running," Rayna cried. "I almost didn't get married because I was fuckin' running!"

I didn't think I'd ever heard Rayna use foul language. She was so emotional. Sundryia handed her a napkin and Rayna dabbed it under her eyes, trying not to rub off her makeup.

"Yeah. But we got through that shit, though," Sundryia added to the conversation. "Clearly, there's some resilience in our bloodline. You overcame that, got into *Duke*, and found love out in Cali. I've been able to make a living for myself independent of any man. Even found one who wanted me in spite of all my shit. And Hayden," Her arm swung my way in gesture. "She done got her degrees, a dope ass job, and just bought her first piece of property. I'm gonna make sure it's not your last."

Rayna sniffled, trying to gather herself. "This is what I mean. You two have always looked out for each other. If I could have stopped thinking about only me, I would've seen I had peers—family—who had been going through some shit, too. Then..." She took a beat to breathe. "...maybe I wouldn't have run."

"And then you wouldn't have met the love of your life. Maybe because I'm so locked in with Maaz finally, I can see how important it is to find a man who sees you in spite of your flaws. The right man will fuck with you. Flaws and all. And not just to fuck you. Like..." Sundryia's eyes met mine. "...these two cats could have had any woman they wanted, but still decided on Louise's great grands. Shit, Maaz's crazy ass risked it all for me."

Rayna spit out a giggle. "Azmir chased my crybaby ass all over the country. Pulled up on me in San Deigo...out here in Jersey—"

"Damn, Ray!" Sundryia burst into laughter.

Rayna followed her. "Yup. Found me in Jersey, had me pack up my things and go with him. Then he had me strip down to nothing." I gasped. "Yup. All to confirm I was pregnant."

"Oh. Damn," Sundryia murmured.

Rayna shook her head. "I'd miscarried by then—remember, I told you that?"

"Yup."

"Yeah. That was my first time being pregnant, and I was so stressed. My best friend had died, and Azmir was stressing me out. So, I...ran." Rayna sniffled then shrugged. "He cussed my ass out sideways when he caught up to me on the other side of the country."

They fell into laughter again, colliding into each other. "Yo, Divine that nigga, yo!" Sundryia shouted breathlessly.

"Yup." Rayna nodded with humility.

"And then he gave you two more at the same damn time!" Sundryia observed out loud. She looked my way. "I wonder if that's what that muthafucka, Maaz, did to me."

It would have been appropriate for me to laugh with them at that time. But I couldn't. I was preoccupied with learning Rayna's first pregnancy ended in a miscarriage. The three of us shared a great-grandmother. Twins ran in our family. I now knew Sundryia was pregnant by Maaz years ago and she miscarried, too.

So, the next time they both were pregnant, it was with twins?

"When is Azmir's birthday?" Sundryia asked.

"June fifth." Rayna sniffled. "By the way, I'm having the event planner send out invitations to his party. You should get it in a few days."

"Where will it be? Vegas or Atlantic City?"

My spine stiffened at those locales.

"Neither."

Sundryia reached to pour herself more wine. "Oh. In L.A.?"

"No. In New York City. *The Garden of LaChateau* in midtown Manhattan."

"Oh. That fancy ass place. Damn." Sundryia glanced my way. "Where's your wine glass? This stuff's really good?" She examined the bottle.

"Yeah. *Chateau Blevin*'s Cabernet. That brand is my new fave," Rayna confirmed. "I brought their Pinot Grigio, too. I love that stuff!" She swallowed back the last of her wine then pushed her glass toward Sundryia. "She hasn't had any yet. Pour me some more, please. I need to get out of this emotional state."

Sundryia's face stoned, but she obeyed. After refilling Rayna's glass, she did the same for herself. As she poured, she slowly proposed, "Hayden, if the reason you're asking about promiscuity is because of what went down in Vegas a few months ago..."

Rayna's head swung over to me. "I forgot all about that."

"I haven't." Sundryia shrugged. "I feel like I judged you—like... not in a 'you did something I wouldn't do' type of way. But in a 'I wanna make sure you're safe and happy at all times' way, and I wasn't there to look out for you." She grabbed a slice of pepperoni. "Not that you need it. Like..." She sighed. "Damn. Getting pregnant changed my ass."

Rayna nodded in agreement. "Yup."

"You get what I mean?"

"*Mmmhmm!*" She continued to nod. "I think it's more than motherhood. I think it's the full picture. When you find your special one, and accept it and them, it like..." Her eyes swept the ceiling. "...opens your nose up like ammonia. It makes you feel things beyond seeing." Rayna shook her head, defeated.

"It's complicated. Love fuckin' compromises you and complicates shit. Anyway." Sundryia tossed her chin my way. "Why aren't you talking much? And you damn sure ain't drinking. What's good?"

"And about your girls' trip," Rayna interjected with a devilish grin. "...was he good?"

I opened my mouth to speak but could only take a deep breath. No words came to mind.

Sundryia placed her glass down on the table. "The fuck, Hayden!"

"What's going on?" Rayna demanded in the softest tone.

"Are you..." She couldn't get it out, it seemed. "That muthafucka gave you something?"

My eyes fell as my pulse raced. I couldn't speak. An underdeveloped thought struck, and I acted on it, lifting my oversized t-shirt I'd managed to run across, likely left by one of my exes. I didn't have many of those, so it would have been easy to narrow down which one.

Sundryia's animated eyes ran busily across my abdomen.

Rayna's torso shot back into the sofa. "You're pregnant, Hayden?"

My eyes, now loading with tears, shifted back to Sundryia.

Slowly, her jaw collapsed. "Oh, baby..." she cooed, voice thickened with tears as she reached over and grabbed me into her arms.

That's when I let my tears go. And why did I do that? A wail I'd been suppressing for weeks broke through my chest.

"Oh, no, Hayden!" Rayna's warm, perfumed-scented body covered me, too.

"Here you go." Rayna handed me a mug of hot tea as I wiped my nose for the hundredth time.

I tossed the facial tissue and grabbed another from the box. Sundryia collected the mountain of soiled tissues and threw them into a bag. Now able to control the wails, I still couldn't stop the tears from my eyes or nose.

"It's okay, Hayden," Rayna assured.

No, it wasn't. I felt helpless, embarrassed, and dumb as hell.

"I feel so foolish," I attempted over a jumpy diaphragm.

"For what? Shit happens." There was Sundryia, once again, trying to protect me.

I shook my head. "No. I'm dumb as fuck—"

"Noooooo..." Rayna tried.

"I should have gotten the abortion. I was scheduled for it last week but didn't go through with it."

"You need a ride?"

"Sundryia!" Rayna scolded.

"Man, listen. I can be the godmother or the damn post-op care-giver and chauffeur. Either way, Hayden got support! She'll never be alone." Sundryia was upset. I knew this by her aggressive presentation.

"Yeah, but it sounds like she wants to keep the baby," Rayna tried to reason with her.

"I don't." I sniffled, shaking my head. "I don't want a baby. I don't want to be pregnant." My throat closed on my cry. "I just wanna do what's right."

"Right for who?" Rayna asked. "You're the only person to be considered now. No one matters more than you."

"Wait." Sundryia demanded. "Is he applying pressure? He wants the baby?"

A fresh round of tears raced down my face. "I don't know that man. I can't even remember his name."

"Oh, damn. That's right. So, both y'all gave fake names?"

I shook my head. "Only me." I could hardly speak. "I was able to figure his name out."

Rayna asked, "How?"

It took me a while to speak. My lungs hiccupped feverishly. "I went to a school event. His college."

Through the corner of my eye, I saw my cousins exchange glances. "Which school?" Sundryia asked.

I took a moment to recall. My brain wouldn't work. "*Panthers...*" I grabbed my forehead. "What's the school?"

"*Panthers*?" Sundryia echoed. "I have no damn clue."

"*Panthers*? Let me *Google* it." Rayna reached for her phone, giving me time to blow my nose again. "*Hmmmm—Ohh!*" She chirped. "*BSU! Blakewood State*?"

"He went to a *BSU* event at Azmir's casino?"

I shook my head. "The *Panthers* had an event there. He used to play ball—something."

"That's easy. I can have Azmir call their events person and maybe get a list of all the attendees from that night."

I didn't respond right away because, at first, I didn't know how. This was so fucked up. I'd heard the fetal heartbeat last week. When I missed the clinic's appointment, I still made my gynecological one with Dr. Brown.

I shook my head. "I heard the baby's heartbeat last week at the doctor's."

"Shit." Sundryia leaped in her seat. "How many weeks are you?"

I wiped my eyes. "I'm in my fourteenth week."

"Fourteen?" Rayna parroted. "You're four months, Hayden." I nodded.

"You're keeping the baby at this point."

Sundryia's depiction made me fall into a hard cry again.

"So, to be clear: you don't want to contact the father?" Sundryia stated.

Father? The reference turned my stomach. Father of what?

I shook my head. "This is on me, Sundryia. I did this to myself. I'll figure it out."

After a beat, Rayna cleared her throat. "Not to sound like Ms. Bourgeois here, but since you are going to keep the baby..." I couldn't see but could hear the movement of her jewelry. "...we need to revisit your living conditions. Right? I mean... I can see you thuggin' it out in this small basement unit alone, but not with a baby."

I scoffed. "You sound like my mother."

"So, Monica does know?" Sundryia asked.

"No. She hates that I'm living down here. And you know you're the blame for it. Right?"

Sundryia rolled her eyes. "Of course. I have no idea why that lady can't stand me!" That made Rayna sputter a titter. "Like... For real! Since we were kids that woman ain't fuck with my ass."

"My mother mentioned how Cousin Monica didn't come to Deena's funeral last year," Rayna noted.

"Yeah. I peeped that, too." Sundryia slapped her knee. "I had so much going on in my own head with having just found out I was pregnant and planning the funeral. I was shocked as hell to see Cousin Samantha there."

"My mother asked if Samantha was there." I sniffled.

"Monica ain't wanna pop out to show support for her first cousin but asking if another first cousin showed? Cold world."

"Yup." Wiping my nose, I shared, "I told her she should've gone if she wanted to know what happened that day."

Sundryia and Rayna laughed at that.

"Hayden be giving Cousin Monica the business!" Sundryia shouted.

"That's why she don't like you, Sundryia. You be laughing at her daughter checking her." Rayna cackled. "But my mother said Cousin Monica don't like her either."

Sucking my teeth, I attempted to explain, "My mom is just..." I rolled my eyes. "...different. She ain't as tough as she thinks."

"You couldn't tell my young ass that as a kid. She was the dragon I had to slay to get to you. I was happy as hell when you got into high school and could move about more. And when you went to college, I felt the dragon was slayed, bitch!"

Rayna howled at Sundryia's passionate storytelling. She was being honest, though. My mother always had a stick up her ass for family. I never understood why.

"*Ahhhhhh...*" Rayna exhaled as she reclined onto the sofa. "This is nice."

"What?" Sundryia asked.

"How we can go from crying to laughing in the span of minutes. How we have a strong commonality like family we can laugh at and not get offended."

"Now, don't tell me yo ass 'bout to start crying again!"

Rayna laughed. "No!"

"Oh. Good," Sundryia sighed. "Because I can't take no more tears. I done took a break from two crying infants just to be around crying ass, grown ass women." Rayna laughed again, and I did, too, as much as my sour emotions allowed. "Nah. I'm fuckin' with y'all. You're right. We're good. I'm gonna hold my cousin down." Sundryia gripped my shoulder. "Always."

"And so am I," Rayna's words spilled with sobriety. "Whatever I can do, I'll do. I'll do even what you don't ask. Louise would be proud. She went through a lot, too, in her journey. Maybe this is God pouring grace upon her descendants. As corny as it sounds, I like it here." She smiled deeply.

"Thank you," I whispered, still at a loss for words.

"And I believe you, Rayna. I didn't really take you at your word a year ago on Shi-Shi's man's boat. But you've stayed true to your word. Thank you."

"We're here looking corny as hell," I murmured. The girls cracked up. "We're looking like the movie *Waiting to Exhale*." I sniffled.

"Count on me!" Rayna sang.

"Count on me," Sundryia playfully countered.

Rayna was right: this moment of not being judged was nice. I didn't tell them about my second encounter with the *Panther* in Atlantic City. I lacked the emotional bandwidth to detail just how reckless I'd been. Besides, conception took place in Vegas and that was what mattered. My dilemma was too complicated for transparency.

'In the meantime,' I'd enjoy this moment with them.

TEN

May

ISHAAN

"Right this way, Mr. Patterson." I followed behind the cheery nurse. The ends of her black, silky ponytail swung in the air. "Mr. Jackson will be happy to see you. He's watching one of those horror movies he loves!"

That put a grin on my face as we passed rooms, staff, and patients along the way. I was tired as hell, and debated staying in bed longer this morning instead of coming here today. But, once again, I pushed through and kept up with my agenda. The vitamins I'd been taking to revive my energy hadn't worked for shit. I had no idea what was going on with me. Still, I pushed through.

Finally, she turned into a room with a huge screen mounted on a wall. Immediately, I caught the image of a woman screaming while running away from a masked man yielding a big ass, bloodied knife. Then I saw there was only one viewer of the film watching front and center.

The sinister beast in me wanted to laugh, but I kept my shit together.

"Look who's here, Mr. Jackson!" the nurse announced sunnily. "It's your brother, Mr. Patterson! *Yaaaaaaay!* I love when he visits." She rubbed his stiff shoulder then turned to me and whispered, "No one else comes to see him. I hate that you two lost your parents and are the only children. Same mother, different fathers, and all are gone. No cousins or aunts and uncles. Just heartbreaking." She shook her head somberly then pepped up, beam returning. "Have fun, fellas!"

She closed the door behind herself. Then I casually rounded him, observing his mobile medical chair, ornamented with poles and tubes for oxygen, feeding and catheter bags, and a general monitoring system. He appeared just about the same as the last time I'd popped in on him. I enjoyed seeing his eyes grow large once fully recognizing me.

I leaned over to get eye level with him. "It's me again. Sorry *your* dead mom couldn't make it. We're still unable to locate your deadbeat father. I'm an only fuckin' child, and I think you remember that." Then my face tightened. "On second thought, you do remember. Your brain is perfectly intact. It's your..." I browsed over his feeble, sitting frame. "...body that broke down on you."

Another scream from the screen had my head lifting. This time, I allowed myself to laugh. When my attention returned to Terry, I was reminded of his alertness. His eyes shifted from the screen back to me, too. That made me smile even more. There's no fun in harassing the maimed. Totally paralyzed and a mute, Terry was fully alert and aware. And I pledged to torture his ass until it bored me.

"Do you have nightmares, Terry?" I winked. "I know you hate horror films. Your scary ass never liked suspense or gore—unless you were doling it out. Right?" I chuckled, remembering the shit he'd done to me. For years. "Do they keep you awake? Do they have you waking up in the middle of the night, wanting to run for your life?"

159

With a big ass smile, I squeezed my eyes shut and pouted my lips. "That's until you remember you can't run. Shit, you can't even walk, my nigga. That locked-in syndrome is a muthafucka, ain't it?"

When I felt my phone vibrate, I stood straight and sighed. "That's work calling." I pulled my phone from my pocket and read the notification. "Don't let me keep you from your next nightmare. I'll just do a little mobile work while horror seeps into your subconscious."

Then I backed away, against the wall, not wanting to sit. I preferred Terry to see me on my feet, pun intended.

Mark: *I'm sorry to have to inform you Ish but if you're changing the day Brielle will not be performing for the grand opening.*

Nick: *Nicki's willing to lessen her aforementioned fee and add a night if you give her Saturday. Did you get the letter? Otherwise, she's not participating.*

I shook my head, annoyed as fuck by two grown, über-successful women trying to one-up each other. I adored Brielle. We'd worked together, amicably, for years. And Nicki and I had a few mutual friends from NYC, and always stood on code. But I'd be damned if I'd let their cattiness fuck up my reputation. The *Sun-Bronzed Maroon Resort*'s grand opening was approaching, and we'd begun contracting acts and vendors for it over a year ago. Both Brielle and Nicki signed the agreement and had been paid their requested deposits at the time of signing.

The two women used to be great friends until drama occurred behind the scenes. Now they'd been quietly off for years. Someone must have leaked the lineup for the opening weekend to both camps. And since, both women have been fighting for Saturday night. Brielle had been booked for the prime time and stage, which was Saturday. Nicki, per her reps, refused to "open" for anyone—male or female. She would not be opening though. She was scheduled for an entirely different show on an entirely different night. However, Nicki sensed Saturday was the bigger event and had been trying to show her claws.

Nicki's request got back to Brielle's camp, causing the mega pop singer to show her fangs, too. Brielle was now threatening not to show at all if she performed before Nicki. The shit was petty and unprofessional. It had been brewing for over a month now in a slow drip. That was until two days ago when my office received a strong-arming email from Nicki's attorneys, offering to lower her performance fee while threatening a no-show as the alternative. I'd had enough experience in my line of work to know I couldn't approach this issue with kid gloves. Bigger than their childish antics, I had a leak in my circle, and that had to be addressed.

Me: Hey, Nick. Sorry for the delay in my response. I needed to make sure I was reading the threat correctly. You tell Nicki's ass she will perform as agreed, or I will sue the fuck out of her. And she knows we have the money and fucking sharks to win. Not to mention it will be yet another unfavorable blow to her plunging rep in the public's eye. Last words: Don't pull that diva shit with me.

Then I moved to my next task.

Mark: Excuse my delayed response. I was giving you time to come back and say this was all a joke. You tell Brielle unless she heard from me or my team that the terms of our arrangements were changing she shouldn't send me threats. That's nasty work. Also, be sure to direct her to the contract where it reads the inconvenience fee she'd incur for being fucking petty. Final words: THE TERMS STILL STAND.

Fucking babies, those two. The number of women—and men— who'd kill to have their career had clearly been lost on them. Perhaps they could intimidate other event hosts with that childishness, but *ADJ Enterprise* had a gang of lawyers capable of destroying careers, even those of Brielle and Nicki's caliber. Not to mention the shit Azmir Jacobs could do to their reputation inside the industry that would have them spiraling into the abyss.

I moved on to extinguish another fire. A cop in my neighborhood had a bone for Mehki and his friends. He harassed them each time they'd run into him. I'd warned the officer once about leaving them alone when I ran into him on my way home one day. When he pulled over Mehki's friend last week and had them exit the vehicle and sit in handcuffs on the curb for over an hour, I knew he didn't believe me, and contacted his commanding officer, the chief of police in the borough of Alpine. I'd been good buddies with him for years, regularly accommodating his stays at *KAHRI Resort & Casino* and beyond. He'd texted me back earlier, but I didn't have the time to tend to it until now. I blocked out violent screams against the sound of a chainsaw to read.

Chief: *Patterson consider the nuisance eliminated. Officer Wright has been transferred to our inventory unit for the unforeseeable future.*

Me: Much appreciated. There's an open chair for StentRo's poker party next Tuesday. Let me know if you're interested.

It was a hot seat folks would pay tens of thousands for. The chief was one of them. Quid pro quo was what I'd mastered in my line of work. I had to keep one in a clutch for every beneficial relationship I participated in. This was my life. From governors to athletes to gang leaders, I maximized relationships.

Yawning on and off, and feeling fucking exhausted, I spent the next thirty minutes texting and emailing as much communication as I could. Some matters needed a call or face-to-face energy. But once I felt satisfied with my visit with ol' boy, Terry, I was ready to leave.

So, I crept up behind him. "I've got to run, T. I know your stuck ass hates to see me go, but no fear. You know I'll always return for my "brother" until the day you meet Mandy in hell." I snorted before straightening my spine and promenading out of the recreation room of the long-term care assistant living facility.

love ∞ belvin

Hayden

"These are so nice, Hayden!" My mother marveled at the

matching satin pajama set and slippers I'd gifted to her. "And these, too." She pointed to the packet of satin bonnets I'd packed in the gift bag as well, along with a bubble bath kit.

My mother didn't like big to-do's when celebrating her, especially seeing her birthday was so soon after Mother's Day. At least that was the excuse she'd given me since I could remember.

It was a Sunday afternoon, and I'd dropped by to bring her gifts and a cake. Sitting up on the sofa, my attention browsed the pictures on the walls. They were mostly of me and my mother over the years. A few captured my grandmother, Marsha. My throat involuntarily closed at the one of Cousin Billy.

"Are you sure you don't want something to eat? I made a big pan of turkey wings, knowing you'd be coming by. You know I hate wasting food, Hayden. I guess whatever Billy and me don't eat, I'll have to freeze. But that's just the meat. What about the mashed potatoes and fried cabbage?"

When she waited for an answer, I smiled. It was all I could do. My mother knew I didn't eat here, much less spend copious amounts of time at her home. I wouldn't begin today.

"I offered to take you out," I reminded her. "You declined."

"Because you don't always have to spend money on food for my birthdays, Hayden."

I sat up a bit more in my chair. "I wanted to take you to *DiFillippo's*. Remember you telling me it was where they had the retirement dinner for your district manager?" She complained of the lowly tellers and local managers not getting an invitation. "Rayna's husband is part-owner of those restaurants. Rayna took Sundryia and me there when she was in town last week."

"So, you think I'd wanna go because Rayna's big, rich husband owns it? She impressed you and Sundryia and now you wanna eat there, Hayden?" She scoffed, rolling her eyes in her Monica way.

My head fell to the side. "You know they think you don't like them?"

Her head rolled back. "It's that Sundryia. She's always said that. I've never said I had a problem with her. And Rayna..." Her shoulders shot up. "I hardly remember what she looks like. Samantha got caught up in them drugs so bad, she let her son grow into a murderer and gave that poor girl no other choice but to flee the state. I used to try to talk to Samantha, you know? I used to tell her to watch out for that Eric. He wasn't moving right. I tried to get her a job at a branch near them projects." My mother shook her head. "And all she could say was God, Jesus, church, church, church. Well, look where that landed her —strung out in them streets just like Angelica! They let them drugs eat away at their souls and bodies. Angelica wasn't as lucky as Samantha. Rayna's husband got her clean."

She scoffed again, eyes cast in the distance with disgust. "Using your daughter's man to get you clean. She couldn't do it for her own kids. She better thank the high heavens those children are making something of themselves now. No thanks to her! It's Rayna's husband and his fat wallet. Got Akeem and the little one..." She snapped her fingers. "Chyna! He got all of them keeping their noses clean. Shameful!" Her lips curled with disdain.

"You don't know that to be true. Rayna's worked very hard to earn the success she has. Don't forget, she's a physical therapist. Akeem has chosen a new path since being released from prison. And Chyna's charting her own path in L.A. now, too!"

"All the while, Samantha's over there with her feet up, eating bonbons she ain't earned!" She sucked her teeth, folding the satin housecoat.

I scratched the side of my belly, eyes cutting behind my mother for the hallway leading to the bedrooms again. "Have you always not liked Samantha and Angelica? I can't remember anything else."

"They're my cousins, Hayden. Why wouldn't I like them? It's just...we were different people. Angelica ran them streets hard. I used to try to talk to her, too. But no." She tossed a hand in the air. "I guess I was too corny for her. So, after a while, you know what I did? I minded my own business. I had you and put everything I had into you. Look how you turned out."

"So, you think you're a better mother?"

"Do you?" She threw right back at me.

I scraped my top lip with my bottom teeth, nervously. "I think women embark on motherhood in different ways. Some never see it coming. They live with a consequence and make the best of the situation."

"Are you talking about your father and me?"

I shook my head, annoyed by his mention. "I never speak of ghosts."

"Your father was no ghost. You know that, Hayden. Don't start."

"I've heard from him but ain't seen him."

"You have seen—" She took a deep breath. "Ernest has some issues but he ain't like..."

"Eric?" I posed. "Monty?" I shot her a pointed gaze. "Those two were imperfect but...around." I smacked my hands together then glanced over her shoulder for the hallway when I thought I saw movement again.

My mother, a thicker woman, tall in height and possibly a size sixteen, was still vibrant at fifty-one. She sat at the edge of her seat, hands clamped on each armrest. "Let me tell you something, Ms. Know-It-All. You don't know nothing. You ain't got no kids. Hell, you ain't never really had a man! You don't get to judge me when you haven't walked a mile in my shoes," she growled with tight lips.

Her posture was threatening, though the woman had no bite in her bark. This, I knew. I'd known since I was an innocent kid needing physical protection.

Dangerously irritated, I hissed back at her, mirroring her exact posture. "What you fail to realize is when you model poor behavior to your children—or in your case, child—they tend to perpetuate some of your poor decisions. And I mean *some* because there are things I'd never perpetuate!"

The movement in the hall happened again. I must have reacted to it physically because it caused my mother to glance over her shoulder to her uncle, Billy, dragging a lame leg behind himself to the bathroom.

"And that being the biggest one," I referred to Billy's creepy ass.

"Now, you wait one second, Hayden! You keep living in the past, you're gonna die there. There you go again: shooting off at the mouth with no experience. You ain't never been a mother, Hayden! You don't know everything!"

"I will!" I shouted, jumping to my feet. "November ninth. I will be a mother and when I do, I'll do better!"

"What?" She couldn't stop staring at my belly. Standing, it didn't look as pronounced as it did when showing it to my cousins while sitting. But I'd always been fit with a hint of abs. The muscles in my lower belly had disappeared, leaving just the top. "When did this happen?"

I swiped an errant tear. "I'm fourteen weeks."

"By who?"

"A ghost. Apparently, mine was one, and I've turned out perfectly fine, let you tell it."

Her eyes shot up to me. My mother wanted to chastise me, but her shock from the news distracted her to a greater degree. "And you're keeping it?"

"Yes."

"Hayden, you just moved into a basement. Your life isn't set up for a baby." she was all breath and no bass. "Is he telling you—forcing you—to keep it?"

"He doesn't know. And I prefer it that way." Another tear.

I'd performed better than I felt. I'd been miserable. This shit still didn't feel real, even with the baby bump. I still had no symptoms—still didn't feel anything inside of me. *Still*, I had to acknowledge it. Announce it. This was no less embarrassing than it was to my cousins, who were married and engaged, and in love with their partners. But sharing with my mother right now was easier because it was delivered with a familiar passion: anger.

She shook her head. "Don't do that, Hayden. It won't be fair to the baby. And with you..." She scoffed again. "Raising a child alone is hard."

"Why she fussin' at you, Monica?" he barked in a slur from the other side of the apartment.

The fucking audacity!

"Yeah. But I'm sure protecting one in their own home—basement apartment or not—isn't that difficult of a task." I turned and left her with a hanging jaw.

Less than thirty minutes later, I was brisking through a restaurant, looking for my friend who'd already been seated. When I located her, I saw the waitress with a pad and pen out, standing at the booth.

"Oh, here she is!" Letisha shimmied in her seat as I slid onto the bench across from her. "What're you drinking? A margarita?" She winked conspicuously for humor.

I placed my purse next to me and grabbed the waiting menu. It was a struggle to narrow my thoughts to the simple task at hand, which was ordering food. This should have been easy considering I was starving.

"I'll have tea. No sugar." I glanced up and managed a forced smile. "Please."

"Okay," the waitress chirped. "I'll get those started."

When she left, I could feel Letisha's demanding eyes heating the top of my head. "No drink-drink?" I shook my head. She didn't speak right away, and I was grateful for the silence. Something was burgeoning in my chest. I needed time to manage it. The menu was no help. Trying to keep my shit together, I couldn't even read the words. A burger? Pasta? Soup and salad? My eyes roved all over. "What the fuck is going on?" Letisha asked, motionless.

"What?" I glanced up. "Trying to figure out what I'm going to eat."

"You're off."

"I'm hungry."

"Where are you coming from—oh! Monica? Did she say something to fuck with you?" Then she sucked in a breath. "Did you see Billy's perverted ass while you were there?"

My attention was to the menu when I answered, "Yup and yup."

"Fuck that perv. But what did Monica say this time? And why aren't you drowning your sorrows in alcohol like I'm about to do?"

That's when my eyes swept up to her again. This time, I couldn't find my words. Letisha was typically easy to talk to. However, recently my shit had grown beyond the capacity of judgement. And while I'd been on my transparency tour, telling the people closest to me about my recent and unusual blunder had been difficult—*painful*—as fuck.

So, when my words wouldn't populate, I gazed across the restaurant.

"If you don't spill that shit! Monica's always fuckin' with you and you take it. At least vent so you don't keep bottling that shit up." She leaned into the table and growled, "And order a drink while you're at it."

The levee broke. I dropped my face into my hands, catching my tears.

"Fuck!" I heard. Within seconds, Letisha was at my side, arms encasing me. "That bitch!"

It took a few minutes to catch my breath. I was so fucking embarrassed to not be able to control my emotions in public, but Letisha's aggressive personality made me feel the wall against my back. Life had been the fucking wall for me lately.

I pulled in a deep breath as I lifted my head. Letisha had a napkin ready for me. "What's going on?"

"I'm pregnant."

She scoffed. "That's it? You ain't got the dead disease? Your house ain't in foreclosure?" I shook my head. "Then let's eat lunch then I'll drive you to the clinic. Pregnancies can be a temporary—" I began shaking my head before she could finish.

"I've already tried. I don't think..." Another round of tears raced down my face as I shook my head. "I don't feel like I want that experience."

"You want the experience of motherhood?" She asked with incredulity.

"No. I really don't. It's not been a thing for me."

"I know!" Confidence returned to her delivery. "Me either. I was pregnant."

"When?"

"Back in February while we were in Vegas."

What?

My mind raced to that event. "You were drinking."

"And doing hookah because I knew I had an appointment at the chop shop as soon as we got back."

"Why didn't you tell me?"

"Because I didn't need to. I wasn't keeping the baby, and I damn sure didn't need a pity party. I was in Vegas, baby. Life went on."

Stunned into silence, all I could do was look at Letisha. How could she not tell me. "Who were you pregnant by?"

That's when I saw the crack in her strong veneer. Letisha's eyes swung away. "Chileeee, to be honest with you, I really don't know. I was with Rasheed. Then two days later, Rodney pulled up to my place talking about making things happen for real as a couple, and I fell for the bullshit." She waved a hand in the air. "But fuck all of that with my sucker ass. Who are *you* pregnant by?"

I lifted a shoulder, feeling my stomach roil. "I—*ummm...*" I swallowed with a dry mouth. "I don't know."

"Like me? Like how I didn't know?"

I shook my head. "I know who. I just don't know him."

Her eyes blossomed and face widened with a smile. "Bitch, you been holding out, out. You been having fun and holding back! Who is he? What does he look like?"

His face flashed in my head at that question. Smooth sandpaper skin the hue of peanut butter. Dark, thick braided hair with the sides and nape faded. His long, chiseled frame was bronzed and decorated with ink. His smile was a treasure, and the feel of his heartbeat when he touched me was a wonder. So many things about our encounters didn't make sense. Like how distant he was the night we met until after my test results. How during our second encounter, he'd treated me like we were old, trusted friends. The way I'd given my body to him with the ease in which I had. Twice.

I shook those thoughts from my head. "We're looking weird. You can go back to your seat. I'm fine. Really." With palpable reluctance, Letisha returned to the other side of the table. "You're asking the wrong questions."

"Well, help a bitch out." She whispered hard, "You're pregnant and keeping it, Hayden! I can't believe this is a conversation I'm having with you of all people."

"Which one? Being pregnant or keeping it?"

"Both!" She didn't whisper her answer.

She was right. Neither was like me. I also wasn't the type to cosplay a damn prostitute. That was a detail I wasn't prepared to share with my inner circle. It was a level of bravery I didn't possess. I was ashamed and embarrassed.

"If you don't mind, dropping off birthday gifts and spending less than thirty minutes with Monica has drained me. I'm really not in the right headspace to share more. I swear I will when it doesn't have me looking like a crazed fool in public."

The table went quiet for a few seconds then the waitress returned with our drinks.

"What can I get you two?"

"I'm going to have the herb-crusted salmon over the capellini pasta." I pointed toward the menu. "Does that come with spinach or asparagus?"

"It comes with asparagus, but I can switch it out for spinach if you like." She spoke while scribbling onto her pad.

"Would you? And for an appetizer, I'll have the beet salad with goat cheese."

"Sounds amazing," the waitress replied then glanced over to Letisha. "And you?"

Letisha's eyes were glued to me. She was stumped. And so the fuck was I.

ELEVEN

May

Hayden

I chewed into the last of my apple. *Shit.* It was so good and the last one I'd brought in to work today. Next, I sucked down bottled water before eating my last saltine cracker topped with banana peppers. As I smacked down on it, savoring the delicious taste, I gestured a chef's kiss into the air. *Damn.* The combo had hit the spot once again.

Reclining from my computer monitor, I lay back in my office chair and exhaled. Why was I still here at almost six in the evening on a Thursday? It was because I had no life. I'd only cross the bridge, stop at *Whole Foods* for glazed beets, and then head to Paterson for my basement dwellings for the entire weekend.

The entire holiday weekend…

Rubbing my belly, I exhaled again, decidedly this time. No. I would just stay here and finish the evaluation reports three of our donors required in this quarter of funding. Keeping them happy was paramount for future funding. Getting money from organizations, for some, was an investment. They'd check in with you during the interim to be sure their objectives for funding you were being met. Oftentimes, doing that required answering paragraph-long questions of almost twenty pages. Hey. It was what I was paid to do.

My head swung up when my peripheral view caught a moving object. It was Ezra, Lex's husband, ambling down the hall for her office, I was sure. That made me sit up straight in my chair. I didn't want to appear like a slouch to the pastor of the church my organization belonged to, even in passing. And thank goodness he'd passed. I wasn't in the headspace to engage with him. The man high-key intimidated me.

Pushing my lips out, I blindly read over the last paragraph when there was a knock at the doorframe.

I managed a smile, "Pastor Ezra."

"Ezra's just fine." His voice was deep and raspy, speed of words measured as he smiled with his eyes. "Burning the midnight oil?"

One side of my mouth lifted grimly. "As much as I'm reminding myself this is a holiday weekend, I just can't seem to put one foot in front of the other to leave this office."

"Do you have any celebratory plans?"

I shook my head before sharing, "My cousin—the one you and Lex met in *Macen Beach* last year?" His eyes glazed over, and brows met. I thought to go further. "The one Lex apologized to?"

"Angelica?"

I snorted. "That's her late mother, yes. But her name is Sundryia."

"Sundryia," his timbre more confident. "You'll have to forgive me. Though there are none in Christ, I speak to strangers almost daily. Most of which slip from my mind as seamlessly as I am able to share with them."

"Well..." I chuckled. "...you sure did share with her! Anyway... She's since given birth to a set of twins. She and her fiancé, Maaz, closed on a house down there on the same stretch of land where you and Lex stayed. Sundryia invited me down to help start redesigning their home."

"But?"

"But..." I gestured to my computer Vanna White-style. "...work is calling."

Ezra strolled over to the chair in front of my desk and took a seat. "Work doesn't have an owner. It's only assigned. I tell people all the time to remember work is just a tool. It's not to be prioritized over the fruits of life."

"And what are those?"

"Family. Friends." His brows lifted. "You. Your fruits in life are whatever nourishes you. Replenishes you from..." He gestured to the computer again, too. "...that thing."

I wanted to change the subject. Work had actually been a godsend over the past few weeks. It was the only thing I felt I still maintained control over in my life.

"What are you and your family doing for the weekend? If you say traveling to *Macen Beach*, I'm going to scream," I jeered.

"Oh, no," he murmured, escaping my joke. "We will not be in South Carolina this weekend. We'll be home. This evening, I'll be attending an appointment with Alexis then taking her out to dinner. Tomorrow, we have activities scheduled with the girls virtually all day. Then I'll have my bride to myself overnight. I'm taking her to *Crystal K's*."

"The spa in Central Jersey?"

"That would be the one. We'll leave there and join the girls for a barbeque with their friends. Of course, church is on Sunday where we serve. And on Monday, we will rest our feet. No work."

My face warmed with a grin, and I pointed toward him. "I see what you just did there."

"Did you now?"

"Yup." My head bobbed up and down. "You've just demonstrated the work/life balance."

"Ahhh!" he breathed, long, thick beard lifted while his head tilted back. "Is that what that was?"

Ezra's sense of humor, though dry, was slipping. It made him endearing. I could see how a woman could fall for him.

"Yes. While reminding me of how single I am, might I add."

"Single? Being single has its benefits. There are worse missed opportunities than being single."

"Like what?"

"Like never having been loved, and in a woman's case: never having been covered by a man. But I don't sense you're ready for that conversation. I'm feeling you're not concerned about being partnered with."

Involuntarily, my hand palmed the side of my slightly raised belly, though Ezra couldn't see it. "No." I thought. "I've never had a problem being single. I mean…" I chewed on my lips as I considered it. "I think getting married one day would be nice. I don't think I've ever determined the distance of 'one day.' But if I never marry, I don't think I'd be greatly disappointed. I've done well. Still have goals I'd like to meet."

"I've spoken to you in the past about those excessive goals. If you don't mind me asking, is your mother a single woman?"

I noticed he didn't ask if my parents were together. He went directly to my mother.

"Yes."

"Has she ever been married?"

"No."

"Are you an only child?" He shot off questions while his eyes were toward the floor. Weird, but this was Ezra.

"Yes."

"Was your father present at all?"

Why is he asking 'at all' as though he knows my father's presence has been a problem?

"Kinda."

His eyes were still elsewhere. "Your mother and you. Did you two have struggles?"

My lips protruded and I dipped my chin. "Marginally."

"*Hmmm.*" I could sense something behind that simple, verbal gesture. "You know, sometimes with young women, when they see their mother make something out of nothing while coming up, they lose the ability to see the benefit of having a useful man as a partner. Sometimes, when mommy doesn't fail alone while being single, it defines your need for partnership as a young woman."

My face folded. "And why do I need a partner?"

"Because you're susceptible to depression." Finally, Ezra did peer my way.

My eyes ballooned then I found myself blinking. "Depression?"

He nodded. His hand lifted and he pointed over my head. "I see them. Three demonic spirits lurking over and around you right now. Isolation, lack of trust, and the ability to forge ahead during calamities instead of addressing the calamities head on all attract them. You're not a community woman because you weren't raised to be one."

Ruffled, I smiled. "What makes you think that?"

"Did you attend lots of family gatherings coming up? Attend a church or belong to religious gatherings weekly or more? Social groups of any kind?"

"No."

"Did you attend sleepovers as a child? Host them?"

I swallowed, remembering what Lex's husband did often. He read people. This wasn't my first "prophesy" from him. He managed to blow my mind with that one. He'd even told my cousin, Sundryia, accurate shit he couldn't have known. So, why had I been challenging him today?

"No."

"Do you have an active family unit or support group outside of work?"

I thought for a few seconds. "My cousins. The one I mentioned to you: Sundryia. And for a few months now, our other cousin, Rayna, has been coming around to build a bond."

"But this is all new?"

My heart galloped. And out of nowhere, Lex appeared in the

doorway. Her *Louis Vuitton* tote hung from her shoulder, energy was small, and she sported a familiar grin. She likely knew her husband was doing his…"thing" again.

I nodded, answering Ezra. "What are the demons going to do to me?" I cleared my throat, feeling hella uncomfortable.

His eyes brushed across my desk as he shook his head softly. "Nothing if you don't let them."

Panic rose from my belly like bile. "Then what should I do? The last sermon you preached touched me. You spoke about staying put 'in the meantime.'"

I watched him stand. Ezra shook his head. "That has application for all of us at some point in our lives. But this thing, I feel, requires a different approach. Hosea chapter four, verse six says God's people perish for the lack of knowledge. You need to know, more often than not, we sit in the seat of circumstances made by our own decisions—good or bad. The proverbial 'devil' cannot make us do anything we do not want to."

Our existence was suddenly swathed in peace when Ezra leaned down to kiss Lex on her forehead, greeting her. I didn't miss his left arm snaking around her waist and his hand on her ass cheek as he pulled her into him while doing it. Then his attention returned to me while still physically linked to his wife.

"In the sixth chapter of Ephesians, the Word tells us, 'We do not wrestle against flesh and blood, but against the rulers. Against the authorities. Against the cosmic powers over this present darkness. Against the spiritual forces of evil in the heavenly places.' Don't beat yourself up for making bad calls every now and then."

"But what about…" I turned in my chair, peering up at the ceiling. This was some scary shit. "You said I don't need to worry. How can I not?"

"Don't give them an entrance opportunity by way of your heart or mind." He pointed over my head and behind me. "Those are parasites with no power, just an assignment. The book of John, chapter ten, verse ten tells us 'The thief comes only to steal and kill and destroy. The Lord, Jesus, came that we—*you*—may have life, and have it abundantly.' Sometimes your abundance is your community. Do you talk to God through prayer?"

Embarrassed, I cleared my throat again. "I mean. When you pray in church, I repeat after you."

Lex snickered. It wasn't malicious, but it didn't dull the shame a bit.

"When you're alone, just talk to Him as you've entertained me this evening. Share the concerns of your heart. Request provisions for a community. Its arrival will quickly approach thereafter." He tried to lead Lex out of the doorway to get on their way.

"Wait." Lex demanded softly, humor danced in her eyes. "Baby, do you know her name?" Her beam brightened even more. She was teasing him.

With confusion coloring his face, Ezra turned to me. That glaze covered his eyes as it had when I asked if he remembered speaking to my cousin last summer. Then Lex broke into a cackle, "reading the room."

"Babe, you've got to at least ask for their names before spooking them. Remember?" she groaned softly. Intimately. Once again, her husband pivoted so they could leave. Then she turned to me, nose scrunched. "Ewwww, Hayden. Why don't you open up that window? There's a slight stench in here."

"She's expecting, beloved. Show some grace."

"What?" she screamed mere feet away from my door.

ISHAAN

As sweat flung everywhere, my grunts were rhythmic, syncing

with my body movements. The sound reverberated from the walls of my gym. Next to me, Mehki wasn't as verbal, but his ass was wiped out, too. We were finishing up our mid-week workout with box jumps. It was a great conditioning workout for balling, but they were the fucking devil! *Shit!* When the alarm sounded, I completed the last rotational pivotal jump. My torso dropped and hands slapped against my knees as I tried catching my fucking breath.

"Damn, man," he heaved. "I ain't think your old ass was gonna finish."

I ignored his jab.

"Yirp!" A call rang through the gym. StentRo was strolling in with Neil, his assistant. His smile, per usual, was so big, it exposed all his pearly whites and disappeared his eyes. "Good to see you puttin' in the fuckin' work. Now, let's get the next level done!" He began placing his things against the wall. "You had a late night, Ish?" He was asking about my condition. My damn chest was on fire.

This was strange and had begun a month ago. Simple tasks and even familiar, rigorous ones, like working out, had been taxing my ass notably. It's been concerning, and without solution. I performed some fashion of intense workouts ranging from cardio, to weightlifting, to mixed-martial arts training, to yoga five—sometimes—six days a week. Nowadays, a trip to the damn bathroom exhausted me.

I managed to stand and walk over toward the bench for my towel and took a seat there. Mehki began putting away the equipment we'd just used for his pre-training conditioning. As I downed water, StentRo approached me. Stenton Rogers, a former forward for the *League*, a three-time MVP, a six-time champion, and now assistant coach for the organization, was a trusted friend and neighbor.

Stenton reminded me of what could have been if I'd just stayed at *BSU* and trusted the coaching staff who said my time for the *League* would come. Even still, I wasn't as good as StentRo, LeBron, or Kobe. Back then, I low-key knew I didn't have to be. The *League* was filled with talented, yet subpar performers. And I'd known, Stenton. Had followed his journey into the *League*. He was one of the best the basketball *League* had seen.

New Jersey, small in size, is an extremely condensed state. Being a part of the upper-echelon athletic community shrunk it considerably. At thirty-nine-years-old, he was just two years older than me. We attended many of the same camps and had even played against and with one another before he was recruited. He was now a retired player and had entered into a new facet of the game. He was also a family man, married to a dope ass woman.

Stenton and I didn't become close until after my college days and when I'd gotten into the entertainment concierge and protection business. I made a few arrangements for him and was paid accordingly. Then, I purchased a home here in Alpine where he'd owned. With Mehki being into basketball and admiring the champ as we all did, I started reaching out on more personal matters and our relationship shifted from professional to personal. He'd taken a liking to Mehki and had been coaching and mentoring him for years. About twice a week, off-season, StentRo would come over and coach him on the court.

"You ready for this work?" he asked.

Wiping my face down, I replied, "I wish I could. I'm fuckin' zapped."

He laughed his ass off. "Again? Man, what the fuck? You need to see a doctor?"

"I've seen her like four times."

"Since you got cut in the back, your stamina's been trash."

I didn't say, but it had begun before then. I'd been feeling way off.

"The man getting old, Unc." Mehki approached us, dribbling the ball between his legs. "He 'on't want this work. He ain't able to keep up with me working out." His smile was big as hell.

"You know he's only two years younger than me. Right?" StentRo reminded him.

"Then you should talk to ya boy. Give 'em game, O.G."

Stenton grinned my way. "This nigga. You can house and feed them and still gotta check they chin."

I scoffed, "Especially once they sprout some fuckin' hair around their dick."

"Dawg!" Stenton agreed. "I be ready to toss Jordan's little ass the fuck out when he gets froggy. My guy used to be so chill and cute.

Now, he's full of know-it-all answers and fuckin' hormones. Yo, sometimes that lil nigga think he can school me."

"On what?" Mehki asked, curiously. He was only a year older than Stenton's son, Jordan.

"On shit!" Stenton spit.

"On nothing, nigga!" I agreed. "Y'all don't know shit yet other than what we teach you."

"Y'all still in student mode."

I received Stenton's dap as I followed-up. "If y'all know like I know, you'd stay seated at your desk and in student mode as long as you can. Because..." I exhaled. "...man, when life comes at you—especially as a Black man..."

"It'll have you wondering what curse was put on our ancestors to make Black men the most at-risk species, man." StentRo exhaled.

My attention went to Mehki. This was a constant topic of conversation for us: be patient as I teach you how to navigate this cold ass world.

"You been on your A-game, Ki?" Stenton asked him.

"Always. I be tellin' Poppy and Nanu they be worrying too much. I be straight chillin'. Poppy be acting like he don't remember what it was like to be young and free." Mehki laughed.

"He is free." Stenton pointed his thumb toward me. "He single."

Mehki's eyes went wild convincingly. "That's what I be saying! I be like, 'Poppy, at least you ain't got no pussy shackles like Uncle Ro!' You know what I mean?"

Both Stenton and I fell out laughing. That was Mehki with his humor. He clowned us, and I couldn't even be mad. The kid was charming and knew not to let this masculine humor spill out in front of women, especially my mother.

"The fuck?" Stenton couldn't breathe as he hollered.

"You know I'm just fuckin' with you, Uncle Ro. But for real. Poppy getting old, man. I think he letting it rot off."

"Rot off?" Neil joined us.

"Yeah, man." Mehki shook his head, getting into character.

I shook my head. "This guy, man," I whispered, wiping my face again.

"I bet Poppy can't remember the best piece of ass he's gotten—don't bring up my moms, bro!" he warned.

That made them laugh again and harder. Mehki had no worries about me doing that. I couldn't remember the last time I'd thought of Mandy in a sexual way…with me.

"See!" Mehki continued. "He can't! Uncle Ro, what was the most memorable pussy you ever got?"

"The fuck you mean, youngin'? The one I wake up to every damn day. How you think she got to Alpine?" Cracking up, StentRo gave me more dap.

"Man, don't disrespect Auntie Zo like that." Mehki swung his hand dismissively. "I mean before her."

StentRo took the time to think. One thing my friends and I did with Mehki, understanding his circumstances, was keep it real with him. Once he turned ten, we let the leash go on the topic of drugs to prevent him from getting into them. Ki went to school with mostly white kids. White, rich kids. They had access to everything, as did he if I wasn't careful. We allowed him a safe space to talk his shit on girls at fifteen. He could ask us anything so long as he did so with respect—and out of my mother's earshot, which was challenging.

"NormaJean," StentRo answered.

Neil's green eyes grew large. "Rest in peace to the greatest of all fucking time."

StentRo nodded. "True indeed. She was a real one. A beautiful soul, man."

"She's dead?" Mehki asked with squinted eyes.

"You're showing your age, son," I warned. Every Black man knew about the queen of porn, NormaJean.

"Nah. Nah. Nah. I know her. She was here at one of your parties. I think it was your birthday party."

"A party here?" I didn't have many.

"Yeah. I remember because that's when Uncle Trent had just got home. And remember how…different he was. He wasn't talking much, but I saw him kickin' it with her."

"What the hell were you doing there?" Stenton asked.

"Sneaking." Mehki shrugged. "Poppy caught me that night, too. He was too tipsy to be mad. But wasn't she old?"

"Nah." I shook my head. NormaJean and I were really cool. We kicked it a lot. "She died way too fuckin' young." I still couldn't believe the homie was gone.

"I remember going to her memorial, being fucked up." Stenton shook his head.

"Whom the gods love, die young," Neil murmured. "I still have her work saved to my computer."

"Send them to Poppy." Mehki pointed at me. "He can use them shits."

I leaped his way. "Get the fuck..."

Mehki jumped backward, hands defenselessly in the air.

"Get ya ass on that court," Stenton demanded. "Layups and finishing tonight! Let's go!"

I turned to give Neil some love then StentRo.

"Yo, you don't wanna stick around and torture this lil nigga together?" He laughed.

"Nah. You and Neil got my man on your own. I'm about to hit the shower then my office for some work." I sauntered toward the door, pulling the scrunchie from my head, releasing my braids.

First, let me stop in the kitchen for banana peppers and some artisan crackers...

My stomach was rumbling like a motherfucker.

June

Hayden

"The bottom line is, we have a bottom line. Enrollment is up. Beds are being created. Funding is pouring in, thanks to..." My boss, Lex, used both her hands to gesture to me, standing in the corner of our conference room during our staff meeting. "We more than met our goals for the first quarter, and I'm beyond confident we've exceeded that in the second one we're closing on. The board is happy." She gave a fake smile then fingered her long, dark wooly hair behind her shoulder. The room snickered at her shade. "I'm thrilled. And you should be, too." She went to her clipboard. "Any questions before we close?"

"Okay. Everybody's happy. So, when can we talk raises around here, ma'am?" The room found that funny.

"Well, dang, Mika!" Lex shook her head. The room broke into side chats, some laughing, and others affirming her inquiry. "Okay, guys. Okay. You know there are regulations around increases. It is not at my discretion, though I do have the power to push it up the agenda for the board. If we can keep our intake numbers up, continue to go out giving education and resources as outreach workers, and if some of the ideas Hayden has shared with me about potential donors can happen within the next six to eight months, we can be looking at increases next spring into summer—" My colleagues' excitement turned loud, overpowering Lex's strong delivery. "How much, I can't say or guarantee! Any more questions?"

A few people were stuck on the increase possibility. Others shared gazes for more questions. Honestly, I never had an issue with my income. It was more than enough for my lifestyle. Did I endeavor to earn more? Hell yeah. But my pacing had been good. Now, with my current predicament, I could use more money.

"Okay, well..." Lex gazed around the table. "...if there are no more,

183

I have one announcement—well, Hayden has a final announcement —and then we're free to go to lunch."

Heads whipped my way fast as hell.

"You leaving, mama?" Eduardo asked aghast.

Tamara, another outreach worker, yelped, "Oh, no!" and covered her mouth in shock.

"Man, hell no!" Lex hissed. "Just call her Paul as my Annie ass boards her up in that office until I don't give a shit about none of this anymore!" I knew she was kidding, but understood her passion about keeping me on, too.

"Damn," Laura breathed.

"Please let her speak!" Mika rolled her eyes. "My nerves are too bad now!" she pumped her palms in the air.

I tried to use her humor as yet another moment to brave myself. Then, it was time to execute. "No, guys. I'm not leaving anytime soon. At least not permanently. But in late October, I should be taking some time off." I snorted, "Knowing me, working from home much of that period." I forced a giggle. It was useless, based on the expressions on my colleagues' faces; they were so confused, no jokes could break their moods. My shaky hand pushed my blazer to the side and brushed across my dollop-shaped abdomen. My chest pounded as I shared, "I'm seventeen weeks pregnant."

"Seven—" Mika gasped, yanking her short torso to face me with a quickness I didn't know she was capable of. "That's four months!"

Struggling to continue to brave myself, with pinched lips, I nodded.

Tamara cleared her throat and chuckled nervously. "Forgive me, as I've never had a child. I don't understand weeks or trimesters. At four months, are you in your first trimester or your second?"

"She's in her second." Lex's jaw twisted.

Was this going bad? We were a small staff. There wasn't much we weren't forced to share about our worlds. This was not corporate America. It was grant-funded—including governmental supple- mented—work. The formalities weren't as black and white.

"Oh!" Laura chirped. "Okay."

"You're due early November," Mika mumbled, no longer facing me.

"*Ah*—I didn't even know you were dating anyone. He never got my approval."

He never got mine either, Eddie. And that's likely because I didn't date. Nope. I just found him magnetically handsome, abandoned my mind, and gave my body to him on two occasions. By the way, the first time we ran out of condoms but couldn't stop playing the pokey game.

"If any of you were around during my first pregnancy, you know how sensitive of a time it was for me, which also included announcing it to you all." Lex advised, "Let's reserve our personal questions. Hayden will share as she feels comfortable. She simply thought it was time. Let's respect that and keep it cute."

Her protective tone came from knowing the details. Last week, after her husband chastised her about criticizing the stench in my office from my favorite snack as of late, she marched back in, demanding details obverse of what she'd just demanded. I broke down bad. I sobbed while sharing my secret. I, of course, didn't detail my prostitute role or how we went without condoms, or how we'd fucked again the following month. I simply kept it to the main event. I'd had a one-night stand with a complete stranger, in a distant state, whose name I had no clue of. And I didn't want to. The damage had been done.

"Guys, I won't lie. I'm not dancing on cloud nine. I am decided and will be the best...mother I can be. I'm just putting one foot in front of the other right now." I drew a wry smile. "I just wanted to share my condition with my peeps because the changes are rolling in." I rubbed my little belly.

"I umm..." Mika stood from the table. "...need the potty." She walked past, leaving me a memory in her dust.

She'd aborted her revered baby a few months back. *Shit*. Mika and I had gotten pregnant the same night, under the same circumstances.

Fuck.

Fuck.

Fuck.

"Well, thanks for sharing, Hayden," Melanie warmly offered with a smile. She was one of the registered nurses on our team. "If you need anything, just let us know. We're overdue for a baby shower around these parts."

"True that," Eduardo seconded.

"*Yaaaay!*" Laura clapped.

Lex smiled, appearing to have relaxed.

That was it. My 'in the meantime' was over. I'd decided to put on my big-girl panties and face my consequence. I'd survived so much as a child; it was a mode I was conversant in. I'd roll up my sleeves and make the best of my situation.

Besides, with having announced it to everyone who mattered in my life at this point, the most difficult task of being ashamed was over.

Twelve

June

Hayden

The sales rep handed me the shopping bag. "You have a wonderful evening. You're going to look amazing. You and your tummy."

"Awww!" I couldn't help my beam. My face warmed immediately. "Thanks so much for your patience with me today."

"The pleasure was all mine." She gave another neck bow. "I'll always be the person who helped you select your first pregnancy dress."

She was right. It took some time, but I'd picked a dress for Azmir's party tomorrow night. And while it wasn't a maternity piece, it was certainly one hiding nothing. The off-white dress was fitted, backless, and exposed my growing midsection. I loved it from the moment I tried it on.

"Thanks again." I turned and left the boutique, feeling confident about my selection.

When I'd made it out into the mall, I thought about how I'd be using Azmir's birthday party as my "exposure event." I now had a little pouch, though no weight had sprouted anywhere else on my body. When I sent Sundryia a picture of me in just my bra and panties, she agreed I was "all belly." A cute little one at that. Other than that, I still didn't feel pregnant. I had no food aversions, no sickness, no itchy belly, and I was not particularly exhausted. All I had was my raised pouch.

I stopped at the window of a *Janie and Jack*.

Damn.

Without thought, I sauntered inside, and my senses were overtaken by the sight of little people's clothing. They were so cute and... miniature. Stripes, solids, and polka dots. Tiny denim jackets and shoes. Burping cloths, hats, and—

"Socks," I whispered to myself as I held a pair with shaky hands.

They were so delicate and tiny. I checked the size. They were sized for newborns. There were white, yellow, pink, blue, and green ones. How could mothers decide? Did they spend as much money on these cute little fabrics as I did on myself? I felt dizzy with wonderment.

My phone rang. Unable to take my eyes off the tiny socks, I placed the shopping bag on the floor between my legs and reached for it in my purse.

"Hey..."

"Hey! You need a mani and pedi?" Rayna asked. "I do. I didn't want to get one alone."

"I... *Ummm*..." I turned the pure white socks over in my hand. "... have an appointment for tomorrow after I get my hair done."

"Cancel it. Come over to the City and get yours done with me. My treat."

"MiMi's gonna be mad," I warned.

"Tip her more next time. I'll even throw in dinner." She sighed. "The kids are with my mother in Jersey. Azmir's working late. I don't want to be alone."

I sniffed the socks. "Where are the kids?"

"Are you even listening to me? Wait! Where are you? What are you doing?"

That's when my eyes blossomed open, and I glanced around me. "In the mall."

"Did you find a dress?"

"Yes."

"Something to go with your *Bottega Veneta* "Lido" mules?" She murmured, "Those are so cute!"

"No. The metallic *Gianvito Rossi* 'Bijoux' sandals. I need to break them in."

They were the last designer shoes I purchased before closing on my house. Having Rayna in my life had been fun because she was a shoe-nista. Sundryia said we both were, but I didn't have a collection anywhere near Mrs. Jacobs'. I window-shopped a lot.

"Oh!" She chirped. "Okay. Girl, don't let my husband see you in those heels."

I whispered to a sales associate, asking where the register was located. "Why?"

"Because he has this thing about pregnant women wearing heels. Them being dangerous and all."

"But I'm not big?"

"It doesn't matter." I heard the eyeroll in that statement. "Anyway... What time can you get here? You know where our apartment is. Right? What are you doing?"

Smiling, I pulled out my card to hand over to the sales associate. "Making my first move out of my old 'meantime.'"

And damn, did it feel good.

189

ISHAAN

We walked down the hall of a basement in the police station. The air was cold and stale, and there was an eerie scent of indifference to life. It was always this way here. I followed the lieutenant into a room where close to two dozen bodies lay out on metal tables, covered with white sheets. Some were solid like the one we approached. A masked and uniformed employee who'd been expecting us stood next to the metal table. And with a simple nod from Lieutenant Grands, she pulled the sheet from the top of the table down to the middle.

Damn.

It was him. Lavonte Harris, one of the top-ranking runners for the Marinos, an Italian family who'd, once upon a time, ran Atlantic City and some parts of Philadelphia. The mob was still alive in Jersey, just not as powerful since the nineties, beginning with Gotti's successful takedown by way of R.I.C.O. violations.

But this dumb ass motherfucker still found value in running for a weak ass family who'd been struggling to survive by violating innocent people for scraps. Before working for the Marinos, Lavonte ran drugs out of his uncle's tire shop in Camden for years. When the uncle died, the wife used the money from his insurance policy to buy a small house in Pleasantville. Lavonte, being the useless and talentless man he was, moved in with his aunt. Low hanging fruit will find its way to familiar terrain. In Lavonte's case, it was the streets. Local to Pleasantville was its next-door neighbor, Atlantic City. After running through several hustles, including pimping, he landed work with the Marinos. That was over twenty years ago.

And here was where it'd landed him.

I nodded, observing the two bullet wounds still fresh from his demise. Lavonte was a deadly color gray, and now without a pulse. His eyes were yellow and the skin around them were a grayish black I'd only seen on the expired. His mouth was open, jaw misaligned. The bullet hole on his right breastplate was near a tattoo: a heart with the name Paris inside. I mindlessly wondered if she was a special lady to him or a daughter.

"Yeah." I continued nodding.

Then I turned to motion Tillman, who I'd brought along for this. I didn't allow Munchie to see this side of the job. Some things about women needed to remain pure for their nature of nurturing the young. Tillman shot a few pictures with his phone. When he was done, he nodded to me, and I did the same to Lieutenant Grands. Grands followed the same act with the masked coroner's staff.

Grands led us out of the room then turned to me. "Greggs said I needed to get you here before the coroner took him up to the medical examiner. We'll have to wait to hear back from him to determine what happened."

"That's cool." I knew this side of the game. "What do you know so far?"

"He was pulled out of the water. Water patrol found him floating near a pier post around three-fifty this morning. Cash and jewelry in place and fully clothed except for his upper torso, which is why we can see the bullet entries." He sighed and shrugged. "The list for who could be responsible is endless. Hell!" he scoffed. "We know how adamant your boss has been about the trafficking. We heard you guys had a go at him back in March. One of my detectives named Jacobs as a possible."

It was true. When we'd detained Lavonte after seeing his attempt at sneaking onto the property for the third time, I beat his ass pretty bad and let my fighters have a go at him when I was done. He was hospitalized for a couple of days. I didn't want to off him, but to tattoo Mr. Jacobs' sentiment in his mind. I hadn't heard from him since.

I shrugged. "That's fine, too."

Tillman tapped his watch, which meant I had to go. There was a jet fueled up and waiting for me at *Atlantic City International*. That caused me to prompt Grands, who was nearly as tall as me but almost double my weight, to lead us down the hall. I caught him giving me a full once-over but played it cool. In a royal *Tom Ford* 'Original British Mohair Atticus' suit, I was dressed for an evening event rather than a day of identifying bodies of local miscreants.

"You know," he chuckled. "...the guys and I were talking about working for Jacobs after retirement. A sergeant said our ships have sailed on that. We're old as hell, seeing the type of shit you do. You can't be married. Can't have no kids either. No time for a life at all."

"I've got a youngin'. But yeah. It's my main bitch."

"No time to eat or shit. Huhn?"

I yawned as we waited for the elevator. "Pussy will never run dry with a gig like this. But missing anniversary celebrations and double dates are guaranteed." As we walked on to the car, I advised, "*ADJ Enterprise* always has room for trained eyes and loyal soldiers. The work is never-ending, and the pay is a motivator for allegiance."

By the time I landed in New York City and had arrived at *The Garden of LaChateau* in midtown Manhattan, the place was electrified with music flowing and countless people vibing. Balloon chandeliers dropped from the skyscraping ceilings resembling pulsating jellyfish. They fell in a rhythmic speed toward the floor then retracted back up toward the high ceiling.

I'd been to this place a time or two, including a wedding of a friend of mine, Jackson Hunter, a public relations executive. The first time had been for an awards event the practice honored my mother and a few of her colleagues at a few years back. High-end with visible security—and not so, considering the celebrant—lots of glass in the structure, particularly in the solarium. There were flowers galore, keeping with the needs of the facility. Brass fixtures highlighted the lush and purposeful ambiance.

"You look great." Munchie cleared her throat. I glanced down and found her adjusting her silver pleated dress again. "I'm glad you chose that suit over the taupe *Kiton*."

With a wrinkled face, trying to hide my humor, I leaned down to ask her, "Why?"

Without giving me eye contact, she pushed the frame her glasses up her face. "Because I'm not alone in an electric color here."

I gave a cursory glance to the entrance of the room where the party was happening. "You wouldn't have been, Munch. Chill."

"*Mmmhmm!*" She sniffled, fortifying herself. "I know. It's just that... You know."

Her weight. Munchie was a beautiful, rotund woman. She was one of the smartest people I had around. Fuck her weight. She was powerful and useful for her employers, namely me. I hated how she struggled with her social self-esteem. Events like this made my assistant being a woman beneficial. We could work under light conditions, and I'd have feminine energy to balance me.

I stopped a passing waiter carrying a tray of champagne flutes and passed one to Munchie. "If it makes you feel any better, it's work for me, too. I made you my plus one to break up the monotony of the intense shit we do."

That's when she did peer my way. She blinked those dark, long lashes behind her lenses. "I'll locate Mr. Jacobs. Keep your phone engaged."

After a sip of the champagne and deciding to have something else, I smirked then winked at her. "Don't pick up no fuck boys on the way."

Munchie rolled her eyes, huffed, and took off down the stairs. I was right behind her but decided to head to the bar. It was packed, but being a tall man gave me the advantage of seeing over most heads cutting through to an empty area. I ordered *Mauve* neat, knowing it was a primary sponsor for this event. Of course, seeing familiar faces, I spoke to a few people in between answering texts on my phone. My drink was ready in no time, and I cut back through the crowd.

The moment I left the shore of bodies awaiting the bar, my path was cut by Jenise Taylor's fine ass. She was average height, brown-skinned, with a sexy ass smile she paid tens of thousands for, and it worked for her full lips. The top one had a scar on the side, which was a major tell-tale of her cosmetic dentistry. She'd likely had a tooth or two knocked out. Other than that, there were no other physical indicators of her story. In my line of work, I had to recognize everyone's story before they could share it—if they shared at all.

"Mr. Patterson." Her eyes twinkled, full lips bold in burgundy.

"Esquire Taylor."

She giggled, following me as I left the bar area completely. "No one says that quite like you, you know. How have you been?"

After raising my glass in greeting to a familiar face, I peered down at Jenise again. Her dress fit like a second skin. A wide, metallic gold belt exposed her hourglass shape, and her hair, in long loose curls, draped over one slender shoulder. I'd learned, about two years ago, she was the sister of Coach Launz's old lady. I'd known Jenise for over five years, and she'd been trying to fuck for just as long. However, with her peculiar, aggressive personality and profession, I decided to look into her after a year or so. I learned she had a severely disabled son, who lived in a facility in D.C., and that was the gun she'd shot herself with moving forward.

I smiled her way, admiring the view. "You know me."

"All work and no fucking pussy. At least, not mine."

"Is that why life's so damn mundane for me?"

"You know it," she singsonged then ran her tongue across her teeth.

I wouldn't fuck Jenise because I couldn't trust her. Any woman you know for years, have been in intimate settings with them discussing various aspects of life, and she doesn't speak of having a special needs child is the one you don't get close to. It's antithesis of a woman to not mention her kids in some capacity, including an accomplished, educated one like Jenise. If I'd engaged her, it would be purely in a fucking capacity. And, to me, Jenise was the type to sue you if you didn't deliver the dick to her on time.

"I heard what you did for Jules Richards. That was good work."

Jules was the mayor of Paterson, New Jersey. He'd been unlawfully pulled over and detained in a traffic stop in Wycoff last year. With her at the helm of Richards' legal team, the ruling was made in January. They sued for an insane amount, and he pledged to donate the money to various organized efforts committed to fighting recidivism and assisting Black and brown men and women into education and the workforce.

"Well..." She tugged at one of my lapels. "I'm good at so many things. I don't want you to only experience me in that one arena." She dropped her head to the side, watching me push a lollipop into my mouth. "Why are you still single, Ishaan?"

With a closed-lip smile and a wrinkled forehead, I squinted while exhaling deeply. I needed to figure out how to answer that question for Jenise Taylor.

Hayden

Maaz had just returned to our table with drinks for himself, Sundryia, and Rayna. Azmir was off greeting his sea of guests.

"Are you sure I can't at least get you a club soda?" Maaz offered as Sundryia randomly stood from her seat to kiss him.

She typically didn't drink much but had been all over him tonight. Maybe she'd had a drink too many. Either way, it was cute seeing her so affectionate.

I shook my head. "I'm good for now."

"Awwww!" Rayna rubbed my back. She looked amazing with her beautiful eyes lined with white at the bottom waterline. She was killing it tonight with a white mini dress, showing off her toned thighs and legs with metallic *Christian Louboutin* 'Iriza' pumps. Her cleavage exposure was ample and nicely defined. It was clear Rayna worked out and likely ate well.

Damn, I was in for wreckage of my body. I, too, worked out. Not that I was a gym rat, but with my mother's height, I'd always been afraid I'd take on her size as well. So, since college, I'd been working out, at least, weekly but not necessarily regularly. My eating could be improved, but I was cognizant of overdoing it. I wasn't like Sundryia, who didn't work out much but looked absolutely amazing. She was a tall woman like my mother and me. She was an athlete as a child and still maintained the muscle structure from it.

Rayna continued, "That was the worst thing about being pregnant for me. Azmir has such a compact social schedule. It was hard to watch everyone drink when I couldn't."

"I didn't miss it much." Sundryia had let Maaz loose and was straightening her high-waisted shorts, revealing her beautifully shaped thighs. She'd just given birth five months ago to twins and her stomach was virtually gone, at least enough to wear a body suit, showing off her shapely boobs. The suede, block heel, strappy ankle, high-heeled sandals she wore only enhanced her feminine physique. "I think if I missed anything, it was my privacy. I couldn't be alone anymore. Someone had to know where I was at all times or even be with me." She rolled her eyes as she resumed her seat next to me.

"Maaz?" I asked, grateful to switch thoughts.

I'd been eyeing women all night, observing their bodies. It had to be the pregnancy. Self-consciously—or clearly—I was mourning the loss of the shape of my body. My shape and size had always appealed to me. Yes, I had my imperfections, but appreciated what I had to work with. Now, my best shape days could have possibly been behind me. Even my boss, Lex, had been in talks on finally getting a tummy tuck after having three kids. I didn't know how to feel about it. Was I panicking? Maybe. My fitted dress most definitely exposed my announcement to the world tonight. It was what I'd looked forward to. But being here and seeing all these fit women tonight, including my cousins, had me in my feels.

Sundryia took a sip of her drink. "Girl, Maaz, his mother, his weird ass cousin, Rhonda, his housekeeper in Connecticut, Dora—every damn body."

"Including me." Rayna winked sheepishly and laughed.

"Yup. You, too." Sundryia shook her head laughing. "I'm the type who likes to escape the world."

"That's completely over for you!" Rayna did the cutting gesture at the neck.

That made me smile. Resting my chin on my tented hands, I added, "I do not and will not have a baby daddy or his crew breathing fire over my head. I have complete freedom to turn off my ringer or power off my phone." I swung my arms in the air. "And if I can stay away from Azmir Jacobs, I can wear heels down my driveway to the mailbox with no criticism." My cousins laughed at that.

"Ain't he a beast with that!" Sundryia trilled. "I hated going out with A.D. while pregnant. Even if he didn't say anything, he'd give this fatherly look. He was so disappointed." She cracked up.

As I chuckled, I caught Rayna rolling her eyes. "That man. But how 'bout when I'm not pregnant, he looks at me crazy if I'm *not* wearing heels!" As we laughed, she shook her head.

"This is my song!" My head swung left to right as I tried to remember the artist.

"What you know about Jeff Red, youngin'?" Sundryia quizzed.

"Ain't this from that old movie?" Rayna snapped her fingers as she bounced in her seat.

"*Strictly Business* with Halle Berry." Sundryia danced in her seat, too. "My mother couldn't stand that lady, but I loved her."

I jumped up. "Forget all that. I wanna dance while I can still move, and before your intimidating husband comes back looking for you. Come on!" Moving around Sundryia, I made my way to the dance floor with my arms in the air.

My body may be damaged come November, but my 'meantime' of deciding on motherhood was over. I had to live my life. Fighting for some happiness had to be my focus.

ISHAAN

As we were on the second level of the ballroom, a bit away from the crowd, suited-security created a barrier for us. Azmir studied the picture from my phone.

"And the locals think it was me?" he asked. I nodded in the affirmative. He sighed, standing straight and handing me back my phone. "Then let them." I knew he'd say that. "It's been my practice to stay away from violence as much as possible in this line of work. But you know, there will always be that one or two who don't understand I'm a polite executioner.

"In this case, I didn't have to deliver the hammer, but the sooner they understand I'm capable, the sooner we can get to a peaceful coexistence. Because at the end of the day, my vision will prevail. I don't give a fuck if it's in Atlantic City or Timbuktu. We don't randomly choose a city to set up wonderland in. We do our due diligence and research its history. Its leaders. Its problems and its weaknesses. So, hell yeah, we'll take the blame for this if that's where it rests."

"Yeah, but our address would have been far more spectacular."

Azmir raised his palm for a dap, chuckling. "We deal in grandeur."

I caught Munchie's messaging eyes as I leaned into my boss. "The shit nightmares are truly made of." Which was why we'd made an attempt to avoid violence at every turn. "Pardon me."

I fully turned to address Munchie, who was leaning over the railing with the lower view. With her eyes, she directed me to the first floor. I placed my lollipop back into my mouth and strolled over to the railing a few feet away from her. It took a few seconds, but down on the dance floor were Azmir's wife, Maaz from the *Connecticut Kings'* lady, and...

My eyes squinted just to be sure. But heels and a skintight dress was her uniform for me. I glanced back at Munchie, who gave a discreet nod.

"Is there a problem here, Patterson?" Azmir asked, joining me at the railing.

love ∞ *believe*

Hayden

I laughed my damn head off while Rayna was trying to teach Sundryia and me the choreography for Tyla's "*Water.*"

"Wait!" I grabbed my chest, trying to catch my breath. "I can do it!"

"Then let's do it!" Sundryia demanded next to me.

"Then can you not be so serious?" I hooted again. Sundryia wasn't a big drinker, and it was clear to me that tonight she'd had too much. "Relax your face."

"Okay." Sundryia blinked and pouted her lips over and over.

"Sundryi*aaaa*!" Rayna cried, laughing. "Y'all, come on. The song's gonna be done soon!"

I had no idea how we had so much room on the dance floor. Likely because it was Rayna's event for her husband. People cleared the way, dancing around us. A few were in line, learning with Sundryia and me.

Sundryia clapped her hands then arched her back. She looked so damn good. "Okay! Okay! I'm ready."

"Alright!" Rayna clapped, getting into position. "Come on!"

I was ready, rounding my hips to the beat, waiting for the chorus to come back around.

And when it did, Rayna counted down. "Five! Four! Three! Two!"

Then we went to town, angling our spines and jerking our hips to snap backward into the air. We repeated it throughout the entire chorus. Once done, we broke into celebratory dances, hi-fiving each other and the others who appeared in our cypher out of nowhere.

"You look so cute!" The apparently effeminate man in pink pointed to my belly while shimmying.

I blew him a kiss and mimicked his movements, swinging my hips left to right while holding my little protruding belly. He cheered me on, and I was game. Tonight turned out to be a great one for me. Getting out with my cousins, playing dress up, and dancing had been just what the doctor ordered for my blue state as of late.

"Hey, Boo-baby," was breathed sensually into my ear.

Simultaneously, three things happened: one movement and three sensations. My entire frame steeled and shivered. My clit pulsed, and the baby moved. *It moved*. It wasn't a kick, I didn't think. It felt more like a jolt. Like an announcement.

Finally, I turned, wafting in a masculine fragrance at the forty-five-degree angle mark before seeing what appeared to be bespoke royal blue. I'd forgotten how tall he was, and—*holy shit*—he was fine as hell. I'd forgotten. It had totally skipped my memory how captivating his beauty was. *His hair*. It was out of box braids and crinkled, styled to one side of his head. The exposed side was cut sharply into a flawless fade. The front was tapered with precision. *Goddamn*. This man was suited to be a modern-day Fabio cover model. He was perfection. And it wasn't superior features alone. The man had a swag about him. Like the wicked gleam in his dark eyes as he gazed down on me avidly.

He pulled a lollipop from his mouth and smiled so damn roguishly, insulting me with his full lips and gorgeously white teeth. Those piercing eyes roved down my face and onto my body before he stepped into my personal space again.

"You've got some 'splaining to do to daddy," he singsonged in a whisper I could hear every syllable of.

Unable to control my lungs and keep my eyes opened, I argued, "I don't. I don't even know you."

His smile slowly returned, widening his peanut butter-hued face. "You may not remember my name. But, oh baby, you *know* me." His eyes traveled down to my little bump.

Nervously, I glanced around, shame suddenly encroaching. Sundryia was laughing with someone, and I didn't see Rayna.

I turned back to my intimate stranger. That damn lollipop was back in his mouth, eyes were still glimmering with sensual threats. "Can I tell you a secret?" Before I could answer, he leaned down and whispered in my ear, causing my spine to jolt, "I'm so turned on by your body. I don't care whose baby's in there. I wanna fuck you *so* bad, Boo-baby."

When he reclined, straightening in his stance, his eyes were locked onto me, paralyzing my entire frame.

"You two know each other?" Another masculine voice interjected, causing my neck to snap to the left.

Azmir's tall figure was there, wearing an expression of confusion and wonderment. I noticed he stood closer to... Jesus, I didn't know the man's name—didn't remember.

Out of nowhere, Rayna appeared, her brows knitted with curiosity. "What's going on here?" She tried to smile. "Hey, Ish!"

Ish?

He wouldn't take his eyes off of me, even when he returned, "Hello, Mrs. Jacobs."

"Who this?" Sundryia appeared on my right.

Shit.

My lungs filled until I had no choice but to expel the pent-up air.

His magnetic beam broadened. "All these check-ins and no name. Not even Jane." Even the red dye on his tongue was annoyingly alluring.

"Who the hell is—" Sundryia's eyes popped wide. "The fuck!"

The beam on his face reduced to just his eyes. "Let's go somewhere private for a tête-à-tête. *Huhn?*"

I glanced around at my cousins and Azmir. Maaz had joined us as well as a woman who I believed was the one who'd approached me in Atlantic City, soliciting for him.

If I could open a portal on the damn dance floor to swallow me up, I would. But I couldn't. I needed to gain control of this situation, at least for the next few hours.

I cleared my throat before saying, "I'm open for a chat, but now's not the time. We can set up a time to do that later. Tonight, we're celebrating my cousin's husband—*my* cousin." I swung my eyes over to a pensive-appearing Azmir. "I take it you know him. You're at his birthday party."

"Ishaan's Azmir's partner at *ADJ Enterprise*. He's the COO, in fact."

What?

My attention went to Azmir, who seemed to still be awaiting an answer of sorts. Then when I glanced over to "Ishaan" that gleam remained in his eyes, and my body once again reacted to it. A damn COO of Azmir's company with *Mielle* perfect hair?

"What the fuck is going on here?" Sundryia sounded irritated.

"I'll call you," rushed from my mouth. This needed to end.

"You don't have my number." Ishaan wouldn't stop smirking.

"Well, seeing we know someone in common, I'm sure I can get it."

He turned over his shoulder and mumbled something. That brought the tattoo on his neck into vision.

The eagle.

How could he be Azmir's—anyone's—chief operating officer with such an exotic presentation?

Ishaan returned to me, carrying a business card I knew came from the woman I'd met in Atlantic City. That made me wonder if Azmir knew his partner used women to solicit prostitutes for sex.

I glanced down at it long enough to capture *Ishaan Patterson*. That was his name. I couldn't recall, and likely would have never from February.

"Thanks." My one-word response was awkward, but that was all I had for him.

Before I could move my cemented feet to leave this conundrum,

"Ishaan" reached for my face. He pulled my hair back over my ear. "I'd like to talk tomorrow. If you don't call me, I'll contact you."

"You don't have her number!" Sundryia's tipsy ass rolled her neck.

Ishaan turned to her and smiled. He proffered his hand. "Ishaan Patterson. I'm great associates with Zyad. His older brother and I were conversant."

My eyes grew wide as did Sundryia. Ishaan swiped my chin with his index finger before taking off. The hippie "schoolteacher" followed behind him.

"Are you okay?" Rayna appeared closer in my personal space. It was free now that "Black Fabio" had vacated.

"I'm good," I snapped because I wasn't.

"What that muthafucka mean, he was conversant with—" Sundryia shook her head then took me by the hand. "Let's go have a breather."

Azmir and Maaz remained there wordless.

"Yo, what the fuck was that?" Sundryia shouted before the private bathroom door could close and John, Rayna's assigned security's face, disappeared behind it.

We were inside a plush powder room. I assumed on the other side of the room were the bathroom stalls.

Moving directly into my face, Rayna demanded, "Is that him? Did you sleep with Ishaan in Vegas?"

Sundryia shouted, "And what the fuck did he mean by bringing Amir up while introducing himself to *me*?"

"I don't know," I tried explaining with a tight throat. "I don't know that man."

"So, he's not the guy you slept with," Rayna didn't pose as a question, but was damn sure asking for clarification.

"That nigga is fine as shit! From afar, I would think he's a pretty boy." Sundryia was pacing in her heels, using her hands to communicate. *Yup.* She was intoxicated. "But when you got up in the nigga's space, you could feel ain't shit soft about him. He gives sniper vibes."

"He's the COO of Azmir's company. Whatever Obi-Wan Kenobi to Luke Skywalker, jedi mind trick you got is what he gets paid for. He's unassuming. And while I don't know much about the operations of my husband's multitude of businesses, I do know the chief operating officer is responsible for entertainment and security. He's supposed to be Dr. Hyde and Mr. Jekyll."

"You mean Dr. Jekyll and Mr. Hyde," Sundryia corrected as I propped myself onto the vanity.

Unphased by the potential embarrassment, Rayna mumbled, "Yeah." Then she peered my way. "How did you meet Ishaan?"

"Why you asking her that? What the hell do you know?" Sundryia gasped. "Yo, Rayna. If we're gonna do this cousin shit, you're gonna have to protect Hayden. That's the name of the game."

I blinked hard. "Protect me? Don't we all need protection?"

"Nah. I'm good!" Sundryia clenched her fists together and did the wrestler's pose by broadening her shoulders and clenching her teeth.

I closed my eyes, trying to erase her silly ass expression. My cousin couldn't handle alcohol. She wasn't a libations type of girl. She once told me it was because her mother was an addict. At most, she'd smoke a little weed every now and again. I'd shared a few blunts with her, but that was as far as Sundryia would go. Drunkenness was out of character for her. I wondered how Maaz was feeling about it.

"Ladies, I'm fine." I massaged my temples. "I really am. I don't want to spend a bunch of time in here, taking away from Azmir's celebration. It's enough that he knows I have a sprinkle of whoredom in me along with my—whatever the hell he thought of me before tonight. Let's just get back to the party."

"Do you wanna leave?" Rayna asked. "You look so frazzled now. You don't have to feel obligated to stay."

"Of course, I want to leave. I wanna go home and have crackers and banana peppers, but I won't. I'm here celebrating my cousin's rich, fine ass husband." I tried for cheerful.

"Are you sure, Hayden?" Sundryia asked.

"Yessssss!" I giggled convincingly. "Listen. I fucked up. I did some stupid shit I need to address and fix. But that's not going to happen tonight. Tonight, Rayna's gonna show us how she flirts with her man in a room full of people to get him to fuck her in the car. Right?" While Rayna wasn't violent tonight, her level of intoxication wasn't that far off from Sundryia's. I needed to keep this crazy ass discovery tonight under control. So, I hopped off the vanity. "Come on. Let's get back to the party."

As I managed to arm the sexy ladies out of the powder room, one thought screamed in my head.

I can't believe I felt my baby move...

Thirteen

June

Ishaan

"That's her. Huhn?" Munchie asked from the balcony.

I watched the door Hayden and her cousins left out of for their girl chat. "Yup."

"And she's... What? Three...four months pregnant?" Her head shifted from right to left as she observed the lower level.

"I wouldn't know."

"It's hard to say." I caught the shrug in her tone. Munchie was trying to keep an alarming predicament calm, following my lead. "One sister was showing at two months during her first pregnancy. The other one of mine didn't pop out until her sixth. That's because it was the other sister's second pregnancy. But what do I know?"

The hairs at the back of my neck stood straight when I saw the women strut back into the room. Among a few other things, Azmir mentioned they were cousins when they'd left. Hayden and Maaz's fiancée were undoubtably tall women, but all three cousins were toned and fit. All three were also extremely attractive women. Azmir and Maaz were wealthy men by all measures. I knew Rayna was from the projects in Jersey but had only experienced a woman of class and decorum. Her mother was a recovering addict I'd see during holiday parties or impromptu meetings while Azmir was with his family. Rayna's brother was now home off a lengthy prison bid for murder. Rayna's family was conversant with the streets.

Maaz's girl was from Paterson and ran with shooters from the Fourth Ward and Down the Hill. She carried them, sold them, and pulled out heat when she had to. She eventually matured and went legit by becoming a real estate investor and opening a couple of daycares in Paterson. They were shut down because of the *FED*s running down on her partner's boyfriend, Dante. We knew him as D-Bricks on the streets. I didn't know if Maaz's fiancée had business with D-Bricks, too, but I'd damn sure find out.

Until I learned who was responsible for swelling Hayden's belly, I'd find out everything I needed to know about her family. Knowing everything would tell me why such a beautiful woman, who worked in grant writing, would pose as a damn sex worker in Vegas—and in Atlantic City—for shits and giggles. It couldn't have been for money; she'd returned it all.

Munchie finally turned to me, sighing, "So, when do we start digging?"

"Tonight. Hope you don't have plans." I stepped off to leave.

"And what about you?" She asked over my shoulder. "Where are you picking up?"

"I'm going to check with Sam to make sure we're clear on security here then head out."

"But..." I vaguely heard her sigh of frustration. "Sir, it's pretty late. Sir?"

Hayden

"I think those edits from the last draft were perfect. I know when *New York-Presbyterian* sees numbers written out instead of in numerical values, they'll automatically return the application!" I slapped my forehead, slamming my back into my office chair. "Remember they pulled that shit on me a few years ago?"

I glanced up at Mika, who was sitting in the chair across from my desk. Her face was to her writing pad as she doodled. "*Mmmhmm.*" Her response was as spiritless as all the others before it in this meeting.

"Did Adam Perry from *Johnson & Johnson* return your email?"

"No, boss lady." Her eyes remained low as did her volume. "I tried calling him yesterday before I left for the day. Nothing yet."

"That's strange. Adam gets a kick out of you like we all do." I twisted my mouth, making a mental note to call over there myself. "I wonder if he's away on vacation."

"There was no bounce back email indicating that. It wasn't mentioned in his messaging for his voicemail either."

"Hmm." I massaged my fingers, not knowing what to say to my assistant.

If she'd been out of character since having an abortion back in February, she'd definitely been off even more since I announced my pregnancy to the office.

"Mika, I can't help but notice your energy has changed with me. Have I done something to offend you or hurt your feelings?"

"Is that my boo?" Darnell, one of the drivers for *Christ Cares*, craned his neck into the doorframe of my office.

Shit...

Not now.

His eyes were soft and his cheekbones high as they always were when we interfaced. Darnell was my office husband. He'd been flirting with me since I started, and I let him. The energy was light, so I allowed it. It was common knowledge around here. Once in a blue, we'd have lunch here in the building together. The "date" would be filled with harmless jokes about his failed dating life and some of the clients he transported to job interviews, work, and doctor appointments. Here at *Christ Cares,* we serviced women with a gamut of issues from addiction, housing insecurity, and domestic violence. The stories were endless.

"Hey, Darnell," I returned softly, sans my typical smile.

"I was just dropping in to tell you today's my last day."

What?

Even Mika swung her head around.

"Are you serious?"

He stepped fully inside the doorjamb. "Well, you're pregnant, *and it ain't by me,*" he whispered the last part. "What good am I here? I'm humiliated."

Oh, no...

My attention went to Mika.

She gathered her pad and folders to her chest and stood. "Excuse me." Abruptly, she stopped and turned back toward me. "Unless there's more on the agenda."

Exhaling deeply, I shook my head and Mika jetted out.

"She okay?" Darnell asked, pointing over his shoulder.

I shook my head softly. "There's a lot going on around here."

"Damn. My bad. I gotta go myself. I was just coming to mess with you." He cackled sillily. I snorted, rolling my eyes. Darnell backed out of the door. "No. Seriously. Congrats. He has to answer to me now." And he was out.

Continuing to shake my head, I tried processing all the energy I was just intertwined with. It was too much. I had no idea what to do with Mika, or if there was anything I could do. Was I responsible for her disposition? I shouldn't have been. Then, I thought to check the time. I grunted again, dropping my head back into the chair. It was after one in the afternoon. I had a call to place.

Slowly, I stood from my desk and traversed my tiny space to close the door. Before dumping myself back into the chair, I grabbed my cell phone. His business card had been in a tray on my desk. It had been three days since I'd seen, "*Ishaan Patterson,*" I mumbled, reading from the business card. I told myself to call him on Sunday but had been too tired from the party to do it.

Then, I'd gotten a call I let go to voicemail. He'd left a message inviting me to speak with him again. His voice was so silky and firm as I wondered how in the hell he got my number. That's when I was reminded of him being Azmir's business partner. There were a number of ways he could have tracked me down, Rayna sharing it with him being one. *But she would have said...* Either way, I told myself I'd call yesterday, but couldn't build up the nerve to. Today had to be the day.

With a trembling hand and pounding chest, I picked up the phone and dialed the numbers.

Flexing my ankle and watching the pointy tip of my pump, I decided to check the time again. It was only two minutes later than the last time I'd checked. *Three more minutes and I'm out the damn door.* I chewed the stale gum to keep my mouth from going dry. Rubbing my lips together, I checked to be sure they were still well glossed. My stomach was in knots, had been since agreeing to this. The door opened again, and I turned on the sofa to peer over my shoulder. It was a Hispanic woman in uniform, wheeling in a tray of food. She nodded, making her way to the long table against the wall and underneath a mounted screen. I watched her transfer food and beverages.

A swanky ass hotel in Midtown Manhattan...

The room smelled and looked clean, professional. Glancing

around as she worked, I wondered was a meeting about to take place in this lush conference room. It was rather large, with the traditional conference table and a dozen or so chairs on the opposite side. I was across the room in the lounge area, with semicircular sofas and chairs around an S-shaped coffee table. In between were smaller companion tables. It was where I was invited to sit when escorted inside the room by one of the concierges at the front desk.

The uniformed woman left as quickly and quietly as she'd come. Again, I was left alone waiting. With one more minute to go, I began gathering my things. I took my time standing, pulling my dress pants from between my thighs to straighten them out. Idly, I wondered if I'd been gaining weight. The adjustment was more than I was used to. Just as I tugged down the matching suit jacket, the door opened.

The zoftig "schoolteacher" toggled in first, hips wide and femininely curvy. She wore her smart glasses, ballerina shoes, floral A-line skirt, and wide belt over a three-quarter sleeve camisole. Behind her, he seemed to rush through the door, long legs in a black suit and white dress shirt with the first few buttons undone. His hair was braided back in cornrows. The sides were neatly tapered as usual.

"Hayden." He spoke my name as if we were companions to some degree for quite some time. "I do apologize." He peered behind me. "Please tell me you've eaten something." His one golden hand defensively in the air.

"I haven't," my tone icy. "I didn't come here to eat."

"I understand." He closed the door behind him. "I was in court this morning down in A.C. It ran a few minutes behind and the traffic coming into New York was crazy as hell."

"And now, I have to get back to work."

"I did text you explaining."

I turned my attention to the "schoolteacher." "*Someone* sent a couple of text messages, and I did receive them. Still, you're incredibly late, and I have work. Your message on Monday convinced me you wanted to have this 'talk' expeditiously. I agreed to it and have availed myself, although it's totally unnecessary."

Deftly, he unhooked a button, releasing his suit jacket. "Why do you view it as unnecessary?" His dark eyes brushed down my body, likely in search of my belly. Too bad. It was hidden behind the standup-style suit jacket.

I sighed, frustrated. The fact of the matter was, it was my lunch hour, and I was hungry. I never intended to meet with him for long. I had my own agenda. Now, my message had to be rushed to delivery.

"Listen, I get what this must be like for you. I get it, and I'm truly sorry. But I'm not asking you for anything here. As far as I'm concerned, we've never met. Nothing has ever transpired between us, and we can go about our lives as though they never intersected."

His brows hiked as he stood stock-still, managing once again to appear like a model. This time, an urban runway model. "So, there is a possibility you conceived back in February—"

"Or March," the "schoolteacher" interjected with a screech then cleared her throat.

"Or March?" Ishaan echoed.

"What I'm saying is it does not matter. I'm sorry. You don't have to worry about me disturbing your life whether I did or did not."

"Have you had sex with other men before, in between, or after me?"

My face turned to stone, and I spat, "That's none of your damn business!"

Then that sinister beam opened, and his beautifully aligned, white teeth appeared. "Apparently, you don't have any business to keep to yourself because you're no prostitute."

My head whipped over to the "schoolteacher." Her eyes were pointedly on me. Did she know, know? Was she judging me?

"Your name escapes me." I tried for a smile.

Her eyes swung between the two of us before sharing, "Munchie."

I snapped my fingers. "Munchie. That's right!" I declared convincingly. I had no memory of either of their names until being told again. "I don't know what your relationship with Ishaan—"

"It's *Ish*-shon," he corrected with a smile. "Not E-Y-E-Shan."

"Ishaan," I tried again. "With Ishaan is, but seeing how you and I don't have one and never will, do you mind giving me a minute alone with him? I promise not to lay a finger on him. As you know, I'm pregnant."

Without looking at her, Ishaan gave Munchie a nod, dismissing her. With pinched lips and a hung head, she left the room, closing the door behind her.

"You can still lay a finger or two on me—pregnant or not. In fact, I'd like to see what that's like," his words poured like spiked honey.

He was so goddamn good-fucking-looking. What universe had he sprung from? I'd never felt an energy like his before. Never seen a tatted man at the chest, up to the neck, and with the crown of his head topped with long, thick, black hair falling inches down his back in a suit with the title of chief operating officer. But before me, he stood confident as hell, worldly, and as though he understood the space he occupied very well. The man could bottle it up and sell me some confidence.

"I'm sorry. I know I played a nasty joke in Vegas and fell easily into character again in Atlantic City. But I'm not that girl. I'm an educated professional, employed by a religious organization. I could be fired for the shit I pulled. Not to mention, the position I unknowingly put my cousin in by coincidentally hooking up with her very powerful husband's business partner."

"Then that makes two of us." He gaited over to the single sofa and sat on the armrest. "You mentioned your cousin. Her husband is my—"

"Business partner. You told me in Atlantic City you were a W-2 type of employee."

"Because I am," he scoffed. "I didn't lie to you. I could be fired tomorrow just like any other expendable employee."

My eyes shot wide. "I'm sorry."

He stood but didn't come into my personal space. "Why do you keep apologizing? I was there, too—both times."

"Because..." I thought for a second about how heedless my behavior was—twice.

"Look. I'm willing to cooperate however I can. I don't want to be dismissive. I just want to know if there's a possibility the baby isn't mine."

"And how can I supply you with that peace of mind?"

"It's why I asked if you'd had sex just before, in between, or just after me."

I understood that to be a reasonable question. However, answering it would disclose my personal sex life, and that topic was not open for discussion. Perhaps it was easy for prostitutes to divulge that information because of their line of work, but I was no prostitute.

"Again, I'm not about to answer that."

"Can I ask why?"

"Because I'm a woman. I know I didn't behave like a modest one, but I am a lady. My vagina is not up to being dissected by you or your boss, who's married to my cousin. My sex life is sacred to me. It's an essential part of my femininity. I will not make that a conversation with a stranger. That's why I am sorry. I've given you the absolute wrong impression of me."

His thick brows lifted. "Now what?"

I shook my head, frustrated to a new degree. "Now, nothing. Now, this is me." I grabbed my belly. "Now, I deal with my circumstance."

"And what if the baby's mine, Hayden?"

The way he said my name.

Familiarly. Ultra-masculine. Pleading. Authoritative.

"Now, you go back to your day-to-day life. You have no adjustments to make or surprises to expect or have your life thrown off-kilter. You're free."

Ishaan's chin dipped, and he shook his head as he peered deep into my eyes. "I can't do that. As much as I would love for the baby you're incubating to not be of my DNA, you need to know I am not off the hook until I know for sure. I understand you're not making any demands and don't want shit to do with me, but until I know the paternity results, I'm not off the hook morally, and damn sure not professionally. My career is at stake here. My employer knows I've engaged with a prostitute on our property. Twice. That shit ain't flying. So, tell me. What do I do in the meantime?"

The fucking meantime...

Taking a deep breath, I hated feeling sympathy in any way for this man. But I did. And taking a moment to think about why, I recalled my culpability in this. I'd willfully fucked him on two occasions. He didn't force me or push. I wanted him.

I scratched my brow. "Again, I'm sorry. I guess I didn't see it from your perspective. As far as I'm concerned, you did nothing wrong. I've been consistent with that when I shared some of what happened with my cousin. I don't even think I told her about the prostitute thing."

"And the money?"

I cupped my forehead as that memory slapped me hard. Then I let out a groan. Collecting myself, I shared, "I haven't told anyone about that. It wasn't my finest hour."

"Is that why you gave the money back?"

"*Yea*—no. Maybe. *Ah*—I don't know. I didn't expect the money. It didn't belong to me."

He took a step closer to me, humor dancing in his eyes. "You sat on that money for a whole month?"

"I couldn't sleep knowing I had that money. It didn't belong to me. I was happy to give it back."

His face softened and eyes sparkled. "You're a horrible prostitute. You know that?"

I scoffed, feeling ridiculous. "I'm not a prostitute."

He pointed to my belly region. "That's clear."

"Look." I sighed again. "I've got to go. I'm on the clock."

"Did you drive yourself from Harlem or take an *Uber*? Or did you take the train?"

"Why? And how do you know where I work?"

"Because I was going to offer a car service to get you where you need to go." Ishaan walked over to the buffet table where the food was laid out. He took what looked like a prosciutto cheese roll and bit into it. My stomach growled and flipped at the same damn time. I needed to go. "And it's a facet of my job to know shit about people."

That was alarming. I switched weight on my hips. "And what else do you know about me?"

He smirked, glancing my way. Then he stood straight. Damn. He was tall. As a lengthy woman, it was difficult finding men taller than me that I was actually attracted to.

"Why don't I propose this? Until we learn more about the baby, maybe we can be...friends—platonic, of course."

"And what does that look like to you?"

He casually shrugged, flipping his chin. "I don't know. Maybe just checking in with you regularly. Perhaps I'll go with you to your next doctor's visit?"

My head bounced back, and I blinked hard. "That's rather personal. Don't you think?"

His eyes squinted and smile blinded me when he expressed, "I think we've jumped the line on personal already. Huhn?"

It was time to go for real. "I'll think about it," I muttered, heading toward the door. Powering through the lobby, I kept my head down. My mind was reeling with what had just taken place. I walked a block to a parking lot where my car was located. By the time I locked the doors and pulled on the seatbelt, my phone chirped.

+1(973)555-0980: *I'm sorry about having you wait. Here's my personal cell number.*

+1(973)555-0980: *Oh! And you looked cute today boo baby.*

I slapped my mouth with my palm, trying to catch the scream shooting from my belly. Tossing my head back, I laughed so damn hard and loud.

Then I cried. Like a baby, in the next breath, I cried.

ISHAAN

"*Kiiiiiiiiiiiiii!*" I shouted, turning into the dining room.

Ms. Green, the housekeeper, giggled as she arranged serving

dishes. "You remember those days. Before paying bills was your main challenge in life, it was your social currency that was prioritized."

Qiana Green was twenty-nine years old. So, when she made comments like that, it revved up my curiosity of how she went into housekeeping at such a young age.

I grabbed a homemade, miniature donut from a tray as I whisked past the buffet on my way to the door leading to the balcony. My mother was already at the table, gazing into the night air beyond the lights lining the deck. A few trees were covered in white lights as well. It was always a picturesque vibe out here, year-round. There were endless forest views beyond the acre of manicured lawn.

"You good, Ma?"

"*Mmmhmmm.*" She sighed. "I love it out here. I'm so glad you hired the landscaping architect when you first bought this property. This is so peaceful." She reached for her wine glass. "I wish I had a daughter-in-law to share it with."

I didn't react. The timing of that conversation wasn't great at all.

"Yeah, but you *Apple Cash*ed him. Right?" Mehki came blustering onto the deck, speaking loud as hell on his cell phone. "But you could've *CashApp*'ed him, too."

"Hold up, now!"

"Nah!"

My mother and I responded to his rude ass at the same time.

"Off. Now!" I told Mehki, looking him dead in the eye.

He rolled his eyes, huffing. "Maury! I gotta go. Family time over here. A'ight. Peace." The call ended.

"You just walked Jessica to the door, and I told you to hurry for dinnertime. Your poppy just called you again, and you're coming out here on the phone?" my mother complained as he kissed her cheek, finessing her ass.

"Sorry, Nanu." Mehki took the seat to the right of her, facing the house. "I had some bit-ness to take care of before having dinner with my number one girl."

"*Hmm,*" was her remark.

Ms. Green came out to load the table with food. We fixed our plates and engaged in conversation while we ate. Still being trained for proper socialization and communication, Mehki spoke the most because my mother and I asked him lots of open-ended questions. It also helped with learning what was going on in his head and life outside of the house.

Dinner eventually slowed. Mom was done eating and Ki was still picking at his mostly empty plate. He always saved the vegetables for last.

"Hey, you two..." I started, sitting up in my chair, placing my elbows on the table and threading my fingers together. "I asked for us to have dinner out here tonight because I have something to share with you."

"The cartel found out where we live and they're coming for us?" Mehki asked, partially joking.

My life had been pretty private, including my home address. It was covered by a shell company through an LLC. Someone would have to dig deep to find me. So, I didn't sweat a rupture in security. I'd put things in place to ensure the safety of my family.

"Nah." I shook my head. "A few months ago, I met a young lady. It was random. We attended a *Panthers* event at *HAYDAR*. We had a few drinks, vibed...and decided to explore the rest of the night together. I'll put it like that."

My mother lowered her chin. "You mean adult time?"

I scoffed, feeling weird about sharing my sex life in front of my family. But hell, Ki was old enough to know I fucked. He just didn't need to know how much or with who.

"Yes." When she didn't have a follow-up question or comment, I continued. "Well, it's come to my attention recently that she's expecting."

"What?" My mother chirped.

"Wait. Wait. Wait!" Mehki waved a hand in the air. "Poppy, you be getting ass like that?"

"Mehki!" my mother scolded in a grunt.

"Ki."

"Sir?"

"Chill."

Exhaling loudly, he used his fingers and thumb to create a fist, intimating he was cutting off the wild energy. "Yes, sir."

After a beat, I continued. "I'm only sharing this because of the complexity of the situation."

"What? You having a baby?"

"We don't know that. I won't know for sure until we do a paternity test," I explained. "It's complex because when I learned of her pregnancy, I also learned she's Azmir Jacobs' in-law."

"Daaaaang! Poppy, that's messy!"

I shrugged. "It is."

"And what's Azmir saying about all of this?" my mother asked.

"Well, we haven't spoken much since we learned about the situation, which was the same night at the same time. We were all at an event."

"His party," Mehki surmised.

I nodded. "Yeah. And I'll be meeting with him about it. He's been out of the country, and I've been inundated with shit down in A.C."

"You think he's gonna fire you, Poppy?"

"Your father is the COO," mom reminded Mehki. "It's not that easy to get fired."

"Yeah, but it's possible. There are details I'm purposely leaving out because it doesn't need to be shared unless it needs to be shared. But he's not happy about it." I knew this because of how Jacobs and I parted ways that night. I knew the man, could follow his pulse. Azmir had been protective of his wife and family since he looked me up and began to slyly "screen" me for my role. The man was calculating. Hayden mentioned two days ago, when we met in the City, how she didn't tell Rayna about the prostitution lie. If that was true, perhaps my impending conversation with him wouldn't be as intense. "Either way, we'll be fine financially as a family. My purpose in being transparent is in case we have staff changes around here along with your personal detail." I expressed the last point to my mother in particular.

Security was supplied to me by *ADJ Enterprise*. Azmir had his assigned detail because of his status and former life. I had mine due to the nature of my work. It was essential to my job. I was the face of the enemies of *ADJ Enterprise*. My sleeves got rolled up when there was an issue. My combat team pulled up when there was a threat. Azmir may have been the commander, but I was the enforcer. With that role came risks of safety. Nothing mattered more to me than these two people at the table. They were my community. They reminded me of my humanity when I came home bruised from the latest war on behalf of *ADJ Enterprise*. I would never keep them in the dark about their security.

"Is that it?" Mehki asked, exhaling.

Leaning back in my chair, I considered his question. I'd shared more with Mehki than normal. Anytime I talked to him about women, or in his case "girls," it would be in past tense out of respect for his deceased mother. This reveal was different.

"Yeah, man. That's it."

Ki stood and picked up his plate. "Be easy, big homie. That baby ain't yours, ya heard?" He rounded the table, coming my way. Then he placed a hand on my shoulder. "You ain't messy, big homie. These chicks see a cat with money and exotic hair and its cha-ching ching. N'ah I mean?" Then he continued inside the house.

I took a deep breath. "If that kid could be serious for just a damn minute."

My mother tossed her napkin into her plate. "Maybe if you were more forthcoming, he'd understand the gravity of this situation, and would be serious for once."

I chuckled, kicking my jittery leg out beneath the table. "Forthcoming? Ma'am, isn't that what I just did? Isn't this behavior right up your alley?"

Mom scoffed. "You can't game a coder. You're telling us in the event our security company is going to change? Boy!" she mumbled, rolling her eyes.

Feeling tired as hell, I was in no condition to take on Dr. Nancy Patterson.

"What're you saying, Doc?" I yawned. "I'm simply preparing my family for a change that may or may not come."

"That's not why you shared. It's not what you did at all." She stood.

"Then why did I just spend minutes here laying out my personal fuck-up to my family?"

"Because there's a part of you—perhaps the tiniest part of you—that believes you're the father of that baby."

"No." I shook my head adamantly. "I'm not. If I thought so, I'd share that."

"No, you wouldn't." She stopped at the door. "Because in your mind, it would put a chink in your tough armor. It would expose your Achilles heel. Overachievers like you don't like that. You can't admit a weakness or imperfection every once in a while."

I turned to face her. "That's not true, Doc, and you know it."

"Tell yourself that as you go down a half a gallon of ice cream and finish off those crackers and banana peppers in there." She turned and walked inside the house.

FOURTEEN

June

Hayden

I switched weight on my hips, leaning onto the reception booth. Each time someone sauntered down the hall from behind the desk or breezed through the revolving lobby doors, my head whipped in full attention. On a determined mission, I'd been waiting for over twenty minutes this morning.

My phone rang, annoying the shit out of me.

"Hello?"

"Well, damn!" he laughed. "Work fucking with you already?"

I closed my eyes, further frustrated. "Something like that. Can I call you back? I'm in the middle of something."

"Well, I'm calling because I'm in Harlem. I was hoping to see you. Let's catch up. Maybe take you out for breakfast as an early lunch break or bring you a couple of bagels."

My eyes burst open. If Kenny was good for anything, it was always a decent meal and superb gossip. And in my current condition, it was difficult to turn one down. However, today was impossible. And until I told him about being pregnant, I had to endure these calls. Plus, now was not a good time. "I can't do either."

"Why not?"

"Because, Kenny, I'm not in Harlem. I'm in New Brunswick this morning." In my peripheral, I saw a small group of people ambling down the hall, toward the desk. *Fucking Adam Perry.* He was smiling goofily as a woman of Asian descent was messaging something he found humorous. "I've got to go. My meeting has just arrived."

"I'll be in the City until about six tonight. Call me if you want to hang—."

"Okay. Bye!" I charged over to Adam and crew, my heels clacking with each step until I was square in his face. "Mr. Perry."

Adam stopped his stride abruptly, his gray eyes blossoming as he attempted to recognize me. "Well, hello, Hayden! I can't believe—" He glanced around, thin lips spreading. "—the wind blew Harlem in! I was just on my way to a meeting, darling."

"Because you seemed to be too busy to return our calls." I jerked my head. "The deadline is approaching, and you know if smaller donors don't see names like *Johnson & Johnson* on our list of primary funders, they're liable to pull out."

Adam turned to his colleagues. "Give me a few minutes, will you?" On cue, they rounded me and continued across the lobby to another hall.

"I've been here for over twenty minutes. How long were you going to make me wait, Adam? I didn't know we'd turned contentious. Have I done something to offend you?"

"Honey..." He took me at the shoulder with one hand, guiding me near the floor-to-ceiling windows to the side for privacy as he swiped his slender nose with the other. "Listen. A lot of shit has been going on."

"Shit preventing you from just returning an email—"

"I'm freezing you out." Those gray irises sparkled as his expression stoned.

"What has *Christ Cares* done to deserve that? We've maintained a solid relationship for five years. We've remained above board—"

"It's not them. It's you."

"What about me?" I panicked. "What have I done?"

Adam sniffled, bringing a fist to his waist as he attempted to block off the energy of the lobby. "You're good, Hayden. Really good! Don't you want to get out of the private sector and come over to the big league? There's a position opening here. It's a sidekick role to mine. Do you know what I could do with a mind like yours, securing funding on this end?"

My chin dipped. "You're freezing out *Christ Cares* to get me to come to *J&J*? You'd do that to the small guy?"

"Oh, come on!" he whispered forcefully. "The church will find another grant writer."

"That's not right and you know it."

His eyes twinkled wickedly. "It's life. And don't be foolish." He began whispering again, "What're you bringing in over there anyway? Fifty—maybe fifty-five grand a year?"

"No. I earn well."

"The base for this role is ninety-three. That's ninety-three to one hundred and one. You're not making anywhere near ninety thousand a year and never will at *Christ Cares*. I swear I was going to call you this week. I've been working on this. You can start by September first."

I grabbed my belly. "I'm twenty weeks pregnant. I can't jump insurance plans."

His face spread in pure shock. "Holy shit. When did that happen?"

"Apparently, twenty weeks ago, Adam. So, as you can see, my jumping ship isn't possible."

"*Pssssst!*" He flipped a limp wrist in the air. "We can work around that. When's your due date?"

"November ninth."

"Your benefits would kick in by then, Hayden. Shit, you can negotiate to have them within thirty days of your start date. The deal would be pretty sweet!"

"And if I say 'no'? Will that mean a disruption in *Johnson & Johnson*'s relationship with *Christ Cares*?"

"*The Foundation* is loaded with requests for grants right now," was his confirmation.

"This is fucked up. What does this mean for my team? You know them. Shit. You love Mika! Or so we thought."

He spit out a dry chuckle. "Bring her along. We can work out something for my girl." Adam thought he was being charming.

With the pads of my index finger and thumb, I rubbed my eyelids. "I'm sorry." I sighed. "This bullshit was not on my bingo card this morning."

"Look. I've gotta go." He tapped my shoulder. "We'll be in touch. Think big, kid!"

Twisting my mouth, trying to process what the fuck had just happened, I made my way to the doors. My stomach grumbled in the parking lot while I made my way to my car. Steam shot from my head under the beaming sun. Once inside my car, I ignited the engine and pushed for a blast of coolness from the air-conditioner. Sighing, I sat back in the driver's seat with one question on my mind.

What's for pre-lunch?

I was hungry, having had only a few pieces of cutup fruit before hitting the road for New Brunswick. *B-Way Burger* had a breakfast menu, but I really needed to think of healthier options. There were a couple of restaurants in Harlem where I could do a high/low, which for me meant ordering both something good and bad for balance. Maybe a Lox bagel with fresh pineapples. Or—*ooooh!* Strawberries and blueberries—

My phone chirped.

+1(973)555-0980: *Morning. I was hoping to catch your next doctors appointment with you. If I'm not mistaken you're 20 weeks. I hear that's when the ultrasound picks up the sex of the baby easily. Send over the address date and time. I'll be there.*

"Shit!"

Reading the message with rapid speed, I leapt in my seat, accidentally dropping the phone.

ISHAAN

Pulling the lollipop from my mouth, I shook my head. "No," I responded to Munchie's rundown of another candidate for a security guard role.

My attention swiftly returned to the contract I was signing. There was actually a stack I'd put off for over a week and was finally combing through.

"Merkel Marks," she moved to the next while standing on the opposite side of my desk, holding a clipboard and remote control. Referring to the image on the big screen, she shared, "Twenty-four, two years of experience, former police officer, one arrest on record for felony assault."

"No."

"Well, are you even going to consider him first?" she lamented.

Now, with the lollipop wedged between my cheek and molars, I glanced up at her. "I have. Next."

"Why is he a 'no'?"

"I guarantee that assault charge is why he's off the police force, the tightest gang in America. And if they let his reckless ass go, he's trouble my ass don't need. Next."

I heard her deep sigh as I flipped the page of a contract I was currently reviewing.

"Maurice Holmes. Thirty-two. Martial arts phenom with notable armed combat decorations. Married without kids. Six dogs, two cats. No record."

"Move him on to the next phase."

My phone rang. Munchie's head whipped toward me at the desk where she stopped to pick up the handle. "I'm sure I told you we were not to be disturbed—"

My office door opened and in strolled the C.E.O. Munchie slammed the phone down. Then she straightened and cleared her throat. On approach to my desk, Azmir grinned.

"Munchie," he greeted her.

"Mr. Jacobs, sir. Pardon me. It's just..."

"No worries. I know you're the best at assisting and guarding Ishaan." He stood at the front of my desk. "Do you mind if the chiefs have a moment alone?"

Munchie's eyes swung over to me, and I gave her a nod. "Sure, Mr. Jacobs. Can I have the admins bring you anything?"

"I'm fine. I have a flight to catch." His attention roved over to me. "I believe Ish does, too."

"Of course." Munchie took off for the door.

"I've been awaiting this chat." I placed my pen down. "Should we have it over brown juice?"

"As tempting as that shit sounds, I don't think I need oil or any preamble for this. I can't lie; I'm still confounded as fuck about you hooking up with Hayden. I don't even know how that shit happened."

I sat back in my chair and stretched my arms out. He was right; soon I'd have to head over to the airport for my flight back east. "I'd rather not say."

"You're grown. I don't need to know. But it sounds casual as hell."

I nodded. "It was."

"And now it looks permanent." Azmir watched me closely.

"It can be." I scratched a brow, not wanting to discuss this shit, but knew I couldn't avoid it. He'd given me time since the blow up at his party over a week ago. I knew he'd catch up to me. I damn sure wasn't going to him.

Azmir moved to perch on my desk. "So..." He scratched beneath his bottom lip, taking a pause, likely to consider his words. "I've been in a situation like this before."

"Oh, word?" My brows lifted on my forehead.

"Yeah. With my ex. It was long and unnecessarily drawn out. I'd just met my wife and didn't need any shit from my past fuckin' up what I was trying to build with her. It wasn't the wisest decision I've made, but I waited until after my ex gave birth to do the paternity test. And Rayna..."

"Shit. You ain't even gotta say."

Azmir chuckled, but I could tell there was no humor behind it. "Yeah, man. Dark days. Anyway..." He exhaled. "...that was mad years ago. Technology is even better now. I don't know Hayden that well, but haven't heard anything making me believe she's..." He hesitated. "Well, that she's...immoral. Never heard about her being out there like that." Shaking his head, he shrugged. "And I won't ask. It's not something I really give a fuck about. But what I will say is she's family, and this shit feels...messy. I trust you'll do what you need to do to maintain a good-standing reputation as an executive leader at *ADJ Enterprise*."

He didn't know about the prostitution angle. At least, it didn't feel like it.

Slowly, I responded. "It's being addressed. In fact," I sighed before collecting the few contracts I had left to go. I'd finish them on the flight over. "I'm flying out to Jersey tonight. I have an obstetrician appointment tomorrow."

Azmir didn't say anything at first. He only stared at me. When I realized it was blatant, I returned the gaze.

"I'm addressing this shit very delicately, Patterson."

"And I appreciate it."

He chuckled, swiping his nose. "I know you, and you know me. Perhaps I'm getting old. I truly try to avoid trouble with those closest to me, but don't take my light tread as a sign of my indifference. You parked your shit too close to my home—"

"I get it. Jacobs, I swear I get it. I also appreciate your choice of soft words. Like you said, I know you. I fucked up. Okay." When I realized I had let my emotions slip, I took a deep breath. He was right:

A.D. and I, corporate suits and luxury business buildings aside, could both get to it. The unique thing about my boss was he was with the shits either way you called him. He could pay sharks to eat your ass up legally or he could box you to sleep with his hands. We shared that unique dichotomy. And while my money was nowhere near the length of his, I, too, was a wealthy man. I could leave *ADJ Enterprise* and not neglect a bill for a long time. But I enjoyed what I did. It was an honor to sit at his right side on the throne. "I'll make good on this. However it goes, you don't have to worry about this becoming more off-putting than it was the night you learned Hayden and I knew each other." I proffered my hand, closing the conversation.

Azmir took his time, but he eventually stood from my desk and took my hand for a firm shake. "Indeed, Patterson. Indeed." After I returned his succession with a nod, he bade, "Safe travels."

As he strolled out of my office, I called out, "You, too, Jacobs."

When the door was closed. I fell back into my seat.

Fuck!

love ∞ believe

Hayden

Walking into the doctor's office, I froze while holding the door.

He's here.

He's really here.

And he's early.

There, sitting in the waiting area, Ishaan was reading a pamphlet. My belly jerked again, similar to the way it did at Azmir's party, but even more intense today. Feeling awkward, I decided to ignore him and head over to the reception desk to check in.

As I stood waiting for the attention of one of the two girls, the hairs on the back of my neck rose, chilling my spine. The moment I made eye contact with the smiling brunette, I sputtered, "*Hey—*Hayden." I cleared my throat. "Hayden Washington here for my one o'clock with Dr. Brown."

She began typing on her keyboard. Seconds later, her beam returned. "Of course, Hayden. Have a seat. One of the girls will bring you back shortly."

I nodded my thanks since my tongue didn't want to cooperate this afternoon. Stiffly, I turned and tried not to look directly at him. But, damn it, something paranormal compelled my attention straight to the man. And *shit*. Ishaan's dark irises were directly on me. I caught his onceover before he stood.

"Hey..." His smile was blinding.

"Hey." I was all breath, no lungs.

He was so damn tall. So fucking fine, it all felt like a farce.

Then his mouth closed, robbing me of his gorgeously aligned teeth. But the smile in his eyes brightened while his devilish grin took over. "It's good to see you."

As I ambled toward him, his scent wrapped around me like a warm hug. But my wits had returned. "But under much more undesirable circumstances than the first two times you saw me."

With an expression of sympathy, pressing his lips together and cocking his head to the side, he reached for me with one hand. Taking it, I allowed him to direct me to the seat next to him. We both sat. Ishaan resumed reading the pamphlet.

"Oh. Multiple births." I read from the cover. Then I found myself rubbing my belly. "I don't need that bad juju."

"According to this, twins happen once in every two hundred fifty pregnancies. Triplets—once in ten thousand. And quadruplets occur once in every seven hundred thousand pregnancies. I think you're safe."

I sighed, eyes toward the reception booth. "Not necessarily. It's hereditary."

"Pardon me?" I felt the heat of his gaze on the side of my face.

"Twins run in my family. Fraternal."

"Damn."

"Yup. My great grandmother had multiple. Hell, even my cousins, Rayna and Sundryia."

"You're right. They do have twins," he mumbled with concern.

Then I turned to him. "You really don't have to do this. I'm still offering you a pass."

His head angled again. "And you know I cannot take it, Ms. Hayden."

"So, my connection to Azmir gives me V.I.P. attention?" My eyes rolled over to him.

"The fact that you shared your body with me earns you my full attention to see this thing through with you." His head dipped and lips pinched together. "The proximity to my boss is a secondary inspiration."

"Ms. Washington," the nurse announcing my name from the door closed the conversation.

For now...

I left my seat for the door then thought to turn around. Ishaan was still standing at his chair.

"You coming in for this part or nah?" I joked.

"Is it okay?" He rubbed his hairy chin.

"This is *the* part." I wanted to laugh. The man was too fine—too immense in presence to exude even an ounce of uncertainty.

I still remembered what his dick looked, felt, and tasted like as he sauntered my way. Ignoring that inappropriate fact, we followed behind the nurse who directed me to a room where she took my weight and temperature. Before she was done adding the information to my chart, Dr. Brown was knocking on the door while coming inside the exam room.

"Why, hello, my favorite grant writer," she chirped not so spiritedly.

"Hey, Dr. Brown."

She stopped in her tracks, eyes wide as hell behind her glasses. "And who do we have here?"

Ishaan stood and offered his hand.

"This is Ishaan, Dr. Brown. I told you he may be in attendance today." I tried keeping a formal tone.

"Ishaan Patterson, Dr. Brown," he droned. "It's a pleasure to meet you."

"The pleasure is all mine. Interesting you made this visit in particular. It is the one where we should clearly be able to see the gender of the baby." Her eyes on him were examining.

Dr. Brown liked what she saw. I couldn't blame her. He looked good as hell in a collared button up, solid slacks, and a casual style of sneakers appearing to be a premium designer. What was exposed of his arms were wiry with ink running from beneath the sleeve down to his hand. It reminded me of how his delicious, bubbled abdomen was ink-free.

When I glanced up to his face, Ishaan's eyes were on me. They were expectant. Seconds after gazing into his irises, he asked, "Do you?"

I blinked. "I'm sorry." My attention went to Dr. Brown. "Did I miss something?"

"The gender reveal. Is that something you two want to do today? Or do you not want to know?"

Dumfounded, my head rotated back over to Ishaan. "I haven't given it any thought. I…"

"Okay." Dr. Brown went over to the sink and began washing her hands. "Well, today I'll measure the baby's size, examine all the major organs, and get an idea of the amount of amniotic fluid in your uterus."

"Will you also check for multiple babies?" Ishaan asked, wide eyed.

I covered my mouth to control the burst of laughter upending my belly.

Rinsing her hands, Dr. Brown nodded cautiously then smiled. "Why, yes. We can look for more babies. Hayden shared with me her family's history of twins."

"Yeah. She just dropped that bomb on me today," he muttered with a grin while appearing shook at the same time.

Why? He didn't have to assume the responsibility of my fuck up. My body, my consequence, my problem.

"How have you been feeling lately?" Dr. Brown asked. "Increase in appetite?"

I considered that. "Not really. Pretty much the same. When it's time to eat, it's time to eat. Still eating weird things and combos."

"Headaches, heartburn, indigestion...leg cramps or swelling?" She tossed the damp paper towels into the trash then approached me. "Lie back, please."

"No. At least, I only think my midsection is swelling—"

"Whoa!" she chirped. "You've grown, woman!" She referred to my belly as I pulled my shirt up to my bra line, exposing it.

Although her physical reaction was less spirited than her words, it still left me feeling a little self-conscious. I found my attention creeping over to Ishaan. Once again, his eyes were on me, only this time they grazed over my pouch. The muscles around his eyes were relaxed, soft. Then his eyes swept up to mine, head unmoving. My belly jerked once. Then again. And then again.

"What was that?" His brow line tightened.

I turned my attention to Dr. Brown, who tucked a paper down under the elastic waist of my leggings to protect them and then picked up a tube of gel. "Why does my stomach jerk?"

"Has it been happening a lot?" She squeezed the tube over my belly, causing the warm, wet matter to splatter.

I shook my head. "It happened once at the top of this month. I thought it was the baby moving, but when it didn't happen again, I figured I was wrong. But since I've been here today, this is like the fourth time it's happened."

"Looks like your baby is kicking," she advised, placing the handle thingee on my stomach while studying the ultrasound screen. "What were you doing the first time you felt the baby kick?"

Stupidly, I glanced over at Ishaan. This time, his attention was on the screen. Then he turned to me.

"I...*uhhhh*..." I didn't know if I wanted to share all of that. This was all too awkward. "I was on the dance floor at a party." My words dripped slowly because that was when I, too, realized Ishaan had been present when the kicks occurred. Like now.

"Yup. The baby's kicking. Look at where the legs are positioned."

I squinted at the screen and saw a mass of something. It was possible for me to make out what could be a leg. The image looked like an alien.

"That's the femur portion of the leg." She informed as the screen quickly changed. "Here's the baby's profile. You see the mouth moving? I guess you have a singer and a dancer. Music industry, are you ready for your next superstar?" That made me smile. "The head is measuring well. Let me take a look at the organs," she spoke slowly. "While I'm checking, please make the call on the gender reveal in case it becomes really obvious we're dealing with a male child here."

I froze. I wasn't ready to make that call. The baby moved today. Before that, it was just a growing belly I'd been adjusting to. Ishaan being here had me flustered, my brain off kilter. I didn't want to share such an intimate experience with a stranger.

Then I felt the weight of his big hand on my arm. Ishaan leaned in. "Do you want to know?"

Now?

Today?

I shook my head, scraping my lip against my teeth, feeling so damn anxious.

"If you don't mind, I'd like to know." His voice was so tender.

"Why?" I whispered back as if Dr. Brown couldn't hear.

"Because we're trying out this buddy thing. Right? And as your bud, I find this fascinating." He stared me straight in the eyes.

But his tone didn't match his claim. Ishaan's delivery was too soft and sentimental. Did he think my life was an open book?

Like your legs back in February and March? Maybe...

I closed my eyes, feeling a nasty blend of anxiousness and shame.

"You mind if I record it?" Ishaan pushed. "I won't show you until you ask me."

Rolling my eyes behind my lids, I hissed. "Do what you must."

"As you can see, only one fetus can be detected," Dr. Brown

continued with her vocal guide through my uterus. "The baby's very close to the placenta. Do you see that?"

"Yeah. Is that the nose?" Ishaan asked, voice thick.

"Yup. And the fingers."

Things got quiet for a minute, and I refused to open my eyes. I didn't want to rush anything in the process. I may have no longer been in my "in the meantime" of deciding what I'd do about the pregnancy, but I'd evoke another ITM period to experience this at my own pace. Maybe I'd want to know the sex of the baby later on tonight, perhaps next month—or maybe not until it announced itself from my vaginal canal. I didn't know. But I didn't need to make that call now. This shit was moving too damn fast.

A strong, vibratory rumbling sounded from the back of Ishaan's throat. My eyes burst open, and I looked his way. With wide eyes, he peered at the screen.

"You see that?" Dr. Brown asked.

"*Eh*—I do." He blinked hard.

"Is everything okay?" Panic swelled in my lungs. "Something wrong with...it?"

His big, warm hand was at my arm. This time, he gently rubbed it.

"Nothing's wrong, mom. The baby wanted its gender revealed. I guess it's showing off for Mr. Patterson here."

My eyes burst wide, and head whipped over to Ishaan. Feeling my gape, he turned to me and winked. Ishaan didn't split his attention too long because he went back to the monitor. Suddenly, I felt left out. This was my body after all.

"Can I look now?"

"Give me a moment. I'll take a few pictures for your chart. Then, I'll go back up to the heart." She continued to rove the handlebar over my midsection. "Okay. It's safe to look now."

Yeah. But now, the alien view had returned. I waited and watched the last few minutes of the tour. When she was done, she handed me paper towels to wipe down my gelled midsection. I could feel Ishaan's gaze on me but ignored him.

As I cleaned myself, Dr. Brown put away her tool then asked, "Do you have questions for me?"

Again, I was flustered as hell. "No."

"You taking the prenatal vitamins?"

"The delicious horse pills?" I strained to sit up on the table. "Oh, sure."

"You're in your fifth month. You'll be done with them before you know it. Your tummy is officially here, I see. I would advise maternity clothing or at least something comfortable around your abdomen. Something you don't have to push down beneath it."

I wanted to roll my eyes. Instead, I muttered, "Duly noted."

"Okay." She pulled in a deep breath then walked over to the small desk in the corner near the computer. "As for you, Mr. Patterson." She picked up a file folder and opened it. "Hayden requested I discuss a bit of her testing history in your presence. As you know, by law, I cannot disclose this to you directly. However, understanding the uniqueness of this situation, I'm going to share it with you both." She sat down on her rolling stool and placed a document on an empty portion of the exam table next to me.

"She's tested for sexually transmitted diseases regularly, which can be noted here." Dr. Brown pointed to various years. "However, in February of this year, she was tested more than usual given..." She cleared her throat. "...her activities and exposure. Here is what she's been tested for. As you can see, it's the full gamut of sexually trans-mitted infections. Now, disclosing her testing activities does not prove who she's been with sexually or the frequency. It can, however, demonstrate the pattern of testing changed this past winter after your first encounter."

Ishaan followed her index finger and listened to Dr. Brown with patience.

"I appreciate this, Doc—and Hayden." He quickly thought to include me. "I know this is an unconventional situation we're in. But I hope it's understood, I'm in no way judging Hayden or requesting her to jump through hoops all because she's the gender between the two of us who holds physical proof of us being intimate. Although we engaged, she shouldn't be the only person under scrutiny." He used his long fingers to gesture himself. "I'm not being required to rundown such personal information, and that isn't fair." He peered at me. "I'm sorry for the invasion."

Defensively, I offered, "I just don't want you to think you're being trapped, or you had sex with a real prostitute, unknowingly."

His eyes softened and cheeks spread. "I don't think I need to remind you of your lack of acting skills."

I did roll my eyes this time.

"Okay," Dr. Brown brought us back on track. "Is there an issue of questionable paternity?"

Ishaan nodded. "I don't mean to be offensive, but of course, there is. Hayden and I are not married. Neither do we know each other personally...yet."

"Okay. Fair enough." Her head bounced up and down. "So, let me broach the subject of paternity testing. With today's technology, it can be done in utero."

"Really?" Ishaan asked with his chest.

"Yes. Really. It's called non-invasive prenatal paternity testing. The test is viable beginning at seven weeks. And, as you can see, Hayden is well beyond that."

I shook my head. "It's totally unnecessary. I'm not looking for a father for my child. I told you I wouldn't pursue you that way."

Ishaan's face darkened. "And I don't think you understand. You don't have a choice in the matter. If there's a possibility I have a child on the way, I will pursue the answer of paternity. There ain't a place on earth, heaven, or hell where I have a child and it's not cared for by me. That ain't V.I.P. treatment, Ms. Washington. That's Ishaan Patterson one-oh-one."

My skull tightened. I was angry but understood I couldn't lash out. Again, this shit was a lot to process.

Ishaan peered pointedly at Dr. Brown. "I'd like more information on that."

After a single, deep nod, she sighed, "Okay." Dr. Brown stood, gathering the papers inside the file folder and placing it close to me. "I'll have my girls get that information ready for you. It was a pleasure meeting you, Mr. Patterson."

Ishaan stood and offered his hand. "The pleasure was all mine. Thanks for this today. I'm hoping to see you at the next visit."

Next visit?

"Very well." My doctor smiled, taking a dramatic pause before verbally observing, "Your hair is gorgeous. It demonstrates your confidence, sir. Call if you need anything, Hayden," she offered before leaving us alone in the room.

As I scooted over the table to get down and straighten my clothes, Ishaan noted, "I heard your stomach growling. Wanna grab a bite?"

I could only gape at him.

He scoffed. "I know you don't know me. I'm a straightforward type of guy. Don't take shit I say personal unless I dish it that way."

"This *is* personal." I grabbed my belly. "Ain't shit about this not personal. I don't even know you." Before I knew it, my body trembled. Tears clouded my sight before racing down my face. Embarrassed, I leaped around, turning my back to him.

While struggling to get control of my emotions, I felt two hands on either side of my shoulders.

"We'll get through this," he droned over my head. "I swear."

FIFTEEN

June

ISHAAN

The waitress began delivering entrées from the tray balanced on her arm. "Loaded beef nachos." She placed the toppled plate in front of Hayden. "And the pollo asado con frijoles y arroz."

"Thank you," I returned.

"Okay. Anything else I can get you?"

Hayden shook her head, still emotional from earlier at her doctor's office.

"That'll be all. Thanks."

Hayden pulled out a bottle of hand sanitizer and squirted some

239

into her palm. "You peeped how she spoke my dish in English, but yours in Spanish?" She rolled her eyes.

Ignoring her accurate accusation, I reached over the table with my hand out to prompt her to share the hand sanitizer. After seconds of hesitation, she did.

"You know I'm not trying to be your enemy here."

"I never said you were."

I rubbed my hands together, watching her do the same. Hayden wouldn't look at me. In fact, I was surprised she agreed to lunch.

"I don't know," I mumbled picking up my fork. "It's the vibes I'm picking up."

"Again, you don't know me." She bit into a stacked nacho.

"I'd like to change that."

"By showing up to every O.B. visit, knowing you don't believe the baby's yours?"

"Would you rather I ignore your pregnancy?"

She took a deep breath, gazing somewhere behind me in midair. "Maybe. You do know Azmir is an in-law, not blood. Right? You're not obligated to do this."

I chewed my food. "I own a floating fleet."

She glanced up at me. "A what?"

"A floating fleet, also known as a fleet of private planes. It's small." I shrugged. "I operate out of seven major locations across the country. It's been about five years since we've been successfully up and running. I also have a private security company." I pushed my food around on my plate. "High-profile people call us up for protection at events and such."

"Why are you sharing this?"

I continued eating. "Because this is how two people begin to get to know each other." When she rolled her eyes. "I'm not asking to be your BFF. I'm simply trying to make the best of an unexpected situation. Until we find out the paternity, why can't we pursue civility?"

"How can civility be in question when the purity of my uterus is the subject matter? It's not an easy conversation to have for a woman."

"So, let me ask you this: do you believe the baby is mine?"

"I know how and when I got pregnant, Ishaan."

Okay...

"Was it back in February?"

"I think we both know this after visiting my doctor."

"And were you with a man other than me during the month of February?"

Hayden didn't respond right away. She ate more nachos, avoiding eye-contact. And *shit*. She was beautiful. A redbone with jet-black hair parted in the center of her crown, falling down past her shoulders. Her makeup was minimal today. High, defined cheekbones with long, dark lashes, and lip gloss glistening her lips. The top was flat and the bottom lip round. That Dr. Brown was right. Hayden's stomach had really popped out. It was even more pronounced since I'd run into her at Jacobs' party just a couple of weeks ago. But she was still slender in the shoulders and face.

"No."

"So, you believe the baby's mine." That wasn't a question.

"No. I believe the baby is mine. I made a rash decision, and the consequence is mine."

"Twice." I corrected. "You made that decision on two different occasions." I continued to eat.

Damn. I'm an asshole...

I couldn't help it. I knew people. Hayden, here *with her sexy ass*, was fighting for a steel wall to be between us. She was embarrassed. Unlike a decent sex worker, she was self-aware and self-conscious of her risqué behavior. Prostitutes I'd encountered at work didn't give a fuck about their latest herpes diagnosis or recent trip to the chop shop for an abortion. Shit. They'll disclose their john count for the night without an ounce of shame or guilt. The only thing they wouldn't whisper a word about was the money they collected or earned for the day. That was not this woman sitting across from me.

"Why talk about the companies you own specifically?" she asked just before biting into another nacho.

"To demonstrate my earnings beyond my role at *ADJ Enterprise*. I'm not making attempts here from fear of losing my job. In fact, I wouldn't lose my job if I didn't act responsibly. I'd simply lose the respect Azmir has for me. Losing my job is a far more complicated task."

"That's what you made me believe last week."

"It's called humility." I smiled. "But I'm not under any obligation to do shit I don't wanna do."

"So, what do you want?" she asked while chomping down on her food.

"To lessen the tension."

Rolling her eyes, she mumbled, "What tension?"

Placing my fork onto my plate, I left my side of the booth and slid into hers. Hayden sprang in her seat, eyes ballooned. Ignoring her natural response to my abrupt action, I reached for her neck, gripping the muscle connecting the back of her skull to the spine. I kneaded even deeper when I realized how tight she was. Her wild eyes scanned the area around us, revealing her unease at being touched intimately in public.

"You're so fuckin' tight," I croaked.

That's when her eyes closed then squeezed with emotion. "I'm so fucking stressed."

"*Shhhhh...*" I urged her, loosening the muscle.

In less than two minutes, Hayden's head fell forward. She was allowing my touch.

"Do you want to take the paternity test?" she mumbled.

"Of course, but I'm not rushing you."

"You should."

"Why?"

When Hayden wouldn't reply right away, I moved on to the opposite shoulder. "How old are you?"

"Twenty-nine."

"Interesting."

"Why?"

"Because I'm thirty-seven."

Her head shot up and Hayden studied my face. "Is that bad?"

"What?"

"That you're eight years older than me."

"Why would it be?"

Her eyes fell, expressing a lack of security. "Well... You know how they rag on older men/younger women relationships. Not that we have one or will. I'm just saying..."

I chuckled. "I think that's more of your generation than mine. Plus, I'm not old."

"I wouldn't have guessed your age."

"Because I'm not old."

"You're an old millennial."

"And you're a younger one." I caught a short groan leave her throat. "A very tense one."

"You must have a girlfriend or a wife."

I wanted to laugh again but knew it would kill her relaxation. "What makes you assume that?"

"Because you're too good at this."

"Thanks. But you're wrong about both. What about you? You have a man?"

I regretted that question as soon as it left my fucking mouth.

Hayden's head popped up. "So, now I'm a whore and a cheater?"

I'd ruined our ceasefire.

Taking a deep breath, I withdrew my hand. "Your food's getting cold. Excuse me." I scooted off the bench and returned to my side of the table to finish my food.

"So, you're a grant writer?"

Her face stoned. "How do you know?"

"Easy." I snickered. "I heard Dr. Brown address you as her favorite grant writer."

"Oh." She exhaled. "I wrote a small grant for her office once. No big deal."

"How long have you been in the industry?"

"Almost five years."

"Did you go to school?" As I ate, I measured her body language against her delivery.

Hayden nodded. "*Kean* and *Rutgers*."

"Bachelors and masters?"

Hayden still didn't want to look at me as she chomped on nachos.

"A double-bachelor's degree from *Kean University*, and two masters' from *Rutgers*."

"All that needed for a grant writer?"

She shook her head again. "I have a few certifications for that."

I couldn't help myself. Sitting back in the booth, I laughed.

With her top lip curled and eyes squinted, she asked, "What's so funny?"

I grabbed my belly. "I met you at a *Panther's* event. You were a damn chatty patty with my peers. I peeped it but didn't get alarmed. You made me feel like you were a fish out of water. Now, I see they were more of your peers than mine with your hyper-educated ass."

"Why do you say that?"

"Because I never finished *BSU*. Remember?"

Instantly, her face warmed, eyes shifted, and lips pushed together before she busted out laughing. That made me crack the hell up all over again. Although the shared humor was short-lived, it was cool to disarm Hayden. Her pout was cute, but her laughter was a trick I wanted to pull off over and over again. In less than a minute, we returned to our food.

"Well, education isn't everything," Hayden murmured, still not giving me full eye contact. "You seem to have turned out well...considering your many jobs and businesses." She was still pouting, but trying to come out of her funk, it seemed.

"I've done well. My parents were educated. They raised me well. Sent me to the best schools—the *Ellis Academy* accelerated institutions. They invested in my basketball talent. I owe them financial independence at the very least." It was all true. But I wasn't done pulling information out of her. "Have you spoken to your parents about this? What has your father said?"

Chewing, she shook her head then swallowed her food. "I told my mother. She's..." She rolled her eyes, and I could instantly feel sadness emitting from her. "...still adjusting, I guess. It's not something I'm tripping over. Like I said: my deed, my circumstance."

"And your father?" I wanted to know what male energy influenced her.

"No." And that was it.

"Where are you from?" I forked the last of my food.

"Passaic."

"Is that where you live now?"

Swallowing, she shook her head. "I live in Paterson."

"How long have you been there?"

"A few years. I rented from my cousin for a while until I closed on my own place in April."

"Congratulations."

"Thanks."

"Do you have a support system?"

Hayden hesitated. "Of course, I do."

"Who?"

Her head rolled, expressing discomfit before she blurted, "My cousins."

"Oh. Okay." I nodded, not sure if I believed her. "That's cool."

I'd pushed her. I didn't know Hayden at all but knew enough about people to know she'd been emotionally taxed in my presence today. Her visit to the doctor would likely have been easier on her if I'd not been there. I had no damn regrets but understood the invasion of her privacy. My string of "investigative" questions didn't help either. It was time to give her space from me. She'd need it because, until we learned the paternity of her baby, I'd be around.

Done with my food, I decided to check my phones. There were three. I'd silenced them all, something I never did unless I had them laid out on a table in my face. This afternoon, I decided to turn off the world to tap into Hayden's. I didn't fully trust her and needed to attempt to get to know more about her than what was presented in a file.

Shit...

I'd received a gamut of fucking emails pointing to a severe problem on *Red's Island* with the *MC2* gang. Munchie had been freaking the fuck out based on her last text sent two minutes ago.

Munchie: *Where the fuck are you? Code fucking 10!*

I had to go. Now.

Remaining calm, I reached across the table for Hayden's free hand. "I'd like to support you as much as you need."

Her lips parted. "What do you expect to come out of this?"

"If we conceived together back in February, my answer is 'the start of the best partnership we can provide a kid.' If the baby turns out not to be mine, the answer is 'to show you humanity beyond having had your delicious body.'"

She squeezed my hand before turning her head to hide her face as she cried.

"I'm gonna get back to work now. I know me hanging out with you has overwhelmed you. But I'd like to do it again. You have my number. Call or text."

Sniffling, she nodded. I let go of her then pulled two bills from my pocket and placed them on the table before leaving.

Hayden

Mika gasped, eyes as wide as saucers.

"That fuckin' prick!" Lex grumbled.

"Boss lady!" Mika cried.

My hand went into the air. "Well, in this instance, she's playing the right role because...fuck him. He's going to freeze us out for no reason!"

"Oh, he has his reasons." Lex folded her arms beneath her breasts. "That's so fuckin' unethical it's not even funny."

"I thought Adam Perry was so cool," Mika sighed. "I thought he was my guy."

It had been four days since I'd visited Adam down in New Brunswick. I waited until Lex returned from her vacation to break the news to her and Mika. When she got in this morning, I could tell she was busy fighting through the things which needed her attention ASAP. When her assistant told me she had a few minutes to meet, I asked both Lex and Mika to my office to break the news.

"If *Johnson & Johnson* withdraw their funding from us, it can put us at risk of other donors backing out as well." Mika smacked her face. "How did I miss this about that white man?"

"Well, I'm going to make sure his bosses know about him," Lex vowed nastily.

"What are we gonna do, boss lady?" Mika asked as I wiggled my pen between my fingers, having the top tap rhythmically on my desk.

That was the million-dollar question. It was my turn to collapse my face into my hand. I couldn't overdo it thanks to my makeup and lashes. "I haven't had the full capacity of my mind to think about it yet."

"Baby brain?" Lex guessed.

Exhaling, I admitted, "Kind of. This is week twenty."

Lex pulled in a breath. "You find out for real, for real what you're having! Is your appointment today?"

"It was yesterday." Why did I feel uneasy about discussing this?

When I chanced a glance over to Mika, I was reminded why. Her attention was below at her wrestling fingers on her lap.

"Oh!" Lex clapped her hands then peered down to a sitting Mika to join her choir. Mika didn't. "What's inside the oven, girl? Do spill!"

A feather stroked my spine, and I shivered at the memory. I twisted my lips before admitting, "I don't know if I want to know."

"Awwww!" Lex swiped loose strands of wooly hair over her shoulder. "Why?"

Because I feel safe in an "in the meantime" bubble and knowing would expose me to a new level of feeling fucked up about the stupid shit I'd gotten myself into.

A cheesy ass smile opened on my face. "It's all happening too fast, I guess."

"I understand." Lex offered a wry smile.

A rap sounded. At the doorframe, Eduardo appeared, craning his neck inside. "There's a delivery here."

"For who?"

"You, ma'am." Eduardo moved into the frame more, offering room for an older, silver-haired gentleman with the most perfectly arched brows to come into view. He carried a huge ass *Neiman Marcus* shopping bag.

He smiled at all three of us in the room. "Delivery for Hayden Washington."

"She's right here," Mika instructed while pointing my way.

Lex asked, "Who's this coming from?"

As he traveled inside my tight box of an office space, his beam never faltered. "I'm Nash from *Neiman Marcus*. I was instructed to deliver this to you. There's a correspondence card inside." I received the heavy ass bag from him. "Have a wonderful day." Then he turned to leave.

"Open it," Lex demanded.

Mika agreed. "Yeah!"

"If it's from that damn Adam Perry, I'm pulling up on his ass in New Brunswick today!" Lex hissed.

There was a card inside. I pulled it out and placed it on my desk. Then I went for the bright yellowish-orange box inside, struggling to lift it in the air.

"Damn," Lex spit out.

"Is that *Fendi*?" Mika asked with obvious incredulity.

Quietly, I removed the lid then grabbed the dust bag holding the mystery item. By the feel of the object inside, beneath layers of tissue paper, I could tell it was a bag of sorts. After sitting it on the desk, I ripped through the black paper. It was a *Fendi* bag for sure.

"Why would someone send me a big ass bag?"

Fendi or not, I didn't get it.

"It's a baby bag, Hayden." Lex lifted it from the desk. "You see the different compartments for bottles, handy-wipes, and stuff like that?" She modeled the bag. "I had a *Gucci* one for my girls. A gift from their la-di-da father. Now, we wouldn't be caught dead in *Gucci*."

Damn...

Okay.

I moved on to the envelope. Inside was a card with a typed

message. As soon as I opened it, a gift card and receipt slipped out, falling to the floor.

"Tell me it's from that Adam!" Lex was serious as hell. If I wasn't so curious, I'd laugh while picking them up.

Boo-baby, I know yesterday was a lot. And in the spirit of owning our "circumstances," I thought a great gesture would be to help you look forward. Your tomorrow is bright. You have something wonderful to look forward to. Dr. Brown suggested you start wearing maternity clothes. Call me. Maybe I can be your hype man while shopping.
I.P.

"*I.P.*," I whispered, low-key smitten.

"How much is the gift card for?" Lex demanded again. "That's how many lashes I'll give his pink ass."

I opened the receipt. It was for fifteen hundred dollars.

Peering over to Lex, I finally answered, "It's not Adam. It's..." I reached for my belly, mouth twisting. "It's...*ummm...*"

"Excuse me." Mika jumped to her feet. "I forgot about a call I was supposed to make before noon." Then she scurried out of my office, cutting an immediate right instead of a left where her cubicle was located.

"What the hell was that about?" Lex whispered while putting the bag on my desk.

Tears welled in my eyes, not having much to do with Mika, per se. "Excuse my French, boss lady, but life can feel so fucking blue it crushes your lungs."

The tears escaped.

Damn!

Ishaan

"Mr. Patterson, I need a few more days," the commissioner of police of *Red's Island* begged with a modest accent. "I've been in contact with a relative of Eli. I'm going to request a meeting with him tomorrow. My men are working out those details now."

Peering through nighttime goggles into the *MC2* gang's village where Eli, all of his crew, and their kind lived, I chuckled, "Right now? At four in the morning, Commissioner?"

"*Ye*—well... You know, sir, the hour is indecent, but given the sensitivity of the matter, my team has been working round the clock. There will be a search crew out in two hours to recover the Brucker kid."

Behind me, Lynn whispered, "I see Kell. He's motioning he has eyes on Eli. The target's good."

It was, indeed, four in the morning on *Red's Island*. One of Eli's top-ranking gang members kidnapped a nineteen-year-old guest of the *Sun-Bronzed Maroon Resort*. His father, a wealthy banker from Switzerland, reported him missing the night I'd flown from Vegas to Jersey to attend Hayden's obstetrician visit.

The Bruckers, along with other exclusive guests, had been invited to stay at *Sun-Bronzed Maroon* to experience the amenities without cost. It was a marketing ploy regularly used as we'd been developing a reputation in the resort and entertainment industry. Apparently, the younger Brucker had been a rebellious kid and decided to leave the resort to find drugs. One of the gang members encountered him. The *MC2* gang decided to abduct him for ransom. The dumb fucks contacted the *Sun-Bronzed Maroon Resort* to make their wishes known.

I'd landed eighteen hours ago, measured the predicament, assembled and strategized with my team, then finalized a plan of action. One of the first things I did before landing on the island was contact the commissioner of police. I allowed him to think he was offering a solution. Predictably, it was passive, which landed me here in *Port Tesce* on *Red's Island* during the resting hours of the morning.

Seeing Carver at a shed, giving the signal that he'd located Brucker, I alerted the crew in the bullet-proof van, also known as our combat home. "In two hours, the Brucker kid could be dead, Commissioner."

I gave my team a finger motion to begin engagement, and, within seconds, Lynn announced, "Go time!" into the van and walkie-talkie.

Two men discharged from the van. From my nighttime binoculars, I could see our other combat unit rushing into the village. My crew announced our descension, guns blazed.

Hearing the shouting, the commissioner questioned, "What is that ruckus I hear, Mr. Patterson?"

I stalled him, keeping an eye on Carver, who had just burst through the shed where Brucker was being held hostage.

"That, Commissioner...," I spoke very slowly, making sure to maintain my eagle eye on the operation. "...is what we do when there's been a breach in the agreement Mr. Jacobs set up with law enforcement and the scoundrels before investing in your land. We're bringing you tourism and millions in revenue—a means to develop wealth for your families and to strengthen your government. We've already provided generous means to increase your infrastructure—employing hundreds of your residents."

Fuck...

I paused at the sight of several people—older and younger—male and female—scurry out of the small hut as bullets riddled the sky. Women screamed in terror, running out of their homes, some half naked. Men popped from hut doors with machetes, bats, and other weapons of choice. None traveled far. Some were struck with bullets to the head and others to the chest. The village of about fifteen shacks, huts, and trailers was filled with unredeemable miscreants. *Port Tesce* was the most vile and dangerous underbelly of the island, and it was lit up like the fourth of fucking July with blood splattering everywhere.

"The kidnapping caused this commotion, Commissioner." I did

my final round of observing the shooting points of my team. Everything seemed copasetic.

This had to be done. Eli proved it with the kidnapping. Quickly, the disruption had begun. However, only one thing rang alarming to me: the motherfuckers had imprisoned more than the Brucker kid.

"*Eh-eh*—Mr. Patterson, what exactly is going on?" Panic rang out in his inquiry.

Through the radio, Kell announced he had Eli and asked if it was safe to walk him out. When Krys confirmed the area was secured, I left my station, grabbed my *Barrett REC7*, and hopped out of the van. While the commissioner remained on the line in my ear, Lynn followed me.

"So, what I was saying, Commissioner, is it's unfortunate that after the years of negotiating and laying out terms of law enforcement, crime, and order as a result of *ADJ Enterprise* bringing a multi-million-dollar business to this island—" As I spoke loudly, under the last of the gunplay, Kell was approaching me, escorting Eli with his hands over his head. "—all we asked for was help from the respectable leaders here. Leaders from government to the street. We even took out the trash for smaller gangs both you, Commissioner, and Eli here declared as difficult and less likely to get on board."

Kell pushed Eli to his knees in front of me. His long, thick locs were covered with a layer of white matter, likely from his seizing. His eyes were red from the odd hour, lips curled into an evil sneer.

The Commissioner sputtered in my headpiece, "*Bah*—but Mr. Patterson, there was no breech on the government's part—"

"There is when you take too long to cut the snake at the head." Holding my rifle over my shoulder, I bent to get on eye level with Eli, seeing his sneer deepen. "Mr. Jacobs has been clear and generous. He's been a lot of things. However, one thing the man isn't, is a liar." I stood and gave Kell the nod to proceed.

Turning away to head back to the van, and almost in slow motion, I caught the sight of a wailing toddler being carried off by one of my men, Tyler. A few feet away, a pregnant woman with the most beautiful locs I'd ever seen falling past her ass was tottering to a different destination by my girl, Krys. She looked to be ready to deliver at any second now while screaming obscenities in her native tongue. I could've felt concern about her condition; however, I kept one thing in mind since making the decision to annihilate this small town. Everyone here, with the exception of hostages and children, decided to be in the most dangerous neighborhoods of the island. They couldn't be spared.

My mind immediately went to my "predicament" back in the U.S.

Before I could dwell on it, I heard **POP, POP, POP, POP!**

Still in motion, I turned to see Eli's lifeless body face down in the dirt.

"Now that our class clown has been eliminated, let's revisit the agreement, Commissioner."

"Mr. Patterson," he choked out.

Sixteen

July

Hayden

After pushing a saltine cracker topped with banana peppers into my mouth, I exhaled with closed eyes.

Damn.

So damn delicious...

Sitting up straight with crossed legs in my bed, I gazed around my bedroom. I had lit candles around the apartment. They say "pregnancy nose" is a real thing, but since yesterday, I'd been smelling a foul odor. *This, though...* This one symptom of my pregnancy cures all. I chomped on my favorite snack.

My phone rang. When I saw the name of the caller, I thought to retract my claim.

"Hey, Ma."

"Oh. You answer this time?" When I didn't reply, she let go of a long breath. "What did I do, Hayden? What did I say to make you not want to speak to me? Why am I feeling shut out? Did you expect me to scream congratulations about having a baby?"

My brows lifted. "That's a thought."

"You didn't give me a chance, really. Did you even think to realize you haven't even been dating anyone to get pregnant by? Or at least, you haven't told me about anyone you've been dating."

"Does that matter? I'm twenty-nine, not nineteen. I'm an independent adult. What is wrong with me having a child right now?"

"You don't have a husband."

"Neither did you."

"Which made it so hard for me, girl!" she shouted into the phone. "You don't think that's the first thing I think about when my single daughter ups and buys a house—in Paterson, of all places—to live in the basement then come to me weeks later saying she's pregnant? Was it random, Hayden?" Her inflection changed as she thought out loud, "It had to be. You haven't mentioned a man to me since Raymond."

Raymond?

Ewwwww!

I rubbed my lips together. "Ma."

"Yes!"

"What were you hoping to gain from this conversation?"

"For you to simply speak to me, Hayden. I haven't heard from you since you stormed out of my place when Uncle Billy came out the room!"

The sound of his name. She spoke it with reverence and innocence, making me cringe.

"Well, I think you've accomplished that. I need to go now. I'm working on something important, and it's already late."

"Well, can you call me tomorrow so we can hash all this out? You're an adult, Hayden. It's time for you to act like one. Communicate how you feel. I'm your mother. I'm not your friend. I'm here to help you make the best decisions in life."

Closing my eyes, I pressed my lips together, trying to suppress the desire to go off. "Thanks, Ma."

She sucked her teeth. "Goodnight, Hayden!"

She killed the line, and instantly, my scalp began to loosen from the tensioned grip that had begun when she spoke her first word. I wanted to cry but I also felt the urge to scream. Shaking my head, I quickly made myself another loaded cracker, going to the saucer on my lap. After stuffing my face, the big shopping bag on the floor caught my attention. It had been sitting there since Friday when I received it at work. The memory of it caused me to look down at my bare belly beneath my breasts caged by a bra.

"Do you have a support system?"

"Of course, I do."

I'd lied to that man.

Then I picked up my phone.

ISHAAN

Standing at the conference table in one of the boardrooms at the *Sun-Bronzed Maroon Resort,* I spoke to Jacobs on a screen.

"Fatalities?" he asked, flipping through paperwork in his office in Long Beach, California.

"We're estimating less than twenty-five," I answered.

His head popped up, face expressing shock. "You don't have an exact number? Does the commissioner?"

"There isn't much left of the village. It was set ablaze once we wrapped."

His chin dipped and brows hiked. "Before the police arrived?"

"Yes, sir."

I had his full attention now. "Casualties?"

I shrugged. "Not much. Hines suffered a nasty cut from a machete to the arm. Jones has a bullet graze to the shoulder. But that's pretty much it. They weren't expecting us."

Finally, his brow line jumped as he sat back in his office chair, tongue pushing into his molars. "Well..." He tossed his hand. "We made the terms clear to the government, law enforcement, community, and the nefarious subset. Crime affecting those associated with the *Sun-Bronzed Maroon Resort* won't be tolerated. I know how rigid you are about adhering to the rules." Shaking his head, he mumbled, "That fuckin' Eli couldn't even wait until the grand opening to show his hand."

I shrugged with my forehead. "We had to make an example out of *MC2*. What's left of them now understands who we are."

My phone rang. Instantly, a sensation swelled in my brain. "Jacobs, I gotta take this. I'll hit you up when I have more of an update."

He nodded before muttering, "Indeed."

The screen had gone dark by the time I answered. "Hey."

"Heey," she breathed into the phone, kind of sounding as though she was laughing.

"Everything good?"

This time, Hayden did giggle. "Yes, Ishaan. 'Everything good.'" She teased me. "I wanted to say thanks for the delivery."

Silently letting go of a breath I didn't know I'd been holding, I slipped into one of the rolling seats at the conference table. The problem was, as quiet as my expression of relief may had been to Hayden, Munchie, across the big ass room, whipped her head my way. Her face was tight with curiosity at my sudden lax display.

Decidedly, I ignored her. "That was two days ago. You're just now saying thanks?"

Hayden didn't speak right away. "I'm sorry." Her inflections revealed her guilt. "I've been..."

"Nah. It's all good. I'm just fuckin' with you, Hayden." That shit was funny to me. That was until I found Munchie staring at me again. With all the people coming in and out with updates on the *Port Tesce* takedown, she had time to check for me? Ignoring her was easy when Hayden was the cause. I could use the distraction. The past few days had been heavy. "It's good to hear from you. And you're very welcome. When are we going shopping?"

I knew she wouldn't take me up on the invitation but thought to throw it out there.

"That's the other reason I'm calling. When are you available?"

My head reared back. Not expecting that, I tried to think about my upcoming schedule. But it didn't matter; the shit was impossible. "When did you have in mind?"

"*Ummm...*" She stalled. "I'm free on Tuesday after work."

"Then Tuesday it is."

There was another pause before Hayden asked, "Is it that easy? Can't be!"

"What's that?"

"Getting time on a COO's schedule. I have an idea of how busy Azmir is. You're really giving me V.I.P. treatment here."

"I'm not Azmir, Hayden. And yes, I'm good with making you a priority."

I have no damn idea why...

I could hear her pull in a deep breath. "Okay. Tuesday it is."

I scoffed. "Can't wait."

"Aye. Be careful with me," she warned playfully, childlike. "I'm a good time."

I smiled slowly and broadly. "Oh, I know. You forget that?"

She spit out a hard guffaw. "Bye, Ishaan!"

"Bye."

Hayden

I toed out of the dressing room holding the polka dot, babydoll dress at the sides. Across, in the lounge area lined by long mirrors, Ishaan's thick and neatly woven hair could be seen. His head lifted from his laptop then brows raised.

"*Daaaaamn*, that's cute! See! I was right. Right? It may look big on the rack, but once you put it on and fill it out, you see it fits."

A grin of embarrassment tickled my mouth, and I rolled my eyes. "Yeah. You were right." I examined myself in a nearby mirror, grateful not to have to share it with anyone, compliments of Mr. Ishaan Patterson. I still couldn't believe he'd arranged all of this. When he picked me up at my place in a damn *Audi R8*, I had no idea he'd arranged a private shopping experience here at *Neiman Marcus* in *Garden State Plaza Mall*. It came with two shopping assistants who walked the racks with me to pick out pieces and who'd run out to get different sizes and accessories. This was the obscure man with the *Richard Mille* I'd encountered in Vegas who'd paid me fifteen thousand dollars for one night at my body. I should have known. "I like this a lot."

"You can rock that at your baby shower."

I froze. Instantly, I found myself in a daze.

A baby shower?

"Did I say something wrong?" he droned from across the room.

Stammered, I admitted, "I haven't even thought of a shower."

"You're five months pregnant...twenty-one weeks. I mean... You have time."

I smiled. "You talk like you have so much experience at this."

His eyes widened. "At this?" He pointed to my midsection. "No." Ishaan scoffed. "Nah. Not at all. This," he tried whispering. "...ain't my M.O. I thought women planned shit like this as little girls. You know. Like your weddings and the names of your five kids and two dogs."

I hummed, thinking. "I don't think I've ever planned any of those things."

"Then what was your imagination like as a young girl?"

With a shrug, I answered, "Survival."

"That's heavy for a double master's-prepared achiever."

I winked. "A double bachelor's, too." Ishaan's head tossed back, and he laughed. "Okay. I think I'm a bit over my budget at this point. Let's settle this bill finally." I knew I'd have to shell out a couple of hundred dollars at this point. It was all good, though.

Today had been unexpectedly fun. When I thought Ishaan would be impatient and awkward—as I was, at first—he turned out to be energetic, optimistic, and an exceptionally patient cheerleader. He didn't "pick out" much. Once we arrived, we were shown to the dressing room where Ishaan parked himself, setting up his laptop to work. The shopping assistants and I went out into the maternity section and selected pants, skirts, shirts, and dresses.

When we returned to the dressing room, and I walked out to model the pieces we picked out, Ishaan expressed his opinions, which were mostly positive. The only critiques were about the clothes, never my body. The way he'd look at me belied his "friendship" proposal. The man was attracted to me. It was clear. The fact was also unsafe because I was still very much attracted to him, too.

Like now, as he examined me as I did myself in the mirror, Ishaan's jaw twisted, exposing those big, white, beautifully aligned teeth. From the mirror, I could see him. His eyes were low on my toes, and then climbed up to my ass hidden by the silk-like material of the dress.

I turned on my heel. "I guess we're done!"

Those dark eyes lifted to my face. "What about swimwear?"

"Swimwear? For what?"

"It's the summer. Don't you go swimming?"

I pushed my lips out, expressing incredulity. "I work."

"And that's it? How many jobs do you have?"

I grabbed my belly and laughed. "Unlike you, only one." That shit was hilarious, forcing me to cover my mouth. When I opened my eyes,

I saw Ishaan was taking pictures of me with his phone. "What are you doing?" I couldn't straighten the muscles in my face.

"Documenting your journey. You should laugh more often."

"How do you know I don't laugh?"

"Back to the swimwear. You have time to find some?"

He totally ignored my question. And I let him. "You're encroaching on my dinner time."

"I can take care of that for you."

"I can take care of it myself, Mr. Patterson. But I think we've exceeded the amount of the gift card. Plus, I don't want to waste money on things I won't wear."

His face wrinkled. "It's July and you haven't been swimming yet?"

"No."

"That's sad. And you don't think you'll go swimming at all this summer?"

My eyes rolled up then down. "No."

"We need to do something about that, Hayden."

I laughed. He was cute. "We? I'm fine, Ishaan. I know I'm unexpectedly and unconventionally pregnant and I work like a dog. And I don't have any plans to vacation or go swimming this summer, but I'm not suicidal. I swear."

He closed his laptop and stood. "Pick out a few pieces. You don't even have to try them on. I have a call to make. I'll meet you out front." He winked.

The guy actually winked, and it was so fucking sexy. I couldn't help watching his delicious ass gait as he left the lounge.

I stirred the straw in my glass when I asked, "Are you single?"

Ishaan chuckled, holding the dessert menu across the table from me. "I guess that's a fair question to ask. Again." He looked me in the eye. "Yes. Yes, I'm single."

Yes, I asked again. Men lie every day. Every damn hour.

"Why?"

He laughed again. "What do you mean why? Because I choose to be."

My eyes narrowed. "Why is that your choice? Please don't be one of those airheaded men who don't believe there are any good enough women around."

Please. Ugh!

"I'm not sure who's around. I haven't dated in years."

Slowly, and with uncertainty, I asked, "How many?"

"Over ten years ago."

"If you don't mind me asking, why didn't it work out?"

Ishaan's beautiful features expanded as he grinned my way. "The last time I saw you, you wanted me out of your space. Today, I dropped a few bands on you, and you're asking me about my ex?"

Embarrassed, my eyes slipped away. "I'm sorry."

"No need to be sorry. I'm still getting to know you. Remember?" His energy felt sincere as he peered me directly in the eyes. Then Ishaan lay the menu down. "We were together on and off since we were kids—probably too damn long. I went through a few life changes and learned I wasn't the man for her."

"Was the breakup hard?"

With his eyes to ceiling, he shook his head with pouted lips. "I can accept loss. What I can't accept is deception."

"She cheated."

He shrugged. That was as far as Ishaan wanted to go on that topic and it was fine with me.

"That doesn't answer for why you're still single." I glanced outside of the booth in the darkly lit restaurant twenty minutes from the mall.

By the time I'd come out of the dressing room, and made it to the register, I was told everything had been paid for. Ishaan wasn't in sight, so I asked for the receipt as the bags were being collected to be taken to the car—I didn't even know that service existed. When the receipt was given to me, I learned my math guesstimation game wasn't as strong as I assumed. The bill came to just over three thousand dollars. So, of course, I was insistent on paying for dinner, to which he agreed.

"We're still on that. Huhn?" He chuckled again. "Okay. Well, I'm pretty much a straight up dude. I'm real about myself...my lifestyle." He spoke, flashing his long fingers over the table. "I can't commit to a full-time relationship. Marriage isn't something I desire now. Most women want that—even the ones who say they don't then change their mind after a year or two into the relationship. And that's just not something I can offer at this point in my life."

"You're still not saying why."

"I did. I mentioned my lifestyle. I work around the clock. I've lived bicoastal for some years now, developing then launching the resorts in Vegas then A.C. My work is my true companion. The shit is demanding and would compete with date nights, foot rubs, and anniversary celebrations."

"But you're here with me." I stirred the straw in the glass, not so confident about my arrogance.

"I'm dealing with a consequence of my behavior. Isn't that how you put it?"

"You seemed to have fun earlier doing it. I think you'd make a good boyfriend."

Shaking his head, Ishaan softly scoffed, "That's because you have no idea of my workload, sweetheart."

"What exactly do you do? And don't give me that line about making sure people have fun and be safe while doing it you did a few months ago in Atlantic City."

His smile should have been illegal. Pregnancy hormones or generic attraction, every detail of the man's countenance appealed to me. I hated it.

The rumble in his laughter made me smile. "What is it exactly that I do? Okay." He inclined toward the table, interweaving those fingers. "As the chief operating officer of *ADJ Enterprise*, I'm responsible for just that: the operations. We're an entertainment business, so I'm responsible for the various spokes of what we offer our guests."

He began to count off on his fingers. "Stay, dining, gambling, live entertainment, and activities like the aquariums, zoo, water show, golfing—all amenities. Then there's social engagement like the clubs on our properties, which can bring in riffraff, specifically from the locals who frequent them regularly, unlike tourists. I make sure everyone not only has a good time with the hosts, deejays, and artists we bring in, but they get home safely as well. All the nuance of what makes the operations run smoothly falls on me: lighting, toiletries, security, food and beverage, and community relations."

"For marketing?"

"No." He shook his head, brows lifting. "For law enforcement. There's no way I can do even half my job without providing a stringent level of law enforcement. To do that, I have to work with who the government deems as the authority for that. It's my job to forge a partnership for the safety of our patrons."

I spit out a laugh. "Dawg, I don't know what all that means. But it all sounds heavier than a motherfucker!"

Shrugging with his head, Ishaan agreed. "It's a true commitment."

"What's your work schedule like?"

"I'm never off duty." His face hardened and he appeared to be in deep thought. "I truly can't remember the last time I was 'off duty' and inaccessible." He used finger quotations.

"So, where's your office?"

"In Vegas and Atlantic City."

"Where do you live?"

"I have living units where I work. You've been to two." His eyes darkened.

Shit...

"In Vegas? That was your place?"

Ishaan nodded. "One of them. Yeah."

"And in Atlantic City. That was your place?"

He nodded again. "You've been getting V.I.P. service since the day we met, girl." He winked.

It made me think of the maid in the kitchen back in Vegas.

"They can't be your primary homes."

"When I'm in Jersey and not in my office in Atlantic City, I go home to Alpine." My eyes bulged wide.

"Like..." I swallowed, hand suspended over the glass while holding the straw. "As in Bergen County where Trent Bailey, Chris Rock, Eddie Murphy, Stevie Wonder, Stenton Rogers, and the like live?"

Glancing away, Ishaan chuckled adorably. "I can't confirm all those names but can assure you it's the address on my driver's license."

"So, your house is empty most of the time while you travel around the globe chiefin' on operations?"

"No." Ishaan never lost the smile. "My mother lives with me. I have a seventeen-year-old there, too, Mehki. She's been helping me out with him."

Huhn?

So, he's a father already?

That would explain his quickness to support me on this journey.

"Where's Mehki's mother?"

"Dead." He used the side of his index finger to rub that obscure spot beneath his bottom lip. Ishaan watched me closely.

My eyes fell to my cup as I murmured, "My condolences."

"I appreciate that."

"I'm feeling silly right now. You asked me about my parents and support system when I never considered how this may affect your life." I scratched the nape of my neck.

"Don't sweat it. You've had to divulge personal shit. I don't mind giving up a little bit about myself. I'm single. I've been single since Mehki's mother because all I have to offer a woman are temporal things. My time, my body, my attention are all on a timer. It's the best and most I have in my arsenal. I understand this, and don't see the need to lie about it."

"I wish more men would be like you."

"Is that why you're single?"

It was my turn to shrug. "I haven't wanted in the game in so long, I don't know what I want anymore." That made me think. I was absolutely fucking lost on my desire for a relationship. "And now since I have..." I looked down at my pouch. Having a laugh at my expense, I shared, "I don't think I'll have to think about why I'm single for many moons to come."

Ishaan didn't crack a smile. "You're so fuckin' beautiful, though. Smart and ambitious."

"Oh, please." I rolled my eyes. "And a bag of issues." Nodding, I admitted, "I'm good but nobody's prize. At least, no one I know."

"What issues?"

Oh, hell no, Ishaan!

"Well, they seem to continue." I pointed to my belly.

He appeared to be rubbing his thighs beneath the table. "You're so damn hard on yourself, especially in front of a man who clearly ain't no better than you in the potential baby-making department."

I wanted to roll my eyes. "You're far too kind, Ishaan," my tone was dry.

"Seriously. And I appreciate how you've already decided to lay dating aside for a while, considering you'll have a small child. I've been conscious about that with Mehki. Yeah, I've dated since his mother, and seriously, but nothing passing that benchmark. You know?"

I got lost in his eyes. His maturity—if Ishaan was being truthful—appealed to me more than I wanted him to know.

"How many siblings do you have?"

He picked up a vibrating phone. "Only child." He tapped into it for a while then as he lay it back down on the table, Ishaan asked, "How about you?"

I cleared my throat. "Same."

"Are your parents excited about becoming grandparents?"

"I don't have a father."

"Oh. My condolences. I lost my father, too." His thick brow line furrowed as he blinked successively.

"No need to waste condolences. But please accept mine. I'm sure your father would be proud of the hard worker you are and the father you've become."

"You sound like my mother."

That broke the tension as we snickered. "Good. I need to get my practice in early."

"You really want to raise the baby alone?"

I leaned in to sip from my straw. "It's what I'm prepared to do."

The muscles in his handsome face loosened instantly.

We pulled up in front of my house, and Ishaan turned the volume down on the stereo. Him peering my way felt like a cue.

"Thanks so much for this. It really was a...spirit booster I didn't know I needed."

He nodded. "We should do it again."

My head pushed back. "Shopping again? For maternity clothes?"

He scoffed. "No. I mean hang out."

"Well, after you paid all of that for my clothes, I feel obligated to say 'yes.'"

"Don't. I said hang out. Maybe we can go swimming."

My chin dropped toward my chest. "I guess I feel obligated to say 'yes' since you bought swimwear. Where do you go swimming?"

He shrugged with his lips, rocking his head as he peered straight ahead. "Lots of places. My backyard, at the shore, *HAYDAR*, *KAHRI*..." He shrugged with his shoulders then looked at me. "Lots of places."

I laughed. "Okay. I'll let you figure out the destination, but maybe we should stay away from your place." I glanced around to my house. "Speaking of which, I can get everything in myself."

My intent wasn't to be rude. However, I didn't want to give Ishaan the impression sex with me again was possible. I'd given it to him easily twice. Now, in my predicament, I wouldn't disrespect myself by having sex with him, giving him the impression I had no dignity. Hell no. I respected myself too much for that no matter how fine he was. If he found that rude, oh well. We'd both simply have to live with it.

When I turned back to him, Ishaan was leaning over the center console. He reached for the back of my head, deluding me with his charming scent. Helplessly, my eyes closed in relent. Then he kissed my forehead and retreated. "I'll be in touch."

That's it?

He'd be in touch.

Okay...

I opened the door to let myself out. Ishaan was out of the driver's seat and to the ascending trunk door—which was in the front of the *R8* in the hood area. He unloaded the shopping bags from there then went inside the car where a couple were behind the two seats. Ishaan gathered them all and walked them a few feet up my driveway.

"I'm assuming you'll be entering the same way you exited," he announced as his lengthy frame moved and long braids swung in the air.

Even his damn walk was bad ass and sexy. And when he gaited past me for his car, he planted another kiss on my forehead, "Goodnight," sounded to be a grumble.

I watched him close the hood of his car then take off. Pulling in a deep breath, I turned toward my driveway and grabbed as many bags as I could to walk to my back door. Then I returned for the rest. Once I had everything inside my place, I found myself huffing again, dropping to the sofa with exhaustion and another emotion I wasn't quite ready to face.

I grabbed my belly and whispered, "Not a damn peep about the paternity test today."

My phone rang. Slowly, I leaned over for my purse to dig for it. Excitement zinged through me. In my crazy ass mind, I hoped it was Ishaan calling to say he forgot something—anything. I didn't register the name on the screen until it was too late.

"Hello." I reclined on the sofa, collapsing my head.

"Yo, did I do something wrong?"

It was time. He was overdue for an answer, and I was over dodging his calls and texts.

Rolling my eyes, I explained, "Kenny, I'm five months pregnant! I know I've been out of the mix but, as you can see, I've been dealing with some shit. Real shit!"

There.

"Well, daaaaaamn!"

SEVENTEEN

July

Hayden

Out of breath, I guzzled back bottled water. I bent over next to the *Stairmaster* to grab my purse. My attention went straight to my phone. Oddly, a call had been coming through.

"Hey!" I panted.

"Where are you?" Rayna asked.

I glanced around. "The gym. Why?" Now done with my workout, I moved out of the cardio section of the gym toward the main entrance. "Did you hear Cousin Patsy passed?"

"*Nuh*—yeah," she sounded to hesitate. "When will you be home? When did you even join the gym?"

I snickered. "I've been a member, just an inconsistent one. Sometimes, I'm here just once a week. Girl, that scale's going up, so I try to get here at least three days a week when I'm not too exhausted and can barely make it back over the GWB."

"What time will you be home?" she asked again. Something felt off.

I'd just made it out of the gym when I stopped and scoffed, "I'm leaving now. Everything okay?"

"Yeah. Are you going straight home?"

My first panicked thought was my mother.

"Rayna, you're killing me. What the hell?"

She laughed. "Girl, my bad. It's been a long day with these kids. I just wanted to vent." *Vent? To me?* "I wanted to be sure I had your undivided attention when I do."

With a wrinkled forehead, I relented. "Okay. Give me about twenty minutes. I'll call you as soon as I get there."

"Okay!" She sounded more relaxed, cheery even.

On my way to my car, I noticed missed calls from her as well as texts from Sundryia asking my whereabouts. I texted Sundryia back before igniting the engine.

"You guys are wild," I snorted, glancing around at my cousins in my living room.

Rayna, sitting with crossed legs on one end of the sofa, looked like an *IG* model with a *Chanel* neck piece, floral *Dolce & Gabbana* matching short set, and beautifully shaded hot pink lips. Sundryia, sitting in the single sofa chair, wasn't much different, just slightly understated with an *Asè Garb* logo, white tank, and cute denim hot pants showing off those long, toned legs she'd been known for. The matching fresh *Retro Jordan 1 High* was the icing on the cake for her look. Just about all of her mommy pooch caused by the twins was gone at this point. It had been six months since she gave birth. My cousins were goals. And they had snuck up on me with food and gifts.

"I feel so awful!" Rayna cried dramatically.

"Why?" After lighting the last fragranced candle, I resumed my seat at the opposite end of her and went back to my plate loaded with several of *DiFillippo's* signature entrees. They really knew how to woo a pregnant woman. The stench had returned to my place. It was so bad, Sundryia suggested I have a plumber come take a look at the pipes. She was currently looking for the number of one she'd been using. The house had been newly flipped when I purchased it. Having to put more money into it so soon wasn't ideal for me at all. "I'm okay. Really."

Rayna shook her hanging head while closing her eyes to a squeeze. "We haven't been by to spend time with you in a while. I feel terrible. I really do."

"We need to plan your baby shower."

With a mouth full of food, I parroted, "Shower?"

"Yeah. You know." Sundryia's head rolled. "The party given in your honor to help you prepare for the baby? By the way, I just sent you the plumber's information."

"It's only July," I argued. "And thanks."

Rayna laughed. "But we have to get started. You did have the doctor confirm you're carrying just one baby. Right? You know how tricky our genes are with that."

I nodded, not wanting to give away just how fucking terrified I was of having twins. I wasn't even cut out to be a mother of one. What in the hell would I do with two?

"Y'all, this is too much." I chewed my food. "I'm good. I know you two have extremely busy lives. Rayna, you live in Cali. You have a mogul ass husband, three kids, and a job. And Sundryia, you've been building houses and planning a wedding."

"I know," Sundryia argued. "But we usually speak like every other day. Now, I feel like I've gone weeks without really talking to you. I feel bad as shit."

I waved a dismissive hand in the air. "You just had twins at the top of the year. I can't expect you to be on the phone with me like we used to do."

"You know what made me remember?" Rayna asked. "A girl at my practice is expecting in September. So, they want to give her a shower at work. My office receptionist, Sharon, asked for my input. When I told her I didn't know anything about planning baby showers, she asked how far along I had gotten with yours."

"Mine?"

"Yes. I told them my cousin was having her first baby during a meeting last month." Rayna smiled. "They're not used to me talking about personal stuff. But I was so excited, I shared. I told them I was hoping Sundryia would ask me to help plan it." She looked over at Sundryia who did the fake baby pout.

Rayna had come a long way. She continued to prove she wanted in this cousin circle for real. Learning this swelled my heart.

"I haven't thought about it, honestly," I admitted, sounding so damn pitiful.

"Has Cousin Monica mentioned it?" Sundryia asked. "Does she want to do the shower?"

Rayna pulled in a deep breath. "I didn't even think of that. You think she'd let us help?" Her lips stretched in an expression of embarrassment. "I don't think Cousin Monica likes me or my mom. God, I shouldn't have said that!"

Sundryia laughed. "Monica only likes two people: Hayden and Cousin Billy."

I rolled my eyes. "I haven't been in touch with her much since her birthday."

"Does she know?" Rayna asked.

"Yeah. And her response was...shady as hell. She was high-key judgmental. Plus...seeing Billy there always fucks with me. So that day, it was just a bad combo for me. She's been calling and texting, but I've been..." I whipped my head, brows high to express my hectic life as of late. "I'm going to call her. Maybe I'll take her out to dinner."

"Then you can tell her we're doing your shower, and if she wants to help us to let us know." Rayna's tone was sharp with *big* authority.

"Damn!" I shouted.

Sundryia and I fell into laughter and Rayna gave us an "I don't give a damn" expression.

Cracking the hell up, Sundryia asked, "That's what you sound like at work, Ray?"

Rayna shrugged. "Maybe, but I don't want no drama. I just want to make sure Hayden has everything she needs to take care of that baby. I hate that I'll be so far away." She tossed an index finger toward Sundryia. "You're not even here in Paterson anymore. You're up in Connecticut with two little ones. And I imagine with how Maaz is, you'll be traveling with him this season. Hayden, I hope you and Cousin Monica can work something out."

"I'll be good either way. My mother can't be a trusted party for me as a parent. The day she slips up and takes my baby to her house around that disgusting motherfucker, I'll have to kill him and slap good sense into her. Then I'm going to jail. So, what would that mean for said baby?"

The room shifted into silence. I knew what Sundryia may have possibly been feeling. We'd been open about our shared abuser. As a new mother, she understood the need to protect your children from predators. My mother did not.

Rayna croaked, "Would you ever consider moving to California? I know we can find you a job out there. You and the baby can stay in my guesthouse until it gets older and you're sick of me. Then we can get you a place not too far from me. But I swear you wouldn't be alone. My mother, Keeme, and Chyna would help you get settled out there, too."

"You are so melodramatic, Rayna! Anybody ever tell you that?" Sundryia howled in laughter. "She has friends and family here. No, it ain't me, but she had a life before flying out to Vegas and acting grown."

That chastising jab was funny. I had to laugh, mouth full of food and all. "No. I'm good. I'll be fine."

With a purposeful stare, Sundryia asked, "What's been going on with dude?"

My brows shot up. "Dude?"

"Old boy," she returned.

Rayna cleared her throat as she rubbed the nape of her neck. "Ish."

I snorted nervously.

Him...

I gathered the last bit of food on my plate. Red sauce mixed with pink and white. Two pastas with shrimp and a small piece of lobster would end my palatal festivity. And I took my time savoring each magical morsel. Damn! Pregnancy had ignited my inner-fat girl, and I loved it. "What do you mean?"

"Like, has he been in touch?"

"He went with me to my twentieth week visit," I informed with natural casualness.

Then I reached over to place my empty plate on the side table.

I didn't want to talk about Ishaan. It had been a week and a half since our shopping venture, and I'd honestly began to feel his actions were insincere.

"To the doctor?" Rayna gasped.

"*Mmmhmm.*" I nodded.

Sundryia's gape on me was demanding. "And that's it?"

I shrugged. "He took me out shopping for maternity clothes last week."

"Holy crap!" Rayna croaked.

"And?"

"And what?"

"What else? What's he saying?"

"He's saying he wants to be my friend."

"He should!" Rayna damn near shouted.

"Why you say that?" Sundryia asked her. "What type of dude is Azmir saying he is?"

"Azmir hasn't said much other than asking me a few questions about Hayden and if I knew they'd hooked up. I don't know a lot about Ish. Like I said, he's one of those people you can't take at face value. And even with sharing that, I've never heard anything bad or immoral about him. He's a cutie. We can all see that. But I don't think he plays off his looks."

Sundryia asked, "Have you seen him with women? Maybe he's gay."

I cocked my head to the side at her. My cousin shrugged.

"I've seen him with women at formal events. I really don't know who he's actually dated. But he's never given me gay vibes. I recall hearing he had an ex-girlfriend he was with for years. She died in a car wreck or something. I remember hearing it was bad. There were rumblings about her having cheated on him, and it was bad. People questioned if Ishaan had something to do with it." She shook her head. "I don't know. It was so long ago."

"Wait." Sundryia's face tightened. "Why would he have something to do with the accident? Was he in the car?"

"No. I can't remember. I feel like the guy she was cheating with shot him or tried to shoot him...or kill him." Again, Rayna shook her head. "I don't even like speaking on it. It sounds so much like episodic television." That made me snicker because it truly did sound theatrical. Then I recalled Ishaan sharing about a dead ex. Was this his son's mother? "I don't usually talk about my husband's work because, in his line of business, the unthinkable happens. I'm just happy he has a COO, taking a lot of potential danger and violence off his plate. Azmir has a history that made him all too familiar with thriving in the underworld." She shivered her disgust, making me feel there was a lot more she wasn't sharing.

"Well, seeing how he slickly mentioned Amir at the party, he could be grimy." Sundryia rolled her eyes.

"That's my point. I've never heard he's grimy. And trust, Azmir has a lot of grimy characters around him. It's a part of the entertainment business. But he'd never partner with one." She shook her head vehemently. "Not at *ADJE*. Nope."

"I don't know. I hate that we don't know someone who knows him," Sundryia shared. "Someone who could vouch for him. That Amir mention was wild."

"But it's Ish's job to know random stuff on people." Rayna added.

"He watches over a lot of people and things. He's at the helm of security."

Ishaan mentioned that, too. Then a sudden thought occurred.

The eagle on his neck...

"What do you think about him, Hayden?" Sundryia asked.

"He's nice. You ready to rip into that crème brûlée or the tiramisu?"

"Whoa! Whoa! Whoa!" Sundryia barked out.

I turned to her. "You're very much giving male energy tonight, cupcake."

While Rayna laughed, Sundryia explained, "Because I don't play when it comes to you."

"Awwwww!" Rayna found that endearing.

"I don't. Hayden deserves the world. She's always been level-headed and good hearted. She didn't let obstacles force her to make questionable decisions when she was coming up. I don't want this guy to think how he got her is who she is."

"Thank you, cousin, but this was totally my fuck up, and I'm fully prepared to accept the consequence of it alone."

"Alone?" Rayna chirped as I, once again, attempted to get up for dessert. "You don't want him sharing the responsibility?" She appeared alarmed.

"He doesn't have to."

"What does that mean?" Sundryia sounded surprised, too.

"I mean my doctor told us about paternity testing in utero, and how safe it is. He said he was interested but hasn't uttered a word about it since. It's just weird to me."

"He's denying he's the father?"

I shook my head, hating to even talk about it. I'd rather use my mouth for other things like dessert. "He said he's sticking around to find out and 'in the meantime—'" I rolled my eyes. "—wants to be friends. He even bought me bathing suits—*stupid* bathing suits—so we can go swimming."

Rayna's face folded. "What's wrong with that?"

"I don't know him. And like Sundryia said, he seems like a damn algebraic conundrum. I'm about to be a mother; I ain't got time to figure out all the shit he doesn't want me to know while deciphering the palpable shit he feeds me. That would be like...dating." I shook my head, feeling my emotions cresting already.

Fucking pregnancy.

Rayna giggled. "You remind me of my husband. I can't decide if you're a brilliant professional or a ratchet soul with the way your vernacular goes back and forth. Oscillatory expressions."

"You do geek out sometimes, Hayden." Sundryia agreed with Rayna. "Anyway. If this Ish guy is playing nice, I don't get why you won't let him. You said you don't have any expectations of him."

"Because...after having him with me at the doctor, sharing two meals with him, and going shopping with the man, I realized I find him attractive as fuck."

This was the conclusion I'd come to since our *Neiman Marcus* excursion. I was very much attracted to his fine ass on this side of our bad decision. His appeal to me felt incongruent with my current predicament. Being attracted to Ishaan got me into this trouble in the first place.

"Oh. Okay..." At first, Rayna seemed to be at a loss for words. "Well... If you feel—"

"Is it that farfetched that you find him attractive?" Sundryia's face was tight. "I'm sure he thinks you're the shit now. What's wrong with finding him attractive?"

"The fact that I'll end up fucking him again." I started to the kitchen. "You picking up what I'm putting down now, protector?"

Stirring from a deep sleep, I could hear my phone buzzing on my nightstand. Lazily, I reached for it. Reading the name on the screen, my belly jolted.

"Hello..."

"It's late and I'm sorry," he droned stoically into the phone.

"You don't sound sorry."

"You're still getting to know me. I'm sorry."

"How can I help you at—" I tapped my phone for the time. "—two-thirteen in the morning?"

"By being nice to me as I apologize." His voice was deep, thick, and silky.

Was it because of the hour? How many women experienced the virile tease of his tenor?

"Be nice to you? I left a tantalizing dream to answer the phone. That's beyond nice. It's gracious."

"What were you dreaming about?"

I yawned. "I was sitting at a bar and a fine, chocolate brother approached me. His suit was Italian, and cologne was French. Maybe *Dior* or...*Le Monde Sur Mesure*. Something. But his conversation... Damn, it was refreshing, educational, and...arousing."

"Shit," he uttered lazily. "What was the nigga saying?"

I yawned again. "I don't remember. Honestly, I don't think I heard a word he said. I just knew he said something good to me."

I was delusional from exhaustion.

"It's been twelve days."

"Hmmm?" I asked with closed eyes.

"The last time I saw you, I asked you to call me. We're trying this friendship thing out. Right? Then why haven't you called me in twelve days?"

"You haven't called either, buddy."

"Because I'm trying not to be forceful. I've already been aggressive with your time. Reciprocity goes a long way."

My tight, swollen eyes opened. "You haven't asked about the paternity test."

"What about it?"

"You said you want to do it."

"I do."

"When?"

"Whenever you're ready."

"Why are you so lackadaisical about this shit?"

I could hear what sounded like ice cubes clinking followed by a deep swallow. Damn. It sounded good. And the visual was dangerous.

Where was Ishaan? Why was he awake at this hour? What type of life did he have?

"I put out fires for a living, Hayden. Some—minor backwall kitchen scorches. Others—explosive block fires. I can define the degree of an emergency. The paternity of your baby is important but not an explosive code ten. It's more of an adjustment for you because of the 'code ten' changes happening to your body. But for me, it's more of a two—perhaps a two-point-five."

"Is it because you don't think it's yours?"

"No. I was there with you in Vegas. I remember each position, each stroke, and every explosion." There was casual seduction in his delivery. "My actions, my fire to put out. It's just not the end of the world for me, Hayden."

I swallowed hard. "Understood." I maintained my tough veneer.

"Thursday. Let's hang out after work."

That was a switch in moods. Seconds ago, we were discussing our reckless behavior. Now, he's asking me out in the next breath.

"I'll let you know."

"Why can't you tell me now?"

I yawned again. "Because it's after two in the morning, Ishaan. And I'm so out of it, I don't know if I'm really having this conversation or if I'm lost in another dream."

The low rumble from his mirth was even sexy as hell.

"Hayden."

"Hmmm?"

"If I ever pop up in your dreams in a pleasurable way, promise you'll share each detail of it with me. I'll make everything you share come true. I'm a realist and an exceptional taskmaster. Don't limit me to your mind. We can have fun in other places and realms." My eyes popped open. "Please let me know in the morning if Thursday afternoon works for you."

"Okay."

"Good night, Hayden." The call disconnected.

My face wrinkled and I whispered, "You mean 'good morning.'"

ISHAAN

The young man hit a high note to end the song. The chorus sang strong behind him, and the orchestra playing beneath the stage created a bold sound, complimenting them. It only took seconds before the room exploded in applause. The stage eventually darkened. Moved as much as others in the room, Hayden damn near jumped to her feet, clapping her hands with emotive enthusiasm.

My eyes went to her ass first in a mini denim skirt. Her legs were long and firm. The high-heeled sandals she wore highlighted her feminine posture. Then my brain took over and my attention traveled up to her expression of excitement. *She really enjoyed it.* Hayden stood through the final bow, when the lights came up again, and until the cast waved while leaving the stage.

Then she turned to me, flushed with high emotion. "Wasn't that amazing?"

Smiling, I stood and sidled next to her to speak directly in her ear, "You're amazing."

She was. We were at an off-Broadway play in New York City's theatre district. We'd just finished watching a new play about a kid abducted at four and moved to New York by his abusive captor. A few years later, the boy ends up killing his kidnapper and running away to live on the streets. He struggled not having a place to stay or food to eat. The kid didn't know anyone because he wasn't from the City. In fact, he didn't even know where he was from because he was too young to remember those earlier years. He spent years on the street, navigating abusive relationships, the government learning of his lack of a custodian, establishing his sexuality, and gaining his independence—all while maintaining a pure heart and faith in humanity. He eventually grows up to become one of the most successful fashion designers in the industry, though. Throughout the play, the little boy in him never leaves his side.

Perhaps that's what had Hayden climbing up my arm almost the entire play. She grabbed my thigh at times, too. Now, I'd never been a starving man. I got pussy when I needed it, which was regularly. But I damn sure was a hungry man, responsive to the touch of a soft woman. An attractive woman. An exceedingly educated woman. And recently, I learned, a pregnant woman. This one was sexy as fuck.

"Awwwww! C'mon! You can't tell me you weren't moved by that!" she argued with the cutest smile, lips glossed to highlight their unique shape.

She had me in a bad way; her perfume was now rubbed into my skin from the contact. I leaned down and rubbed my nose against hers. Not expecting it, Hayden's breath caught then it was released at our contact.

"Come on." I pointed toward the aisle to the right of her. "They're requesting us backstage."

Her eyes were wild when she argued, "Not me. Maybe you."

Nudging her softly at the small of her back, I shared, "We'll just have to see."

Hayden walked over to the young man wearing three badges hanging from his neck. He verified my name, introduced himself, and asked that we follow him backstage. We trailed behind him through the droves of people leaving the auditorium. Backstage, we passed dressing rooms, costumes on racks, and stage crew members. He led us into a large room, which looked like a dressing and storage room. Turning from one of the well-lit vanity desks was a tall figure who annoyed the fuck out of me when he wore a face full of makeup.

"Oh. This nigga finally came?" LeRoy rolled his eyes over high ass cheekbones that weren't there the last time I saw him.

Botox again, man?

On sight, I was annoyed. My friend was gay. I got it. He would always want to have sex with men. And as a straight guy, I accepted that so long as he didn't share details. LeRoy was free to be who he wanted to be. That is, until he wanted to play dress up like this with a face full of femininely-accented makeup coupled with a dope ass linen suit and the latest *Asè Garb* moccasins. They went hard. His makeup did not.

"And who is this?" He reacted to Hayden.

With a shy grin, she peered up to me.

"I didn't see you in the play," I noted out loud.

LeRoy's head snapped back. "Because I'm no actor. I'm the producer, dear. And you know this."

"Why are you looking like a character?"

He gasped, bringing his painted nails to his chest. "Are we having a sibling brawl in public or deflecting from this gorgeous reveal?" He blinked, lashes longer than Hayden's slapping together.

Annoyed, I finally performed the introduction, taking her at just above her hip. "This is my buddy, Hayden. Hayden, this is my good friend, LeRoy."

She transferred her beam from me to a dramatically expectant LeRoy. "Hi, LeRoy. The play was phenomenal. I was moved to tears, but..." She caught herself, hands going to her belly. "I'm also loaded with extra hormones I don't know what to do with." Her airy laugh was so damn sexy.

LeRoy's attention went straight to her belly, and, at first, he seemed to be at a loss for words. "Oh, *okaaaaay!*" That's when the motherfucker straightened. His inquisitive eyes bounced between Hayden and me. When he saw I wasn't letting off any explanation or information, he skipped over it. "Well, hormonal or not, you're lovely. And I'd like to think the reception of this play will be stellar. The actors are top tier. Passion pouring from every pore of their beings. We've been working so hard and long on this production," he yapped on. "It's very near and dear to my heart."

Because you embellished your own life's story...

"We've poured millions into this," LeRoy continued. "As a matter of fact, when we hit a dry wall in funding about seven months ago, I called around and asked my friends for help. Would you believe only one answered my call and wrote a six-figure check?" His limp wrist gestured to me.

That, of course, brought Hayden's attention back up to me. She snorted, "You don't say!"

"Girl, I say! I say, chile." LeRoy acknowledged me as Hayden tittered about his feminine dramatization. "You want to meet the cast, Ish?"

Hayden peered my way again for an answer. "Nah. It's getting late. It's a weeknight and she has to work in the morning."

"Well, it's not late." He checked his *Rolex*. "I mean, I know even production wouldn't mind meeting a sponsor."

"I'm sure you can see she's pregnant. I need to feed her before calling it a night."

"*Ooooh!*" Hayden playfully wiggled her shoulders. She'd been in a good mood tonight. I didn't feel the guards she'd put up since I learned she was expecting. "First, he makes me cry, then he feeds me."

"Oh," LeRoy croaked, attention still going between us. My friend was reading our energy and chemistry. "Well, I'll be a third wheel. There's something I need your advice on." *Huhn? What the fuck?* "Let me just wrap up a few things here. I'll be right behind you."

The sommelier poured LeRoy a glass of wine as the table was quiet. When he was done, LeRoy cheered. "Shall we make a toast?"

Giggling, Hayden raised her glass of water, garnished with a lemon wedge, over the table. Since I had a fresh glass of wine, I figured I'd play along.

"Well... First, to the precious new life growing inside of Hayden's beautiful belly," LeRoy began. "Then, to the continued success of '*Stolen Black Boy: from Captivation to Fashion Week.*' Lastly, to my brother, Ishaan, for doing yet another great Black thing in the Caribbean. Your mind is brilliant, bro. Cheers!"

"Cheers!" Hayden echoed.

I took a sip, enjoying the *Chateau Blevin* white blend.

"What are you doing in the Caribbean?" Hayden asked shyly, lashes batting.

"A new resort launch."

She gasped. "Where exactly in the Caribbean?"

"*Red's Island,*" LeRoy answered. "I've seen the pictures and videos. It's divine—no pun intended." That made Hayden laugh, too. "Yes, Ishaan. I've been raving about it to all my friends across the globe."

Sharing the same bench across the table from LeRoy, she leaned into me. "Sounds nice."

"You should come," I murmured before taking another sip. I felt her eyes on me.

"What's your deal?" LeRoy asked suspiciously. "You've been really snappy all night."

Sighing, I rubbed my eyes, being partially honest. "I'm tired, man."

"I heard you've been complaining of being tired a lot. What's up with you? Are you taking supplements?"

I nodded, not wanting to discuss my health. There was nothing major going on. I'd just been feeling lazy lately. It had been going on for a few months now.

"You've gained a few pounds."

"Get the fuck outta here!" I laughed.

Aghast, LeRoy's palm went into the air. "I design and dress men around the world. Not to mention, I'm very gay. A very gay man. I study male anatomy professionally and personally, hunny. You've picked up a few pounds. It's okay. You're lean-brawny." He picked up his glass. When Hayden snickered, he pushed. "Isn't he?" LeRoy winked. "Y'all go crazy about that long curly mane, but I know the real tea must be between them legs."

Hayden's hand flew to her mouth.

I warned, "Chill, L."

He sipped again and shrugged. Damn. I was glad dinner was over, and we could wrap this up soon. LeRoy had been on one tonight, and I'd been fucked up experiencing Hayden's familiarity to me. I wasn't expecting that energy from her.

After his dramatic swallow, he placed the glass down. "Okay. On to serious matters. You've been one of my closest friends for years. You, unlike most of them insecure ass straights, allowed our friendship to happen fast and organically. I trust you with my life, Patterson. Not to mention, you can beat a muthafucka's ass close to death with one hand tied behind your back. Hell, you'll carve a dagger from a rock like *MacGyver*!" *The fucking dramatics.* I knew LeRoy. So much that I sensed him being out of character. The question was why. "I need your god's honest opinion on something."

"Shoot."

"I want to adopt."

"No." I thought some more. "Hell no!"

"Now, why such adamant opposition, Ishaan Dawl?"

I lifted a finger to him. "Don't start your shit."

"I'm just asking why. I expected my best friend, with his religious, close-minded ass to shun me, but you?"

"Yes. And you know why."

LeRoy was a gay man who sometimes wanted to be a woman. He enjoyed being taken care of. He owned nothing but had likely seen every wonder of the world on a downlow man's dime—many of them. He was in no position to govern innocent lives. He hadn't always managed his own well, jumping headfirst into bad relationships. LeRoy loved fast and hard. He wasn't much of a thinker. He only felt the love he'd always desired since he was a kid. He'd tell you himself.

"Please..." He rolled his neck. "Enlighten me."

"I'm not doing this in front of Hayden."

"No!" He snapped. "If Hayden is in your life, she must be worthy of a private conversation between you and a close pal. Tell me," he enunciated each word.

"Because you have a shitload of unresolved childhood trauma. You don't even have a partner. A child needs to be raised in a household with a fair balance of feminine and masculine energy, no matter the sex. You don't need to be a parent right now, bruh."

"You're a single father."

I retracted my glass from my lips and scoffed, "Yeah. Why do you think my mother's living with us? She'd rather be off, enjoying her damn sunset years. But she understands what's best for Ki. And sidebar: you know me having Ki was due to circumstances beyond my control. I didn't choose this life; I stepped the fuck up."

Looking to recoil, LeRoy tucked his tail, nodding his head. "You're right, and I'm sorry."

"Excuse me," Hayden interjected nervously. "I'm going to use the little girl's room. Be right back," she whispered, scooting from behind the table.

LeRoy and I watched her glorious walk from the table. *Shit!* Those legs did things to me. I could still smell her perfume on me from the show earlier.

"Muthafucka, that baby is yours!" LeRoy whispered hard across the table, his eyes bearing into me.

I shook my head casually, going for my glass. "I didn't ask you that."

"Yes the fuck you did by bringing that fish to my work. You don't operate in mess. You casually hanging out with pregnant fish is fucking mess, sir. If you felt that wasn't your baby, you'd never spend a moment of your time with her. Yes the fuck you *did* want me to confirm what you already feel. My question is: 'When will you officially know?' There are safe forms of paternity testing in utero. They're hugely reliable, too." He stabbed a finger onto the white cloth tabletop. "So, what's the hold up? Or are you in my presence tonight to make an official announcement that you're having a baby?"

I pulled up in front of Hayden's house, parking in front of the driveway. When I cut the engine, I looked at her.

A sad smile lifted from her face. "Thanks for picking me up from home and driving back out to the City."

I nodded. "Thanks for the stamina to ride back over the bridge."

"This was fun." Then she pulled in a deep breath. "The play, the food, LeRoy..."

I leaned into her, crossing over the middle console. When my lips met hers, Hayden's parted, and a cool waft of air hit my mouth. I met her flesh with an aggression belying my strange and wicked desire for her body. It reminded me of how damn odd it was for me to even be attracted to a prostitute on my damn property when I'd been clearing it of street level-sex workers. I was still drawn to her. I pushed my tongue into her coy mouth the same way I did that first night when I sensed her imposter act.

Beyond all reason, I was drawn to her. Look at how tonight turned out. This was the first time she'd relaxed around me since Atlantic City. And now, I was ravishing her fucking face with pure intent. I tasted the roof of her mouth, spurring her tongue into action with my own. When she danced, Hayden's mouth moved sinuously against mine, her head bobbing to let me fuck her orally. She tasted good, but sensually deprived. The sound of our sucking and licking reverberated in my ride. The feel of her chest lifting told me she enjoyed this.

Damn.

The shit I can do with you.

To you.

For you.

But I didn't. Instead, I retracted my tongue, sucked on hers, and gently gave her lips a final kiss. When I pulled back, Hayden's eyes were still closed.

Slowly they opened, and I watched her take a deep breath. "You... *ummm*...wanna come inside?"

I knew what that meant. Hayden was breaching her boundary of not entering each other's personal space. She wanted to avoid fucking, and I understood. That's what got us in this precarious situation.

I shook my head. "You need time to know if that's what you want."

A smirk softened her face. "What do I want?"

Glancing down to my swollen lap, I answered. "Trouble."

"How do you know I didn't simply want you to see my new

place?" She made a silly face then opened the door. "Good night, Ish. Thanks again."

I performed the military hand salute. There was no need for words. My dick was hard and throbbing. I wanted to plug every sensual entryway of her body with it, and knew she'd enjoy it. But instead, I watched her saunter down her driveway as those toned thighs and ass switched in heels. The night light flashed on, bringing my attention to the stream of water rushing toward my car.

EIGHTEEN

July

Hayden

Holy shit...

I opened the door and saw it. At least five inches of water was covering my floor. Where did it come from? And it reeked. The scent I'd been tolerating the past few weeks was loud and present. It was the water. My head swung left and right. *My floors! My furniture. Shit!* My entire apartment was flooded. I had to take off my heels. My feet were so wet, I could slip in them.

Who to call?

My first thought was Sundryia. As her phone rang, I remembered she and Maaz were traveling with the twins to Greece. I ended the call. Panic rang in my ears and my chest pounded.

Fuck!

I lifted the phone again.

"Aye!" I turned to find Ishaan's long frame in the doorway. Immediately upon recognizing him, I wanted to cry—I almost cried. But I didn't. I knew if I weren't pregnant, I'd be more pragmatic about how I felt in the moment. I'd get through this. "Is this your unit?" Dumbfounded, I nodded. "Let's see what's salvageable so we can get it out ASAP."

Bravely, he stepped inside onto my flooded floors while pulling out his cell phone.

"So, who's responsible for the damage?" I asked the firefighter.

He glanced up from filling out a form. We were outside of my house with so much damn traffic all around. "It was a city line that burst, but it depends."

"Depends on what?" I demanded, feeling Ishaan's narrowed attention on me.

It was him, after all, who knew a pipe had burst and to call the fire department. It took almost an hour, but they learned a pipe had burst next to my house, backing up into my property—specifically, my basement.

"On your insurance coverage," the firefighter answered, still writing the report.

"I have homeowner's insurance." So, they wouldn't put this on me.

"You need specific coverage for this type of catastrophe," Ishaan advised.

The firefighter nodded while pointing to Ishaan with his pen. "He's right. It's a line item called water backup or..." He hesitated. "I think sump pump overflow. A lot of people think it's included in their property insurance bundle, but it isn't."

"How would I know if I have the coverage?"

"Is your safe on the truck?" Ishaan intervened again, motioning over to the *U-Haul* truck he'd managed to have someone drive here before the police and fire units arrived.

The two guys who drove here with the truck helped Ishaan. We were able to remove as many non-damaged things as I could find. I figured I'd add them to the storage unit I'd been renting since moving in here. All of my things from the place I leased from Sundryia couldn't fit into this basement apartment. When and how I'd get them there was beyond me at the moment, similar to the particulars of my insurance coverage.

"Yes."

"Are your insurance papers in there?"

"Yes," I snapped.

"Okay." Ishaan walked off toward the moving truck.

"So, here's the preliminary report. I'll work on this more and have it finalized within three business days. You'll receive a copy and so will your insurance company, if you have the water backup coverage."

"Three business days? So, what happens to the water?"

"You'll have to get a plumber here to pump the water out. They'll explain the entire process to you." He ripped off the top layer of the document and handed it to me. "That's it for us. Have a good night."

That's it?

Have a good night?

I turned and saw the police car pull off, having turned off its siren lights. The *U-Haul* truck, opened in the back, was still being stacked with my things. Then the fire SUV took off as well.

"Do you have everything you need?" Ishaan was just over my shoulder.

Shrugging, I answered, "I guess."

"They can park the truck in the driveway." I went down for my phone.

"Why?"

"Because it'll be fine here until I can take care of it tomorrow. How much do I owe you for it? How long do I have it for?"

The soft shaking of his head didn't match my heightened emotions. "You don't owe me anything, but you also can't do shit with the contents on the truck by yourself."

He was right. I glanced down at my bulging tummy. "I'll get someone to help me."

"You don't have to."

I scoffed, "What do you mean I don't have to get help? I'm pregnant. I get it: I can't lift heavy loads. But I can damn sure get help." I put the phone up to my ear.

"Who are you calling?"

"My cousin, Sundryia." The voicemail picked up almost right away. "Damn!" I sighed.

"Why are you calling her?"

"I want to know if she has a vacant apartment, but she's out of the country. I'll try my girlfriend."

Letisha, pick up...

"Just come to my place."

My eyes went wild and an unexpected fucking loaded scoff left my throat. I may have allowed my guard to drop just enough to possibly fuck him earlier, but that ship had sailed. I had a fucking emergency on my hands right now. I was effectively homeless.

"Come again?"

"I have a guest bedroom. You can stay and get a good night's rest before you tackle your next move. I can find someone to drain the water."

"I can do it. You've done enough with getting my things out and staying with me this long. Really, Ishaan." I just needed a moment to breathe.

And his gargantuan, looming, authoritative aura didn't give me space to think.

"Hayden."

"Yes!" My eyes closed to a squeeze. "I'm sorry. I don't mean to be snappy, but this is a lot and..." My hand went to my belly. "It's all a lot. And the bottom line is we're strangers, Ishaan. As much as I may seem irresponsible in your eyes, I really am self-sufficient. I can handle this." Even if I didn't have all the answers in the moment.

"I don't doubt you are. But think about this one thing."

"What?"

"You're twenty-three weeks *pregnan*—"

"I know that—"

"Which means you're six months."

"When are you going to start with the shit I don't *kno*—"

"You can't bring a baby home to the basement unit. The drainage and repairs will take months at best. You need to prepare for the baby. If you stay at your cousin's place, is that the home you're gonna bring the baby to? For how long? If you crash at your girlfriend's now, will she have space for you as a pregnant woman?" He pointed to the *U-Haul* truck where the guys were now waiting. *On me!* "Does she have enough space to possibly house you and the baby? For how long?"

"You're not offering solutions here." I scoffed. "It sounds like you're sneaking jabs. This is my problem. Not yours."

"My suggestion is to come to my place. Take some time to think."

Feeling stuck, I licked my lips then calmly stated, "I don't think that's appropriate, Ishaan. I can get a hotel room."

He pointed to my drenched driveway. "For how long?"

"And how long am I to stay at your place?"

"Until you get a few good hours of rest in. You can't make any reasonable decisions right now."

I dropped my face into my palm, crushing the report.

"Come on. I'll drive you," his delivery was raspy, reminding me of the late hour.

"No. I need my car."

"Then follow me. Do you have your keys?"

I nodded. "I need to lock up."

He stretched his arm, prompting my next movement. Damn. I must have looked weak and needy. As I made my way up the driveway, Ishaan warned, "They're bringing the truck to my place. I have your safe in my car. If you change your mind when following, it may be an inconvenient call for you. I'm going home to get in the bed so I can be ready for tomorrow, too."

I wanted to roll my eyes so damn bad. But instead, I used my energy to keep the tears inside my heart.

He lived in Alpine, *Alpine...*

I followed Ishaan into a gated, beautifully lit community at just after one in the morning. The *U-Haul* truck trailed behind me until we all arrived behind another gate encasing a vast estate. *Shit*. Another potential bad mistake on my part. This place looked otherworldly. What was I doing here?

Ishaan parked his car then directed me to do the same. After I cut the engine, I saw him speaking to the gentleman in the *U-Haul* truck behind me. I hadn't realized there was a car following behind the truck. One of the movers was in there. The driver of the truck got into the car, and they pulled off. Ishaan ambled over to my car and opened the door.

He reached for my hand. "Let me show you to your room for the night."

Still unsure about this, I allowed him to help me out of the car. He even retrieved the duffle bag I was able to secure when moving my things out of my flooded apartment. Ishaan led me into the house—rather mansion—from a side door. The corridor we entered through was dim, but immediately, I experienced a burst of potpourri. The place was quiet at this hour as we turned to a staircase and hiked up to the second level. It opened to glistening hardwood floors covered by floral runners. The bedroom wasn't too far off the staircase. As we approached the door, I could see over the loft into a great room with endless views of what I could only assume was the front of the house.

Ishaan turned on the light, illuminating a gargantuan, carpeted room. He moved to the opposite side to shut the curtains, closing off what appeared to be a garden, though I couldn't quite tell. He placed my duffle bag on the coffee table in front of a sofa in the corner of the room.

He pointed to a door, "Bathroom. It should be fully loaded. Let me know if you need anything. I'm going to get your safe from my car."

I watched his lengthy frame leave the room with the ends of his long braids swaying over his neck as he moved. Feeling awkward about being in a strange home, I moved toward the door. Peering out, I saw when Ishaan hit the staircase. When my attention lifted again, it wandered until landing straight ahead. I wasn't alone. There was a young man, brown-skinned and rather tall, staring at me.

He wore only basketball shorts and had abs for days as he rested against a distant doorframe. His expression was deadpan, though I could tell he was an extremely goodlooking kid. *This must be his son*. If I wasn't so sure, I'd think the young man was shooting me flirty vibes with how hooded his eyes appeared and his relaxed posture, showing off his athletic physique.

Shit...

I backed into the room and walked over to the dresser where I parked it until Ishaan returned a few minutes later. When he entered, his strength was evident as he carried the heavy box over to the sitting room, too. Curious, I crept back over to the doorway to see if the kid was still there. He was not.

"You good?" he asked while panting.

"Where's your bedroom?"

"Down on the first floor."

"Who else is up here?"

"My mother and Mehki." My mouth twisted. Likely sensing my angst, Ishaan brought his palms to the back of my skull beneath my ears and massaged deeper than I'd ever experienced. The touch was so aggressive at first, I froze, tensing all over. But at the first sweep of relief, I leaned into his ministrations. His fingers kept moving, pressure so perfect I could cry. "You're safe here. No one will bother you." So relaxed, ensconced in his hold, I collapsed into his chest and cried. "*Shhhh...*" He soothingly demanded. "It's been a long day. But you're not alone."

ISHAAN

I knocked on her door. While waiting, I took a deep sip of my morning tea. I was still tired as fuck but had to address this first thing today and then attempt to get inside of Hayden's head.

Within seconds, she opened the door, her expression soft. "Good morning."

"Good morning," I returned, reaching forward to pull her hair from her beautiful face. "You ready?"

We'd been texting since six this morning when she'd apparently woken up. Initially, I wasn't going to bother Hayden until she awakened, understanding the long night she'd had. But when she hit me up, I explained since she was awake, I wanted to introduce her to my family. It was only right since she was a guest in their home. She agreed and said she'd be ready by eight.

Hayden nodded and I offered her my hand. When she reciprocated, I led her down the primary staircase of the house, unlike the one we took last night when she'd arrived. I noticed her eyes bouncing all over, and understood it was a lot to take in if you weren't prepared. My home was close to nine thousand square feet, situated on over three acres. This was why I'd never been in the habit of bringing women home.

We're beyond that now...

We made it into the kitchen. "Morning, crew," I greeted.

My mother shuffled around in her chair at the breakfast nook. Mehki was leaning on the island in the main area with one leg crossed over the other, picking his hair.

"Ms. Green's gonna have your ass if she finds your hair in this kitchen," I warned him playfully.

Mehki sucked his teeth and straightened while virtually rolling his eyes. He'd stopped with the hair picking but I didn't like his attitude. Quickly, I brushed it off, especially because his attention settled on Hayden. When she, too, saw him eyeing her belly, she began to cradle it, likely a self-conscious act of protection.

"Ma," I began. "...Ki, this is my friend, Hayden."

"Good morning, dear," my mother greeted with her professional tone as she smiled.

"Good morning, Mrs. Patterson," Hayden returned.

I corrected her, "Dr. Patterson."

"Oh." She peered up at me. "I'm sorry. Dr. Patterson."

My mother shook her head and waved a dismissive hand. "I don't think formality is necessary in this instance. I'm just glad to meet you, Hayden." Then my mother regarded Mehki. "Your poppy just made an introduction, young man."

A cheesy ass grin widened his face. "My bad. Hi." He scoffed, "This just feels so weird."

"Hi, Hayden," I prompted.

"Hayden!" Mehki corrected himself. "Hi, Hayden. My bad, Poppy."

"It's nice to formally meet you, Mehki." She initiated a handshake, something I'd taught him to never allow to happen.

Again, I dismissed it. The situation was precarious enough for us all.

"I heard about the flood," my mother began. "I'm so sorry. I had one due to an HVAC malfunction. It can be an expensive nightmare."

Hayden giggled nervously. "I slept so well in that bed last night, I haven't even fully processed the damage. I found my insurance papers and called the company. My cousin gave me a number for a plumber last weekend. I'm actually going to meet them there in a few."

"I can't imagine what your parents are thinking. I'm sure your family will meet you there in droves."

Hayden gave a nervous titter. "Oh, no. I'll be fine."

"You'll soon learn how motherhood ends when we close our eyes for the final time." Mom winked. "I'm sure your mother's worried like crazy."

"I haven't even called her."

Finally sensing something with Hayden and her mother was off, my mother wisely changed the subject. "Your belly's beautiful. And you're still in heels. When I was carrying Ishaan, I practically wore starchy, figureless gowns. They didn't have cute maternity pieces available."

Smiling deeply, Hayden returned, "Thanks." As she cupped her belly again.

She did look cute in a fitted white tank top with loose jeans shorts hanging low on her waist. She wore thong heeled sandals with it.

Hayden sighed, "Well, I just wanted to say thanks for having me last night. I slept well."

"Will you be having breakfast?" My mother asked. "Ms. Green makes delicious waffles."

"No. I'm going to get out of your hair." Hayden turned to me. "I've been texting back and forth with my cousin about him coming to pick up the *U-Haul* and helping me unpack my things into my storage unit."

"You can't put everything in there," I thought out loud. "What about the things you'll need until you get settled?"

Her beautiful ebony eyes bore into me, communicating something I knew I wouldn't like. Hayden had a lot of decisions to make. If no one in her circle could convince her she did, I would do it.

Moving along this awkward introduction my mother kept attempting to save, I explained, "I wanted you guys to meet Hayden since she'll be here for a bit—"

"I'm about to leave now," Hayden blurted.

"Well, I think he means staying over. It can take some time for those repairs to be completed in your home. If my memory serves me correctly, we had to live above that mess for months."

Hayden glanced up to me again, clearing her throat. "I'll be fine. I'll figure something out. I always do." Then she turned to an unusually quiet Mehki. "It was nice meeting you. Sorry if this has been awkward for you...especially last night."

Last night?

Mehki sighed, standing straight. "Nah. It's all good. Hope...everything... You know...work out."

"Thanks, Mehki. Thanks for having me, Mrs. Patterson. Your home is lovely."

"Oh, I have seniority here for obvious reasons, but this is Ishaan and Mehki's home. I'm just taking up space until I'm no longer needed. Best of luck to you, Hayden."

Then Hayden peered up to me as I swallowed back my tea. I noticed when her eyes tarried at my lips before ascending to my eyes. "Thanks for everything," she mouthed.

Then she left the kitchen.

"Welp!" Mehki clapped his hands together. "It's looking like a pool day to me. Jessica's pulling up with subs and sodas in a few. Holla at'cha boy if you need me."

Mehki took off in the opposite direction of Hayden, leaving for the back staircase.

I turned to my mother, expecting her to chastise me about letting Mehki break off so quickly and easily.

Taking a deep breath, I warned, "Not right now. I'll get on his ass."

"And what about hers?"

I glanced over my shoulder to nothing in particular. "Hayden?"

"That would be the one."

I took a sip of my tea to hide my frustration. "She's just stressed out. She's been dealt a lot of surprises this year."

"Oh, I don't doubt it. But even more: after spending less than five minutes in her presence, I can sense that young lady has trust issues. Possibly severe."

"Don't we all."

"You do, yeah. But imagine yours on steroids. How much do you know about Hayden? Who is she connected to? If she's indeed carrying your child, you've got some educating to do for yourself."

Try regulating, Ma...

I turned to leave so I could see Hayden out. "Roger that, Doc."

By the time I left the kitchen, I had my plan laid.

When I made it back upstairs to the guest room, Hayden was packing her duffle bag. I tapped on the open door.

"What do you need help with?"

She glanced up at me then blew out a breath, appearing taxed already. "The safe. If you can get that into my car, I'd be grateful."

"You can leave it here. I swear no one will touch your things."

She shook her head. "Until when, Ishaan? I get all the salient points you made last night." Hayden walked up to me, energy softening with each step. "You were right. I was tired and needed some sleep." Her gentle hand rested on my chest. "Well, I'm rested up and have my wits about me again. I've got it from here."

Studying her beauty, I reminded her, "You don't have to. I meant what I said about us being friends. You were so cool last night...before we pulled up to your place. I thought we'd turned a corner."

"We did and have since then." She swung an arm behind her, gesturing the room. "I've stayed at your place. I'm grateful for your..." She grabbed her belly. "...friendship. Now, I've got some shit to deal with. It's life. You know?"

I pulled a lock of her hair into my hand and sniffled. It smelled of hot appliances and her natural odor. *Damn.* I wished we could've awakened with this in my face this morning. In my bed.

"My mother says you don't trust me."

Her head whipped up to meet my eyes. "What type of doctor is she?"

"A psychologist."

"Then she's not off." Hayden shook her head. "I don't trust most people. Nothing good has ever come from trusting folks."

"Leave your safe here, at least. I'll bring it to wherever you decide to settle."

Hayden stood motionless, eyes examining mine for a long while. Then her attention dropped to my mouth. A shaking hand appeared in my peripheral, and she gently touched my lips. My dick swelled so fast, and eyes closed in immediate arrest. I so fucking wished her soft fingers were coated with the secretions of her pussy, caressing my hungry lips. This woman had been fucking compromising my unyielding nature.

"Let's make a deal," poured raspingly from my lips as my eyelids grew heavier and heavier. Coincidentally, so had my dick.

"I can't stay here again," she whispered.

When those sexy ass chocolate irises struggled to find my own, I leaned down and kissed her. Taking her at the back of the head, I tasted her toothpaste. I sucked on her glossy lips, then fucked her mouth with my tongue. My inner beast roared, needing to take her to bed and bury my fucking wood deep inside of her pussy. Hayden's belly pushed against my lower abs and crotch, and I felt a kick from it. A gush of air pushed from her mouth as she clasped my chest, trying to keep up with my tongue and lips. The girl wanted me, too, perhaps as much as I had her. Should I prove it to her?

Then there was a tap at the door. "Yo, Poppy!"

Hayden jolted against me, and I used my hands to keep her in place.

Smoothly, I pulled from her opened mouth. "Yeah."

"You busy?"

I licked my lips, studying Hayden's panicked expression. "What do you need, Ki?" my delivery croaky as hell.

"*Ummm...* I can't find the rolling cooler. Ms. Green said the last she knew, you cleaned it."

Panting against me, Hayden's eyes squeezed closed as though she was ashamed.

"I'll be out there once I'm done with Hayden, Ki," I bit back.

"Oh. My bad." I heard the disappointment in his reply. Then I heard when he took off.

I couldn't deal with him right now. There was a far more pressing matter collapsed into my chest right now. *Two.*

"Leave the safe in the *U-Haul*. Don't trust us? Take the keys with you. But you can't be fuckin' driving around with a safe in your car. It's not safe. Take out what you need and leave the rest."

Hayden's eyes rolled then closed, "Ish—"

"I'm going to call this morning and schedule the paternity test." I watched as her expression grew wild. "If you don't want to be friends with me, I'll acquiesce understanding I'm not even the father. I'll respect your privacy and desire to be fuckin' done with me."

Hayden pushed off from my body. Her nostrils spread and lip curled. "Help me with my safe. Please."

She'd decided.

And pissed me the fuck off.

Hayden

Yawning at my desk, I was thankful to end a *Zoom* meeting with the state so I could get on to my next task. As I checked my email, my phone rang.

"Hey."

"Hey, Hayden. What's going on?"

Sighing, I sat back in my seat, one hand reaching for my belly. "Work, girl. What're you up to today? Wait..." I checked the time. "It's like eight-thirty in the morning over there. Or are you home?"

"Yeah. I'm home. I just got the kids off to school. Haven't even started my day yet. I needed to call you first."

"Why?"

"Hayden, Ishaan called Azmir around five-thirty this morning." My eyes grew wild. "He told him about the flood in your apartment. I'm so sorry to hear that."

His ass!

"It's not a big—" Then I stood to close the door to my office. "Life lifes, you know?"

"I do. Where are you now?"

"At work."

"Work?"

"Yeah. I stopped by the house to meet the plumber. I gave them access to my apartment to start pumping the water out." Sitting back in my seat, I rolled my eyes when sharing, "They want eleven fucking grand for it."

"Sheesh! Eleven! What's your insurance going to pay?"

"Nada." I wanted to cry. "It isn't covered. A fucking city line burst, backing up into my basement, and they only pay for their line, not my damage. That was the odor I'd been dealing with."

"Yeah. I remember Sundryia telling you to call the plumber."

"Yup. I put it off, and now I wonder if I'd moved faster, could I have prevented all this shit."

"Speaking of which, where are you going to stay?"

"I was hoping Sundryia had an available unit for me. I'd been calling her since it all went down last night—"

"But they were in the air."

"Yeah. She did get back to me today saying she didn't have anything available. Not even my old apartment."

"So, what are you going to do? Did the plumber say how long before you can move back in?"

"Nothing definitive other than it has to be fully dried out before I can go back. It can be months. Apparently, there's a whole process. The other units are unaffected. It's just my illegal apartment. I guess there's something to be grateful for."

"Hayden," she singsonged.

"Yeah. I know."

"No." She groaned. "You don't."

"What do you mean?"

"Ishaan's calling an audible."

"An audible?"

"He wants you to stay at his place. He said you did last night."

"I did but who does he think—" I lowered my voice. "Who does he think he is to call my cousin's husband?"

"A wealthy, powerful man who's used to getting his way," she sounded sad.

"And? I don't even know him."

"He's not exactly a stranger to you anymore. Plus, he's not one to me or Azmir. Azmir trusts Ish implicitly."

"That's good but I don't. Do you know he had the nerve to go take the paternity test today? The lab called and asked when I can come in to submit mine, as though that's going to change anything!" I whispered hard into the phone. "It feels like he's trying to trap me here!"

"He's not. At least, it doesn't seem that way to me...or Azmir. It sounds like he's trying to be responsible, Hayden."

"He has been! He's done a lot. Spent money and even tripped me up in the head a little bit." *I invited him into my place last night in a moment of weakness brought on by his sexy ass prowess. That could have been disastrous.* "That doesn't mean I have to answer to him. Act like we've been in a relationship for years." I bit my lip, anger bubbling out of nowhere.

"Do me a favor."

"What?"

"Take a deep breath. I need for you to try as hard as you can to relax. It won't be a *Crystal K Spa* type of escape. But it will be beneficial to my little cousin baking in your womb."

"Rayna, I'm sorry to worry you. I know I seem a mess, but I'm really used to finding my way through obstacles." I tried to laugh. "I swear I won't be jumping off the *GWB*."

"I don't think you are. But I know what I know. And what I know is survivors of trauma navigate through subsequent traumas, sometimes, all their lives and never realize how it changes their brains and hearts. We don't realize we deserve a break. We stay in combat mode for too long stretches of time." Rayna paused and it felt heavy. "We believe being tough and emotionally independent is a flex. We wear it like a badge. Ain't nothing cute about loneliness."

"I'm not lonely."

"You're not connected either."

"What do you mean?"

"Who are you close to except for Sundryia? Have you spoken to your mother lately? Does she know about the flood? Who has your back?"

"Rayna—"

"Every word I just described was me. It still is me, which is why I work on myself daily. Why do you think I've been trying to get into the cousin circle with you and Sundryia? That tough, *I hold myself down* shit is for the birds. Hayden?"

"Yeah."

"Stay with Ishaan."

"I can get a hotel room," I shared dismissively.

"For how long?"

"Until my apartment is ready. I'm not married to a millionaire but I ain't broke either, cousin."

"If I thought you were, I'd have you stay at our apartment in the City or in the *Ritz Luxuriate Hotel* until you said when. I'm halfway tempted to now, but I know you'll decline. Ishaan will not beat or murder you. If you go get a room, your hotel expenses will rival the plumbing bill." My face dropped into my palm. "Whenever life throws you a break, catch it. Take the blood test. Let's put this detail behind us so we can raise this baby better than we were, and without the insecurities we've developed along the way. Please."

Tears spilled from my face and my diaphragm quivered hard.

Nineteen

July

Ishaan

I strolled into the kitchen to find my mother washing dishes. Headed straight over to the counter for hand sanitizer, I asked, "Why are you up so late washing dishes?" Mehki mentioned to me she cooked for them, something she rarely did nowadays.

"Waiting on my relief to arrive and take over. Then my shift ends."

I scoffed, "Ma, he's seventeen. He's fine at home. I was just back there, checking in on them. I didn't catch any hanky-panky." If I wasn't so fucking tired I would have laughed hard at my own damn joke.

"Eh..." She glanced down at the frying pan soaked in bubbly water

306

as she scrubbed with a sponge. "He's still a child. They've been out there all day."

I understood. It was close to eleven at night. Even for me, the day had been long. I walked over to the pantry for a pack of crackers. Then I headed to the fridge for a jar of banana peppers.

"You look knackered." She watched me pull out a plate from the cabinet. "I have some leftovers."

"I'm good."

"I hate to be the nagging mom, but I'm worried."

Rubbing my eyes with my wrist, I murmured, "Ma, we're good."

"Oh," she chirped then nodded. "Okay."

Stuffing a pepper-loaded cracker into my mouth, I asked, "What's up, Ma?"

I gripped the sides of the broad, marble island. If I knew anything about Dr. Nancy Patterson, it was that she'd always have the last say, even if it wasn't as soon as she wanted to. She was patient with her subjects.

The faucet was cut, killing the water. Then my mother dried her hands with a towel near her. She then turned to me, leaning against the sink herself. "I know what you do for a living. You don't share, but I know how dark the work gets. I know how high-risk your job is. I know how, although you've gathered the strongest team you believe you could, anything can happen in combat."

I stretched my forehead, trying to go for a smile. "I know you're not telling me to quit my job, lady."

"I know your work is high stress. High stress career work leads to an early death for most people. Look at your father." *Bingo!* "Constantly in combat, never being able to just relax. I wanted more kids but knew better. He took care of you exceptionally well financially, but you and I both know children need more than money to flourish in life."

"Do you need me here more often, Ma?"

"Oh, you're going to have to consider it, young man."

"Ki will be eighteen soon. He'll be away at school. I can touch him easily wherever he goes in the U.S. He knows this."

"It's not really Ki I'm concerned about."

After eating another cracker, I asked, "Are you going to get to your point before midnight, Doc?"

"Hayden."

I tossed my head back and scoffed. At this point, I was done being forceful with her. When I pulled up and saw the *U-Haul* still parked in the driveway, I made a mental note to arrange to have it parked on her block. I'd play this shit Hayden's way: from the back. This morning, I went to one of the labs her doctor referred us to and gave my blood. What Hayden would do with it before having the baby was up to her. But after the baby was born, we'd definitely learn the truth. At that point, she'd grow the fuck up and let me fill my role as father, or I'd know I'm not and move on from her.

I loaded banana peppers on another cracker. "What about her?"

"Do you think it's your baby?"

"If she participates in the paternity testing, I'll know for sure. I did my part today."

"But what is your gut telling you, Shan?"

"I haven't used my gut for women in years."

She slapped her palms together. "And that's where I'm leading up to. You have a handicap with women."

I shook my head. "I'm cool on women. Have no issues with them, ma'am."

"Oh, you just banging the headboards with them doesn't cover the full gamut of women!" she grumbled with tight lips.

"Doc," I scoffed, "I've been patient with that girl. You know I have. I brought her home, offered her a place to stay. I went to the doctor with her. I even took her maternity shopping. I've been trying to be an ally to her. My mother taught me well. I've been understanding." I popped another cracker into my mouth. "I haven't judged her. Shit." I swallowed. "I even offered for her to stay here until she had the baby. She lives in a damn basement apartment. Me, personally... If the baby turns out to be mine, I wouldn't want them in a damn basement."

As I went about fixing another cracker, I caught my mother's knowing grin. "You like Hayden."

I shrugged with my lips. "She's cool." Then I thought. "Especially when she ain't...fuckin' cagey. If the baby turns out not being mine, it would be unfortunate. She's a cool girl. I can see myself being friends with her."

"Translation: you can see yourself taking on an intimate relationship with her as long as she allows you to keep a barrier of emotion between you."

"Yeah." I nodded, annoyed, like a fucking kid. "Because she got trust issues." She'd said it the second time we'd fucked in Atlantic City.

"No." My mother pointed dramatically. "Because *you* have trust issues." I scoffed, forking peppers from the jar. *Here we go...* "Mandy did a number on you. She tried to kill you, Ishaan—they thought they did kill you. Left you for dead!" she tried whispering. It was something we practiced out of respect for Mehki. My history with his mom was peppered with nuance he'd likely never understand.

"It's a pain you'll never forget," my mother continued. "A betrayal you'll always be reminded of. You see it every day you lay eyes on her son, Mehki. And you feel it each time you rub your hand against those tattoos, feeling the scar." She patted her chest, an area near the shoulder. "You think *you* don't stand a chance with that young lady's trust issues? She may be dodging a bullet with avoiding *you* with yours."

I found that funny. Again, I was too damn tired to laugh.

"I tried, Doc. I tried the mature route with Hayden. She's not interested. And you know what?" I closed the lid on the banana peppers. "I'm too damn exhausted to give this anymore headspace for the day. I offered. She opted out." I shrugged like the childish kid I could only be around Nancy Patterson. Then I returned the peppers to the fridge.

"She didn't exactly opt out." I heard the confusion in my mother's voice.

At the same time, two of my three phones were vibrating in my pocket. It told me I didn't successfully shut one of them down. I paused to do just that, not even giving a fuck about the notification. Then I carried the crackers back into the pantry.

"What do you mean by that?" I hadn't heard from Hayden all day, and that was all good. "I see she didn't come back for the truck. I'll have it driven back down to wherever she is in Paterson."

"Mehki didn't tell you? Hayden came back around seven. She looked not dissimilar to you now. She was hungry and exhausted—emotionally." She motioned to the kitchen. "I cooked up some pasta and seafood Ms. Green had here."

"Mehki and his friends ate pasta and seafood?"

"No. But when he got wind of me cooking, he asked for wings."

"Wings? You fried him wings?"

She nodded, going back to the sink. "Ms. Green's going to get me for overstepping. But I fried wings and made mozzarella sticks, too. Hayden liked those."

"When did she leave?"

"She hasn't." My mother tossed her chin upward. "She's upstairs."

Shit...

I took the staircase off the kitchen up to the second floor. My movements weren't swift, but my intention was clear in how I moved. I didn't have to knock on her door. It was ajar. Unable to find her from the view of the cracked door, I opened the door. This room was the third largest in the house. It was a full suite with a view of the garden. Finally, I could see Hayden sprawled out on the sofa sleeping. One leg was hiked up on the seat, and the other was stretched out. She looked fucking exhausted.

On approach, I noticed the opened laptop near her. How long ago it had gone to sleep, too, I'd never know. Her overnight duffle bag was on the companion single sofa chair adjacent to her. *Shit.* Hayden had really come back. Did she have no other place to go? That would have been fucked up. Where the fuck were her parents? When I'd put in the call to Jacobs this morning, it was more of a call to have Rayna and their family step up and help Hayden. She sure as shit wasn't allowing me to.

She was so fucking beautiful. Laying there with her lips parted and belly visible in a fitted dress drawn up her thighs from the way she was positioned. Light-skinned, tall chick, who was a little nerdy, and slightly gangster. Hayden was dope as fuck. Mean as hell when she wanted to be, but adventurous and humorous when she'd lower her guard.

Taking a deep breath, I turned for the ensuite bathroom. I started for the tub then remembered pregnant women shouldn't take hot baths at some point in pregnancy. Realizing it wouldn't work either seeing how tired she was, I turned on the shower instead.

Back out in the sitting room, I rubbed her cheek. "Boo-baby," I called out to her. A part of me took that approach because I didn't want to startle her from her sleep with harsh energy. The other part felt it was a natural approach to her. "Time to get up." Hayden stirred, then too quickly sat up. "Whoa," I chided gently, taking her at the shoulder and arm. "You can't be moving so fast now. Remember?"

"What time is it?" she whispered, rubbing around her long lashes.

"It's after eleven. I've got the shower running. Go get washed up so you can get in the bed."

"I—" she yawned. "I'll just get in the bed."

"Nah. Washing off the bullshit from the day can help you get to sleep faster and for longer."

Hayden studied me warily. She observed me from my shoes and suit pants, all the way up to the opening of my button up shirt.

It made me scoff. "I ain't proposing nothing sexual." I pointed over my shoulder. "I'm heading back down to my room to do the same shit. Come on." When she stood, I brought her duffle bag to the table so it would be closer to her. "You need any toiletries?"

Hayden nodded her head. She plucked a few things from her bag then wobbled into the bathroom and closed the door.

Thirty minutes later, down in my bedroom, I yawned while studying one of the many monitors I had set up in my bedroom. There was remote surveillance to all three resorts. It was just a matter of signing into the respective account. Just after leaving the bathroom from a hot shower, Munchie called with a problem at *Flare* in Vegas.

The Drake brothers, owners of *Drake Casino and Hotel* in Las Vegas, had a security breach in one of their clubs last week. There was an organization selling hard shit, causing a few of the patrons to fall ill. Luckily, there were no fatalities. Incidences like that were a huge liability to the club. Local law enforcement had to get involved.

However, a good resort has local ties. The Drake's team was able to tap into their resources and find the perp. The problem was, they were ahead of local law enforcement. This meant the group had not been detained and only banned from *Drake Casino and Hotel*. This left the problem of them being free to set up their operations at other popular clubs. *Flare* would invariably be on that list.

Today, I flew down to Atlantic City after giving blood, and worked there for a few hours before flying back. I'd prepared my team for tonight, after receiving whispers about *Flare* being one of the targeted clubs. The director of security wanted my take on identifying someone and had Munchie plug him into my private line.

"Zoom into eight," I requested remotely. When the directive was followed, I noticed a few things. "That's him." It was Rob Whitter, former promoter for *KAHRI Resort & Casino* in Atlantic City, New Jersey.

"Shit," D'Angelo, my director of security swore. "I didn't even recognize him. What the fuck is he doing on the West Coast?"

"Go into four, please." I asked. "It's because he didn't want you to. We have a breach, guys. Someone on the inside allowed him access." I didn't like this shit a little bit. "Yup. He's doing hand signals."

"Fuck," D'Angelo swore. "I'm bringing them both in!"

"Nah." I yawned. "Whitter wants to be smarter than us. Let him be. Meanwhile, he may tell us if Rocky's crew is in there. Watch him for the rest of the night. Put our best floor people on him. Don't fuck this up."

"I won't, sir. Not on my fucking life," D'Angelo pledged.

"My guy," I affirmed him as my personal cell vibrated near the monitors.

Imposter: *Can you come up to chat for a minute?*
"Munch..."

"Okay, D'Angelo," Munchie chimed in. "Mr. Patterson has to go. If this situation escalates, you're to—"

I disconnected the call and stood from the desk to stretch. Raising my hands and arms above my head, I strained, yawning at the same damn time. *Shit!* I was tired as fuck. This had been so different for me. Before, I could go thirty-six hours without needing to rest. Over the past few months, I barely made it to eight. But I had another situation to tend to. This one in my home.

So, I dragged my heavy body into the closet and grabbed a cotton shirt from the dresser drawer. As I pulled it over my head, I was on my way out of my bedroom. In my hand, my phone rang again. It was Ebonee. Not having the mental capacity to speak to her tonight, I didn't send her straight to voicemail but did think to kill my ringer.

I knocked on her door.

"Come in," she called out in delayed speed.

Slowly, I opened the door. Hayden was in bed, snuggled beneath the bedding. She wore a silk head scarf. I noticed the dark spots beneath her eyes. She was tired as hell, too, it seemed.

Join the fucking club.

I leaned against the doorjamb.

She waved a facial tissue in the air. "Here's my white flag. I come in peace. Come here, please."

Pushing off the frame, I ambled over to the nightstand. I faced her, chin low.

"You don't feel hospitable."

"You said you didn't want my hospitality."

"Yet I'm here." She gestured to the room. "Resting in your bed."

I nodded, realizing her humor. "My bed's downstairs, Boo-baby."

She smiled. A cute smile. A girly smile. Something confusing the hell out of me with Hayden.

"Good. I want to talk about this."

"What?"

"Me staying here."

Readjusting my stance, I sighed, "Stay as long as you need. The offer's still on the table."

"Thanks." She nodded softly. "I was going to address that. I spoke with the plumber this evening. He's still not giving me a timeframe. All he can say is there was lots of water and I need to be prepared to be out of my place for at least a couple of months."

"That's cool. Stay as long as you need." I brushed my hand down my face.

Hayden's head fell to the side. "Really?"

"Yup."

"So, it was an audible."

"I don't understand."

"You reaching out to Azmir today. You called an audible...on *me*."

I snorted. "Oh, Boo-baby, you have yet to learn about me. My audibles are direct. I don't need backdoors for them. And trust me, I call them every day—sometimes more than one."

"So, why did you call my cousin's husband?"

I pulled in a breath and found space on the nightstand to squat. "Because you're stubborn as hell, Hayden. If you wouldn't let me help, fine. But where's your family? Azmir's wife is your blood. You need somebody to look out for you."

"Okay. For starters..." Her palm splayed in the air. "...it's just as you said. Azmir's wife is my cousin. I don't know him. Furthermore, Rayna and I may be cousins but we're just getting to know each other as adults. We're building something new, so to have her call me about something so personal—while I'm pregnant—angered me to the point of tears. Crying isn't a sport I enjoy."

She'd cried. Tough girl Hayden cried. That shit didn't sit right with me.

Leaving the nightstand, I climbed onto the bed. Hayden shifted over to give me room but soon learned my intent when I pulled her into my arms. She had to adjust because she was beneath the covers, and I was on top of them.

I wrapped Hayden in my arms and rested my head on top of hers.

She giggled against my chest. "This is nice but wholly unnecessary. I'm fine, Ishaan. I'll figure my shit out. I always do."

I sighed, "I get it. You're tough. I just hate that you have to be."

"That's life. I'm truly blessed, though. I have more than I should

314

compared to my peers. I've gotten far. Alone." She sniffled. "You, too. You own this estate alone."

"I do, but my motivation has been the people who live in it. They're here far more than I am. They're my 'why.'"

Things got quiet. Then Hayden whispered, "My 'why' is baking."

I nodded over her head. "It is."

"And I know you're thinking if the test results come back eliminating you, I'll be taking care of the baby *alone*, too."

I fought back a yawn. "I don't."

Hayden's head moved as she looked up at me. "So, you do have doubts?"

Shaking my head, I told her, "I don't."

"You're confusing me."

"And you made me mad earlier, Boo-baby."

"Please don't call me that." That's when I peered down at her. Her expression was hard. "Because it...blurs the line."

"What line?"

"Of who we are to each other."

"Who are we to each other?"

"Strangers."

I chuckled, abs vibrated while my legs were crossed. "Sorry to have to tell you, but we're beyond strangers now. I know what you taste like, honey." I studied her eyes.

They closed as she exhaled. "I didn't want to stay here—don't want to—because just as we crossed the line the first two times we saw each other..."

My arms tightened around her in a hug as I kissed her forehead. "I still want to fuck you, too, Hayden. I get it."

When she went quiet on me again, I glanced back down at her only to find her long lashes. "I didn't say that," she whispered.

"But it's what you meant. You said it yourself; we acted out our attraction for each other our first two encounters. Our chemistry is animalistic."

Again, Hayden went quiet.

"You weren't going to tell Rayna about the flooding?" I asked, breaking the silence.

Without skipping a beat, she returned, "I'm sure I would have. It *just* happened last night. I hadn't told anyone who couldn't help me at the time."

"I thought you called your cousin, Sundryia."

"Yeah. Because she owns properties. Apartment units. I rented from her before moving into my own house. I was hoping she had a vacancy. She hit me back today saying she didn't."

"What about your mother?"

"I don't want to talk about her. Let's just say, our relationship is nothing like yours with Dr. Patterson. She's really nice, by the way. Intimidating but nice."

"She's a head doctor. The lady's hard to get comfortable around because she's always reading."

"Was that bad for you coming up?"

I yawned. "Nah. She was chill. She gave me tools. It's how I can read people myself."

Hayden pushed out an arrogant titter. Looking up at me, she asked, "What's your 'read' on me?"

I studied her face, seeing she'd washed her makeup off for the day revealed an intimate access to her beauty. Hayden was a redbone. Her cute narrow nose, and mismatched-sized lips were all proportioned perfectly. Her voice was croaky, slightly deep, and a total contrast to her soft features. Her body was artful, too. Before getting pregnant, those long legs were the first to catch my eye in the lobby of *HAYDAR*. Her bite-sized tits, small waist, and plump ass may sound like an odd attraction on paper, but in person she personified perfection.

How had she escaped a man's grip all these years? Yeah, I knew she was headstrong and ultra-independent. Hayden was fucking stubborn, which would be challenging for my alpha nature if sharing a child. Either way, beneath all of the noise of what made her so distrusting was a vulnerable girl who wasn't indifferent to me. Behind those dark irises was a blazing fire no one saw. I wasn't even sure her cousin, Sundryia, knew it was there. Hidden deep were her passions, vulnerability, desire to be loved, ability to be doted on, need of connection, and the ability to return it.

Fuck.

How had I gotten myself in this predicament again? I was at a crossroads with Hayden. I could be the father of her child and try something exclusive with her. Or, I can accept I'm not the father and pursue something exclusive with her. I didn't want either. My work was my main and side bitch. I didn't have to schedule or prioritize with my mistress.

One thing was for sure, Hayden wasn't going away anytime soon. I'd have to decide.

As she seemed to search my eyes, I murmured to her lazily, "As long as you're here, you don't owe me shit. Not in money or pussy. I don't need shit from you but trust. Don't lie to me, Hayden." Our pupils bounced between each other's—me challenging Hayden, her measuring me. "Ever. It's far worse an offense than revealing shit you're ashamed of. I'll protect and respect you. All I want is for you to take it easy in life. Just be easy."

When I caught the gloss in her eyes and saw her throat bob, my stupid ass leaned into her, catching that thick bottom lip. I caressed it with the tip of my tongue. Hayden's warm breath met my face. Pushing my tongue in her mouth, she moaned, and quickly reached for my shoulder. She felt like silk against me. In this way, Hayden softened to me when I touched her, yielded to my masculinity. And I could temper her with my tongue for hours, condition her femininity.

When Hayden's little hand cupped the hard shaft of my dick through my pajama pants, the bubble burst. I grabbed her arm, bringing her hand to claw across my belly and chest until I kissed her fingers.

"Don't lie to me, and I'll always protect you."

Her jaw dropped. "I…"

"Let's get some sleep, Hayden." I pushed myself up with one hand.

Hayden shifted, grunting along the way. "I'm sure you'll have more success doing that. The baby's up." Her hands were on her belly. "It's probably going to be up, doing leg day exercises for a while now."

It…

"You still not ready to know the sex yet? I still have the video."

Licking her lips, Hayden shook her head. Seeing her in this position reminded me of her loneliness. I lay back down next to her.

"Can I touch your belly and feel the baby move?"

With visible hesitation, Hayden nodded, biting her lip. She pushed the comforter from her torso and pulled up her shirt. The moment I lay my curious hand on her round pouch, I felt movement.

"Shit," I scoffed, fucking amazed. She moved my hand to the lower right region where it felt like the baby was kicking me purposely. *Stay away from my mom.* "And this happens every night?"

"Often enough. It's cool during the day when I'm up and going about my day. But when I'm ready to turn in at night and it's ready to turn up, it's misery."

I liked it. The baby was demonstrating strength and rebellion. My hand roved all around her naked belly, enjoying the energy.

Most people didn't know I had a problem maintaining relationships with women. I was heralded as a good fuck but a difficult guy to connect with. Only one woman ignored my dry personality due to being raised by a high-ranking infantryman. She was the one I now watched soaking in a jacuzzi, ass naked, with a member of my combat team.

From the door of the cabinet, nestled in the ville of Za'Ka, Québec I'm watching. So wrapped up in kissing and petting, neither Mandy nor Terry sees me here sucking on a lollipop.

Mandy leans into Terry, kissing the tip of his nose. "The Exorcist."

"No!" he pretends to be upset but is totally under her spell.

Mandy giggles, "The Shining." Her index finger trails down his chest onto his belly as she's done to me for years.

Terry shakes his head adamantly. "No fucking horror films, babe. The last time I let you make me watch that shit, I stayed up all night for almost a week."

Mandy's head falls back, and she laughs toward the ceiling. "You're shitting me, T!"

"No." He shakes his head again. "No shit. I'm terrified of horror films. Always have been."

"But you..." she kisses his lips. "...kill people for a living."

Caressing her back as Mandy holds a champagne flute in the air, Terry clarifies, "I've killed people in the line of duty. I don't just 'kill' people, sweet cheeks." He shifts forward and tongues her neck.

"Mmmmm..." Mandy leans into it. Then, as the wisecracker she is, she moans, "You keep this up and I'll only make you sit through Psycho."

Enraged, a familiar emotion heightens to the point of me blacking out. Not in a losing conscious manner but moving into an out-of-body experience. Terry's head draws up, but before he can respond to Mandy, he finally sees me. I don't feel shit but rage and can hear very little. I'm no longer here but in full control. Flashes of me slowly approaching the tub and seeing the shocked expression of the two begins. Then Terry attempts to leave the tub. I help, grabbing him by the arm and flinging his naked body from the water to the adjacent wall.

"Wait! Ish!" Mandy cries, delivery shaky. "Please!"

I'm speaking casually, in a low manner, as I lift him up by the neck. I see the moment reality kicks in for my boy and he swings on me. I'm able to dodge it and toss a hard one to his nose. Blood splatters as he throws another jab. I uppercut him, catching him in the chin. Terry's head flies backward.

"No! Stop, Ish! Stop it, now!" Mandy screams behind me.

Angered now, Terry charges at me. I duck and take him by the waist to flip his ass, slamming him into the ceramic floor.

"Ahhhh!" he howled, wet skin smacking into the hard material.

The thickness of my winter coat padded my impact. When I move to roll onto my stomach to grab him, the bitch pulls at the ends of my braids. I pound his face with my fist back-to-back—back-to-back while wincing from the pain of his grip. Then I manage to move so I'm over his lying body and stomp him in the groin.

"Fuuuuck!" bursts from his lungs and my hair is released.

Now free from Terry's grip, I slide his wet, bowed body across the bathroom by the neck to the wall. I try to get him to stand but he's still ailing from the blow to his dick, tightly curled into a fetal position. I speak to Terry again. While I'm out of breath now, my tone is still fair.

*And just as my arm cocks back for me to punch him in the face, I hear a **POW** followed by a clamping sensation to my back.*

That's when I black out.

At some point, I was able to regain consciousness and could hear voices.

"Come on, baby," she strains. "Come on." It's Mandy.

Of course, I recognize the voice of the woman I've been with since we were kids in high school.

"Is he..." Terry grunted. "...dead?"

"If he is, he deserves it. Come on. Is your back broken?" Terry mumbles something. "I've got your shoes, pants, and coat. We have to go, Terry."

"Is he dead?"

"I don't give a fuck, Terry! We have to go! Now!" Mandy's panicking.

Shit...

Should I be? I can't move and don't think it's wise to try to right now.

"Give me the gun," Terry pants.

"Why?"

"So—"

"There you go," Mandy coats. "You're on your feet now."

"Give me the fucking gun!" he demands.

"Why, T?"

"So I can make sure the motherfucker's dead. I'm gonna put one in his head," he squeals while panting.

"He's dead! That's it. Now, if you know anything about Ishaan, you know he planned his visit here and ain't alone. We need to go before his backup pops up!"

Then I hear shuffling and stomping. The sound grows distant. I don't know where the strength comes from, but I'm able to roll over onto my side and stand. My whole body's fucking tingling. I see the blood on the floor. It isn't all Terry's. Taking my time, I listen and limp to the front door of the cottage. It's open, arctic air blowing snow through. Outside is nearly gray in the late morning hour. The snow is pouring.

Next, I feel myself in the armored Tahoe. I'm racing behind their BMW 3. My body's still shaking from losing blood. My head's spinning from the betrayal. We'd been miles in at high speed. And for him to have her driving in these snowy conditions with this speed confirmed what I felt. These two deserve each other. With one hand on the steering wheel, the other was clamped around a pistol.

PLOW!

My eyes fluttered open, but I could still see the *330i* shoot into the air, flip, and plunge back down, landing on its roof.

My head whipped to the left where I heard soft, steady breaths.

Shit...

I'd fallen asleep in Hayden's bed. Feeling vulnerable and highly charged at the same damn time, I shifted until I was off the mattress and onto my feet. I cut the light on my way out then shut the door. This couldn't happen again. Whatever feelings I thought I had for Hayden...however I'd been softening to her need of support or what the fuck ever...the shit had to end.

My baby or not, I wouldn't take a risk with Hayden or any other woman like I did...that other callous bitch.

TWENTY

August

Hayden

"Burning the midnight oil again, I see." The familiar rasp had my head jerking up from the computer screen.

Surprised at missing a visitor in my peripheral, my lungs expanded as I acknowledged, "Pastor Ezra."

His head shook softly. "Ezra's fine. How have you been making out?"

Teasingly, I asked him, "Do you remember my name?"

He smiled with apparent charm. "Hayden, yes. My beloved will only be able to embarrass me once. Besides, I've heard about the primary funding issue for next quarter."

I pulled in another breath, reclining in my chair. "Which is why I'm here on a Friday night, burning that midnight oil."

"And how's life outside of here?"

That made me think. Being silly, I glanced over my left shoulder then right. Finally, I peered up toward the ceiling. "I think those companions are still there."

Ezra didn't smile. "They have no power, Hayden. Have you been praying?"

Folding my arms over the desk, my smile was wry when admitting, "I did at first. Like... For weeks after our last conversation."

"And what exactly did you communicate with the Father about?"

"Exactly what you said. Community. I asked Him to expand my community."

"And?"

I grabbed my belly. "And life continued to life so fast, I completely forgot all about praying."

I saw when Ezra took notice of my belly. "You should be in your second trimester." When I sputtered laughter, Ezra's hand moved to his chest. "This is not prophetic. After having my daughters, I have a clue about the length of pregnancy. It was just an educated guess."

I nodded. "The last week of it. Yup."

"Do you know what you're having?"

That, too, gave me pause. "*I* don't know but..."

"He knows?" His palm pushed into the air this time. "Another educated guess."

I nodded, feeling a little emotional.

My life was becoming more and more out of control. Yesterday had made two weeks since I'd been staying at Ishaan's estate. While the home was beautiful and weirdly inviting, the host himself had not been. Mrs. Patterson had been great, inviting me down for evening tea a few times in her gorgeous garden. She made sure to learn what I liked to eat to be sure Ms. Green, the housekeeper, purchased foods for me.

Ms. Green had been amazing, fixing my favorite dishes. She was a young, Black woman. I found it strange for her to work as a house-keeper. But after speaking to her last week just before she clocked out,

I learned housekeeping was her family's business. The family had an LLC with an established payroll. They'd been serving wealthy families for generations. Ms. Green, or Qiana, which was her first name, lucked up with a wealthy, Black family. She'd even shared her father's cancer journey. So far, things had been looking up for him, thanks to early detection. We talked and it made my stay there bearable.

Ishaan and his son, Mehki, were another story. Mehki would always speak when he saw me around the house, but never with his eyes. It was delivered rudimentarily, reminding me of his home training. Mrs. Patterson didn't play with Mehki, and apparently neither did Ishaan. The father spent time with his son though, playing basketball in their home gym. Stenton Rogers even stopped by to train Mehki. Imagine that! Nonetheless, the two Patterson men hadn't been as warm as the two women of the house.

So, being reminded of how intimately connected Ishaan and I were—because I knew, without a shadow of a doubt, he was the father of this baby—made my pregnant ass emotional in front of the preacher man.

"Yes. He does."

Ezra nodded, gazing at the wall. "Remember what I said about your vulnerability to depression?" I nodded with tears in my throat, *because...let's not mention that!* "There's an increased chance of you transitioning into that dark state of mind while pregnant by seven percent. May not sound like much, but let that be the factor spurring you into prayer more often. Declare your desires to the Father. You have to make the time, Hayden."

A sharp cry left my throat and I hung my head.

"*Awwwww*, E," I recognized Lex's voice, too. She must have just arrived. "Is everything okay—"

"No!" This time my palm shot into the air. "Nothing is wrong. Your Ezra is my weirdo bestie is all that's going on here."

"Why him?" Lex hissed playfully. I saw her peering into his eyes as he gazed into hers before kissing Lex reverently in a greeting with his hand splayed on her ass and hip.

"Good evening, Alexis," he whispered.

Her long lashes batted in response before turning back to me. "I treated you to *DiFillippo's* this week, and this guy gets that title?"

Then the tears wouldn't stop. "He's been the kindest, most distant person to me during this crazy, fucked up ordeal. He owes me nothing but gives me so much hope."

A rap at the door snatched my attention.

Damn.

Ishaan's tall body curled at the door, his head lazily resting on the frame. I noted the tumbler of honey-brown juice in his hand. His eyes were low, and hair loose from braids. It was damp in curly ringlets framing his oak-hued face.

"Still working?" He took a sip, referring to the laptop and writing pad in the bed with me.

I found myself snickering, thinking of Lex's husband. "That seems to be a common observation of me." I shrugged. "Work has to get done. Mine has to get done or no one gets paid. The mission isn't met."

"There's always tomorrow."

"We have a crisis on our hands."

"How so?"

I was happy to have his interest again, even if it were only for a few seconds at the door of my appointed room in his home.

"One of our primary funders is backing out on us. Without them, several others could follow if we don't find a replacement ASAP."

"Why are they backing out?" Ishaan took another swig then licked his lips.

I rolled my eyes. "Because he's an asshole." I dropped my face into my hands over crossed legs. "He doesn't give a damn about the little orgs affected by his corporate antics."

His brows met. "What does all that mean?"

Oh.

I was speaking non-profit lingo. "He wants me to come aboard. I told him 'no.' He's not committing to renewing our funding again."

"He wants you that bad. Huhn?"

"He wants his way. Doesn't care about who gets hurt in the interim."

Ishaan nodded, licking his lips—*lips I knew were comforting, delicious, and downright fucking arousing*. "Well, I just wanted to let you know, I'm going out of town in the morning. I'll be back on Tuesday."

Suddenly embarrassed, I pushed on anyway. Smiling, I asked, "Vacationing?"

Ishaan tossed his chin, referencing my makeshift workstation. "Working."

"The Caribbean?" I recalled the resort LeRoy mentioned.

"Miami."

"Oh."

"The DNA test results will be available on Monday."

Pulling in a nervous breath, I replied, "So they say."

"How do you want to handle it?"

"How do you?"

Ishaan shrugged, switching position to lean on his shoulder on the doorjamb. "I'mma take the pussy route."

That confused me. "What do you mean?"

"When I filled out the paperwork the day I had my blood drawn, I gave them my mother's contact information for the results."

My face lit up in shock-humor. "Your mother's?" Then I thought. "Shit. I should've done the same."

"Given your mother's info for the results?"

"No. *Your* mother." We both found that funny, laughing together. "I wonder if it's too late."

"I'm pretty sure it is, Boo-baby." Ishaan was sober again.

I nodded, serious now, too. "It is. They're going to email me. I opted out of the texting option. I'm just not going to open it."

"Why do you keep dodging shit about your baby?" He asked,

swirling the tumbler in the air. "You don't want to know the gender. Now, the paternity?"

An errant tear slipped, and I quickly caught it. "Because this isn't my finest hour." I shrugged, smiling falsely. "I've never been so…not in control. Not careful. High risk." I shook my head, maintaining that safe facial expression. "But I'm going to be alright. I'm in my new 'in the meantime.' I'll have to face the noise soon. I know."

Taking another sip, Ishaan nodded. "Good night, Hayden."

Hayden?

"Good night," I managed to squeeze from my tight throat.

Ishaan took off.

She took a sip of her lemonade then wiped her mouth. I could feel my mother tensing up to share something she didn't find easy to say. Then she glanced out of the window of the pizzeria where we'd had lunch on her break and into the streets of Clifton where she worked.

"Hayden, I don't know what to do."

Her plate was clean except for the two crusts of pizza. Mine was completely empty as I'd devoured my two veggie slices. I planned on grabbing a slice of cheesecake I'd seen in the refrigerator bakery display at the counter.

"I'm not asking you to do anything."

"I haven't seen you in four months. I have so many questions."

I stretched my arms wide. "I'm here now. What do you want to know?"

She hesitated, clearly irritated. "*Wu*—Well… What are you having?"

"I don't know." I cleared my throat after jerking my head to remove the hair gathered near my eye.

"You don't want to know? Why?"

"Because it won't change anything. The baby's coming in November. I'll have to prepare whether it's a boy or a girl."

"When are you going to start preparing?"

"I don't know. I'm having an issue in my apartment right now."

"What?"

"Flooding. A waterline burst near my house. My apartment got flooded."

Her forehead stretched and lashes clapped successively. "Well, it *is* a basement after all."

Moving her judgement right along, I asked, "Is there anything else you wanna know?"

"Where are you staying, Hayden?"

Instinctively, I reclined on the hard bench, my hands going to my belly. "A friend's."

It was Monday, and as promised, the DNA test was emailed to me just before nine this morning. As I'd told Ishaan, I had not opened the email. Silly me had been so emotional about receiving the gender reveal, paternity results, and having nothing to celebrate, I thought this scheduled lunch with my mother could distract me. *Actually*, that's not true. A *stupid* me thought maybe she'd be so...different. So supportive, so motherly, I could share the confirmation of paternity. But having just shared a meal with her, Monica gave the same Monica vibes she had since my teenage years.

"The father?"

Embarrassed by the lack of answer, my eyes diverted to the street. "A friend's, Mom."

"Look... Hayden," she shrieked. "I'm very offended you didn't ask to stay with me."

My head whipped to face her, and I grimaced. "What? Why would I do that?"

"Uncle Billy's old, Hayden. That elderly man can't even make it to the bathroom on time. He can't hurt nobody."

"He doesn't have to. He already did," I shared through gritted teeth.

"Hayden, you really need to mature past that," she whispered, reprimanding me. "There's a bigger picture at hand. You're having a baby! Are you saying your baby won't come visit—"

"Not on my dying bed," I grounded out. "Let's get this straight right now. My child will *never* visit your home while Billy's living there. I understand you chose him over me, but I would slice my own throat before I'd allow my child near that demon."

She huffed, tossing her hands in the air. "Here we go! I'm the worst mother on the planet. I'm choosing his side. Blah. Blah. Blah. Is that what Sundryia told Angelica? Does she resent her for Billy the way you do me? Billy is Billy. He's the last of his siblings. The one with no kids. Maybe having him live with me when I was raising a daughter who'd never lived with her father is where the mishap took place."

"He molested me." Tears swelled my throat. "That was no mishap. It was evil. You not believing me has been deplorable. You still denying it is disrespectful. I'm done." I shifted to leave.

"Now, wait a minute, young lady!" She gripped the table and bench, turning toward me. "I may not have been around to know what really happened because I worked long hours—two jobs—to take care of you by myself. You're not going to make me feel guilty for raising you by myself, keeping a steady roof over your head, feeding you, and making sure you went to the best schools.

"No one can take away my hard work and focus! You think that Sundryia or Rayna can say that about their mothers? You had the best, young lady—from me only! Do you blame your father for Billy, too? Do you resent him, too, Hayden?" She tittered bitterly, face-tiously. "No, you don't. You blocked him out of your life when you were twelve. Remember that? Now, you want to do the same with me?" Having enough of her shit, I walked away. "It's you, Hayden. You're the one with the problem!" she shouted to my back.

I was out of the door a second later, feeling the owner of the small restaurant watch the spectacle my mother had caused.

Fuck that cheesecake…

I took the rest of the day off. At the sound of my voice when I called Lex, she practically threw me off the phone, saying to take care of myself. I had no idea what that shit meant. When I pulled up to the Patterson estate in Alpine, I saw a white *CLA Coupe* parked directly in front of the house in the circular driveway. Mehki sat inside the driver's seat, his long legs kicked out as his girlfriend, Jessica, stood leaning against the door. Through the car, they blasted some Future song I'd heard before but couldn't name in my current headspace.

I really didn't want to run into him, especially in my current emotional state. Still, I shouldered through.

"Hey, there!" I greeted with a mild smile as I slowed near them. It was all I had in me at the moment.

Jessica motioned for Mehki to lower the volume of the music. Once he did, she looked my way and smiled. "Hi." Her wave was short and fast.

"Hi." Mehki supplied after her.

Seeing they weren't for much conversation, I pivoted to move on. "Nice car. Is it yours, Jessica?"

With a beam still in place, she shook her head.

Mehki took Jessica at the bare thigh in her mini skirt, pulling her into him. "It was my birthday gift when I turned sixteen. Poppy did me right."

He wouldn't face me. Mehki wore sunglasses, but I could still sense he gave me no eye contact.

"Oh! Nice. Your father really loves you." Moving along, I bade, "Have fun, guys," hating how shaky my voice was.

"*My* father?" I caught Mehki scoffing by the time I landed on the first step.

I heard Jessica snickering in response. On a normal day, I'd pay the antics of teens no mind. But on this day, I was pregnant, homeless, and motherless as far as I was concerned. Thankfully, the door was unlocked as I had no key. Inside, I walked through the grand foyer with my head hung, diaphragm threatening.

Shit.

Can I make it to my room first?

Feet away from the staircase, I felt like I needed to vomit—with tears.

"Hayden?" rang out beneath the vaulted ceiling.

I froze, no longer able to keep it together.

"Sweetheart," she called out pleadingly. "Something's clearly wrong. Is it with the baby?"

That was it. I lost it. A cry ripped from my throat, "No!" I answered her, internally berating myself for being weak in public—*in front of a stranger*. It didn't matter. My body convulsed as I wept. Mrs. Patterson was behind me. She used my shoulders to turn me to face her.

"You're home early, Hayden. Where are you coming from?" I couldn't speak. Even communicating with my hands was a feat as I wailed. "Who were you with?"

"*Mah*—my," I breathed. "My mother!"

Deep concern colored her face. However, Mrs. Patterson's tone was calm, soothing against my meltdown. "Did you two fight?"

I was only able to nod. "She's so fucking *cry*—critical!" I managed through tears. "*Fu*—gging *tok*—toxic to me! Always!"

"Okay." Her hands went to the sides of my face. "Okay. Look at me, honey. Does she love you, Hayden? Do you believe your mother loves you?" she demanded with authority.

As silly and ill-timed as that question was, I felt like a child, automatically following her lead. "*Ya-esssss...*" I cried.

"Then we can work from there." She released my face. "Let's get you some hot tea. And tell me what you will."

She took me by the hand and did as she proposed. Mrs. Patterson served me delicious chamomile tea. And through blabbered tears, I told her about *most* of the lunch with my mother.

Perhaps the delicious tea was sedating. Per Mrs. Patterson's advice after our chat, I soaked in a calming, warm bath, which she helped prepare for me. That had did the trick. I'd turned in early, falling asleep as soon as my head hit the pillow.

Now, I was up at midnight, and starved as hell. I grabbed my phone and saw I missed a call and text from Sundryia. Letisha sent me pictures of Shi-Shi from *TikTok* on a small yacht with her daughter. They were cute together. Letisha knew I stanned Shi-Shi. She also sent me a link to *Spillin' that Hot Tea*'s Instagram page. There was a post about Ebonee Williams. She was on a red carpet in Miami promoting a new show. She looked...pregnant.

My baby kicked.

The video was muted, but I read the caption below. As I suspected, the blogger did, too. Ebonee wore a pleated, purple baby-doll blouse. She'd put on weight, too, though she still looked beautiful. She and Shi-Shi were boss babes.

There was a text from Rayna, too, but my bladder screamed, so I shifted out of bed, grunting each inch as I progressed. Leaving the covers, I realized I was naked. After that bath, I had no energy to put on my pajamas. I toed into the bathroom, straight to the toilet. After washing my hands, a hunger pang struck.

Shit...

Then they came back-to-back. I grabbed my phone for the time again. It was now close to one in the morning. Figuring no one would be awake, I shouldered into a housecoat, being sure to wrap it around my belly as secure as possible before tying it. Then I toed into my slippers and crept out into the hall. Taking the back staircase seemed more appropriate. It was less airy. The house was quiet but still well-lit to a fair degree for the hour.

Once I made it to the kitchen, I headed straight to the fridge for banana peppers. I sucked my teeth hard. There were none. Then I thought to look in the pantry. It was where I'd get the crackers from anyway.

Mmmmm... Buttery, crisp crackers. My mouth salivated.

I used the flashlight from my phone to search for the elements of my cuisine while begging my stomach to be patient. *Yes...* I found everything and easily. Within seconds, I was stacking peppers onto a cracker. *Shit.* It was so good! Exhaling like the foodie I'd become, I leaned into the island there in the pantry and rubbed my belly with my free hand contentedly.

I'd made it to my fifth cracker stack when I heard a door slam. It sounded like the side door of the house near the garages. Quickly, I toed over to the door of the pantry and pulled it closed. The lights from the kitchen still shown through the shutters. Chewing sounded so loud in my ear. I realized the flashlight from my phone was still on, and reached for it. After powering it completely off, I dropped it into the oversized pocket of the robe.

The steps grew closer to the kitchen, and while I wasn't afraid, I still didn't want to be found. I stood frozen, hearing the refrigerator door being opened. Ishaan sputtered expletives, slamming the door shut. That made me spring in place.

Then he was nearing me. His long frame was approaching, shoulders swaying with each step. When he pulled the door to the pantry open, his torso jerked back a little, braids swinging in the air. We locked eyes for a while. I'd been caught. *The man offers me a place to stay for free, and I'm nibbling in his pantry like a greedy night mouse.* And *damn*, did I feel like one. Slowly, I turned to close the jar of banana peppers. It was time for me to go. When I glanced back up to Ishaan, realizing he hadn't spoken a single word, his attention was on my snack. He stepped inside and removed the jar from my hand, studying it. Then his head whipped down to the crackers. Suddenly, I felt embarrassed.

A grin of embarrassment warmed my face just before I explained, "Looks gross. I know. But pregnancy can change your palate, making gross shit so goo—"

Ishaan leaned into me and planted his soft lips onto mine. The swift, intimate contact had me bracing. His brows were knitted as he kissed me, his tongue arrowing into my mouth. The man smelled so good—tasted amazing. My body began to tingle the way it did the first days of exploring my sexuality *with* consent. The time I was new to a guy's welcomed touch. As his tongue rolled over and over mine, this kiss felt different than our last two. There was an energy Ishaan was radiating. There was a hunger fueling his heated body.

He pulled from my mouth, eyes still narrowed, jaw relaxed. I watched as Ishaan's attention roved down my body. His hand went for the belt and unraveled it. My breath caught when the housecoat loosened and opened. What Ishaan couldn't see, he pushed aside the cotton to reveal. And here I was, bare to him in his damn kitchen pantry.

My panting was as audible as the blood rushing in my head. When he dipped to stroke the peak of my right nipple with his tongue, my neck gave out as I clasped the cool edge of the granite countertop. The bristles of his beard swept against my sensitive skin when he switched to my left nipple. It sent chards of pleasure to my groin.

My abdomen contracted, unrelated to the baby. Heat swelled between my thighs when his mouth and beard swiped down and on to my swollen tummy. His hands joined his face, touching it with such reverence. Ishaan was on his haunches before me. My head rolled back, the ends of my hair swaying against the housecoat. Animalistic sensual energy had my body vibrating, my groin churning. His explorative touch told me my body appealed to him. I felt sexier than I had in months. Feminine, and worthy of desire.

Then Ishaan lifted my left leg, drawing my thigh over his shoulder. The first stroke of his tongue in my cleft had my knee buckling. My eyes squeezed, mouth stretched wide, emitting muted moans of pleasure. He cupped my ass with his big hands, providing me a seat. It was useless. Ishaan stroked me two more times with a wide tongue and stiff tip. By the fifth stroke, my pelvis was vibrating, and helpless mewls poured from my throat. I was cumming, and so hard into his mouth. I felt a burst of liquid splattering on my thighs and smack against the floor. I couldn't help it. My pussy kept riding his face, upswinging and squeezing greedily. It went on and on until my clit had, had enough and I pushed back against the island.

Panting with a spinning head, I could make out Ishaan's frame growing in stature as he stood at his full height. He grabbed me at the front of the neck painlessly but with intimidating mastery and pulled me toward him. My hand slipped from my body, momentarily weakening when I watched him open his mouth and pour a concoction of liquid into mine. His saliva and my excitement mixed together. Before I could think of what to do with it, Ishaan's tongue was diving into my mouth. Together, between silky tongue swipes, Ishaan and I both managed to swallow our secretions.

My shaking hands reached for the waist of his dress pants. The fastener was beyond my knowledge, and I couldn't release him. Ishaan quickly brushed against my knuckles to assist me. This confirmed he wasn't adverse to me making yet another reckless decision of fucking in his kitchen. When he turned me around, yanked the back of the housecoat up over my ass, and pulled me back at my hips, I knew it for sure.

Panic struck when I felt the wide crest of his dick against my soaked, swollen folds, lubricating himself.

"*Ish*—" I swallowed, tasting and smelling us as I panted. "We don't have a condom."

"*Shhhhh...*" He hummed against my neck, "We're beyond that now."

He breached me, beautifully bruising my sex. It was blunt, conversant, and deliciously arrogant. My hips were tense as he stroked deep then shallow. My lungs couldn't keep up with the pace of the deep plunges, and I didn't give a fuck.

"*Shiiiit*," he grunted, thick cords vibrating. "You feel fuckin' amazing, Boo-baby." My eyes squeezed tight when the pads of his fingers stroked my pebbled nipples. "I've been wanting inside you for so long. I don't remember it being this wet...this soft...this hot." His tongue crept up the rim of my ear, another sensation igniting another storm in my groin. "So fuckin' tight. Just for me," Ishaan whispered seductively. "Just." He stroked. "For." He stroked. "Me." Then he plunged intrusively again.

My legs vibrated. Ishaan was losing his shit, too. I knew this by his breathing pattern. They were coming out short and shallow. He was trying not to cum. Had his last time been with me as mine was with him?

Hell no, girl!

Suddenly, the thrusts stopped, and he *shhhh*'d me, still at my ear. "Someone's in the kitchen," he whispered with no base in his delivery.

My eyes burst opened. A light had been cut on inside the kitchen, just on the other side of the cracked pantry door.

"Girl, quit playing!" Mehki chuckled quietly into the phone. "All your girls wanna get with the kid." Things went quiet as my groin churned. "Damn. Ain't shit to eat in this bitch. Wait till I speak to my housekeeper," he mumbled.

Ishaan began to thrust again, this time slower. Shit. Were we really doing this? The insistence of his fingers strumming my tight nipples answered the question. Surprisingly, I wasn't panicked. My need to release dominated every other emotion in the moment. It felt intoxicating as Ishaan stopped thrusting again, listening. A ringing in my head was increasing, and the play of my nipples revved me deliciously. *Fuck*. I was ascending, only needing a few more of his strokes—plunges preferably. I squeezed greedily around him, pushing back on his pulsing firmness.

Then I was cumming. A tsunami of pleasure licks stroked all over me. I pressed my lips together, thrusting my ass into him. Ishaan tightly encouraged my orgasm, stroking my breasts and nipples now, reclining his torso to feed me more of his dick.

"Boo-baby," he cried in a faint whisper into my ear.

I tried not to breathe as my body was being wracked by pleasure, the covering of Ishaan's heat and scent. It all dizzied me, buckling my knees.

Then one of them hit the damn wall of the island. The soft thud scared the shit out of me, and I wisely pushed back into Ishaan. But my neck was lazy, and spine and shoulders wouldn't stop jerking.

"Hold up!" Mehki hissed. I could see as he slowly walked over to the pantry, his pace expressing his guard was up.

My heart hammered in my chest.

"*Shhhhh*..." Ishaan commanded breathlessly again.

Mehki stood there for a few seconds while Ishaan was behind me, making infinitesimal movements inside of my sex.

"Poppy, that you in there?" The boy actually sounded like a kid instead of an immature, young adult.

A grumbling pushed from his throat, "Yeah."

After another beat, Mehki inquired, "If I open this door, would you beat my ass?" His voice cracked with what sounded like fear.

"Yup."

Without another word, Mehki backed away. And as the distance between him and the door grew with each step, his father's plunges returned and intensified. Ishaan slammed into me, causing our flesh to smack against each other. Since I'd orgasmed just seconds earlier, I was still sensitive deep in my canal. So, while the impact was intrusive, each bite was luscious.

"Oh, fuck," sloughed from his lungs. Ishaan's hips locked and his pelvis began to wobble as he shot deep inside of me. "*Goddamn*," he whispered, collapsing his face onto my shoulder. His heart pounded on my back.

ISHAAN

"*Fuck...*" I moaned as the water sloshed around the tub, her narrow shoulder caving around my head, tits inches away from my mouth.

Hayden's eyes were closed as her full tits bounced in the air. Her thighs pressed into me. She was riding the hell out of my dick. So responsive to my touch. Who knew pregnant pussy was this spongey and messy? When I ate her pussy down in the kitchen, Hayden squirted all over my face and the floor. Had she been this sexual all this time? Possibly. I could do this. After quickly cleaning "us" up down there, I brought her into my bedroom and washed my face and mouth. Then I ran us a bath and washed her down.

Her body was beautiful, lewd even. Those perfect teardrop-shaped boobs were swollen, and their apexes shades darker than I remembered them back in the winter. Her belly was gorgeous, reminding me of just how slippery life could be. How could she hide all of this from me?

I'd been off of Hayden for a few weeks now, opting to give her space, especially in my home. Although I knew I could, I promised I wouldn't try to fuck her, and had kept my word. Then I received a call from my mother this afternoon while I was in Miami. I was anxious at first, knowing she'd received the DNA test results today. Her call was about Hayden. She explained she'd had a breakdown. My mother had been sensing Hayden's loneliness and lack of support for some time now but didn't pry. Today, it was confirmed.

Apparently, Hayden and her mother were estranged. The daughter hadn't felt supported by her during this pregnancy. Damn. Her not going to stay with her after the flood was a big red flag. But Hayden had been so goddamn cagey. I didn't want to push my aggressive nature on her. She'd already said she didn't want to co-parent had I, in fact, turned out to be the father. Dr. Patterson called my ass home. She really didn't have to. I'd been messaging my team about my impending departure since hearing the start of the details of Hayden's situation.

And then to find her eating my favorite snack as of late while I'd been looking forward to it for hours. The sight of that shit turned me the fuck on to dangerous degrees. My lack of energy. The weird ass taste for banana peppers and fucking crackers. It finally clicked. I'd been experiencing pregnancy symptoms. We'd had a connection all these months and didn't even know it.

Her arms stretched aside me began to shake. Hayden turned her pussy upright, grinding harder and faster. The vein at the center of her forehead almost aligned with the middle part in her hair. I slurped one of her knotted nipples into my mouth, sucking and licking it. Hayden's head fell back, hips straining around me. She moaned as her tight walls convulsed around my dick, squeezing me like a fucking vise grip.

Shiiiiit...

I could do this. I could give Hayden the support she needed to help raise this baby. I didn't know how successful I'd be at tending to her needs, but if she gave me a try, I'd do it.

I pushed my arm from the water, sticking two fingers in her mouth. She peered down on me, crying around them.

"Suck." Then I grunted, "Be mine. Give me a try."

With enthusiastic speed, Hayden nodded, sucking on my fingers while riding out her orgasm.

"Just don't betray me, baby," was a whisper from the recesses of my mind.

Inevitably ElleBee...

August

Hayden

I'd just returned from the lady's room when the waiter was placing our food on the table.

"Yummy." My stomach roiled, telling me to hurry as I was eating for two now. "Soul food!" I rubbed my hands together once back in my seat, surveying the smothered, fried pork chops, macaroni and cheese, and small porcelain bowl of mustard greens. I hadn't had this type of greens since I was a child when my grandmother used to cook them. "It's been a minute. Now, I'mma go back to the office with the damn 'itis.'" I laughed, reaching for my utensils.

"You know," Kenny squinted my way from across the table. "You're really glowing."

My head angled and chin dipped. "I am?"

I *did* feel good. A total contrast from just twenty-four hours ago. Ishaan. We'd...collided into our bedfellow of recklessness once again. I told him I'd 'be his' and meant it. I hadn't been in a relationship in so long I didn't know the protocol. But once we finally discussed the paternity results I still had yet to open, we could figure that out, too.

He'd called me beautiful in the tub as I rode him, feeling empowered by our juxtaposition. He called me beautiful in his bed over and over until I passed out from proper exhaustion. Ishaan wasn't lying to me either. His touch, and the sparkle in his eyes as he watched me orgasm into oblivion, told me all I needed to know.

And I didn't realize just how much I needed to be told those kind words. At six months pregnant, I needed affirmation. I needed peace and a sense of belonging. I'd been baking a whole human being by...a stranger. Mrs. Patterson was right: I'd been carrying a lot and alone. Being intimate with Ishaan last night gave me a sense of connection. So, yeah. I likely had been glowing. Ishaan had injected into me last night into this morning. He'd poured a lot.

"You are. Shit. It's making me wonder why I didn't push to take you to this new level in your womanhood."

I rolled my eyes, scoffing. "We both know why."

"Cill?" He laughed guiltily. "Man, please."

I prayed over my food then forked baked macaroni. It was delicious. "So, which club was your interview at again?"

Kenny was a club owner just before I met him a few years back. He'd lost it and had been managing musical groups and night clubs since. A true hustler, the man was connected, too. He'd gotten Letisha and me into a few concerts and clubs. He'd called me yesterday before I left the City for Jersey to have lunch with my mother. He mentioned he'd be in Harlem today for an interview at a club and needed to share some scoop with me. I was all game for his type of tea. Could certainly use the distraction.

"*Club Sin.*" He bit into his fried chicken.

My neck snapped back, and I shimmied. "Okay, big dog! *Club Sin* be poppin'! I've been there a couple of times. I saw Young Lord there once. He performed live."

"Yeah. It's been popping for a minute. Leading in revenue, too."

"Well..." I winked. "I hope you get it." I raised my peach iced tea in the air. "To you running one of the dopest clubs in New York City." With a wry grin, Kenny met my glass with his own. "Now, let's get to the tea. What's been going on since I've been..." I gestured to my midsection. "...doing me?"

"Before we get into that? Who the fuck are *you* pregnant by?"

I fed myself some of the greens.

Mmmmm...

Smiling, I shook my head. "Gossip first. Then maybe I'll share about my rollercoaster of a life." My hand caressed my belly with fondness.

"Okay." Kenny's head bobbed side-to-side as he smiled, holding his fork over the table. "Your sister..."

I rolled my eyes. "Of course."

"She's been indicted."

My eyes blew the hell up. "The credit card scamming?"

He nodded, grinning—not necessarily in a gloating manner—with his eyes to his plate. "Yup. Wire fraud and aggravated identity theft. I tried to tell her that shit was gonna catch up to her."

"I told you it would. Priscilla was getting too cocky with it—" My hands flashed open. "—well, first, let's acknowledge how illegal that shit is." Kenny nodded. "She went to Aruba twice last year and bought all those designer bags, the *Rolex*es...that *Bentley!*"

"Yup." Kenny's head wouldn't stop bobbing.

He would know. He'd been fueling me information about her since we learned of our connection. When I met Kenny, he tried to talk to me—romantically—and I half-heartedly entertained him. That was until Letisha found a picture of him on Priscilla's *IG* page about two years ago. They'd been dating for a while by that time. So, after I contacted Kenny to bust him, my toxic heart kept him close because he'd share gossip with me about my "family." Kenny and

Priscilla had broken up and gotten back together a lot over the years. In my opinion, things had run dry between the two, but they kept in touch, and would occasionally fuck. Those details were of no interest to me.

"But those aren't all the charges."

Cutting into one of my porkchops using a knife and fork, I was confused. "What else?"

"Bank fraud."

My stomach flipped. Bank fraud was a serious charge. *How in the hell did Cill get involved in—*

I sucked in a breath, suddenly recalling, "The townhouses in Hoboken!"

Kenny's head fell to the side, confirming my memory. "Come on, now! Didn't I tell you I warned her! And she almost got your other sister, Amaya, in that shit. Amaya was like, 'Hell no. Sounds fishy as fuck to me.' I told Cill to chill, but..." He shrugged.

"So, who's going to help her out of this hole? Momma Melba?" Rolling my eyes, I sipped my tea through a straw, not knowing which was better: the food or the entertainment.

"Amaya told me your father said this would be the last time. He's gonna have to take out a second mortgage to cover Cill's attorney fees. Between me and you, he said he's cutting her out of his will."

I blinked hard. "Not precious princess Cill getting the ax."

"Yup." Kenny shrugged with a smirk. "I didn't say this to your sister, but that just means there'll be more money for you and Amaya when the old man croaks."

Just when I was about to remind him I wanted nothing to do with any of those folks, including money, I felt a strong energy on my right side. Before I could look, he was sitting down next to me. His enchanting, virile scent had my lungs hiccupping before I could fully recognize him.

"Well, damn, Rob. Just when I thought your weaseling ass couldn't get any bolder in my orbit, here you are in Harlem, another place you shouldn't be." His tone so calm, his aura so conversant with Kenny.

My heart slammed in my chest, stomach toiled nastily at the

attractive scent of Ishaan, who wouldn't even look at me. His eyes were unrecognizably dark and pinned to Kenny.

Kenny initially appeared scared shitless. Then he huffed, throwing his chicken into the plate as he reclined in his chair. "The fuck, bro. I'm not here bothering nobody!" Then a suited, buffed gentleman sat in the chair next to Kenny. His posture was fucking intimidating. Kenny caught on and muttered, "I'm minding my business."

"Is Rob minding his business?" Finally, Ishaan peered at me.

Now, shaking from every limb, with a dry mouth, I asked, "Who the hell is Rob?" My throat almost closed up from anxiety just after I was able to get that singular question out.

Ishaan turned to Kenny. "Who is Rob? Why is she asking that?" Ishaan then asked me. "Who do *you* say he is?"

My eyes welled with concern. "Kenny," I whispered, clearing my throat. "...why is he calling you Rob?"

Kenny sucked his teeth. Abruptly, he tried to stand, but the heavyset guy to the left of him used one hand and violently slammed Kenny back into his seat. I thought the chair would break, the act was so harsh.

I turned to the right of me. "Ishaan," I called out, chords trembling. "...what's going on here?"

"That's what I wanna know. Who's this guy to you?"

My brain hiccupped. Suddenly, I felt any answer I gave would displease Ishaan. Anger lanced my chest. "Jealousy doesn't look good on you." I was doing nothing wrong.

Ishaan let off a casual scoff. "And commitment and integrity doesn't wear well on *you*, Boo-baby." There was no charm in his reference of me.

I was right. He'd placed me on some sort of hot seat. Ishaan was fucking angry. *I* was, in fact, being indicted—or had been.

"Don't do this, Ish," Kenny either begged or warned. He was so heightened emotionally in a way I'd never known him to be. "Let's not do this. Clearly, we know somebody in common. But other than that, I don't know what the fuck is going on."

"That's cool." With his eyes on me, Ishaan snapped his fingers.

The big guy grabbed Kenny by the collar of his shirt and yanked him out of his seat. I braced myself, palms hitting the table as he was dragged out of the restaurant effortlessly. When I glanced back at Ishaan, he was pulling cash from his pocket.

Dr. Jekyll and Mr. Hyde.

It was how Rayna explained Ishaan. Was this business between him and Kenny? If so, why the hell did it feel so personal?

"Damn," he exhaled so smoothly. "This is all starting to feel reminiscent of how we met." He tossed a few bills onto the table.

"You don't have to do that," I hissed, body still vibrating with nervous energy from the violence taking place. "I think you know I can't be bought now."

"Maybe." Ishaan stood from the table. His lengthy torso leaned down so he was over my seated position. "But I didn't know you had a father and sisters."

My eyes burst so wide, they hurt. "That's a piece of my life I don't discuss with anyone. No one!"

"Yet, you do it with a man whose name you don't really know," Ishaan's delivery was too calm, accusatory.

"You don't know me! Just because I agreed to...'be yours' last night doesn't mean you get to bust in on a lunch with a guy I don't—"

"I fuckin' told you not to lie to me!" he spoke over me, emotionless. "I told you, it's far worse an offense than revealing shit you're ashamed of." My lungs filled and head drew back. "I said I'd protect and respect you. You say you don't trust men because all they do is lie. What the *fuck* have you been doing to me all these months?"

My eyes closed, overwhelmed with the misunderstanding. "Ishaan."

"Fuck you, Hayden."

It was low, determined, neat, and delivered like a blow to my chest. Ishaan strolled out of the restaurant, leaving me alone without another word.

###

NEXT UP...

INEVITABLY
Love.

THE *complicated* SERIES 2

Available now.

"Is that an eagle on your neck? What does it represent to you?"

"The ability to see sharper than most. Eagles have the wing capacity to soar so high, and the vision capacity to see far ahead. There are times where my sight allows me to see far enough ahead to prevent shit from happening."

"Why do I feel like you're seeing something in me right now?"

"All I see is your next orgasm tonight."

LOVE ACKNOWLEDGES

Christina C. Jones aka CCJ — Thanks for being an active constant, bae. Love you d*ooo*wn.

Interior Artist: Cedeara Ardell McCollum — Thanks, baby girl, for the imagery you've designed for my books! Love you always!

Character Contributor: Bailey West — Thanks for being just a call away for knowledge exceeding my experience. Your turnaround time for the characterization of Ishaan's father was more than I deserve. Can't wait to return the favor!

Proof Reader: Tina V. Young — You're my rock and magic trick. Thanks for your interest and patience with my half a brain. Thanks for the sports contributions and keeping me shiny.

Editors: Zakiya Walden of ***I've Got Something to Say!*** — Thank you for always being patient but never gentle. I appreciate the way you challenge me and never think any question or rivaling perspective is too silly or unnecessary. I truly appreciate you!

Sitara Thomas — The cleanup in chapters 1, 2, 3, 4, 5—Heck! The entire book—was fiyah! Thanks so much for being sensitive to my horrible timing and extreme energy. LOL!!!

MDT: I'm gonna do better. I SWARe it! Thanks for everything!

Master, my ***Jireh***, my ***Rohi***, Proverbs 28:19-20 (MSG): "Work your garden—you'll end up with plenty of food; play and party— you'll end up with an empty plate. Committed and persistent work pays off; get-rich-quick schemes are ripoffs." *The harvest to work has been plentiful. Thank you, Father.*

OTHER BOOKS BY LOVE BELVIN

Love's Improbable Possibility series:
Love Lost, Love UnExpected, Love UnCharted & Love Redeemed

Waiting to Breathe series:
Love Delayed & Love Delivered

Love's Inconvenient Truth (Standalone)

Love Unaccounted series:
In Covenant with Ezra, In Love with Ezra & Bonded with Ezra

The Connecticut Kings series:
*Love in the Red Zone, *Love on the Highlight Reel, *Determining*
*Possession, End Zone Love, Love's Ineligible Receiver, *Pass Interference,*
*Love's Encroachment, *Offensive Formations, Love's Neutral Zone, &*
**Free Agent (*by Christina C. Jones)*

Wayward Love series:
The Left of Love, The Low of Love & The Right of Love

Love in Rhythm & Blues series
The Rhythm of Blues & The Rhyme of Love

The Sadik series
He Who Is a Friend, He Who Is a Lover & He Who Is a Protector

The Muted Hopelessness series:
My Muted Love, Our Muted Recklessness, & Our Reckless Hope

The Prism series:
Mercy, Grace, & The Promise

356

Low Love, Low Fidelity (Standalone)

The Complicated series:
In the Meantime... & Inevitably Love.

EXTRA

You can find Love Belvin at www.LoveBelvin.com
Facebook @ Author - Love Belvin
Twitter @LoveBelvin
Goodreads: Love Belvin
TikTok: Love Belvin
and on Instagram @LoveBelvin

Join the #TeamLove mailing list on my website to keep up with the happenings!
Click here (with Wi-Fi) to join!